BOREALIS BURNING

A NOVEL BY AUDREY SECHREST

BOOK 1 OF THE SEER SERIES

Dedication

To my Grandmothers Rachel and Peggy – to whom I owe all the best parts of my personality. I love you both dearly!

To Sam, Hannah, and Mom, I am so thankful for you all! You went above and beyond and your incredible labors of love will forever make me cry. All the hand-holding and the encouragement. All the support and feedback. This project was only possible due to your kindness. Thank you.

To Matthew Ross, my developmental editor, who took this from rough to diamond!

CONTENTS

Visit Hwei Postcard, 2010
Pre-Pact digital recruitment poster produced and
distributed by BaseX between 2010 - 2025

1 - OVERTURE

(def) 1. an orchestral piece at the beginning of an opera, suite, play, oratorio, or other extended composition.
2. *an introduction to something more substantial.*

THE 22ND MAN

KIERAN

Kieran choked back his disgust at the assembled men in front of him. It wasn't their stench — heavy, funky, inescapable — that burned away his admittedly short-fuse. It was the disloyalty. Perhaps the moniker "men" was too high-praise. They were rats.

That's not to say the stench wasn't rancid, it was. It was worthy of remarking upon at the very least.

The twenty-two gathered union organizers could each brag of a distinct scent profile. Every man's odor combined the last thing they ate, the last time they washed, and their own unique skin flavor to a devastating result. Both the cafeteria and laundry room had been sacrificed to the almighty picket-line, so food and hygiene had taken a inauspicious hit. Jellied semi-meat and paper-towel bird baths weren't doing anyone any favors. Voila, the formula for the stinging aroma for which they all must endure.

As the only clean person in the room, Kieran's suffering was far greater and of more importance than the rest. To make matters worse, it was ***their*** fault that he had to drag his ass down half way across the stars to deliver a message.

In all honesty, the late great addition of their panic-sweats was likely Kieran's fault. The sour armpit dew congealed the initial stank into a new odor that was, shockingly, even more depressing. With a stink like they had, the union leaders nearly accomplished an unheard of feat. They almost made Kieran regret his actions. Almost.

Near regrets aside, he couldn't help but pat himself on the back for a job well done. He'd delivered his 'message' with no small amount of panache. Two big thumbs up for Kieran.

Because despite the continued chants below, the strike was over. It ended in this room at Kieran's say so.

It took five minutes for Kieran to make that point. When these rats exited this room, they would follow his carefully laid out instruction to a 't.' Because consequences of any deviation from his instructions meant another five minute conversation. No one in this room ever wanted to have the misfortune of seeing Kieran again after today's conversation.

Especially the 22nd man.

While, theoretically, Kieran tipped his hat at the only man with enough spine to look him in the eyes and tell him "no". Practically, he just couldn't have that kind of nonsense. So, unfortunately, the 22nd Man became an example.

But with his message deliver, he had a few seconds to spare for a bit of curiosity. He had questions for this man.

Kieran suspected that he might have broken some ribs with the way the man was wheezing. The 22nd man pled for life in a dying tongue. "*El'esses. El'esses. Oeph khemhio.*" Teeth coated in blood, the man could take no more.

"You keep complaining like that and I'm liable to think you don't like me very much." Kieran said, crouched down and took a knee beside his quivering form. He checked his pulse with two fingers pressed against man's neck. "And I don't do favors to people who don't like me very much."

The man's heartbeat was weak. Without medical assistance he was likely to aspirate a lung or bleed out in the before the day was out. Kieran grabbed out his handy-dandy medic's quik-syringe from a small side-loop on his gun-belt. In his line of work he'd started carrying several all-purpose quik-syringe with him for any occasion.

"While I've got you, let's chat. Man to man." Kieran tapped the auto-injector against the man's cheek teasingly to get his draining attention. "Now, I'm just *dying* of curiosity, which you should be able to relate to given your current state. So, while I hate to undo all my hard work, I got a proposal for you. In exchange for an honest answer to my questions, I'll give you the good stuff. One, premium grade, BaseX quik-syringe fresh from the lab. Sure to cure all our aches and boo-boos. The deal on the table is a truthful answer for your life or something like it. What say you?" He twirled the syringe through his fingers. Though Kieran wasn't sure if his showmanship was lost on the purple swollen eyes of the 22nd man.

The bludgeoned man jerked his head down in what Kieran would take on good faith was a nod. Quick, the enforcer uncapped the medipen and jabbed the man in the neck.

His relief was immediate. Groaning as the chemicals raced through his body, the 22nd man rolled and flopped from his side to his back. His face was red and purple, his right eye swollen shut. With his good eye, he gazed passed Kieran with a sheen of nothingness glazing over his vision

"And so, the question is... how did you know?" Kieran asked.

The man gave no answer.

At the end of this conversation, these union agitators would skulk down five flights of stairs and break the bad news to their comrades-at-arms and fellow workers. Twenty-one of the 22 leaders of this strike would assure their unions that they had tried their best and given it their all. That they had not cowered in fear and capitulated embarrassingly fast. They would assure the workers—who had placed their faith in them as leaders–that they

3

had without a doubt not been seconds away from shitting their pants.

Their words would tell one story and their stink would tell another. They were rats, the lot of them.

Except for the 22nd man.

He could walk tall with his head held high because he was loyal to the bitter end. Unfortunately, quik-syringe was a miracle cure, so the 22nd man wouldn't be doing much walking anytime soon.

Since the word go, the 22nd man had been distrustful of Kieran whenever he appeared. And Kieran always arrived in the nick of time. He was their backer. Whatever they had needed, they could count on Kieran to finance and support their strike. And it wasn't just any strike. With Kieran's help, it was the largest, best organized, most collaborative, and successful strike that the Oya Vearro star system had ever seen.

Now, if Kieran was interested in picking a fight, he'd question how much of the strike's success was his to claim. This topic was something none of the organizers were interested in investigating. And honestly, he couldn't blame them. The one-hundred and thirty thousand unionized workers downstairs rattling the walls with their bodies and bellows deserved the lion's share of praise. They had done the hard work, the important work. Money and protective equipment were nothing without the people and persistence to use them. So while Kieran might've been the one to keep their supply chain and intelligence hacking software well-funded, the acclaim was not his to take.

But credit and power have a messy relationship. So he'd take whatever he could get, when he could get it.

There were other choices available to these union leaders. Earlier today, when the order had come down the pipeline, they could've just done what was requested of them. The message was simple -- the strike was "over." The united courisand refinor's fight for humane working conditions and fair compensation must come to a close without delay. The strike had made meaningful victories, the deal on the table was fairer than they had originally hoped. So, now came the time to sit down and shut up.

Apparently, Kieran's holoscroll with instructions had arrived earlier that day to a unanimous "fuck you" from each of the 22 lead organizers. For them, the deal on the table while 'good' was a band-aid on a bullet wound. It would not suffice. The organizers were in this fight for the long haul. A victory in battle is nothing if the war was lost.

Kieran disagreed.

So, Kieran was here for an unexpected visit and had asked for a private audience to deliver the message personally with a bit more urgency. That urgency was communicated in five excruciating minutes. The addendum to the original message was to inform them that they were mistaken. Compliance was not a request, it was a foregone conclusion.

A kinder man might forgive them for their stupidity. But any illusion of Kieran's better angels was shattered about 10 seconds into their little chat. Because until five minutes ago, Kieran was the guy they had all wanted in their corner. There wasn't a task too big, disgusting, or depraved for him not to accomplish with flair. Perhaps kindness is not a word to be associated with such a human, but he was in their corner working for the home team.

The silence stretch between them. The 22nd man's was just barely catching his breathe.

Kieran would hate to think that he was being ignored. As an exquisitely aged man with cheekbones that could cut glass, being ignored wasn't something he was used to or enjoyed. Perhaps the quiksyringe of "kindness", had resulted in the man forgetting the lesson Kieran had so recently been taught him.

"You had me dead to rites the moment I met you," Kieran said. "And I wanna know how. Clearly, you aren't smarter than the rest of them, or else you wouldn't be bleeding all over the floor. So what gave it away, friend?"

The 22nd man swallowed twice around a couple of answers that might've required the full-motility of his jaw. He twitched out what could be considered a head shake. Or a spasm of pain, either involuntary bodily function could perhaps serve as an answer.

Kieran laughed, enjoying the simple pleasure of toying with his food. "What was it? Have we met before?"

A hoarse, barely audible whisper escaped the 22nd man, "Your eyes."

"Really? Do you think they're pretty?" Kieran asked. He knew they were. With towering height well above six feet, pretty blue eyes, and objectively attractive features, his looks normally worked in his favor rather than revealing the devil inside.

"They're hollow."

The 22nd man's answer was intriguing to no end. Unfortunately, Kieran couldn't decide if he enjoyed being intrigued. "Say more." The 22nd man shook his head. "Ah, ah, boss man. I thought I made it very clear. I don't like repeating myself."

In a fit to overcompensate, the cowering man's words raced behind a series of gags and blood-filled hacks, "They — they're, it's hard to describe, but your eyes... it's like looking into a black hole. I've seen one before, a scouting trip out to the next system over. I will never forget it. It was — hollow. Hungry. Full of nothing but it could eat you, eat everything, and still be hungry for more. It scared me. That fear. I'll never forget what that looks like, what that made me feel. When I saw your eyes, it took me a second, but I've seen that kind of hollow before."

Kieran couldn't decide if he was complimented by that little soliloquy.

Most folks saw Kieran as a blank slate. They saw nothing behind his eyes. They interpreted that vacancy as a helpful weapon to point in any direction. The 22nd man saw what others saw, but had a wiser interpretation. He didn't trust Kieran because he saw the void and knew that an abyss could never be a weapon of justice. Any good produced from such a weapon was matched inch-by-inch in evil. Smart. He'd have to account for that in the future.

Kieran tilted his head closer to the man in a mockery of

comradery, like they were friends or conspirators. "Did you warn them?"

The man licked his swollen bottom lip and said, "Yes. They thought they had everything under control." With great effort, he finally raised his head to meet Kieran's eyes. For the first time since they had met, the two men locked eyes with one another. "But only a fool or a god would think they control a force of nature."

"Guess we can all see where you landed on that equation. Gods, you are not," Kieran said.

A timely trill of his ringing commlink broke their connection. Flicking his left wristt palm up, Kieran dropped his gaze to check the GIM data for info on the incoming call.

Sensing that his time in the spotlight had passed, the perceptive little bugger, this 22nd man, subsequently rolled onto his side to curl around his rapidly scabbing-bleeding bits. Kieran stepped over the quaking body of the 22nd man and headed to the front of the room.

Soaking in those last dredges of fear, Kieran took a moment to scan the room and made direct eye contact with several of the more twitchy union members in the group. The huddled mass of unionists, pupils blown wide with adrenaline, tracked his every move.

Trill!

A chirp from his device divided his attention from his efforts in intimidation. Relatively certain even with the interruption that he had made his point clear, Kieran snatched his bomber jacket off the door hook. For good measure and to feed his hunger for melodrama, he bid them adieu. "Fond farewell, boys. We look forward to your compliance."

He exited out past the heavy, rusting door that whined as he heaved. Greeted by an uproar of voices below that echoed louder now than inside the room.

On the final ring, he tapped a single finger behind his right ear to activate the commlink connection.

"You rang?" Kieran's voice was loud to compensate for the long-and-earnest chanting for basic human rights that still echoed through the halls.

A sweet scoff greeted him over the phone.

Cherie.

"Promise you won't gloat?" she asked.

Her greeting put an extra bit of boogie into his step and he practically danced across the rickety catwalk towards the exit. It was good to be right.

"I couldn't promise that. You know I won't make promises I don't intend keep," he said. "What is it this time?"

"You were right. All pretty boys are the same. They'll piss on you and call it rain."

She was talking about the op...

Cherie had called him on a commlink... to talk about the specifics of the Big Plan.

His spine zipped straight and the humor faded from his mouth. She had called him up on his commlink to talk details. Communicating anything but a pizza order over a commlinks was just plain stupid and Cherie was anything but. She was even the one who had taught him to that if it was Pact owned, the Pact was always listening. For her to get this close to disclosing incriminating information when the wolfs were at the gates, meant her side of the op had officially gone FUBAR.

Fucked up beyond recognition.

But apparently it was all Pretty boy McFuck Face's fault. He never trusted the slimo. He was so useless and insignificant Kieran hadn't committed his name or alias to memory, despite his central role in the Big Plan. Cherie had orchestrated everything and everyone down to each ounce of blood, sweat and tears. So, unfortunately, now that the Big Plan was in play, even small, insignificant rocks can make big waves.

Every puzzle piece was to be handled with care. The details mattered so much that Kieran had even hauled his ass out to this Wild's outpost to handle the strike. Two months ago, before the

Big Plan, he would've sent some low-level enforcers and been done with it. But today, these poor unionist got the privilege of a full Kieran experience.

And today, Cherie called on an open commlink because something had gone so wrong the usual precautions were thrown out the airlock.

If he recalled correctly, she was out on Esaa aiming to harpoon a Whale. Kieran wasn't good at high society stuff so he didn't get involved in the details of her current mission. He had voiced his overall distrust of Pretty Boy, then focused on his own work. He couldn't even guess what had happened to result in this kind of breach in protocol.

But, Cherie didn't need him for his deductive reasoning skills. She called her janitor. Kieran was always there to clean everything up and he loved a good scrubadubdub.

"How bad was it? What do you need me to do?" he asked. "I'm done here so, whatever you need. A sanitation, a slash-n-burn, or a 'make sure no one finds the bodies' special. You say the word and I move."

Cherie huffed out a breath. "What needs to be done to fix this... we've never dealt with anything like his. It's a massive... hiccup is the wrong word, but I think I might be stunned. Ultimately I need you on cleanup. But... I also need answers. From both of them," she said, "Cause we sent two of them on this job to prevent exactly this kind of twice-blessed nonsense. Just get here as soon as possible"

"You got it." He jump down of the final steps onto the loading bay where his catamaran was docked, engines idling. He paused before he boarded his ship, the commlink connection would drop this far out from the Central Core.

Kieran's curiosity was getting the better of him today. First his little Q and A with that unionist and now, he wanted to press Cherie for more details. His utter lack of insight frayed at his nerves.

"Just to check that box. What the hell happened?" he asked.

Her end of the conversation fell into silence for a beat to long. Kieran could hear that she was rushing from the sound of her breathe. He could just barely hear the ambient sound of sirens. Chaos was not part of the Big Plan. Eventually when the background noise faded as he waited impatiently for her to break the news.

"Honestly, I'll be fucked... but somehow Dumb and Dumber detonated an Equalizer."

Wow. Unexpected. Fuck.

"They detonated the damn thing under Greene's seat. At least they got that bit right. But the body count... its gotta be close to 400, probably more," she further explained. "The Pact is going to bring the fucking hammer down once they realize how close to home this hit. There were a lot of big names in that theatre tonight. So, get here now."

"I can break some laws getting there as fast as I can." For Cherie, anything. And... this might take everything.

"They've already started station lockdown procedures." Pausing, he heard more rustling. "Call in that favor with Zhou. You're gonna need to be in the belly of the beast for this one."

Ah, Zhou. Now that was a favor. A big favor. While he liked Zhou, it was undeniable that Kieran had a certain taste for rabid animals that made most question his judgment/sanity. Also, Zhou was in deep. It would go unsaid on this phone call that they could only bark up Zhou's tree once. Bad timing with the stakes, this high could be catastrophic.

"Will you be off site by the time I arrive, or would you like to join me in handling our two beloved geniuses?" Kieran asked.

"Oh, I'll be sticking around for a bit," Cherie said. "Keeping my eyes on things. I'll maintain cover and see where this rabbit hole leads. I still have high hope that I can bag me a Whale."

A rare occasion when these two could join together to sow discord in the universe. "Have fun," Kieran said with a laugh.

"Be good."

He grunted and she understood.

He would be anything but good.

THE GOOD FIGHT

02

AURORA

If looks could kill, Aurora was at serious risk of spontaneous combustion.

Between ferociously sporked bites of brownie, her partner, Lieutenant Detective Langston Aster, had her pinned under a glare that could curdle milk. It had been less than seven minutes since they had all settled into the cantina, waiting for the inevitable call to the bridge. His glare remained steady for every millisecond of that time.

As he descended into the crumb phase of his dessert, Aurora prepared to risk another shot at an apology. Because despite his many melodramatic and self-pitying protests to the contrary, Aurora remained reasonably certain that this was not his last meal. Not by a long shot. A little creative interpretation of facts here, an earnest explanation there, and they'd get to the other side of this snafu just fine.

She hoped -- and a healthy dollop of optimism never hurt anyone.

11

Aurora was so determined to get her apology accepted before they faced the firing squad. The metaphorical firing squad... unless they did get canned for their most recent hijinks, then the analogy would be a bit on the nose. Getting fired wasn't outside of the realm of possibility.

Aurora opened her mouth at a couple of attempts of an apology, but Langston's glare had her questioning each approach.

To his right, Liya was no help at all. "It's just so fitting that even when you ultimately, unequivocally, **unbelievably**, screw the pooch... people still shower you in gifts."

The senior forensic analyst of their unit, Liya Grimae, was perhaps the person they worked the closest with after each other. She placed a heckling hand on Langston's back as she nudged him back-and-forth playfully.

Liya's distraction didn't lessen the Lieutenant's heavy-browed scowl in the slightest.

"It's an early, involuntary retirement gift, Liya. Nothing too great to celebrate there," Langston said in a deadpan.

Liya laughed. "You know, it will never get old to see a six-foot-something grown-ass man pout the way you do." Her voice was chirpy and seemed to scratch towards lightening his mood.

He rolled his eyes, but Aurora could see a hint of a dimple winking in humor. The dimple gave up the good fight and dipped into an attempt at a smile, brittle and wry. "You know these feelings won't eat themselves."

Liya hummed in agreement, her hand rubbed across his back. "Then shovel on you must." She turned her attention across the galley table to Aurora and raised her brow in challenge. Liya gave her the *Look* before tapping the time-display on her GIM wrist twice. Message received. She blinked heavily to prevent her True eyes from flashing through. She was running out of time. If Liya could do it, so could she.

It was time to hoist up her big boy pants and just do it.

"Langston–"

"No."

Ooh, ok, Aurora felt the burn of that "no" scorch her as it whizzed by.

"Come on, Langston, I know things–"

His hand came up to his mouth in contemplation that was equally performative and considerate. He grunted out the start of a couple of syllables of a sentence, but didn't get past the beginning. His eyes closed while his hands and utensil gestured about in the failed opening salvo of his attempt to articulate himself. After a while, he made some sort of internal resolution and opened his eyes. Carefully placing his spork in front of the tin on the table, Langston said "Uhhhh, yeah, no. We're not doing this."

That's when the call came in.

A robotic voice crackled over the Mess Hall PA system with the dry report: "Aster and Harlowe. Aster and Harlowe. Report to the Bridge for an incoming call. Aster and Harlowe. Aster and Harlowe. Report to the Bridge for an incoming call."

The mechanized call croaked through the mess, clear as a whistle as every occupant held its breath in unison. This is what they were all waiting for. The incorrigible gossips.

"Saved by the bell." Langston was out of the seat before the message had finished.

Aurora was up and after him, but the mess hall was too full for her to cross over and grab his ear on his way out the door.

Especially considering all the good-natured ribbing that was descending upon them now that the inevitable came a-calling. She couldn't blame them; they had been patient, had put in the time. All five minutes of agonizing time.

By the time Langston had taken the first bites of his pity party soufflé, the mess hall was at full capacity, although dinner had been hours ago. Entertainment like this, even the morsel they would witness in the cantina, was a can't-miss opportunity. Not if half of the rumors they heard what the disastrous mission on Hwei were true. And honestly, they didn't know the half of it.

The partners squeezed and squished down parallel

overcrowded rows scattered between the messy jigsaw of tables that spiraled across through the hall. She looked over at him. Gone was he nerves and self-pity, Langston had shrugged on a caricature of himself like a well-worn jacket. It was a familiar pesona of himself as a swaggering, overly confident Gherrean warrior. Hamming it up, he cupped his hand around his ear, hyping his hand in the air, pretending he couldn't hear the roaring jeers that surrounded them.

Bless their little hearts. The faithful, overworked crew of System Intelligence VP005, "The Socrates," slurped up his dramatics with gusto. He gave an exaggerated bow to his audience before he bolted out the sliding doors.

Aurora had the walk from the cantina to the bridge to get in her apology. Despite his stupid long gait, she was undeterred and jogged behind him to keep up.

She blew out a long breath. "You know... if you looked on the bright side, you might even consider what just happened a victory."

He stopped so fast she slammed into him.

"What? How?"

He turned to face her in profile, an expression darker than his onyx black features settled into the worry lines of his forehead. He had dropped the facade real fast after his exit.

Aurora couldn't help but actually laugh. She reached out to grab his shoulder, "Well, if you remember, days into our first deployment, you tried *so hard* to be one of the guys? Part of the family..."

"And?"

"Just listen to that..."

The sound of laughter and bellows rumbled from behind doors and half a hallway away.

"You made it, babe. For better or for worse, that makes you are 100% part of the family," she said.

Langston scratched at the edge of his brow and scrunched up his face. She liked to think it was in an effort not to laugh. He started up walking again, at a more reasonable pace that she could match.

Ego, posturing, and masks aside, Langston was unlike any other CIC she had worked with. Aurora had been close friends with him for years before this assignment while coming up in the System Intelligence (SI) ranks, the policing and intelligence organization of the Oya Vearro Pact. Hell, she'd even been a groomsman in his fatally doomed wedding. Working with him had been decidedly different from being his friend.

The newly minted Veritas Praeceptorem division of SI had a shoe-string budget and major undertaking, a recipe which didn't lead to success. The goal of the Veritas Praeceptorem program was to deliver the full battery of investigative techniques and practices to the Wilds of the galaxy. It was a mammoth project that was experiencing... complications. To say to least, of the five original commissioned VP fleet, only two had survived a year past their launch. Theirs would be the last of the remaining pair.

While there had been no official word on why VP001, 003, and 004 were scrubbed. But there were plenty of rumors.

As the last of the launched ships, VP005, was larger than the average vessel by several hundreds of square meters, but the additional size was no match for the swelling, overwhelming mass of humans crammed onto the vessel inevitably overwhelmed its architecture and design. After a week and a half in what amounted to a high-tech sardine tin, with consideration of the quick closure of sister ships, the senior staff had made an educated bet tha the inhumane infrastructure had caused the VP ships to collapse.

Langston and Aurora, with a wink and a nod, if not tacit approval from the senior military officers onboard, had abandonned standard military order on board of VP005. Comfort must rule the day. Langston had given the order that anyone willing to put in the work had a carte blanche to redesign the ship's interior to their heart's content.

Major overhauls had started within the first couple of months after its christening and launch. First on the list were the mess hall and the living areas. And, damn, if their squad wasn't creative. The custodial staff had teamed up with the engineering team to construct an airborne second level within the mess hall made entirely of ropes, hammocks, and spare planks of sheet metal. Then the biologists from the tox-lab had undertaken a "greening" project. The result was plants and flora nestled and sprouting from nearly every available crevice they could find among the metallic curves and lines throughout the ship's design. They transformed their regulation barracks, through intention and time, from a cold steel boat into a pseudo amalgamation of a home.

Once all the alterations were made. They held an unofficially christening ceremony for their home. After a proper democratic vote, we dubbed the VP005 *The Socrates*.

Aurora admitted freely that she wouldn't have had the courage to push for something like that. But Langston, with that chip of Core-world guilt as big as Gherre icing down his shoulder, had championed their efforts without blinking.

Sixteen missions deep, nearly triple the flight time as the other scrubbed ships, they were close to realizing the impossible dream advertised in promo reels across the system. Veritas Praeceptorem was the promise of a new, more efficient, and more ethical investigative policing unit for the binary star–Oya Vearro star system. VP shepherded the dream of unbiased, independent investigations—free from the accusations of corruption and laziness that were rising in the shoddy local policing precincts across the Wilds and Utility Belt. The promo reels bragged that the best and brightest were on the case. It was a damn tall order and inevitably meant exhaustion and burnout were part of the package for their team. Most of the crew had been pulling double, if not triple, duty in the face of the constant fear of downsizing.

Downsizing was another plausible reason for prior scrubbed VP units.

Under his breath to no one but himself, Langston said with a resigned sense of certainty. "This just can't be good."

"This isn't likely to be good. Not 'can't'. Don't be so negative."

His silence communicated his disbelief and lack of faith.

Huffing a bit and trying for the easy optimism Langston normally spouted by the gallon, Aurora attempted to give him a jolt of positivity through logic.

"Yes, it isn't likely to be good. I'll admit that. But it could be... ok. Ok is okay." Bumping into his shoulder playfully, Aurora walked slightly faster so that she could spin in order to hold the conversation face-to-face as she walked backward. "'Can't' implies that there is a zero-null probability of the possibility of something good might occur. Which is simply inaccurate and a little fatalistic."

Langston gave her a hard look and searched Aurora's face for something she couldn't quite pin down. "You're kidding right?" He gave a harsh laugh. "I've seen some thing in my eighteen year in the service, and I know two things for damn sure. One, the mission on Hwei was an epic clusterfuck that defied most reason and all good sense. Two, failure has consequences."

Aurora said nothing. He was right.

"I begged for this assignment, Roar. I drank the Kool-aid. I believed the hype. I've seen how rotten things can get with Pact business. Seen it first hand. We could lose all this. You know that, right? That if we get demoted or censured, they are going to send this ship back to HQ and gut it. Everything we built will be broken. No more cantina, no more sciencey folks. All gone... because of us. It seems pretty fatal to me."

Langston had always had this patriotic romanticism for the VP mission. Aurora couldn't have any kind of hope for something that the Pact touched. But he was right. She believed in them, their crew. And she emotionally couldn't handle the idea of starting over.

She caught his eye for half a second. Coughed, unable to say anything to contradict him on that front. She stopped in front of him, forcing him to stop as well, as she grabbed his forearm and gave it a firm squeeze. "Yeah... You're right. This can't be good."

"Hah!" His was a dusty cheer.

"Does it help to know we did the right thing? On Hwei. We're the good guy. You *are* a good guy."

He patted his hand over her and started walking. She fell into step beside him. "I'll be honest," Langston said. "The fact that I really hate that we did the right thing makes me feel like a terrible person. So... I don't feel too '*good*.'"

Aurora didn't have any witty responses to that, especially considering they had just arrived at one of the more treacherous sets of hallways on the ship. As they walked to the bridge, there had been a smattering of techs and crews they'd crossed path with, but as they arrived at the "Blobway", not a single person to be found in splatter distance.

The Blobway was an unfortunate bout of mission creep that was never quite resolved, despite the annoyance it inflicted on every single person onboard The Socrates. When the sciencey staff had asked for permission to conduct their "small" experiment in the northern stretch of hallways closest to the bridge they had mysteriously gotten approval. While, of course they'd asked couple of cursory questions and the project was not what they expected.

That experience taught them a couple of hard lessons. First, there was the clear underestimation of the relative traffic of the area. But more importantly, there was the conflicting definitions of qualified as a small. The experiment involved floating balls of gravity neutralizing sulfur-based goo. It was annoying at the best of times, but bobbing and weaving between the orbs of oniony-gym-sock-smelling goo was the worst way to have a conversation about the emotional complexity of imposter syndrome and morality.

But time waits for no man, so the partners dodged their way through the Blobway.

"So, I've been doing the mental math," Langston started.

"Yeah?"

"Yeah. On one side, I've got every excuse, rationalization or denial I could conceivably offer the XO. Then on the other side I have our laundry list of fuck up both on Hwei and historically. You wanna know how it all adds up?"

"Ow. Yikes. Not particularly, no."

"Well, too bad. The fuck-ups woefully outnumber the excuses."

"Lietenant Detective, come on–"

Langston cut Aurora off with a harsh glare again. He was clearly in no mood and she had, for just an instance, forgotten she was supposed to be eating crow and apologizing profusely.

"Okay. Langston, ole buddy ole pal. When you're right, you're right. And you are indeed right." Aurora said with heaping helpings of faux-positivity. Langston had frequently accused her of pessimism, so she was sure this little performance tickled him pink. "But not for the reason you think. Because —"

Langston laughed as he made his way out of the Blobway and waited for Aurora to catch up. Her crown of kinks and coil, restrained as they were at a voluminous poof at the nape of her neck, still made the Blobway a more trying experience fo her.

"Harlowe, I know that not telling me why I'm right, **but also** wrong at the same time, might very well kill you. Your head might just pop with all the unsaid intelligent deductions you gotta rolling around up there. But let me let you into a little secret. Nine out of ten times, no one cares *why* they are right. As long as, in the end, they're right."

"Langston--"

"Don't be a patronizing asshole, Roar." His words were as sweet as they were final. They'd been friend for a long-time. He had covered for her, been her ally in more ways than she could count. And... Hwei was not only her fault, but it was tragically just as bad as he said it was. But, despite it all, even though they hadn't spoken about it or made a plan, he was going to stand by her side and endure an equal portion of whoop-ass that awaited for them on the bridge.

Instead of apologizing, Aurora said, "I'm not an asshole."

Her tone was soft atonement.

He quipped back, "A patronizing saint, then. Better?"

Smiling, Aurora nudged his shoulder. "Immeasurably worse." For the barest second, she blinked out a glimmer of the *Truth* in her eyes to convey her sincerity.

"See, being right ain't all it's cracked up to be," Langston concluded as they made the last few paces to reach the sealed doors of the flight deck. Langston held up the heel of left wrist to alow his GIM implant to be scanned to unlock and open the fortified doors. With a flourish of faux chivalry, he bowed and signaled her to pass before him.

One after another, they walked into the belly of the beast together.

WHAT HAPPENED
HAPPENED

LANGSTON

There are many things that Langston would deny if called out on. Hiding behind Aurora as they entered the Bridge fit squarely among those many things. The Bridge was Captain Markey's domain.

Captain Markey, the Command Corp flight commander, didn't pick favorites.

But if he did, everyone and their brother knew that it wasn't Langston.

Today, the Bridge seemed gloomier and more foreboding than usual. He walked in past the sliding doors to the main console towards Markey, standing sentinel in his usual spot with a stack of holodecks in hand. He paid Langston no never mind as he approached. The Bridge and flight crew were all CC military officers. They operated on a separate schedule from the VP crew, though they all mingled and gossiped outside of working hours.

Despite his grizzled mug and palpable-if-unconfirmable disdain for Langston, Markey held the laudable position as the kindest captain Langston had ever worked under. It was in the big things like letting the ship's crew redesign and "human-ify" the shuttle to the little things like how he treated the staff.

Kindness wasn't an easy trait to identify as Markey. He was a no-nonsense egalitarian type whose face didn't move beyond the occasional blink. Markey came by his steely exterior honestly, considering he'd risen from the Command Corp ranks the hard way. To go from a Wilds enlisted scrub to a captain was no small feat. The man was clearly proud of his position while also being all too aware of where he came from. Langston could relate for the opposite reasons. He'd argue he was no Gherrean soft-hand, just like Markey wasn't a deadbeat Wilder addict. Both claimed that they were one of the good ones.

However, in the beginning, middle, and end of every day, it would be a mistake to think anyone in the Command Corp ranks had a sweet disposition.

Langston took Markey's dislike personally. Most of their interactions were like projectile vomiting a mixture of oil and water. It made co-management of the crew as the two senior officers on board a constant source of joy and entertainment.

They just couldn't see eye to eye on their approach to anything. Ironically, Langston's inability to ignore the mounting tension was perhaps Markey's least favorite trait of the Lieutenant Detective's. Langston had considered the idea that if he just stopped trying to make nice with Markey, their relationship might heal.

But that wasn't going to happen.

It wasn't in Langston's nature; it wasn't in his stars. So, once again, this time with feeling, Langston attempted to engage Markey in a non-hostile conversation. Casually.

"Captain, you alright?" Langston asked as he leaned against the console.

On brand, Markey in no way acknowledged this greeting or Langston's existence. After it was clear that Markey was specifically ignoring Langston, the Captain mustered up some energy to give a respectful half nod to Aurora. The man then tapped out a series of access codes into the console to open the secure comms channel to Pact headquarters.

The detectives' summons from the Cantina was perfectly timed to account for the time to arrive at the bridge and receive their call from HQ. Langston loved the way the lightning-fast efficiency of the ship's operation viewing it like a bit of poetry.

The productivity was standard across all Systems Intelligence vessels, Langston still loved that faster than light commitment to competence. After all, that's the motto: **System Intelligence -- *The Light Will Find You*.** It was a perplexingly both comforting and terrifying as a motto.

Langston reached over to the control panel and tapped across the display it to pull up the incoming vid call. When the ID verification popped up on the screen, Langston swiped his GIM wrist with his credentials across the scanner to show his IDNA for the incoming message.

"Aster. Aurora." Markey both greeted and dismissed them as he moved back a small foot of space away to give them an illusion of privacy. The courtesy was touching as much as the protocol was insulting. Listening in on every comm between SI officers onboard a CC operated vessel was a typical example of CC abusing their authority. It meant there were no secure calls, outside of the bridge or beyond CC surveillance. Two sides of the Oya Vearro pact dancing in a dangerous duel for supremacy.

So yes, Markey stepping back to give them the illusion of privacy was a class act as much as it was an empty gesture.

Perhaps it was time to admit that perhaps he disliked Markey as much as the man dislike him.

Aurora leaned back, perched on the other side of Langston. She called out to Markey's retreating figure with a friendly, "How's our girl doing today?" Her hand patted the sturdy metal rim of the console affectionately, like a large, beloved dog.

"Right as rain," he said with an impressively somber and impassive tone while a crinkle of a smile shimmied across his leathery skin. He nodded his head before heading over to the other side of the deck, where a crew member had flagged him down. As he walked, he barked out the order, "Comms, pull up Colonel Dean's link up on the big board."

At Markey's command, a pixelated burst of light flared to life from the center console, quickly shaping into a life-sized rendering of one Colonel Jackson Dean. It was a sign of the severity of their overall conduct to have their dressing down so public and so immediate. This call would be formal, tense, and procedural. Langston and Aurora both zapped up to stand at attention, their backs ramrod straight as they await Dean's opening salvo.

To make matters worse, Dean was dressed formally in grays. Dean's baleful, bright-green eyes shone out from the hollow hologram in front of the detectives.

The usual buzzing clatter of activity on the bridge simmered down to a low hum. While all the pilot's eyes were appropriately and professionally on their assigned task at hand, all ears were on the drama that was sure to unfold at the center console.

Seconds ticked away. Dean let the tension between them fester and propagate. Langston saw the tiniest pebbles of glistening sweat collect against Dean's buzz-cut hair line.

In the bloodcurdling elapsed time, Langston clued into the fact that the background noise on Dean's end was louder than normal. Noise-canceling sound equipment came standard, so they rushed and frantic conversations must've been pretty loud over at HQ. It was not the order and ease one typically associated with System Intelligence headquarters.

"Lieutenants."

Jointly, the detectives saluted. "Colonel."

"Are you familiar with the phrase 'to beat a dead horse'?" Dean asked.

Stutteringly, the partners both affirmed, "Yessir," in unison.

If Langston wasn't a top-tier officer trained in military order, he would've shifted slightly and cut their eyes to the right to take in Aurora's reaction. But he didn't. And he was reasonably certain that even if he did that, she wouldn't have had a noticeable reaction. She was a stone when she wants to be.

"To beat a dead horse means to waste time and energy on a situation that can't be changed. As you know I don't waste time." Dean delivered each word with a direct and individual glare that scorched with reprimand. Not one to waste time, zhey continued. "You have a new assignment."

Langston had to take a quick second to register what all this meant. If he was right, it was a damned interesting choice from SI Command. If Dean were to be believed, apparently, Langston and Aurora were not going to be seriously reprimanded for their conduct on Hwei. No need to beat a dead horse with excessive disciplinary action... apparently. So, they were going to get off free and clear, and the partners had only been called up to the bridge to get a new assignment apparently... not to get reprimanded for Hwei. All of this was apparent, and all of this was happening. Because... *apparently*.

If true, Langston could muster up some enthusiasm for this set of events. He'd just thank his lucky stars and keep moving as long as Aurora didn't open her big —

"Colonel, if you could let me explain--" Aurora spoke up.

"No, I won't let you *complain*," Dean said. Zheir voice echoed in stereo as zheir early career as a drill sergeant made a big appearance in the volume of that reply. All things considered, a certain level of volatility was par for the course for all of Dean's interactions with Aurora. "What happened happened. Period. Unless your words will undo your actions?"

Dean waited for several beats too long, daring her to test zhem.

"Thought not. The horse is dead. Move on. Cause I am. Your new assignment: there was a terrorist attack on Esaa Seltenta Station." Dean nodded zheir head off-screen, signaling a nearby aid to send them the case file. In response, the two detectives pulled out their compads in front of them to review the incoming data file from Dean and HQ.

Wow. Out from the pits of Hwei up to Esaa Station, this could be a big assignment for their team. Terrorist attacks were big. They'd been pretty common for a few a year directly following the end of the war some fifteen years back, but Langston couldn't even remember any attacks in the past decade.

For the past few months, the Socrates had just had minor assignments all peripherally related to the rash of labor protests that were popping up through the system. Most, but not all, the strikes faded fast, but there were a couple still raging. So far, the strikes picked at old scabs and dredge up more work for folks like SI investigators.

Esaa Station was renowned as a Pact Monument site. Not only was it one of the most beautifully crafted stations in the system, but it was also where several signature award ceremonies took place.

Langston opened a set of files, the first detailing basic blueprints and information about Esaa Station, and the next was an incomplete file with the sparse details about the attack.

"Captain Markey has the coordinates and is plotting a route now. Esaa Station is a luxury vessel in orbit around the planet, Quo. Based on security protocols and the nature of the attack, initial reports documented a high probability that the terrorists were on board at the time of the bombing. With an actionable level of certainty, the working theory is that the terrorists are contained on Esaa Station. The intel is inconclusive on whether this was a lone agent attack or a member of a larger terror cell."

"These reports don't seem to include information on any details on structural damages or casualties. Is there anything official or perhaps even any unofficial word over at HQ about what we can expect?" Langston asked as he skimmed over the specs of the station. The signature feature of the resort was a glass dome at the vertex of the station. While such a feature was an inarguably gorgeous work of art, Langston had to imagine that such artistry came with some compromise as far as structural integrity went.

He definitely questioned the success of any security lockdowns procedures enacted.

"So far, there are no concerns about hull integrity or any critical breach to the vessel. However, the current estimate is at least 400 presumed dead and counting." Dean pursed zheir lips. It wasn't necessarily a planned pause, but almost as if Dean was struggling with what zhey were about to reveal. Zheir voice didn't waiver though. It was sure and factual. "It was a series of bomb but most of those deaths were in a catabolic bomb detonation. Initial reports show it was a metabolic partiphaser."

Gasps snatched right out from the lungs of half the people on the deck.

Then a complete shock of silence.

Metabolic partiphasers were a popular tool used by Wilder terrorists about forty years back when the Pact had first been establishing order throughout the system. It was a messy, dark period where even the bomb-makers themselves had stopped making the devices because of the inhumane nature of the mass killing. The Pact had outlawed all catabolic explosives in the first set of true laws of the Oya Vearro Pact and Command Corp. The military arm of the Pact had an iron grip on all foundries known to produce the sub-atomic material capable of producing such a weapon.

How the hell did anyone get their hands on such a weapon? And once they did, why use it? It did, however, explain the lack of structural damage that accompanied such a high body count.

Langston flicked through the various files they had given him access to, looking to see if there were any immediate targets given the big payload and inaccessibility of such a weapon.

Nothing so far.

"Any initial suspects or targets?"

"It's the big bubbkis on that one. Onto mission parameters. Point of contact on-site will be Captain Nimco Ahmed, the highest-ranking officer on board." Dean took a breath, shooting zheir gaze slightly off-screen, somewhat dramatically in a sign of perhaps anxiety or surveillance. Interesting.

"Because of the nature of the event and the high-value targets currently aboard, they were able to sequester Esaa Station within minutes from the initial bombing event. We got lucky and there are no departure or arrivals logged within two full hours before the bombing. The station is on lockdown for a single day, thirty hours. The perp is on that raft. It's your job to find them."

Aurora's eyes were glued to her compad playing on repeat. The drone footage from the files. The vid clips compared the original structure of the obelisk glass theatre before and after the bombing. There was no structural damage to the station, which was an enormous relief, but the fire raging bright and blue behind the courisand glass was a sight not to be forgotten. "It's hard to believe people can do such evil to other people, such destruction. Have you seen this footage, Colonel?"

"Of course. It's nothing new. We've all seen the old war footage. It's surprising, but not new. Prepared yourselves. We haven't had something like this in a long time. But we have long memories. We didn't forget how to handle such thing." Dean tapped the compad on zheir side of the holo and pulled up a miniaturized, rotating model of the Esaa Station on holo display.

Esaa Station was a cylindrical station with the signature opera-house crowning the structure in a minaret-style dome made entirely of glass. "The explosion was contained solely to the Santos Opera Hall located at the gravitational south of the station pointing towards Quo. Again a bit of luck here, it's courisand glass dome was designed to withstand planetary impact or several kilotons of seismic impact. These bombs had detonated in any other part of the ship, structural integrity of overall vessel would've caused a station-wide neutralizing event. That being said, this was the opening night of a ZeroG ballet opera event titled... 'An Inch of Flesh.'"

"Opening night, that means--" Langston swiped a hand over his face and pressed his eyes closed for a beat.

"High-value targets, one and all." Dean again glanced to

zheir right, perhaps with intention more likely out of habit. "The metabolic partiphaser plus the ensuing chaos means that so far we have gotten no names of victims on any official reports, but... The Pact is concerned."

Well, that was clearly an understatement.

As well as being terribly trite, it always gave Langston heartburn when people prescribed the government, the Oya Vearro Pact, human emotions. Because they were never happy emotions, like "grateful" or "enthusiastic".

It was always: The Pact is disappointed. The Pact is concerned. You wouldn't like the Pact when it's angry.

It was stomach rumbling that the folks prone to such personification were always people who knew more than he did. It didn't bode well.

Langston, for one, did not like it when the Pact was concerned about anything having to do with him. The Pact's attention was not forgiving or kind. Their concern was a thing of worry.

Langston voiced his own concerns, "No one would accuse me of modesty but I can't imagine we were the ideal team to alleviate the Pact's concerns."

Because any idiot could tell you that this was a big case. This case would probably define politics at least for the next season if not Oyan-year. It needed to be handled and contained. While Langston liked to think highly of the Socrates team, they were still fresh and new. Their unit was barely a year out of the gate.

Prior to their latest deplorable showing out in the wastelands of Hwei, Langston had been planning to campaign to get bigger, more impressive assignment for his team. Be it arrogance or realism until this latest fuck up, their VP005 team had really been holding their own. Solving cases fast, the combination of his Gherrean political adroitness and her Ohahlian intuition was a match made in the stars. They were unmatched when it came to successful case closure rates.

Until... now.

Which made it the worst possible time for this mission. He had fully expected for Dean to send them back to headquarters with their tail tucked behind their legs. But this was... Langston couldn't decide if this was a better or worse turn of events. There was no logical reason, after their last performance, that they would receive such a high-profile assignment.

"Let me guess, we are the closest ship to Quo?" Aurora asked.

Ah, there it is.

Dean's smile wasn't unkind. "Got it in one. Proximity to a problem was your saving grace today. With all the strikes finally coming to a close, the politics of a wasteful fuel-overspend was a nonnegotiable. The next closest ship is 2 sols away from the station. They will be right behind you though." Zhey shot a quick fast gaze off to the right again. Strange.

"Partners or pitbulls?" Aurora asked. Langston appreciated her question; that girl always had her eyes on the prize. Excluding Markey, the woman hated Command Core with a rabid enthusiasm. Langston suspected she had at some point memorized the Westcaneer's Kennel Club dog breed encyclopedia to add more creativity and variety to her insults.

But having a combination of SI and CC hands on deck jockeying for authority tended to make a case messier. She was right to ask. The looming threat of a rabid gang of knuckle-dragging, shoot-first-ask-question-later degenerate 'military investigators' of a Command Corp taskforce was even more incentive to solve this thing before they arrived.

But if the Pact was concerned, a CC Taskforce was the typical prescription to beat their worries away.

"I'm not going to dignify that with a response. Be nice," Dean said. "The closest System Intelligence ship, Command Corp or otherwise, is 2 sols away. So, you two will have the investigation all to yourselves... for the next thirty hours" "

They could work with this. "Markey, what's our ETA to Quo?" Langston asked.

"1.6 hours. We should land at half-past 28hundred hours."

Dean nodded, "Good, good. Mission parameters. Identify and detain suspects as you see fit. A substantial arrest will be enough to end the sequester. But if that isn't possible based on evidence, like I said, Command will be 2 sols behind you. Be advised, Esaa Station has a certain clientèle. The high society folks have voiced opinions to top brass about the lockdown protocol. So it's got to beby the book. Technically the sequester is only legally possible for that first thirty hours, so work fast. Any suspects and detainees will be remanded to HQ for justice once Command arrives. That gives you approximately fifty hours on the ground before the cavalry arrives. Copy?"

"Yessir."

Dean nodded. One last nervous look to the right, "Dismissed."

Aurora followed Langston out of the command center.

He couldn't wait to let the team know about this assignment. They were back in it.

FLIGHT DECK, SI - VP005 THE SOCRATES
OUTSIDE HWEI

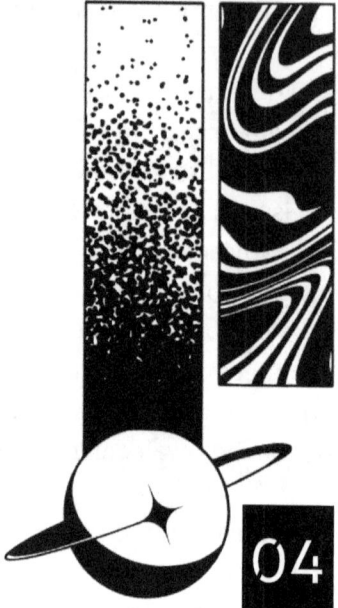

NEVER TRUST A SURVIVOR

AURORA

As they exited the Bridge, Aurora trudged; Langston floated. His feet didn't touch the ground once since they were dismissed. Langston rubbed his hands together fast before clapping three times thunderstrike-loud. The man was gearing up for a classic Aster speech. If he kept this up, Aurora might have to reveal to the rest of the Socrates that he was *skipping* giddy as a toddler through the halls.

He squeezed her shoulders as the doors closed behind them. "This. Is. It." Langston shook her like a rag-doll with each word.

Laughter bubbled from her throat as she squished his face with her hands in response. "I'll guess we'll see, won't we?"

Rolling his eyes, he swatted her hands away. His eyes lost not a sprinkle of twinkle. His huge smile split his deep midnight features in half. He had such easy access to optimism. She pushed down the aching twinge of jealousy. A dark and petty part of her bemoaned another glowing example of Langston's un-traumatic childhood.

"Nah, you are wrong, wrong, wrong! This is it." Langston skated around her as she walked down the hallways. His sweeping gestures artfully dodged the floating ooze of the science experiment as he span, shimmied, and did everything else in between. "The big time. The big kahuna. The big Watch-Out-We're-Coming-For-You-World Grand Slam, Mother of all Beasts, BIG ONE."

Aurora wasn't even sure she disagreed. This was one helluva big case. She was unsure if she wanted to be anywhere near something so big. Big things make a big impact. Impact means repercussions.

"Go get your Big Girl pants on Roar, cause we are In It now! I'll tell the unit," he said. His voice was loud and easily carried over his shoulder as he raced towards the cantina.

Aurora walked alone back to her private quarters with shuffling steps. It was her petulant attempt to delay the inevitable. Her body made the trek through the shuttle on autopilot as she purposefully cleansed her mind to a blank slate in preparation. She shoved her mind into a centered state as she arrived at her barrack doors. Waving her GIM arm opened the biometrics of her doorlock. She rushed in, yanking the cloth pivacy curtain closed behind her. No need to make a shitty day even worse by revealing her inner sanctum to whatever random person was walking into the hall behind her as she opened her door.

Lingering icicles of nerves shattered and broke off as she finally exhaled behind her locked door. She had been prepping for the confrontation with Dean; her nerves and adrenaline were still buzzing, having not actually had that fight.

There was no fight, just the next mission. And as Langston said, it was The Big One. The nerves from before returned. It felt like she was perpetually trying to keep her space in this program. Keep her space on this ship. Keep this eight by eight feet piece of heaven to herself. It was all hers, for now. All her stuff was nice and snug in one place protected by a lock. It was all hers... as long as she solved the next case. And the one after that and the one after that.

The lights automatically flickered on. The lights made it semi-possible to navigate her small little refuge without bumping into too much stuff. Any bunk space not dedicated towards sleep or daily cleansing had stuff on it. There was stuff piled on, stuff touching, more stuff that was leaning against even more stuff. Now, of course, she loved every inch of every item, but even she could admit that this was a lot.

Some would call this an obvious case of hoarding. She reframed that assessment as an enthusiastic curation. She had been in System Intelligence service for a little over six years and she still couldn't stop herself from buying or bartering anything from home. Post-grad as a new SI cadet had been the first time since before the refugee processing center that she had been able to claim ownership over something, anything.

There had been a time when a younger version of her would've loudly taunted that they could pry her things out of her cold, dead hands. In fact, she can recall at the refugee center she had yelled almost that exact sentiment with substantially more curse words thrown in. She had meant it too; wee baby Aurora thought she could spit fire and throw down with the best of them. She was a Harlowe, descendant of six generations of Yavrron warriors — a Truth Seer. There was no blood in her veins, just the raging water of Ohahlia raced within her.

However, life had proved her wrong. Life was the ultimate teacher, and she was a bad student.

Aurora reached out to skim her fingers over the coarse hairy fibers of an embroidered tapestry on the wall, the cold metal glide of the hammered storyteller's bowl on a shelf. Her eyes followed her hands. She witnessed more than felt that her fingers were trembling.

Langston saw a final opportunity. She just saw an ax ready to fall on their necks. Again. No amount of meditation and calming breaths could hold off this upcoming panic.

A lifetime ago, her grandfather had cradled his wrinkle-soft, calloused-leather hands around hers. He told her fingers couldn't shake if you balled them into fists. He whispered "Fight or fly, my girl, but never let them see you quake". Her nails bit into her palms for a second before she shook the achy memory out of her tendons.

There was one last task left for her. While Langston was preparing for the new mission, she had other fish to fry.

The flash of some emotion gurgled up into her unconscious mind, Aurora's *True* eyes sparked into view. Her warm brown eyes blinking out to reveal large iridescent irises. Her hand slammed against her eyelids and rubbed harshly till the *Truth* faded from her pupils. If only there were antacids for emotional turmoil.

Aurora squared off her stance and readied herself for this next conversation. She grabbed a remote from a bowl by the door and flicked it toward the port wall as she tapped behind her ear to activate her commlink. A low-resolution holo pixelated across the wall of her bedroom.

Fake smile firmly in place, she greeted Dean. "Subtly, thy name is Jackson Dean."

Dean's tightly shorn hair slowly came into focus projected across her collage of various imprints and tapestries. Dean sighed before zhey looked up. Pulling at zheir shoulder muscle while using zheir other hand unbuttoned the double-breasted dress coat with the other. Dean glared through Aurora with those sharp sharp eyes of zheirs. A glare was a as good a response as what she was hoping for.

Throughout the briefing on deck, Dean had given her their Signal.

The Signal was a call to arms of sorts. It never meant the same thing twice, but it was more secure than smoke signals orr a public request for a pull aside. Going into the bridge, she had been as prepared as possible to talk her. Langston and the crew out of the shitshow of disciplinary hearings they probably deserved after their last mission. But she was not at all prepared for this. It was out of the ordinary in a worrying fashion.

Originally, the Signal was an inside joke back from her days at the Pressure Cooker, the SI's training program. This was back when anyone who knew anything knew about Dean, the up-and-coming hotshot captain, and Aurora, the untamable Ohahlian with zero education and perfect test scores. The two had the most outrageous rivalry that frequently resulted in comedy. It was the stuff of legend. It was public shouting matches and endless demerits on Aurora's record, and it was all in good fun. Even then, Dean couldn't help zhemselves in giving Aurora special attention.

The joke started when Dean was lecturing her class on assessment protocol for collecting forensic evidence. The lecture was far from riveting material. To Aurora's annoyance, Dean kept glancing towards the back of the room every couple of seconds like a bad tick.

What had started as subtle glances had transitioned into oddly performative head bobbles. However, just the week before, Dean had berated Aurora about interrupting a lecture with non sequitur comments, so she didn't raise her hand. She instead continued to take notes, but her notes were no longer about administrative procedures. No, she was so convinced that Dean was seconds away from an epileptic seizure, Aurora monitored and documented his symptoms. She detailed every instance of a head bobble.

But while Aurora was observing Dean, Dean was observing her right back.

Dean, hotshot captain that zhey were, noticed her attention. This distraction annoyed Dean. The captain then proceeded to slowly and methodically use morse code via head bobs in order to spell out:

F-U-C-K--O-F-F--A-N-D--P-A-Y--A-T-T-E-N-T-I-O-N

This resulted in Aurora bursting out into laughter when she had finished decoding the end of Dean's message.

Later, when Dean had transitioned from teacher to CO, the fire of their previous relationship had cooled. The two had reached an impasse. Dean explained that during that lecture zhey had gotten some insider knowledge that the Captain's supervisor would observe the classroom. So initially all the glances to the back of the auditorium were an attempt to divine whether zheir supervisor was observing Dean's lectures using the internal security cam footage in the lecture hall. Realistically, Dean applauded her observational skills and marked that moment as a start to a new page in their relationship. Theirs was a weird relationship full of coded messages and half-truths. But one each of them valued it nonetheless.

So today, during their dispatch call, she had caught the signs. Dean had made the Signal.

Through the course of their mission brief on the bridge, with head-bobs and glances, Dean signaled: *Call me.*

So she did.

"You can leave out the sass, Harlowe. You know, no matter what context, where we are, or what we are doing, that I'm still your boss."

A light chortle escaped from Aurora, "Of course, my liege. I wouldn't dare forget it."

Dean, however, would never have signaled for a social call. Zheir eyes were serious. The levity between them evaporated as a riptide of tension flooded into the silence. That silence hung abruptly and ominously as a noose between them. She measured her next words carefully. Not abruptly or stupidly. Better to be careful. Dean had given her enough rope to hang herself with.

"How bad is it?"

"Let me be clear. Without this case, if the Socrates came back to base directly after that clusterfuck on Hwei, you would be out. Fired. Gone. Done. End of story. I bought you some time and an opportunity with this assignment. It's a big assignment. I pulled strings and I'm backing you two on this. But Hwei will not be forgotten. It was memorable. Especially with your... background. Because of your background, really. The fact that you got Aster to go along with it, take responsibility for it, might even make it worse."

Zheir words gutted Aurora. Her head jerked down to hide the reflexive flash of iridescent Truth in her eyes.

She hadn't really thought much of Hwei. She didn't let herself, too busy trying to win back Langston's good favor. It was impulsive and earnest and naïve of her to think that "doing the right thing" meant that things would work out in the end.

She knew better. Her history was proof enough of that. Her blood carried that truth. Right and wrong meant nothing if you weren't on the winning side. Langston was allowed to make mistakes. She wasn't. That was just the cards she was dealt.

It would always come back to that.

Ohahlia.

What the Pact did to her people to her, marked her as a lit fuse, whether she liked it. It was so typical of the Pact to make their massacre, their genocide, her problem. Of course, never trust a survivor, for they have vengeance on their minds. The dead are good because they can be mourned, regretted. A dead Ohahlian was decidedly less dangerous.

She cracked her neck to twist out the dying embers of hot-like-burning indignation. She would have to box up those jagged, raw emotions and put it in the same place she put her dignity when she applied to SI originally. Aurora sunk into her bed across from the vid call holo. She knew applying for SI was a gamble. She hadn't realistically thought she would get in. It was that spark of something that smelled an awful lot like purpose that drove her to do it. A fading memory of her grandfather's proud and indefatigable teaching her about the responsibility to do good in the world.

She was under no false pretenses. She understood Ohahlia had lost the war in no uncertain terms. How could she forget when the memories of all that was lost haunted her? There was no going back, not for her. So, here she was, trying to be part of the solution. Trying to do something good. And utterly failing, just like the ones who were lost.

In that box in the back of her mind, she hid her opinions about The Pact being labeled anything close to a solution. They were a solution like death is an answer. Both are true, but neither is preferable. But she didn't open the box in the back of her mind except to shove more opinions in there.

She ran her hand over the fluffy seerkat-fur throw on her bed. She didn't have space for those opinions in this room because all available room was for her Stuff. And she wanted to keep her stuff. That meant staying in the Pact's good graces. That meant no more repeats of the catastrophe on Hwei.

But the idea of doing anything other than what she had done, soured the spit in her mouth. Aurora chewed on a bit on the inside corner of her cheek. She thought back to the Hwei miners' faces. Of the justice that was owed to them. "If you had been there --- If you would let me explain," Aurora said. The pragmatic part of her brain told her they were way past the point of explaining. No explanation would have an impact at this point. "What was happening — I couldn't just... it... it just wasn't fair."

"Aurora. Life isn't fair. I can't possibly be the first one to tell you that."

"Well, you ain't just whistling dixie." She pulled a hand through her coils of her hair, in frustration. "I was hoping with the combination of me and Langston we'd be able to fly under the radar."

"Hwei was a mistake," Dean spoke the incontrovertible truth of the matter. It was a true, raw, and, at the moment, an unkind reminder. But damned if it wasn't an accurate accounting of the situation. That ability to speak with such surety was the foundation their relationship was built on.

Dean rubbed a hand across zheir face in fatigue. "This next case... if you solve this next case with a flourish. You're set. The VP program has seen hills and valleys but your record is solid. Do this. Do it well. And I'll back you. You know my opinion."

She actually didn't. Throughout her entire time in the Pressure Cooker, she had been an outlier. She had assumed that was her connection with Dean was because they were both talented outsiders looking in. But Dean had never confirmed that. In fact, zhey had never even referenced anything till now.

Through design or neglect, the two outsiders didn't speak about such things. Opinions. Feelings. About why Dean had invested in her development. Emotional truth was slippery, and it was unspoken that neither of the two had any time or energy for emotional truth.

"VP... Systems Intelligence, hell the whole damn system. We need you," Dean said.

That's why she liked Dean. "You're lying," Aurora announced, laughing in disbelief.

There are many different kinds of lies. Most people lie so constantly but never for any important reason. Lying to themselves. Lying to be kind. Lying to be cruel. Flattery. Romance. Hope. The way that Dean lied was always interesting to Aurora. It was a clean glass of water. Like zhey knew it was a lie, but that was ok with zhem. A lie you could believe in, like the clarity of it cleaned zheir consciousness.

"Not in the way you would think. Remember that."

Dean was a friend.

"I will," And Aurora knew genuine friends were hard to come by, "I do."

Dean moved to end the call by reaching behind zheir ear to tap the commlink, but hesitated for a blink. "Fast and flawless. Then everything can be forgiven," Dean reiterated.

Aurora almost wished that zhey had said nothing. But of course, she shouldn't be stupid enough to forget that this was not a pep talk. "But not forgotten."

"Don't be shitty, Aurora. Subtleties are for the birds."

She laughed. "Thanks."

NO TERROR

AURORA

A broadcast announced over the Loading Dock PA the beginning of the ten minute docking sequence. It was a four phased final docking procedure the hoity-toity space station that was Esaa Station. It was almost go-time. The Socrates squad had meandered their way out of their bunks to the dock for landing and were all accounted for during the 10-minute final call.

Despite the relative successes or failures of Dean's "pep" talk, Aurora's overall level of nervousness was estimated at mild-to-low levels.

And anyone who would dare accuse Aurora of lying to herself was themselves a damn dirty liar. She had her anxiety firmly grasped and wrangled in her understandably sweaty palms.

Aurora drifted through the various members of the Socrates as they milled around the docking bay, getting ready for touchdown. Several clumped in a tight crowd around the only portal window by the landing door, eager for glimpses of Quo, the twice-blessed second planet from the twin stars of their system, Oya and Vearro.

If one wanted to be a pretentious, pontificating political pundit about it, Quo was a perfect metaphor for what had become of the Oya Vearro celestial system. Though awe-inspiring in its beauty and majesty, if you scratch a centimeter below the surface, there is nothing there. Like all gas giants, it is a swirling colossus of poison and smog. There was no center, no core, no soul. Beauty didn't haven't to be a purposeless monstrosity. But Quo could be described as such... if one wanted to be a pretension pontificating political pundit about it. Which one would never want, of course.

The instructions from the PA system blared their routine announcements and general orders as the VP005 docked at the large cruiser bay on the far north side of Esaa Seltenta Space Station in orbit around Quo.

Aurora pushed the sleeve of her black leather jacket up to her elbow for the fourteenth time in as many minutes. She was perfecting the look. The look had to be perfect.

The rest of the crew was in the customary blue SI fatigues, but her and Langston's authority granted them the luxury of plain-clothes. Which was normally a tremendous relief, as the cool-tone slate blue didn't do her warm hickory brown skin tone any favors. But for a jaunt to the Jewel of Quo, Aurora's normal thrift'd and eclectic fashion would stick out like a sore thumb. So much about her made her feel sore and thumb-like. Her clothes, her armor could do her the passing mercy of helping her blend in even a smidge.

Aurora had picked out a pair of black cotton cigarette pants with the white wildlife embroidery dancing up the outer seam on her thighs and calves paired with a smart white blouse and a leather jacket. The soft-soft cotton of the pants reminded her of something her mother used to wear during special holidays, even though they were a far cry from the hand-woven artistry Mama preferred.

It was the best she could do, and she could only hope that

she hit the mark. This case was actually the Socrates' first case in such a patrician area.

Many would assume that this was simply a result of there being "less crime" in luxury zones than in the poorer plants and the Wilds, but Aurora knew better.

Not that there was less crime, it was that there were different rules, different kinds of crimes. The people who made the law were not enthusiastic about putting themselves behind bars.

Aurora had seen Esaa Station on tourism holos and vacation ads for as long as she could remember. It was perhaps the most recognizable station in the entire system. It was the very definition of wealth.

So Aurora put on her fanciest pair of pants, slicked her high ponytail back with an extra layer of hair gel, and steeled her nerves.

Most of the crew were immune to the nerves that had infected Aurora. It was to be expected; they were civvy's soft hands from Core Planets. Likely, they hadn't vacationed on Esaa Station, but she was sure that most of them had been to one or two vacations on one of the many lesser luxury stations in orbit.

Two bright white strobes of light signaled a successful dock seal and the all-clear signal for unloading. The crew slipped into their regulation four-line formation. She was proud of them. This was not their first rodeo. The crew of the Socrates knew their roles well.

Langston stood looking sharply at the front of the pack. The graphic pattern of his linen button-up was easy to spot in any size crowd. His head had a proud tilt to it as he shrugged on a sharp suit jacket. Langston was entering into the zone, fully prepared to do what he did best.

He had a broad-shouldered masculinity that caused most people to defer to him immediately. Taller than your average grizzly, with thick corded muscles, midnight-black and bright facial features, behind a devastatingly, well-maintained salt-and-pepper facial hair, he glided through life as a son of Gherre. That plus the dimples, and he carried an innate security in his overall place in the universe. At least he used his powers for good.

Langston swaggered down the loading ramp into the hangar. His familiar arrogance settled her nerves a bit. Aurora wished she could steal some of his calm. Maybe she could delude herself into thinking that this assignment was a just a job like any other.

Aurora followed a pace behind him, the squad a pace behind her. Liya, the senior analyst, was at her flank. Military order was as obvious as it was comforting. At least from this side of the police baton.

The landing bay was empty of any other vessel. There was a greeting party of uniformed suits. A man stood at perfect attention in front, his rank on full display in his Esaa-chrome uniform.

"Captain Ahmed, yes?" Langston asked.

Captain Ahmed gave a sharp nod that caused a tendril of hair to fall onto his forehead. Ahmed seemed like the sturdy type who, in any other situation, would present as a welcomingly, competent sort. Today, however, the carefully woven fabric of his calm had rattled apart and was slightly askew. Pushing his hair back into submission, the entire production of his superficial cue seemed to be held together with a recent brushing and more sweat than hair products. The signs that he was pulling it together were evident upon even a cursory observation.

Not that anyone could blame him. Incendiary devices on space stations were just bad news. Captains in particular never liked a bomb on a ship. It was, to put it mildly, fairly dangerous.

Langston introduced the Socrates with his usual flair and efficiency. "This is Detective Aurora Harlowe and I'm Lieutenant Detective Langston Aster, leading System Intelligence Investigative Unit VP005. Colonel Jackson Dean assigned us to this case. We are reporting for duty as of twenty-eight-thirty-four. Based on the Oya Verro Pact Treatise Article 2, Condition 482, we assume unconditional authority over all personnel onboard of this vessel, the Esaa Seltenta Space Station, as run by the Esaa Core Company until this investigation is resolved. Is that understood?"

"Yes," Ahmed said. His eyes dodged nad darted across the various faces of the squadron. He was antsy.

Langston reached down to his belt, unhooked and then activated his compad. He presented his flexiglass screen to Ahmed for several signatures. With a ritualized ease, he guided him through the documentation they needed to have the senior officer on deck sign. "You understand that this is now a Pact matter and that while we all want this matter handled promptly with a thorough and swift investigation, the order's come down the pipe to continue quarantine until further notice. Non-negotiable. Nobody in, nobody out, no exceptions until my unit deems otherwise. Do you understand and agree?" Langston asked.

At these words, Ahmed's shoulder rolled muttered a dejected "Good luck with that" under his breath.

"Do you understand?" Langston didn't enjoy repeating himself.

Straightening and meeting Langston's eyes, Ahmed said, "Yes, Detective Aster. I understand."

Langston nodded in confirmation as he retracted his compad into the small rectangular scroll. Without a glance back, he tossed back his compad over Aurora's head to Liya, who easily plucked the bar of tech out of the air. It was a party trick that was part of the well-crafted and meticulously arranged illusion of Langston's grandeur. To Aurora, Langston's showmanship was less effective as a "I'm so cool" stagecraft, as it was an ode to the Lieutenant Detective's visceral awareness of Liya. She privately thought that it would be fun to see how long it took Langston to find Liya in a dark room while blindfolded and without help.

Aurora had a good guess that it wouldn't be much of a challenge for him.

"Well then, let's speed through this Parallel and get started."

At that, Ahmed's nod dispersed the clean-looking attendants behind him to approach each of the members of the squad. Standard Operating Procedure was to process the team's parallel from least-access to most-access. Each team member presented their left wrist's GIM implant for the Parallel data upload. The Parallel would give them access to the system's network and appropriate security clearance for their position. The Pact-issued half-crescent scanner-mabob thing glowed during a Parallel software update one of three colors: blue for new incoming information, white for general access scans and data wipes, and red for security flags. The devices in use by Esaa staff were newer top-of-the-line models that were less intimidating versions of the ones in use at immigration check points and Pact buildings.

Aurora was next after Liya.

Her eye traced over every moment of the exchange in front of her. It was routine. Based on Liya's seniority, she was to receive a nearly identical level of access to Aurora.

The GIM uplink allowed the ship's network which then did a cursory cross-check against the Pact Archive before uploading new access and credentials for their stay. The Pact Archive was a database they chronicled every Oya-Vearro citizen's personal value -- a non-negotiable history of a human's story distilled to zeros-and-ones in some far off supercomputer.

"Detective?" the attendant asked placidly for her attention.

Despite her wide-eyed focus on the woman's movements, Aurora startled to realize the attendant was now standing in front of her, motioning for Aurora's wrist.

Aurora made every movement steady. Her fingers didn't tremble, her face was blank in a casual way. Because this was normal, this was routine.

She held up her GIM wrist for the parallel access download.

On autopilot, the attendant made her approach to swish the scanner over Aurora's wrist. Then she noticed it. The attendant's breath hissed out, and she yanked her scanner away. They always pull back when they see the scar. It was two inches of thin shiny raised skin that would always mark her as other.

The attendant didn't see Aurora's fancy pants or pinned chest-badge clearly denoting her as an officer of System Intelligence. She saw the scar and that was all the attendant needed to know.

Because there was the lore of the GIM and there was the reality. People forgot that the Last War had ended a mere thirteen years ago. The Pact itself had just barely celebrated its Fortieth Solstice last year. It was a baby empire just out of the knobbly kneed phase, and nowhere near wizened. So Aurora understood the strategic efforts put forth to establish legend through rumors and misinformation.

It was just annoying and inconvenient for Aurora personally.

Quickly under her breath, Aurora said, "It's fine. You'll see. Just scan it." She smiled a practiced reassuring and un-confrontational smile. She presented both wrists this time, a Gherrean sign of supplication to ease the tension.

One of Aurora's particular grudges around the lore of GIM was the common misconception that 'GIM' was an acronym for "genetic identification mod". It wasn't. GIM stood for Greer Intercarpal Mechanical implant. There was nothing genetic or natural about the implant. While sure, 98% of the population received their GIM while in the womb, which prevented any scarring during implantation. That does not a genetic mod make. So, while she got the mythos, she remained annoying. Myths are not born, they are forged. Folktales were quintessential in training a culture on how to distinguish **us** from *them*.

Aurora had received her GIM and the resulting scar tissue at the refugee center. To be clear, the technology needed to close a medical incision without scarring existed; The Pact intentionally inflicted scarring on post-natal GIM implantation to send a message. The scar meant this person is other. This person resisted, this person is dangerous.

For at least the past thirteen plus years, GIM scarring for legitimate reasons was a statistical impossibility. Aurora was perhaps one of the youngest person from the suns to the Wilds to have a semi-legitimate reason to have GIM scar. Or... perhaps Aurora should remember that she was not the arbiter of legitimate reasoning to the Pact.

The attendant held their breath and raised the scanner over her wrist, waiting for what she would expect was an inevitable flash of red.

Blue flash, Aurora nodded and immediately moved away. No need for apologies or further conversation.

Because this was the same anxiety and judgement every damn time. She hated the Parallel update. Hated the necessity of it, in nearly every interaction and at every single mission so far.

Having received his decidedly less dramatic GIM Parallel, Langston motioned towards the entrance. "Shall we?"

Ahmed was quick to comply, and led the group out of the landing dock to the main hallway. Based on the blueprints they had seen in the case file, the main hallway was the central artery of the station. The various floors and levels of the station belted the main hallways in concentric circles surrounding the main hall, with everything being more or less accessible via this path.

Langston and Aurora flanked Ahmed on both sides, eager to get a more thorough initial report from the commanding officer on deck. Liya slid into Langston's periphery, her hand hovering over her compad, ready to take verbatim notes on everything Ahmed said.

"Can you give us an operational update on the incident?" Langston asked.

Ahmed nodded as the entrance hanger doors that slid open to reveal their first glance of Esaa Station in all her glory. Aurora had seen nothing that could match the splendor before her now. The tourist brochures were a pale shadow to its true brilliance. She could dimly hear one of the crime scene techs behind her literally trip over their feet as they took in the first glances of the gilded resort. At least she wasn't alone in her dumb-founded amazement. The archways and artistry on the walls were in the luxe pseudo-Anhkaena style, all angular, sloping archways and intricate geometric detailing.

Numb to the stunning display, Ahmed proceeded through the hall with no hint of ceremony. The crew scuttled back into formation while pulling their collective jaw off the floor.

For Aurora, while the setting was stunning, it was the people that were awe-inspiring. They were all behaving normally. She couldn't help but gawk at the normalcy of it all. Yes, the sights and grandeur were a feast for the eyes, but where was the... terror? The panic? Terrorist attacks were designed to terrorize, it was the widespread production of terror. But Aurora was seeing none of that. Not that terror was a good thing, but Aurora had expected to see some nerves on edge.

As they passed by the different offshoot hallways of the station, the people were at ease. The men lounged at the bar sipping brown liquor from crystal tumblers, a sashimi chef wowed with Zero-G knife work for the surrounding patrons, the constant daylight wading pool filled with dozing debutantes and gossiping mamas.

But there was no terror.

Aurora's attention refocused as one of the station admin staff shuffled by to hand Ahmed a compad. Ahmed swiped his fingers twice across the screen and Aurora and Langston heard a soft ping signaling a file cloud-drop of the newest reports. Now, with access, Langston and Aurora skimmed over the documents as Ahmed began a verbal summary.

"The CO on the Security Deck was able to create an exact timeline of events, starting from the doors opening for tonight's entertainment to when the last body was tagged and taken out of the auditorium. We haven't had enough time to do a thorough dive into the security footage to get any substantive evidence. Until about an hour ago, the primary goal was a simple accounting for the missing and deceased. No interviews, no crime scene investigation. Summary — the first bomb detonated at 11:13 PM, within half a minute of the start of the second act, after intermission."

"Will we have access to all security footage from the station or just the footage of the auditorium and opera house?" Aurora asked. Walking through the hall, she clocked the 360-degree camera installed every five meters. If this was true throughout the entire station, it would be a treasure trove to identify suspects and zero in on the suspicious activity.

"Of course, anything you need that we have, you will get," Ahmed assured.

Behind her, two of the forensic analysts walked right into each other, trying to keep pace while simultaneously stealing lingering glances at the highly renowned aQuorium, the most elaborate nature preserve in the star system. She cringed as she heard the two bumbling behind her.

While she couldn't and wouldn't blame them, the sights were fantastic and encouraged distraction. Decorum was decorum. Aurora cut her gaze to the back, skewering all within her sights. Her eyes commanded the pair of stumbling troops to heel through her silence. Langston was on-brand laser-focused beyond distraction, and completely unaware of everything beyond the case file in front of him.

"It's right up this way," Ahmed said. He gestured several paces away toward the end of the massive hallways they were closing in on. They were approaching the front gate to the famed Santos Opera Hall, the site of the bombing.

Back to his report, "As for the actual event, after the aftermath, we identified it was a series of coordinated bombs rather than one explosive incident. We haven't been able to find the mechanism that allowed for the coordination, but the station jammers meant that manual detonation is the only possibility."

Ahmed said, "So, it was the equalizer and then six firebombs. Best we can tell, first, it was the Equalizer. That monstrosity took out the best part of the center section of the orchestra seating. Then the firebombs took out the 20 private boxes on both left and right of the auditorium. Stampeding fatally injured a portion of people in the rush away from the destruction and we've been getting nothing but bad news from Med Bay about the survivors in the box seats."

Langston, always the perfectionist, asked, "Have you been

able to maintain crime scene integrity?"

A grimace and a shimmying hand wave communicated a negative answer from Ahmed. "We had to send in search and rescue into the box seats and into the auditorium itself to verify deaths and retrieve the burnt and trampled who couldn't exit on their own. They did their best, but one of the security guards fell through the floor in Box 2 so, clearly, we haven't been working with ideal circumstances," he said.

Langston checked the reporting timestamp and tapped his GIM, seeing that the current time was 28:37. "The last status report on the deceased was from twenty-six-thirty-six at the initial hail to SI for help. Were you able to get a confirmed o updated number of casualties?"

Ahmed nodded. "Based on ticket sales compared to a headcount of the remaining patrons. 553 confirmed dead from the blasts, 15 dead in the ensuing rush for the doors, 23 went to the Intensive Care Unit who had either survived the bombing or were crushed during the panic. My med team says we lost 18 in the ICU so far."

Shit, this was looking to be bad news across the system cables. "Total?" Aurora asked.

"586."

That was much worse than expected. While optimism wasn't in large supply, the gob-smacking underestimation in fatalities was a bit shocking. That was nearly a 180 death swing in the casualty count from initial estimates.

"Keep us informed if that number changes any," Langston's voice took on a lower growl. "What was the headcount of the theatre at the start of the performance?"

"Tickets scanned for 1,157 souls, thirty-seven ushers. Orchestra of 66. Actors, 35. Security for the Santos Hall was 16 unarmed guards." Ahmed's last words are barely audible as they approach a rising roar of panicked voices behind the theatre lobby gates. A small deployment of armed guards secured a perimeter around the gate with laser rails surrounding the teardrop-shaped archway. This image was dissonant from the complete lack of any attention anyone from the rest of the pampered station was showing to their goings-on.

It did, however, drive Aurora to one conclusion.

The laser rails and armed guards weren't keeping people out. They were keeping them in.

Ahmed approached one guard and gave a whispered command that was answered with a nod. A pathway was created so the Socrates' crew could make its way past the laser rails without injury.

The doors swung open to reveal the Santos Opera House's Grande Lobby.

The sheer volume of panicked voices layered on top of each other. Every demand, cry and sneer built into an impenetrable wall of noise. While there was clearly more than enough space in the cavernous lobby, most of the large gathering of patrons pressed together in a crashing wave of bodies against the guards at the gate. A riot praying fo a high tide to overflow and escape through the exit. Their was more righteous indignation than ham-fisted insurrection. However, the mass of people forced the squad into quick action. The team rushed down the lobby's grand stairs, following behind Ahmed and a small band of guards.

Scanning the lobby in full, Aurora caught sight of more hostility beyond the patrons. She nudged Langston's shoulder and motioned over to the back perimeter where the guards and frazzled ushers stood with suspicious eyes and clear anxiety. It was a familiar sight for them. The security team on any ship they were investigating was never happy to see them.

Who could blame them, really? It was common practice among the standard rank and file of SI investigators to go for the easy open-and-shut case. Frequently, that meant SI wasn't looking to solve cases as much as they were looking for someone to blame.

Who was easier to blame for a breach in security than the security team? Who was easier to blame than the help?

Ostensibly, the VP program was supposed to address that

issue and be different. However, even Aurora had her doubts about that from time to time.

The endless swell od demands from the patrons at the door really wanted to speak with someone's supervisor. Clearly, to his deep chagrin, Captain Ahmed had been singled-out as the station's 'supervisor.' He was less than amused by the attention.

Once clear of the shouting masses, Ahmed muttered a quick explanation of the barricaded doors with a fair amount of derision. "The decision was made that everyone with access to the bombing equipment, patrons included, would be sequestered in the lobby until further orders. No one in, no one out."

Glancing back at the spitting mad peacocks gathered in the entrance hall, Aurora couldn't contain her laugh. "It seems like some folks have taken an issue with that order."

Ahmed barked out the same soul-despairing laugh he had uttered at the landing dock. "Yeah... Who would've thought my biggest problem today wouldn't be the literal fucking terrorist attack, but nooooooo, my biggest problem is a bunch of elite assholes demanding that we let them out so that they can make their dinner reservation?"

"Who's the genius that gave the order to lock down?" A hint of admiration slipped into Langston's tone.

"That would be me," Ahmed said.

"Hmm, unpopular as that decision may have been, thanks," Aurora returned. She slid Ahmed a bit higher in her internal People-to-Trust index.

Their journey to the back of the lobby stopped in front of an immense, rust-red, circular door delicately carved with the image of dancing bodies.

Aurora took one last look behind her at the gilded masses roving in the lobby. "You should've expected this reaction," she said.

"I did." Captain Ahmed's regrets were accompanied by a humorless smile that spoke of a low opinion in the general humanity of the situation.

Ahmed then turned to the ornate doors to start the door opening sequence. Gears and panels blossomed forward in a mechanized dance, worthy of any ballet. Like the rest of the lobby, the station and the planet below, it was beautiful. Aurora could feel her contempt for the beauty of the various elements of this ship grow with every second she was in the station. She could smell the rot. A scratch below the gilded surface lay something festering below.

The elaborate door opening was made more ethereal by the whisps and tendrils of pitch-black smoke that slipped through the cracks and gaps that appeared between the door's panels.

Charred tendrils of tar beckoned them inside.

SANTOS HALL AMPITHEATRE, ESAA SELTENTA SPACE
STATION & RESORT, GEOSYNC - QUO

THE JEWEL OF QUO

06

AURORA

O nce the awe faded, Auroar had a dark thought: *what a beautiful place to die.*

Ahmed and his small team of guards barreled into the ampitheatre without delay. But her team took their time, soaking it all in.

The jewel of Quo wasn't their day-in, day-out workplace. While the Esaa Corp security staff were immune to its splendor; her team was in awe. With slow, measured steps, they entered the auditoriums as a wonder-struck collective. It was saying something that the artistry was still marvelous while paired with carnage. While everything about Esaa Station was luxe to the extreme, Santos Hall set this resort apart from its neighboring competitors. Her squad was experiencing such a sight in stark juxtaposition of the horror of the crime scene.

An enormous glass dome that extended into space, out of the stage and station in a 270-degree view of the beautiful swirling Quo landscape below encased the amphitheater. Roiling wisps of obsidian fog collected against the glass barrier.

Miraculously, the glass and stage were untouched by the chaotic destruction of the surrounding auditorium. Charred walls and singed velvet drape on all sides. Wet pools of blood squished underfoot. The lingering sulphuric scent of burnt flesh poisoned the air.

Their professionalism finally broke through and the investigative team fell into the routine steps of their crime scene processing. Divide and conquer, small crews formed up to do initial review and documentation. Each unit went to a section of the concentric rows of the circular seating arrangement to tape off sections and laying down initial evidence markers. Liya was on hand to guide them in the initial record-keeping and help in delegation.

Everything was larger than life. Instead of regular stadium theatre seats, each audience member had a swiveling Zero-G seat that was the very definition of luxury. The seats were altogether more like a luxurious pod.

The plush encapsulating pods must've made the ensuing stampeding exit to escape imminent death even the more difficult.

Aurora spotted Ahmed and a pair of his guards in the orchestra pit. The captain beckoned over Aurora and Langston with a waved hand. Ahmed was finishing up the last set of logistics orders to his guards as they approached. Distractedly, Aurora's eyes stole glances at the swirls of smoke that collected in the glass dome while she waited for Ahmed to speak.

Following her gaze, Ahmed threw a quick glance over his shoulder and nodded. He said, "Fifty some odd layers of reinforced battle-tested courisand glass made all the difference between a very bad day and... honestly I can't imagine if that glass gave way during the bombing." A couple of their techs were sweeping the edges of the glass for signs of even the finest cracks or splintering. "I understand the need to double-check, but they won't find any faults in that glass, of that we are certain," Ahmed said.

"How certain?" Aurora asked.

"This is the jewel of Quo, Detective," Ahmed said. A hint of pride and elitism slid behind his words. "There was a significant chance that this structure would be the target of an attack sooner or later. The investors of this station were constantly pouring money into defensive upgrades and parlor tricks. Unlike most stations, they cloaked the airfield with an anti-radio wave field that prevents uplinks from any external communicator. Then, on top of that, Santos Hall Auditorium has an additional layer of frequency blockers just from an 'artistic integrity', at the insistence of the Executive Producer."

"That's why the reporting was so certain that the bomber is on board. The frequency blockers." Langston concluded.

"Yes, we could establish that quickly in our initial assessment," Ahmed said. "Our system can monitor who made the comm and for how long they were talking. We are working to see if there is a way to identify where and who they were talking to, but we hit a bit of a roadblock there. Regardless, one of our first moves was to embargo all departing vehicles from this station. The monster who did this is remains among us. Of that I'm certain." That steely certainty of Ahmed reared its stubborn head. Its surety crisped every word Ahmed uttered. While Aurora couldn't begrudge the captain his death grip on the remnants of his certainty, she ultimately questioned how productive that posturing would prove.

Langston's shoulder nudged her a bit as he pulled out his compad to view a reference guide of the auditorium seating. They looked on his device together. The original diagrams of the auditorium. They were nearly unrecognizable compared to the burnt-out wreckage before them. With the marked exception of the middle section to their left, in a glittering state of perfection.

"Wait, what happened in—Oh..." Langston's voice caught in his chest.

The orchestra center section he'd pointed out lay between the two walls of firebombed double-decker box seats. There was a glossy sheen across the velvet fabric in the middle section.

The lack of explosive destruction in this section was a dead giveaway. It was the equalizer's detonation zone. Massive death plus no damage was the hallmark of the devastating bomb.

"They contained the damage with the fire bombs on the side of the auditorium and that center section got the brunt of the equalizer. Not a lot of survivors. Technically, the musicians and the actors all made it out without incident," Ahmed said. It was a technicality that didn't comfort anyone. Less death was always better than more. "The orchestra's back was to the stage, so they had a front-row seat to the carnage. Good witnesses, I'd think. In addition... I think we have... two or three people from the far most corner of this section who made it. Again, we haven't been able to interview any of the survivors or witnesses, but I can pull the seating assignment and survivors' list so you can talk to them when you're ready." Ahmed wiped the back of his hand against the rapidly collecting droplets of sweat against his brow.

In any other situation, Aurora would've tucked that physical indicator away as a sure sign of subterfuge or worry, but she could feel the heat too. And this was not the metaphorical *heat* to solve the case, but rather the swelter emanating from the orchestra seating section.

The longer they stood beside the blast radius, the more they could all feel the wet heat slap them across the face. It was an Old Stellar's moondust. The rumor that the unforgiving heat produced from the collective evaporation of human bodies could haunt a space. Tales told of the palpable aftereffects of an equalizer blast lingering in a detonation zone for months after the blast. Aurora's fingers danced out to dip through the air into the near physical barrier of heat. Looking at her hand, she noticed the thin glowing ray of security laser-tape. The laser-tape marked off what would've been an invisible wall of moist atmosphere within the detonation zone.

"You've taped it off." The words escaped Aurora's mouth in a whisper without her permission. Her team was perhaps not the only one prone to lapses in decorum.

Ahmed turned to think on her before returning his gaze to observe the roped-off area. "Yeah... it seemed... respectful." He offered the sentiment in a distant and uncomfortable sort of way.

Aurora took a second to consider him. Ahmed was just about the right age. He'd likely know the truth of the matter. He would've been in flight school back during The Pact's *Warm Embrace*. While the official record-keeping of the Warm Embrace favored the 'victors' of the imperialist blitz, anyone with a lick of sense knew that the equalizers were originally the Pact's weapon of choice. Upon entering the Pressure Cooker's academic coursework, Aurora was naively surprised by the sheer gall of the Pact when it came to revising history. No matter what was written in the Pact's bastardized history book, the truth will out. To those who were there, who remembered and who'd survived, the equalizer bombs had all the hallmarks of Pact Policy: Efficient, savage and poetic (if you were a sociopath).

So, back in the early yesteryears, just as Command Corp was established, their first real "success story" was to bring The Wilds to heel. This was the *Warm Embrace*, they were "bringing in the trash" as a couple of propoganda ads phased it. The term Equalizers was a bad nickname several times over and only popped up in military or rebel circles, but not beyond that. Anyone who knew how horrible the weapons were knew the nickname like some sick inside joke. While she was sure Langston was familiar with the term, she was equally sure he wouldn't be able to explain its origins with a gun to his head.

$E = mc^2$. The Equalizer.

The bomb turned people into pure energy. Originally, it was advertised as a more humane way to kill.

Either ironically or maliciously, it proved to be the exact opposite. The Equalizer was a catabolic explosive force that converted all living matter in the blast zone into a fine crystalline dewy mist within the blast radius. The scientific name, the Metabolic Partiphaser, referred to a device unlike any other.

When CC had the monopoly on all Equalizer usage to silence and eliminate dissension, they marketed the device as "humane". But then, when the tides turned and the Wilder rebels built their own bombs, the truth of an equalizer blast became better known. Marketing aside, it had always been barbaric.

"You did the right thing," Aurora assured him. Respect for the dead was both an ineffective comfort as much as it was a necessary half measure.

Langston had called out behind her to beckon over the squad for a quick debrief. Turning away from the bloodless gore, Aurora brought her attention to the present moment.

Their squad of twenty formed up in a semi-circle around Aurora, Langston, and Ahmed. It was time for marching orders.

All eyes were on Langston as he laid out their plan of attack. "Dev, I need a complete reconstruction of the blast zone. Specific attention on determining the design and materials of the bombs used. Collect any trace evidence of bomb particles. Identify the epicenter and placement of each individual bomb. John, take three others to identify any soft points of entry where incendiary devices could've been smuggled in. Torres, we need first-round interviews with survivors who had a good view of the carnage. If they say anything interesting, cut the interview short and report back to me or Detective Harlowe." Each staff member nodded at their assignment in understanding. However, no movement or dismissal followed. They all felt a blip in the air that signaled a slight gap in understanding and confidence that made Aurora wary.

There was something in the air. Insecurity lingered in their eyes. They clearly weren't numb that this wasn't like their other investigations. This was not petty robbery, or corporate intrigue, or a simple murder. This... was something else entirely. To Aurora, it felt like the beginning of something. She wondered if anyone else could pin down that feeling into words.

Without a reason to stay, they shifted in the direction to go forth with their orders. Aurora took a second to deliver some final words to prepare them. "I trust you to do what you always do. Be respectful. Be thorough. Be fast," she said in warning as much as a note of faith. A more confident series of nods followed, as well as a few salutes, and the team was off.

A sharp voice rang out from the back of the auditorium, popping their bubble of efficient police work. "Well, I insist. I must speak to your superior. I am done shooting the shit with inferiority." Each syllable of those last words was spit out under a heavy dredge of disdain.

A trio of burly guards were doing their level best to cage the rather loud, feather-bedecked socialite as he tried to bob and weave between their barricading bodies. Long, lean and, and dressed in a shimmering blue kaleidoscopic suit with a deeply ornate headdress, he was an impossible to miss figure.

Ahmed heaved a heavy sigh and waved a hand to allow the overwhelmed guard to let the man through. "Marius Bell. The bane of my existence. He's the executive producer of tonight's show and the CEO of the Santos Opera House Giving Institute," he said under his breath as context for the senior officers. Bell closed the distance between them with haste.

Beneath the armor of all that ridiculousness, Aurora could tell Marius Bell was a force of nature, not to be underestimated. He was belligerent and completely uncaring of the destruction left in their wake. Beautiful in an untouchable and obvious kind of way. Thick, wavy dark brown hair. Ridiculously chiseled square jawline. Full lips underneath inky blue-black lipstick. His long gait gazelle'd across the distance as he stalked toward the gathering of investigators and security staff.

He gave Ahmed a quick look of routine disgust. "Captain."

"Bell."

Marius Bell's gaze turned on the rest of them in a quick and thorough assessment of rank and authority. Aurora had a running theory that the humans of Gherre had developed a sixth sense to recognize other Gherreans. It was a pseudo-predator instinct from their perch on the top of the food chain; she suspected. All that to say, Bell zeroed in on Langston as the senior investigator. What could only be a signature winning smile replaced his former scowl.

"Marius Bell, at your service," he said to announce himself as he held out his hand to Langston in greeting. "I was immensely pleased to hear that some competence had finally arrived on this station."

To his credit, Langston didn't take his hand and didn't smile in return. "This is an active crime scene, sir. I ask you to leave immediately."

Bell tossed his hair haughtily and pursed his lips out. His smile remained firmly in tack with a determination to win ou this new authority figure. "Sure, sure. I'm sure you all need to hop to it. But you see, someone -- and I won't name names so as to not embarrass the idiot standing next to you -- but someone made the odious decision to hold my traumatized patrons hostage in my lobby. It's a crime, truly, and you must address it immediately."

"You'll actually find that there is a priority list of crimes that occurred today and the five hundred and eighty-six people who died not two feet from where your standing takes precedence," Aurora said dryly.

A sneer roared across his face like a magnoflare before that syrupy smile slurped right back into place. "But you'll find I am decidedly less worried about ticket holders who aren't demanding a refund, darling."

"And they say you can't judge a peacock by its feathers," Aurora quipped, unable to stop herself from the light verbal jab.

Langston clearly felt the same as he took a single large step forward. While Marius' willowy, tall frame was impressive, few could match Langston's sheer height when he wielded it like a weapon. Langston steeled his spine and growled, "Get out."

Marius' eyes narrowed a bit. He tipped his sequined hairpiece. "Fair enough," Bell said with a pivot to leave.

The rest of the investigative squad's eyes followed his progress out of the main doors like storm watchers behind a twister.

Aurora's voice called out to the squad, "That doesn't sound very much like hard work to me." The gathering swung around for a quick salute before the Socratic investigators resumed their work.

Wiping an exhausted hand down his face, Langston muttered through his hands, "Let's go see that footage."

High-end security booths always looked exactly the same. It was almost comforting if it wasn't so devoid of vibrancy. Four walls painted in a light-absorbing blackest black dotted with the glowing blue monitor screens and holo displays from monitors and holo rows and rows and rows of tiny, sad cubicles. The staff working this floor, frequently referred to as drones, all wore black turtlenecks with black cargo pants, which Aurora had always considered a bit as a shame. Turtlenecks and cargo pants were always a good look, but eye bags and depression could ruin any good outfit.

Aurora and Langston, with Liya for support, followed Ahmed down the main stretch of hallway between the cubicles. None of the drones could quite pluck up the gumption to look away from their screens as they went by. But the distinct feeling that all eyes were on them persisted.

At least six screens of live footage surrounded each drone as they typed shorthand notes and flagged any issues as they occurred. Hunched over in their cramped little cubicles, the excitement of it all seduced the drones so they donated a sliver of their attention to the passing specter trio of investigators. They didn't get too many visitors in these parts. Their footsteps echoed and clanged as they made their way through the cavernous darkness towards the main footage analysis station.

Past the near-endless rows of drones and up a flight of stairs, they arrived at the main viewing console station.

The entire back wall, twenty feet up by twenty feet across, was covered in an uninterrupted curve of monitors that illuminated the room. The other walls were glass and gave a supervisory view of the drones below. In the center of the analysis station was a lectern filled with tech from a compad and a remote, to several other gizzmos, was the control booth of the space.

Ahmed approached the lectern and opened up the top fold to review a quick intercom radio box. He tapped a microphone button of the radio on the side of the room's entrance and his voice amplified out to the below security deck, "Tech 110 through 175, please report to the main viewing console for an footage analysis."

Aurora moved to the window to watch the meticulous precision of the drones as they slid out of their console stations and marched up to the viewing booth. Beat by beat, their steps were a syncopated staccato armed with their compads in hand. There was always the open question of whether military or corporate order was more robotized and enforced.

As the drones assembled in front of them, Ahmed turned to Langston and Aurora. "Where do we start?"

Aurora turned to Langston and asked, "The beginning is always good?"

"Yes. Let's start with a basic play-through of the bombing from beginning to the end. Where is a good starting point?" Langston looked to Ahmed for an answer, who in turn deferred back to the line of drones that assembled along the walls.

An alarmingly pretty guard wearing badge #110 stepped forward. "Recommendation to start at the last call for intermission. The bombing starts within 3 mins after doors closed after intermission. Giving us approximately eight minutes of pre-explosive footage until search and rescue efforts began marking the end of the active portions of the attack." As he spoke, the tech's thin-thin-thin fingers clicked across this compad, then flicked the necessary security footage files up to the main console. The still image of the auditorium brightened the crescent of screens in front of them. The footage was from the bird's-eye-view of the auditorium centered above the center most seat in the center section of the orchestra seating section. From this camera angle, they can see the entire crime scene from the farthest balcony box to the first row of seats, a perfect frame for their blast zone. A neon ticker-tape clock blinked the time of the recording at the bottom.

"Can we get an angle that includes the orchestra pit and the stage?" Aurora asked.

"Yes, ma'am," answered Technician #110.

Aurora did an internal happy dance hearing that "Yes, ma'am" in a sweet Anhkaena purr from Tech #110. She did so enjoy pretty boys who respected her authority.

He continued, "This current image is a composite of a selection of the different cameras. To add to those additional angles, we will need to composite the new feeds into the reel. It'll could take 35 to 70 minutes to render a viewable clip. Would you like us to process that request prior to this first viewing?"

"Not at this time." Aurora knew they would ultimately need that on file, but time was of the essence to get the team started cataloging individual movement and potentially identifying suspects. While there was a chance that the musicians or cast would have access to the audience in order to pull this attack off, it was a slim chance that could wait for 35 to 70 minutes of processing time. She finished her thought by addressing the tech. "Please composite that clip for the record and deliver it to Liya, our technical lead at your earliest convenience. What's your name?"

"My employee ID is T-110GZ. I'm the supervisor for the Santos Auditorium security cameras, 110 through 175, and their assigned technicians for the 1500 to 3000 shift. The security technician supervisors handle all footage archiving and composite requests."

"We'll be working closely together to get all this figured out. What's your name?"

T-110 looked at Captain Ahmed, confused by her repeated

question. The tech's full lips frowned down, which pulled his absurdly angular face down with a hint of confusion. There was the largely unquestioned habit of addressing low-level staff by rank and serial number vs their given name in both the corporate and military sphere. Aurora didn't enjoy that tradition much. So she ignored it whenever possible.

Ahmed, at the end of his rope and having dispensed with societal niceties several hours ago, rolled his eyes and nodded to T-110 to give her a reply. The tech supplied her with his given name: "Rhys, ma'am. Rhys Madrid."

"Ok, Rhys," Aurora nodded to him and said, "Arrange for your backup supervisor to take over for the rest of your shift. You'll be assigned to our unit for the remainder of our investigation. SI will, of course, subsidize any overtime. Our team, in particular myself, Lieutenant Detective Aster, and Senior Analyst Liya, will ask for your assistance due to your expertise throughout this investigation. Liya will directly supervise your time with us."

A flicker of brightness with a hint of anxiety flashed through Rhys's eyes in quick measure before he schooled his features back to neutral. He steeled his back and said, "C-Copy, Detective."

She did so enjoy putting pretty boys' nerves on edge. Having Rhys around might provide some occasional enjoyment for her. He was just as pretty as Bell without the bite and ego.

"Ok." Langston pulled focus back to the task at hand. "Now that that is handled, let's see what happened exactly." Langston finished. He motioned for Rhys to start the feed. "Roll the tape, please."

The theater lights wink twice in quick succession. The dimming lights signal to the milling audience that the end of intermission is upon them. It calls for them to return to their seats. Pristinely coiffed and perfectly puffed patrons slowly migrate and settle into their seats. They are all whispered-judgement and delicately gesturing hands.

Just an touch under capacity, it's a full-house. There is barely a sprinkling of empty seats.

They linger, take their time, easy with the complete assurance that time will wait for them. Painted lips part with soft smiles and vicious lies. While their words aren't audible. The poison dripping from every word is clear. There is a languid slowness to their movements. The surety that the worlds revolved around them has them swimming through amber molasses.

The last patron finds his seat and the Santos signature cavern seat sways into its cradle position with choreographed precision.

The lights fade to black. The hall remains illuminated in a soft bath of lavender from the phosphorescent glow on the surface of Quo.

The audience finds stillness. Captivated once again by the drama of the theatre, they breathe as one. One great inhale. All together.

WHIP CRACKING red hot fire explodes in the lower right edge of the hall. Flames licking up to the ceiling. Heads and eyes in the audience are torn from the stage towards the unexpected danger.

Panic spreads as fast as the fire. They fumble from their seats to the upright position and move to the left of the hall.

Another burst of flame. And another, and another. A cannon of explosions spread into back into the theatre. The explosions target the balcony booths, but the blow-back, debris, and fire spreads further and faster.

The four firebombs burst along the right side of the hall. Panicked, the audience stampedes safety, to the left. Except for the center section.

A tree falling in an empty forest. The silent destruction of the Metabolic

Partiphaser rippled out from the center of the orchestra section with the speed of a snap. Silent and deadly. The terror of the reaction isn't is speed but in its chaos. From solid human bodies vaporized into gas then settling in as hot, hot, hot clear moisture. There is no scorch mark, no distortion, no grand explosion. It leaves no mark, just a memory. Just a wet kiss of who was there before.

It's unclear if the frenzied near stampeding masses recognize the horror that was their vaporized compatriots. But regardless of their knowledge of the mounting dread, they rush to the left. To safety.

As they draw close, BOOM, the left erupts into a mirrored sequence of explosions, the fiery waves of destructive blast catching some who had desperately escaped the first set of deadly embrace. A ring of fire surrounds the patrons.

The chaos screams, screams, screams -- never hoarse. It doesn't relent until it breaks into a whimper. The patrons' will to flight is bludgeoned from them. A tired bird in a cage doesn't move fast, it is cautious and knows danger. It will not be fooled again. Beleaguered ushers and security guards eventually led the audience out the back doors.

Clinging to one another, the ushers wave the patrons over with flashlights and arms, faces covered in soot. Signaling for the exit.

From start to finish, utter destruction in 6 minutes. From the start of the performance until the last person exits. Six minutes.

The monitor dimmed, and the lights slowly faded up in the viewing room. In the cover of slowly brightening light, Aurora slipped her hand into the curve of Liya's arm. In silent support she rubbed a quick nipping caress. Langston's presence beside her was strong and equally tense. There was no question about it. This was an extremely well-coordinated terrorist attack.

The main goal was to create terror. They had succeeded.

Aurora and the Socrates would not let them win the day.

07

PAUSE. REWIND. PLAY.

AURORA

"**C**lassic. So, I have good news and I have bad news." Liya's raspy voice chimed out as she twirled a rolling cart of tech into the room. "What do you want first?"

After reviewing the initial footage, Aurora and Langston had spent the better part of an hour slaving over the collection of Esaa Station's initial reports in a secluded back corner of the security deck. Piecemeal bits and pieces of their team's reports were coming back from the crime scene, but nothing substantive has arrived yet. Fluorescent lights cooked their eyes as they flipped through trace evidence holoscrolls that the crime scene techs had been sending over from the Auditorium. The team had produced a few trace elements of the firebombs. Dev, their lead scene technician, was working on cobbling together the first set of detonators. The detonator from bomb 2, 3, and 6 were all heat-activated. This caused the relay effect of the explosions as the bombs progressed through the auditorium. A particularly clever chaos tactic.

Yet there was nothing conclusive, so the impending sense of gloom that hung over their heads hummed. And it was a pretty good guess the gloom was all whispered the same thing: inconclusive. Investigations of this size typically took weeks. There was too much evidence, too many moving parts, too many possibilities. But there was that looming deadline of the Top Brass's pending arrival. So while it was unlikely that they fully solve the case in time, if they broke their back doing it, they might have solid leads.

Aurora predicted that with the present fire lit under their asses they would they might do it.

Unfortunately, so far, they'd ended up fighting for every inch of evidence and progress with a liter of blood and sweat.

The perps were clearly professional. They'd trained for this and, more importantly, they had a plan. But most crimes, even the ones that initially appeared meticulously planned out, always boiled down to crimes of passion. Dark twisted motivation fueled by an ugly internal flame. This horrific event on Esaa Station was a contradiction that was proving hard to disentangle and understand. The contradiction between the icy calculation of a red-hot massacre. It was clearly a terrorist attack, but something in the orchestration made her hesitate.

She had no clear evidence to encourage a more conclusive hesitation. But there was that *pausing* feeling. That, combine with the literal lack of evidence conclusive or otherwise, was at least a cause for indigestion. Which Aurora would argue was clear evidence of expertise, but she knew in a high-profile case like this, her gut would get her nowhere. Hunger from an unfulfilled gut was a familiar friend.

With a strained smile for Liya's antics, Aurora put down her compad to address her damned-if-we-do-damned-if-we-don't conundrum the analyst presented. The detective roughed her fingers across her eyebrows.

"The good news first, please."

Liya leaned forward across the cluttered work desk in between Aurora and Langston with a glint in her eye. "You remember those labor protesters from a couple months back, right? It was basically all the news could talk about for months."

Nodding, they both murmured that they did indeed remember.

"Well, you'll be glad to know that those rabble rousers are still out there fighting the good—maybe a bit pointless—fight, but nonetheless, they are rocking that picket line." Liya delivered this news on a rushed, falsely positive note.

"And... that's the good news?" Langston asked.

"Well, I just wanted to have some good news. So, there you go." Liya shrugged as she sank down onto her forearms on the desk.

Langston shook his head, "Well, that's just great. Exactly the break we needed to bust this case wide open. Thank you. For that brilliant contribution, Liya. What would we do without you?" The lack of progress, evidence, insight, or direction was clearly getting to Langston's nerves. He was more aware than anyone of their deadline. Aurora could practically see an internal countdown clock with the Colonel's ultimatum ticking above his head. However, in regard to Liya's particularly unhelpful "good" news, she agreed. If this was the best news they got, this would not likely be a good showing after that catastrophe on Hwei.

A grimacing wrinkle of her nose at Langston's stinging sass, Liya continued. "But then you forgot, that was the good news. You ready for the bad news?"

Langston dropped his head to the work desk with a hard thud.

"Remember those labor protesters from a couple of months back?"

Langston's head bobbed up to slam back down on the desk in a slow plodding metronome against the metal table as a response..

"Liya," Aurora warned.

"It's topical I promise." Liya, perpetually undisturbed Liya, kept smiling away in pure, unadulterated schadenfreude. She slid her hands back off the desk and started quickly unloading the thin rectangular holoscrolls from the tech cart onto the desk in neat little stacks. "Well, the Esaa Core Co doesn't negotiate with 'terrorists' or 'unionists' as it were. So... they fired all the laborers, top-to-bottom, clean-sweep, and took on scrubs to replace the staff. These holoscrolls right here are the new scrubs' employee files. Soooo, there is not a single entry-level employee on this raft who was on payroll here for more than a month. These scrubs' files are pretty much scrubbed clean of anything usable." Liya plucked a scroll randomly from the stacks in front of her, activating the holo screen with a quick button. The screen displayed was a name, photo, employee ID, unimportant demographic information about age, birthplace, and several bare sections with a header and no substance.

Aurora closed her eyes as she sighed. There was bad luck and there was this mess. This just sucked. Of course, she knew there would not be any easy answers. But at this news, Aurora settled into the looming conclusion that they were going to have to do more than claw their way for every inch gained in this case.

"And that's not actually the bad news."

Aurora was quick to remind to herself: *Don't shoot the messenger. Don't shoot the messenger. You like Liya.* **Don't** *shoot the messenger.*

Langston just came out and said it, "Fuck."

"The bad news is that Esaa Core doesn't run background checks on their employees until their sixth week of employment."

Just no luck at all.

"That can't possibly be legal," he begged, Langston's fingers digging into the tension gathered at his temples.

"Well, it's... not illegal, and apparently it saves a fair chunk of change so it's worth tiptoeing across that line." Liya hedged.

"Fuck." Langston's head dropped again like a hammer on the table again.

"Yup." Liya's smile had tansformed into half upbeat, half beaten-down mess, "Enjoy." She half bowed before standing at attention, ready for her next orders. Because this was the beginning, they had to do something.

Head still firmly planted into the table, Langston started with "Could we run---"

"No, it'd take too long," Aurora said quickly. The case was careening towards the cover-our-asses portion of administrative work. Running background checks manually would be a massive and pointless undertaking with limited functional benefit. "Oh, could we ask---"

"No, we've run out of favors with them," came Langston's reminder.

Maybe he forgot about, "But what about--"

"Did you forget about Hwei?"

Shit, he would never let her live down Hwei.

Langston finally lifted his head to glare at her. "It was yesterday. Literally. Yesterday." He said in disbelief.

Never ever going to let it go.

Hands flat on the table, Aurora blows out a fast rush of air, "Ok. So. We're blind. We go in blind."

"Yeah." Langston's nostril flared out. The idea sat rotten and unseemly, a giant guano on the table between them. He shook out the tension in his shoulder, "Ok, Liya. Send the staff list over to HQ and get them to run the backgrounds and report back on any criminal hits. We know the info won't get back to us in time, but let's just check that box. Let's just attempt to cover our collective asses."

Nodding, she swiped and tapped across her compad, ready to move towards completing that task.

Leaning over to what could be the most useless set of files Aurora had ever come across, she selected a holoscroll at random. Labeled with an employee ID code, a department, and a name, the holoscroll had three main sections. The sections were labeled: history, evaluation, and performance. She selected the "history" icon.

The holoscreen read:

CHECK AGAIN LATER. BACKGROUND CHECK WILL BE
AVAILABLE IN 3.6 WEEKS. THANK YOU.

Well, at least she could say she triple-checked.

Seeing Liya was wrapping up her task, Aurora signaled the senior analyst over to her, "Ok, so, what's in these other two sections if it's not backgrounds?"

Liya reached over her shoulder to tap on the 'Evaluation' section header. A closeup bust sculpture of the employee rendered in shades of red, yellow, and green popped up on the screen. Red on the forehead and cheeks faded out to the yellow section with the largest concentration of green on the nose. "Evaluation has the employee's job interview recordings and supervisor's notes. Then we have Performance. This is where they store all the surveillance tracking data."

Intrigued, Aurora asked, "Surveillance tracking?" Her tone requested more information and with a quick gesture, she called to Langston's attention. He snatched a holoscroll off the top of the pile and flipped the screen of his own to select the performance tab.

With the performance section selected, the scroll displayed a grid of rectangular thumbnails, each labeled with a time-stamp and a date. Liya flicked through the thumbnail and selected a clip at random. "The station's facial recognition software tracks all employees all the time. Anytime any employee shows up on any surveillance camera, the clip is tagged with their employee ID. At the end of the day, each 15-minute section of footage tagged with their name is then compiled and filed. They track the movement and actions of each employee 30 hrs a day, 100 minutes an hour."

Smirking, Aurora said, "I've never been so happy to observe the utter lack of trust the management has in their staff."

Langston whistled out a loud, sweet note of relief. "It's definitely a start."

Aurora scrolled back up to the first row of thumbnail images.

"Do you think you can get this updated to include the past 12 hours?"

Liya nodded, grabbing her compad and moved to the door. "Gimme 10 and I'll be back with the past 12 hours."

In her absence, and with no new information, the pair started pulling and organizing the scrolls. Referencing the list of staff assigned to the Hall in the twelve-hour window prior to the bombing: ushers, stagehand guards, anyone assigned to Santos Hall. Silently, their hands moved to sort out scrolls by employee ID. Perhaps a single step above the rowdy excitement of a stake-out as far as investigative intrigue goes.

Langston's hand settled heavy over hers to stop her from sorting. "Roar, we're wasting time. Which we don't have. We don't have background checks to eliminate even the most basic of suspect. We can't keep going down this road."

He was right. The path they were on was for the long game. Which didn't work for them because the clock was ticking against them.

She slid her hand out from his and continued to sort. She didn't look up.

He said, "I know we don't say it in front of the team or the personnel. But... it was a fucking equalizer. You can't just pick up those supplies at a local mom-n-pop shop. Nuclear biodiesel. Mitoxethum. Slapped together with an insane amount of engineering skills. You can't seriously think some picket-line crossing scrub got all that together and bombed one of the most heavily fortified luxury stations ever built. We need to ditch this shit and start talking to some of them with bow ties in the lobby back there."

Unperturbed, Aurora continued to sort in lieu of a response.

Langston's fist pounded between her orderly stacks of scrolls cause a few to cascade and tumble from their rows.

Aurora finally met his eyes.

"You wanna go through all of this tracking footage for every grunt in that auditorium? That's at least 120 by my count.

And, we don't even know if they have criminal history, gambling debts. Ninety-nine percent of all people anywhere could never do something like this. Seventy percent of that one percent who could don't have the capability to pull this off. So *what* are we doing?" He was out of breath by the end of it, panting out there at the end of his rope.

"Do you want me to contradict you in some way?" Aurora asked.

"No."

"Come up with a magic solution?"

He glared at her like he hoped she might spontaneously combust. "No."

"Then why are you telling me things that both of us already know?"

"We're fucked, Roar. And this time it's not even our fucking fault."

She stole his hands in her own and squeezed, tight with her heart conveying sincerity though pressure. She breathed with him. In. Out. Nice and easy.

"Ok." Aurora flashed the **Truth** in her eyes. "Five hundred and eight-six people are dead. We are going to find the person or persons responsible. That's what we owe them, and we will not fail them." She patted his hand then dropped them and returned to her steady organizing, "And honestly, Langston, if it were easy, fucking Dev would be a lead detective and I'd be slinging homemade trinkets in the Wilds."

A strangled laugh erupted out of him. Still reluctant, he rejoined her in the busy work of organizing the scrolls.

Aurora's hands slowed. Replaying a couple of the highlight reel from Langston's rant in her head. "But... what if they did?"

"Did what?" Langston said.

"What if some random picket-line crossing scab got access to nuclear biodiesel, mitoxethum, and used their engineering expertise to bomb Santos Hall?"

"It's damned unlikely, Roar."

"True." Her mind hooked into the theory like a wriggling bait. "It's unlikely for a whole host of reasons. But maybe... maybe they are counting on us, counting them out. Counting on us not having the background check."

Langston half considered it. "But they'd have to know that the staff would be primary suspects? Despite all evidence to the contrary, here we are investigating the help, although we know the help couldn't possibly be the lead assailant. It's procedural, the smart move. It's like investigating the spouse. You check that box. What you're theorizing would be a... a triple-blind. It's too convoluted."

"But!" Aurora cried out and shot her hand into the air before extending her arms out to him in mock seriousness. "Big booty, big booty. You forget, the spouse is frequently guilty."

"You can't keep saying 'big booty, big booty' every time there is a substantial 'but' in a sentence."

"I can. You'd just prefer I don't."

Bringing the now organized holoscroll to the front of the work desk, Aurora said, "Hidden in plain sight. That means... there's..."

"There's what?"

"Hmmm, there must be... a slightly more obvious suspect then. You can only hide in plain sight if... no one is actively searching anywhere else. The motive is completely lost to us at this point. Other than the carnage, nothing quite makes sense. So, here we are and the staff is the only plausible option."

Langston laughed. "So, equally plausibly, you're spinning stories in the ether with nothing but moondust, huh?"

Mind still tickling, whirling through theory, Aurora pursed her lips before giving him a side glance. "Plausibly."

"Ok, in all fairness, I know that. You know this. But there's more. We need to know what they know, what they are seeing. So, currently, the blind spinning of moondust tales is not the smartest move."

"You're right, you're right." Aurora focused back on the task at hand, sorting and settling into a bit of brainstorming. "You know, I didn't love the angles of the bombing footage. Maybe the surveillance tracking can weave together a better portrait. The staff knows this place. Frequently, their jobs depend upon them being attentive. So I want to see where they were looking. The big question is: what did they see?"

"We could always ask them."

Aurora wagged a manicured black fingernail at him. "Rule number 67. Never ask a suspect a question you don't know the answer to. You taught me that, old man." She turned towards the back of the room sec-deck. "Rhys."

Rhys's perfectly coiffed head popped up among the rows of desk and analyst. The tech supervisor was vibrating with nerves as he scurried over to the duo's workstation. His hands moved a mile a millisecond, clenching, touching, picking, nipping, rubbing in a thousand different tics.

As she would with a skittish animal, Aurora explained their new goal to Rhys with low, slow tones. Once he was clear, he set off on the backend work to prepare for the footage review. Aurora's explanations and demeanor had entranced him. With his orders in hand, Rhys zipped away to complete his assigned tasks. Nerves aside, he appeared to be fast and competent. She mentally patted herself on the back for having plucked an exemplary supervisor from the bunch to keep close at hand for this investigation. Not that she had any actual choice in the matter. He was simply the security footage officer with the most relevant experience, but still.

Together with Rhys, Langston and Aurora organized their staff in the undertaking of processing the footage in a more procedural way. Liya, back from her errand, let them know that all the profiles had been updated with the most recent 12-hours of surveillance footage. That would be put aside and further investigate anyone of interest from the actual bombing.

The clips were organized by the subject's physical placement in the auditorium within the five minutes prior to the bombing. They stacked the holoscrolls into a puzzle picture. Each image slotting into one next to another.

With the supplementary staff of drone techs, they broke into four teams of three and assigned each unit a sector of the auditorium to observe: back, left, and right flank and the orchestra pit. Each unit was responsible for documenting with meticulous detail everything within their section, then flagging any suspicious behavior with either Rhys, Liya, Langston, or herself.

"Shouldn't we define suspicious behavior within this context?" Liya asked.

Aurora looked at Langston to make the call. He said, "Let's go broad. Suspicious is suspicious. I want more, not less. Have the techs flag 'everything' as suspicious initially, and Aurora and I will circulate and give direction and widdle down those options."

Liya worked her magic by connecting the seven different screens to play the footage synchronously. She set the footage to play from the five-minute warning that signaled for the audience to return to their seats' post-intermission to two mins and thirty seconds after the last bomb detonated.

They decided watch without audio to focus on body language and movement. Langston and Aurora weave through the congregated techs as they analyze the frozen still images. They delegated and assigned an assemblage of initial "suspects" to take notes on any suspicious behavior.

Eyes peeled. Finger at the ready, hovering just above compad screens.

PLAY.

They watched it all unfold again.

Warm yellow light cue winks in a dim-bright-dim-bright sweet beckon. The audience sashays drunkenly through the doors in the rear, meandering towards their seats. They settle in for the opening curtain.

The Maestro ascends to his throne and reclaims one-thousand-three-

hundred-eleven audience members' attention with the delicate bouncing of his baton against his cast-iron podium. He opens his arms and welcomes the Act 3 interlude.

The curtains part to reveal the star singer, the Diva, center stage. She floats suspended in zero gravity, feet meters above the stage in the open air. A thousand gentle winds twist and seperate the gossamer tendrils of her elaborate bikini-cape costume. Her hair water-danced in a halo around her. Carried away by her emotions, eyes closed, her mouth opens wide in song. The fuschia glow of Quo dances through the shadows cast in her luscious curls.

The Diva brings her hand up to --

Boom. The cataclysm. People mist away in the wake of the Equalizer blast. That misty stillness is burnt apart by the bright explosive firebombs from all sides. Fires rage across both sides of the auditorium. The flames chase at the audience's heels like a starving animal. Until nothing remains. An empty auditorium and a rage theatre.

The fire crew rush in for search and rescue.

PAUSE.
REWIND.
PLAY.

The light dims, casting shadows across the room.

The ushers shepherd the woozy elite to their designated seats. Once seated, patrons cuddle into the cocoon-like cradle design of the seat. Each seat is enclosed by partitions when in the reclining position, individual audience members feel as if they've escaped into their own worlds within their assigned seat.

A spotlight shines on the rotund bass player and toweringly tall flutist on either side of the conductor. They bow before they take their seats and play in the first chords of the opera's signature sonata.

The audience is transfixed by the music, hypnotized by the madame's artistic pageantry. As one, the audience inhales. A collective, anticipatory breath.

Boom.

Fire. Panic. Death.

PAUSE. REWIND. PLAY.

Lights wink.
Patrons settle.
Song sings.
Deep breath.
Boom.

"Again."

PAUSE. REWIND. PLAY.

Sit.
Symphony.
Beat.
Boom.

PAUSE-REWIND-PLAY.

Entrance.
Soprano.

"Pause."

Aurora's voice echoed throughout the room. She walked over to Liya to check the master controller. Her eyes scanned down to the bottom to find the ticking clock at the bottom of the footage:

26:13:43.

Aurora had an idea.

"Let's play it again butadd in the audio."

"Yeah... ok," Langston easily agreed. "Let's do it. Everyone leaves their current notes where they are and everyone reexamines the footage but focusing in on the sensory aspect for this pass."

Aurora made her way from the control podium to stand within spitting distance of the screens of footage with the most centralized images of the stage. It was behind the equalizer blast and center over the audience.

PLAY.

*The cacophonous buzz of the cocktail hour pervades every corner of the hall. A thousand blurbs of small talk rush into the ears. The patrons are loud, guileless in **Their Moment**. The thoughtless last words of nearly six hundred. Simple small talk. Unsuspecting.*

Tck-tck-tck. The Maestro reigns in the last vestiges of wandering attention with a tap of his baton.

Sharp and haunting, the resonant duet of flute and bass shatters the silence. The flute's ethereal whisper is punctuated by the earthy harmony of the bass guitar grumbling in behind.

The Diva's voice titilates and shivers the thrill of anticipation to the melody. Ping -- the opening keys of a piano join the growing swell of a symphony stretching its legs as the full symphony joins in the sonata. The sigh of a trumpet, the excited whisper of notes on a violin.

Swirling soprano's vocal runs charge toward the Big Note. The High-C.

Then... Boom.

There.

"It wasn't timed," Aurora said. She was sure of it.

Langston went to stand behind her to see what she saw. He motions with a rotation of his hand for Liya to rewind a tick and play it back.

"See there. There is no way for that to be perfectly timed with that note. That's not a coincidence. This is opening night, a thousand things happening for the first time. That detonation is," Aurora snaps her finger, "*perfectly* in time with that big note. The note they were all waiting for."

Rhys interjected, "B-but didn't you find the relay system on Bomb 2, 3, and 5?"

"True... but we haven't identified the detonators on the first or the fourth bomb. We haven't been able to find any of the materials or debris from either of those detonations, which would actually be more helpful to our investigation overall," Langston said. "It is a fair point, though. Liya cut the audio again and play it through till the room clears."

"Wait," Aurora said and turned back to Langston. "Come on, the peak of the high note and the first explosion are both at the same time down to the second. 26:13:42. No one picks a weird time like that."

"That's fucking ridiculous. It obviously could've been on a countdown timer, Roar."

She raced back to the monitor and pulled up the display of the back-stage footage, waving towards the 20 or so stagehands on the still screen. "We've cleared everyone in range to have access to an obvious detonator. No one was in the auditorium, *no one* was behind the stage. So, yes, it could still be a timer, but because of the signal detonator... and I mean the coincidence of it all is grotesque. It wasn't a fucking timer." Aurora turned back to him. "I know we need evidence. But an audio detonator for at least the first bomb could be ou best lead. This deserves serious consideration."

"It's under consideration, then," Langston conceded.

She nodded. "Ok." Given their shared investigative track record, she knew Langston wouldn't be satisfied until there was more evidence. But she was laying the gound wok because they had a standing pact that her "theories" wouldn't be proposed in any official report prior to the appearance of substantive corroborating evidence.

"So. Boom. There goes the MP. Then the first fire bomb. Then boom, boom, boom. Boom," She moves with the wave of the detonations. "It's like dominos. Let's see it again through the evacuation."

The footage rolled through until the auditorium was empty. It's the bare bones of a room once haunting in its beauty that remains so in its tragedy.

"It is a bit flashy, no? Regardless of the detonator, it's all choreography and style. Clearly, they had insider information. The singer's big song. The audience basically holding its collective breath. And then boom." Langston was warming up to her theory.

"Yeah... anything else is... it's *too* perfect," Aurora said.

"With all the evidence, we're operating on the assumption that the perp was in the room. That means they are watching the audience. The play. This was personal. It was perfect." Langston rubbed his hands together before cracking his knuckles and looking down at his notes. "So, you'd just detonated a bomb. What next?" Langston asked.

Aurora hummed. "Do you flinch? Are you anticipating the next boom? Are you a safe distance away? Do you stand stalk-still? Do you have one-foot out the door?" Aurora motioned towards the collected analysts in front of her. "Who noticed any suspicious behavior?"

A beat of silence lingered before folks shouted out their comments and hot takes:

"Marius Bell is *always* acting just a little suspect."

"None of the stagehands were at their assigned posts."

"That's cause they were watching the show."

"I've got nothing. Everyone in my section was geriatric."

"What about the House Manager? Where was she? I don't think he's in the room."

"But only folks in the room are suspect, though, right?"

"But he should've been in this room and he's most likely close. I agree! Add him to the suspect list."

"First, you aren't in charge of the suspect list. And second, the House Manager is supposed to be managing the lobby during intermission. He's not a suspect."

"What about the usher? Everything they were doing seemed suspicious now."

Langston and Aurora took in all the observations and let the rabble make wild guesses and speculation. Slowly but surely trends emerged. The ushers were acting oddly. The pair pulled the techs assigned with the majority of the usher footage to show them the suspicious behavior.

A tech in the back quiet question carried across the room. Aurora and Langston turned to the tech for further information.

"There. All the ushers on the right side were distracted by a loud drunk guy," the tech continued his explanation while pointing out the right side of the auditorium. "The drunken asshole probably saved the lives of all the staff in that section because he basically led the staff quite conveniently out of the immediate blast zone of the first two or three bombs. I can't tell who is more suspicious. The drunk guy or the usher?"

"Both"

Liya zoomed in on the section of footage for the rest of them to see the main monitor with more details.

"See," another tech said as she motioned towards the seven stage-right ushers. "Slowly, they all started kind of nervously inching towards the patron. The first couple of them don't have that much success keeping him contained and the rest of them are almost trying to herd him to the exit."

Another tech catches that— "Look at that one—the one closest to the blast."

The usher has a slight build topped with honey-gold hair

who is looking from the stage to the rest of the ushers nervously. Head whipping back and forth, he crept to the front of the auditorium.

"What's he doing? He's the only one moving closer to the blast than farther away, though, isn't he?"

"Yeah, but he's also just in general... doing the most. It's like—he's... orchestrating something. I'd bet that knows more than the rest of the ushers, that's for sure," Aurora said.

With that statement, everyone developed opinions. Whispers and conjecture exploded from the techs as they produced half-formulated hypotheses based on Aurora's conclusion. Langston shushed the rest of the team before he addressed to Aurora. "You think he's our guy?"

"I think he knows something. Which doesn't make him innocent. But 'our guy'? We'll see."

She leaned over Liya's compad, tapping throuh a couple of different angles to project onto the screen.

There he was, close enough to feel the heat, but not close enough to get immediately incinerated. Goldilocks, a fitting title for our blonde suspect.

Aurora flicked through the different camera angles to get the perspective of the footage shifts to see where Goldilock's gaze was directed.

"Now what are you looking at here... we've got options. He could be looking over here. At Marius Bell," she said. The angle reviewing Marius Bell standing worriedly in the wings of the auditorium, "Or perhaps backstage at the stage manager or..." Aurora zoomed out. The wide angle revealed the approximate epicenter of the equalizer. "Maybe he was looking right at the heart of things, where the MP blew."

Langston considered it for a second before nodding. His agreement with her hypothesis was based on either trust in her instinct or desperation for a break. At the best of times, Langston was impatient, so given their current ultimatum, she didn't think this was a leap of faith on his part. All in all, Aurora would take the win.

"2 out of 3 options, he's probably in the clear," Langston said in conclusion, "That third option... we'll have more questions."

"Yes, indeed, we will."

Langston motioned for the lights in the viewing room to return to full bright. "I want everyone's notes formatted and submitted to file. Please continue to review footage and any other anomalies should be immediately reported to your CO."

The room dispersed into a flurry of activity.

Aurora's eyes remained pinned to the still image of the usher that remained on the big screen. "Can I get a name for Mr. Goldilocks?"

Rhys, who helpfully stayed at heel by her side, swiped a few times over his compad, "Jamie Pope. ID Number 10945."

Aurora took another couple of seconds to look at this suspect. She wandered closer, pausing inches away fom a closeup on his face.

There was something soft and lost in Jamie Pope's eyes. Full of regret, easily breakable perhaps.

"Langston," Aurora called out to draw his attention over to her. He came to sit beside her, looking up at the same close up. "Its gotta be you. You're the one to talk to him," Aurora said.

Knowing the routine, he scratched blunt nails over the scruff of his sand-paper length beard before nodding. "Ok. The usual, yeah? Social biography and then straight-questioning?"

"Absolutely."

A clamoring of hurried, uncoordinated stomping echos up the flight of stair to announce Dev's arrival. Dev, their senior crime scene analyst, burst onto the landing before he beelined towards Aurora and Langston. Out of breath and a sweaty mess, his blue coveralls were tied around his waist in a state of disrepair. He rushed out, "We found something!"

While Aurora was intrigued by Dev's vague enthusiasm, she welcomed the information. "Care to share with the class?"

Dev's enthusiasm was, unfortunately, no match for his lack

of athleticism. Bent over his pencil thin legs, heaving, Dev was forced to choose between wheezing and hyping his discovery as he couldn't do both at the same time. Thought he tried. "If — if I thought that you would benefit -phew-from me describing the damn thing — Oh Oya, pheeeeew-I would have — but... you-you've gotta-."

Yahtzee.

That's all she needed to know. Aurora could finish that sentence in her sleep. She could practically *taste* that next few delightful teases that Dev's huffing and puffing prevented him from delivering. But perhaps the wait increased the payoff because she was chomping at the bit.

Langston shook his head in exasperation. A begrudging smile slipped past his defenses as he cut Dev off. "Don't say it. Please. It's been a long day. It's going to continue to be a long day. And I can't deal with Harlowe getting all excited."

Pressing a hand beneath his ribs in what seemed to be a developing cramp, Dev continued to throw down the gauntlet. "But really this time. You gotta see this."

Everyone knew Detective Harlowe couldn't resist a good show-n-tell moment.

"Let's go see it then."

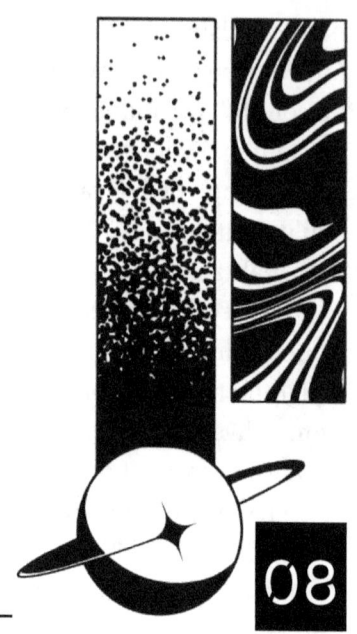

MAKE IT PERSONAL

08

LANGSTON

Langston trudged behind Dev and Aurora through the aisle of the auditorium. They had re-entered the auditorium's seating section to check out Dev's newest discovery. As the group drew closer to the find, amazingly, Dev's energy increased. As he debriefed the senior investigators on the team's progress, he used every appendage available to gesture wildly in every which direction. He looked aboutas coordinated as a spider doing a jig.

Liya brushed past Langston, throwing him a bit of elbow as she hissed under her breath. "Be nice."

"Me?" Langston said with a clear sense of faux affront. It garnered his favorite half-smile from Liya as she continued to follow in Dev's wake. Langston closed the distance, so he was right behind her. Langston said into her ear "Also, I didn't say anything y--"

"It was written all over your face. You had that stupid smile on your face that you always get before you make a stupid joke," she said, staring down at her compad as she continued to walk. He followed close enough to see the reports she was reviewing. Her slim, soft fingers skimmed the screen in a dance. He caught a whiff of the honey warm scent that was all Liya.

Langston was standing too close. It was muscle memory at this point to remember to put space between himself and Liya intentionally. At this point, it was an undeniable fact that he was drawn to her like a magnet.

Trapped in the aisle, his only option for putting an appropriate professional distance between them was to stop walking.

However, Liya stopped walking just a tick after him. She was barely a foot or two in front of him, though she didn't fully look back at him, just a half glance. Her eyes were bright and intelligent, as they always were. He wasn't sure how she always did it, but she could read him like a book. She could almost hear his internal monologue being blasted through loudspeakers. She didn't comment, though. After a couple of seconds passed with their eyes connected, she dropped her gaze and took the few paces to reach where Aurora and Dev had stopped.

Dev was on his knees, pointing at something. "It's right over here." Waving the rest of them in closer, they congregated in the dead center in the middle-most row. Dev clicked on the UV light. "You see this," he said as he shined the light on the back of the seat to reveal a handwritten message scrawled in electric blue under the UV. "We've taken a sample but we think it was written using a combination of a lemon wedge from the bar and a second substance. Because of the theatre's design, they use Blacklight for the exit illumination in the seating sections. So, this message would only be visible during the performance when the house lights were turned off. When it was placed, there should be an easily identifiable with security footage. Most likely, the poor sop sitting in this seat read this message either seconds or minutes before they kicked the bucket."

Scrawled across the back of the curved podchair was a

phrase written in drippy handwriting. It read:

I'm not proud but I am happy.

Aurora crouched next to Dev, who handed her the glowing blue flashlight. Her fingers hovered over the message text before she just sat back on her heels to contemplate the words. Langston, in the aisle behind her, rested his hands against the back of the seats, his focus returning to the case. To his mind, there were the obvious questions that, in this case, were interesting despite being conspicuous. And then the deeper root of those questions that had complexities upon further complication and gave him general indigestion.

The Obvious:

What did this message mean?

Who wrote the message?

When did they write this message?

Then on the more complicated side of things: was this a red herring meant to throw them off on a wild goose chase or an honest-to-goodness calling-card taunt from the terrorist?

It was clear that Aurora was doing her psychoanalytical quiet thing, but Langston couldn't wait for her to tune back into the frequency that the rest of them existed on. He needed to get some facts on the record. Turning towards Dev, he gestured around the section. "I take it that this was the epicenter of the MP?"

"Yes!" The spectacled beanstalk of a man jumped up from where he was shoulder-to-shoulder with Aurora to explain their discovery process. The scrawny technician was sure to make a grandiose point of every praise-worthy accomplishment on his own behalf. Langston listened with half an ear, knowing that any detail he missed would be in the meticulous notes that Liya was writing for the file. There was a dual purpose to stringing this response out of Dev. An accounting of how brilliant Dev imagined himself, was of little import, it bought Aurora time to do some thinking without Dev hovering over her. Thus speeding up this entire process thankfully.

Langston's eyes occasionally drifted to Aurora, trying to gage her progress while her face gave away nothing.

If he let it, this whole genius-detective act of hers might've made a serious impact on his overall ego. Privately, he felt it was fairly selfless of him and a sign of his own deeply secure masculinity. Altogether it wasn't like he had much of a choice. Self preservation demanded that he repress the swift kick to the pride when all eyes of their team unconsciously turned to her when they needed a big answer to a hard problem.

So he patted himself on the back and pretended like it was his choice.

It was a choice, though. He could've made the choice to be a total asshole about everything. He could force his way into the limelight, perhaps steal her glory, after she had put Humpty-Dumpty back together again. In fact, he was sure that some of the team even secretly suspected that he did just that.

But it complicated itself upon more digging. A therapist might call it codependent, but Langston vastly preferred a scientific term: *symbiotic.* Her strengths were a puzzle-piece-perfect fit to his weakness, and vice versa. And to sweeten the deal, they were both great at reading a room and moving people. So, really it was a win-win altogether.

Dev continued to drone on, a portait of a half-broken radio signal that no one much-paid attention. Aurora started mumbling under her breath. After a couple of seconds of divided concentration, he still couldn't hear or understand what she was mumbling.

Dev had somehow clued in on Langston's inattention to his dubiously impressive discovery of evidence at the epicenter of a crime scene. He wondered if Dev realized how obvious this evidence presentation was. It was literally smack dab in the center of everything. An idiot could find it given enough time.

As Dev mustered up the self-control to interrupt his own long-winded soliloquy to his investigative brilliance, he announced. "It's obviously a reference to the opera." Dev swiped a playbill off the floor and thrust it into Langston's hands.

Langston read the title: "An Inch of Flesh." The cover was at once deeply unsubtle and teasingly discrete. It was an erotic image to be sure without displaying outright nudity. It was a great deal more than an inch of flesh. "Raunchy," he said dryly, before he reached over to place the progam on Roar's shoulder.

Still unable to descend from the heights of his own orgasmic intellectualism, Dev continued to ramble. "I'll say. The early preview feedback was a mixed bag, but everyone loved the diva's performance and recently -"

"It's not about opera. That was just a convenient diversion." Aurora said.

With a jerk of his head, Langston shooed away the rest of the team to their duties, so it was just the partners. He climbed over the back of the pod he was leaning on to sit in the seat behind her. Leaning forward against his knees, he settled in for a **Conversation**. That's how they worked best, of course, with a Conversation. She turned towards him and clicked off the UV light.

"But this convenience ain't that convenient, is it? Expand for me, Roar."

"Something about the phrasing... it doesn't necessarily ring a bell, but in this context, I can only assume it has significance above the obvious context here. Does it ring a bell for you?"

"Not that I know of."

"We'll have to do the research on it, but my bet is it's a Gherrean quote. There is no way it's Kaetyene. The sentence is so simple that even a translation would have a different syntax. And I can't imagine what the reverse translation would come out to with words that are this vague. So we just have to *assume* it means something which I don't love. If the average G-men around , ie you, doesn't get the reference, then there is an intended audience that we have to identify. But again, leaving a signature like this is very on the nose. So, the words, the meaning, all of it are a little beside the point for now because it's very existance reveals a fair amount about the person who wrote it. The message is either for us... or for whoever was sitting right there."

She pointed to the seat beside her. Pausing, she got off her knees to settle into the seat she'd referenced. They sat side-by-side in silence for a beat. Looking blankly at the message in front of them. They saw through the eyes of the victim, read the message as they would've seen it. Like it was the last thing they ever saw.

I'm not proud but I am happy.

Langston called out to Dev. "Dev, who was sitting in this seat?" he asked, gesturing to the seat Aurora was currently occupying.

Dev drifted back over their way as he tapped in search of his compad. His mouth opened and closed. He looked up at Langston and said, "It was... Asa Greene."

Langston gave a low whistle.

Asa the Green-Eyed Monster.

It had been a couple of years back, but Langston still remembered the headlines about Asa Greene. The exposés that ran about the conditions in her factories was gut-curling at best. Langston, thankfully, couldn't recall the details of the horrible conditions or deaths written about in the expose. It was rather the complete unflinching lack of apology on Asa's part that was memorable. Greene had weathered the scandal through sheer, dogged viciousness. Her viciousness was more a general principle and business practice.

Langston looked at Aurora. She lived under a rock and it clearly didn't ring any bells for her. She wasn't one for news or recent events. He said to her, "Now, that's a name. She's the founder of HausVerte Domes."—Liya, ever-dependable, stood at attention slightly behind Dev— "Liya, can you pull up some articles on Greene for Aurora? There's probably enough on the unrestricted public domain to give Aurora a picture of who Ms. Greene was."

Liya nodded and complied, passing over her compad

to Aurora. His partner skimmed through a couple of articles, including the famous expose, before she reviewed a lifetime achievement interview article celebrating Asa's 60th birthday last year. She hopped back into a search feature to skim through headlines about HausVerte, which dutifully referenced their exalted leader. Asa was pictured in a few. The victim's face was carved with severity into every crease of the quite elegantly wrinkled features. Greene had a wild, substantive eyebrows that contrasted with her sleek black hair styled in a pompador with a sprinkling of salt at the temples. Langston recognized this woman, though he had never met Asa Greene. He had met people like Asa his entire life. There was something about her appearance, flawless as it was, that indicated wealth, fastidiousness and a deep insecurity.

Sighing, Aurora handed back the device and arched her brow. "What a peach."

Langston couldn't help but agree. "So," he said, "This cat was sitting right at the epicenter. Smells like an assassination?"

"Hmm... What a messy idea."

So, Aurora thought it was possible too–deeply troubling, but possible.

Aurora turned to Liya. It was a default reaction because at times like these, Liya was symbolic for facts and reasons and answers. She was also great at typing fast, so there was that. "Can you pull the official SI file on Asa Greene?" Aurora asked

Dev took a steps forward, inserting himself into the conversation, having listened in with the ability to connect dots. "You can't possibly believe that *all of this* was... what... a coverup meant for one person?"

Langston and Aurora looked at him pityingly.

Dev was soundly ignored.

Liya held up her compad to read a summary of Greene's file for the detectives. "Asa Greene. Bioengineering tycoon. HausVerte Dome Productions. An aggro-business headquartered in Old Delhi, Gherre, with substantial land holding, factories, and operation in. An estimated 68% of the Yemayan GDP attributed to HausVerte. Their cornerstone product -- semi-meat. Originally founded by her father, HausVert started out with a couple of small domes but didn't rise to its current colossus scale until Asa took over. She was known for her aggressive business tactics, to say the least. Very determined. Very cutthroat. She... has never been charged with anything, but there have been a couple of muddy... or hastily silenced complaints. There were a couple of noisy news articles that circulated 2062, three years ago. But as far as SI is concerned, HausVert's produce, semi-meat and... management was above reproach. It might be worth noting that their prices are the lowest on the market."

Unhelpfully, Langston recalled one of the last fights he had with his ex-wife. Near the end, when they had started the dangerous game of being honest, she said something that had stuck with him to this day. He was watching the news with her when a segment about the importance of Yemayan domes and the agricultural output came on. This resulted in a sharp political debate that provided the perfect cover for thinly veiled personal insults. Somewhere in the heat of the argument, she has popped off with: "We all can't afford the high cost of your moral superiority, Langston." And that was the crux of it, wasn't it?

Somewhere along the lines, the folks at the top convinced the System that we couldn't afford better. We couldn't afford to pay the Dome croppois for their labor. We couldn't afford to question the morality of how corporations made what the people needed to survive.

It wasn't that we couldn't afford it. Greene had more money than a god. There wasn't a thing in the galaxy that she couldn't afford. She made her choice. And in a lot of ways, so did the System.

Dev again protested. "I don't care if she owned the worst domes in the galaxy. Nearly 600 people died in less than 5 minutes. Why would anyone do that just to kill one lady? No. Just No. Hasn't anyone ever heard that two wrongs don't make a right?"

Aurora leaned forward in her seat to grab his hand. "We know nothing for sure but... people have done worse to accomplish less," she said. Her thumb made small circles on the back of his hand. He deflated, pulling his hand out of her reach. He plopped into the chair behind him. With all his ego and faults, he wasn't wasting his time investigating various tragedies in the inaugural mission with The Socrates. He was learning. It was painful.

But life was full of painful lessons and being babied by the junior detective of the unit did no one any favors. Langston swatted her knee and gave her the look. Unrepentant, Aurora flashed the Truth in her eyes at him.

"Don't make it personal," Langston said in warning.

The Truth faded from the iced-over, opalescent metallic shimmer to their regular dark hazel irises, black pupils on white. He ignored the obvious traces of petulance as she slammed back into her chair to pout. She winced and her back popped away from the seatback. Reared back away from the seat, she felt along with the center cushion of the chair. Her finger pressed firmly into the velvet fabric. Her hand stopped, but her nails pressed firmly across the cushioning. She found something.

Aurora met his eyes with a quick smile. She called out for Dev to bring his kit to document and investigate this with something she had found. She moved out of the seat onto the floor, hovering beside Dev, who took several photos of the fabric with a small millimeter wide hole in the fabric that was almost invisible to the naked eye if you weren't specifically looking.

Dev pulled out a pair of scissors and snipped at the rip in the fabric. He pulled back the fabric and the cushion plush to reveal... a metal thingy. More photos and then Dev worked to extract evidence and carefully pried it from its position. The device was sandwiched by the cushion foam rather than being stuck on with any amount of glue or adhesive. It was a small metal contraption with a round silver puck-like base and a tiny sharp metal needle protruding from the center. The needle was a good deal thicker than your average needle, but smaller than a straw. The new discovery brought on a smile as he dusted for fingerprints. There were none.

"This is new." Dev handed the device over to Aurora for further observation in the sterile cloth he had been using. "I don't think I've ever seen anything like this before."

"Let's see if this thingy isn't logged in the patent archives," Langston asked.

Liya stepped closer to scan a couple of photos before she tip-tapped on her compad to find their answer. "Hm, it's a soil gage," she announced to the group. "It's used as a fertilization and nutrient distribution device in potted or uprooted plants. They are an incredibly effective and low-maintenance tool. Typically used in agricultural centers rather than home gardens."

She switched over to projection mode on her compad. A holodisplay of a similar soil gage model as the one that Aurora is holding. A holo replica of the flat disk floated above her hand. The holo demonstrated the patented feature, a thick needle-like feeding tube pierced the air before retracting. The "feeding tube" resembles a 5-gauge needle connected to the round base where fertilizer and feed were stored.

Langston could see how these elements featured into the murderous tableau. He rolled his shoulders back. "I'm just going to assume that there isn't plant fertilizer in the puck, so I'd love diagnostics to take a look at that. And how much do you want to bet that this actual model was used by HausVerte?"

Liya frowned and nodded. "Yes, this model was patented by HausVerte to be exclusively used in their domes. The major selling point of this innovation was the timer-based automation feature that's unique to this model. Significant because it cut down on labor costs."

Turning the device in her hand, Aurora asked for clarification. "Automation, you say?"

Liya flipped through a couple more items on her compad

before sliding the tablet under her armpit and wordlessly asking Aurora for the device. Flipping the device over, she used her nail to pry a thin metal back off to reveal a set of rudimentary gage buttons. "You can use these buttons to time when the feeding tube springs out." She pressed down on two buttons at once and a neon clock with the current time appeared and the needle extended to its full length. The needle was approximately a foot in length.

Aurora asked, "Can we check when the last automated spring was scheduled?"

Liya held the gage in her palm. She pinched the base of the needle and turned it twice to the left and once to the right, then flipped it over.

Yellow numbers appear on the disc plate of the gage: 26:12:45.

"So, if we had a body, we can assume there would be a needle-sized hole through her chest," Langston said as his eyebrows furrowed in consideration

He looked at Aurora. Her face was blank while she raised a brow; stubborn woman that she wasn't going to say anything then. She wasn't necessarily pouting, but she played this particular game enough to know what she was doing.

Langston had told her not to make it personal, so she was going to make him regret those words. She was going to let him reach his own conclusions. Withholding her quick conclusions as a petty rejoinder to his chastisement. All an all, it was a game he'd indulge because it had the fringe benefit of skipping the debate on whether it was the logical conclusion or Aurora's semi-activist agenda. Honestly, fair enough, if she said it first, he would be tempted to dismiss it and her.

It was written right there in her eyes, but he'd have to close this loop for himself.

Time to stretch those mental muscles.

"Revenge," Langston said. "Something personal. No matter what went down, if something went wrong if the bomb detonations were botched, no matter what – Asa Greene was going to die tonight."

Greene would've been settling into her seat as the 2nd act started, the lights dimming. The message would be revealed in the fading light and then the stab would pierce through her sternum, piercing her lungs, straight through the heart, sharp. She wouldn't have died immediately, and the bomb didn't blow for maybe another minute or so. Why didn't she scream out.?Did she make a scene? Perhaps she had enough time to riddle the message out in the minute she had left before the play began. Was Asa the kind of person who would've understood the reference?

"We'll rewatch that footage. Get eyes on Greene to see what really happened. There are about thirty seconds between the fertilizer-pokey death blow and the bombing. So I'm interested to see what Asa was doing." Aurora paused in consideration. "To my mind, the person who did this, they wanted Asa to see death coming and not be able to stop it. They wanted it to be slow and painful."

Exhaustion settled into Langston's bones at the idea of re-watching that footage again. "Yah, a puncture wound like this, straight through the heart, will definitely kill you, but... not fast. Not immediately. She would've been the only one in the room to anticipate the end was coming."

Aurora looked up at the ceiling, scanning the stucco to find the nearest security cams. "The question remains... was the perp in the room... Did they watch their masterpiece assassination theatre unfold?"

"Yeah, yeah, yeah. We get it. We're re-watching the footage. Again."

Aurora smirked as she made her way down the aisle towards the exit of the auditorium. Langston followed. He felt Liya's warm presence behind him. "Liya, we need a list of anyone on this station today with personal connections to Asa Greene."

Nodding and taping away, Liya said, "Of c--... Oh."

Liya paused. A few seconds without a complete answer elapsed before she settled her device on his shoulder for him to grab.

Langston took the device and saw the compad screen had an open profile pulled up for him to review. The profile picture of a man was a dead ringer for a younger male version of Asa. He read the name and information of the profile: "Azul Greene. Her son. He was there too? Ticketed for the seat right next to Asa."

"Langston, not just that. He's on the survivor's list," Liya added.

"Now that's... interesting. The man who was supposed to be sitting next to the bomb is stiiiiiilllll kickin'." Langston couldn't help but smile when he realized what this meant. Things were looking a little bit easier. This was a silver lining if he'd ever seen one. Or maybe an "azul"-lining would be more accurate.

A laugh of disbelief puffed out of Aurora as she heard these additional facts. Azul Greene, son and heir to Asa Greene, who should've been sitting next to the bomb, was still alive.

"I think we can squeeze in a quick little chat with Azul before we watch that footage."

Langston bobbed his brow. "Sounds like a party to me."

SANTOS HALL AMPITHEATRE DOORS, ESAA SELTENTA
SPACE STATION & RESORT, GEOSYNC - QUO

DISMISSED

LANGSTON

Exiting the hall for the second time marked the end of the beginning pat of the investigation. All the evidence had been marked and photographed. All the fingerprints cataloged. Now came time for the nitty-gritty work of... finding the terrorist. At least they always left the fun part for last.

Langston could firmly holster most of his deadline-based anxiety in thanks to their two glorious leads.

Dean's deadline loomed over his head. Despite what felt like half-a-century of slogging through dead-ends, it had only been ten measly hours since Dean's initial mission brief. The good Colonel had given them less that a thirty hour day to wrap up this investigation and if their current pace continued Langston would need every last second of the remaining twelve hours. The leg work to get to this point in the investigation had been demoralizing and exhausting. Hopefully, these leads would need to serve as fuel for a long road ahead. Something in Langston's gut warned up that regardless of hope his team was looking at nothing but an uphill climb.

"Ok folks, Aurora and Liya have updated assignments for everyone. We ae down to twenty-two hours on the clock. Let's see some ---

A few feet from the exit, the heavy door swung open, followed by an outpouing of amassed white-clad soldiers. The soldiers stalked forward in a rigid formation that caused some of the Socrates crew to stumble back to avoid physical confrontation.

There in the front left of the platoon of around fifteen was Captain Ahmed who shockingly was even more run-ragged than the last time they'd seen him. The iconic hard-shelled white vinyl chestplate of the soldiers' uniform unmistakably identified them. Command Corp had descended on the station — *the Star's Hammer*.

Ahmed's six foot frame was dwarfed by several of the commandos that flanked him on all sides with one noticeable exception to his right. The exception, a highly decorated major based on the near-orgy of regalia pins on her uniform, stood just barely over five foot. Insignia read "Major Parker Zhou" her specific classification and company designation was redacted in black leather. What she lacked in size she more than made up for in a palpable sense of foreboding. For better or for worse, there weren't many women in the ranks of CC for a reason and rising to any level of seniority was both a laudable feat and a red-flag.

The CC squad formed a blockade between the Socrates and the exit.

They stopped in front of him, several disrespectful inches into his personal space.

They were not suppose to be there.

But they were, they were right in front of him.

Something in Langston's gut clunked hard than thundered fast in his chest. Adrenaline pumped through him. SI officer or not, Langston's natural response was the same as any Pact citizens when confronted with an unexpected visit from CC military command: fight-or-flight mode. The only questions was: how much time did he have to decide.

Fight or flight. Fight or flight.

They were not supposed to be here... but he was. The Esaa bombing was the case of a lifetime. It was **his** case and he was present and accounted for.

So, today he chose fight.

Decision made. Hot, hot adrenaline raged through his veins. Langston had to think faster. React smarter. Because they were not supposed to be here.

The distinction was both philosophical and logistical. Their presence defied the outlined parameters of the mission brief and a fair amount of logic. He dredged his memory for everything he could remember of the mission brief.

Dean's heavy implication suggested that the Socrates was assigned the Esaa case out of pure approximate luck. They had only gotten this assignment cause they were the **only** SI ship within range. In fact, Dean had straight up said explicitly that there wasn't another Pact ship within 2 sols of their location. Time was moving slow but not a single sol had passed since the briefing. Ten hours down. It had been a third of a sola day gone.

So this unwanted CC squadron was here, but *how*? How had this uninvited CC squadron gotten to Esaa so fast? Illegally, that was the only answer -- an unsanctioned burn-and-jump. Something unsanctioned due to the unconscionable amount of fuel necessary for such a move. It was both illegal and not uncommon. Classic CC.

Langston schooled a mild, unbothered mask over his face. Eyebrows at ease, suppress all tension from the corners of his mouth and no one would be able to tell what bubbled underneath.

"Captain Ahmed, we were just about to ping you," he said. "We were on our way back to the security deck. We have a couple of good leads and are ready to proceed." Perhaps if he just refused to acknowledge the platoon, ignore them on focused solely on Ahmed, they'd all just go away.

"No."

The word — the order — rang out. A sharp thunderclap of a word came from the Major. The voice and the command demanded attention. Langston could almost hear his crew's necks crack as the Socartes's zapped their focus onto the speaker. But Langston was reticent.

A lingering mulishness begrudged even the barest of acknowledgement of this new bossy figure, even by sight. He didn't want to look at her. But, dragging out every moment, he turned his gaze to this newest bug in the ointment.

Without any better options he slowly met her gaze. Everything about the major was sharp, the edges of her obsidian hooded eyes, the square jawline cut against high-set razor cheekbones. All that with full lips and a button nose, she was the kind of beautiful typically accompanied an equal measure of crazy. Or so, his dating history would show.

Her unblinking gaze was a crackling caldera furnace, she met his gaze like the challenge it was.

"This is no longer your investigation," the Major said. Her voice was without tone, dry and ominous. She seemed to lack distinct flavor that this person was devoid of the crucial elements of what made a person personable.

Langston wouldn't look away, he couldn't. A person doesn't look away from some things, thing like venomous snakes or rabid chihuahuas.

Despite the brevity, the dead delivery of her message, Langston could detect a cruel edge of humor in her face. Her words skewered him. Oya damn her, she relished in that torment. Her unholy focus was dedicated to soullessly documenting every sign of weakness and discomfort within him.

He hated her.

He wouldn't let her win. She was dead wrong. Whether she acknowledged it or not, this was his fucking investigation, his shot.

Silence and glaring didn't seem terribly effective against her. Perhaps it was time for a different tactic. The big guns. Langston melted into familiar caricature of himself that Roar had dubbed his "PR persona". As the Y-chromosone'd figurehead of their unit, he had an arsenal of schmarm at his disposal. When he slathers on the good stuff, he'd been known to woo even the toughest of cookies.

Saluting, Langston slipped a smile on his face and flashed some dimple. If he was lucky, he could spark a bit of twinkle out of his eyes. "System Intelligence Investigative Unit VP005, Lieutenant Detective Langston Aster." He raised his brow just a tick—a dash past condescending, but hopefully on the safe side of patronizing. "I'm sorry if you were misinformed, but my orders haven't changed. While it's lovely to see such an esteemed group of Command Corp officers such as yourselves, unfortunately I'm going to need to know who gave authorized you to land on this station?"

Silence responded.

Perhaps this was not Langston's best attempt at schmarm. His delivery was admittedly harsh. The oil of his charisma curdled under her glare.

Major Zhou looked him up and down. "You are relieved."

A shiver rolled off his shoulders without his permission. Her eyes ticked up and tighten. It as easy to miss... but she was smirking at his reaction.

Annoyed that his annoyance was showing, he clung to what remained of his composure. "Yeah, that doesn't quite summarize my current emotional state. On whose authority are we relieved?"

That finally cracked her face into what could be technically identified as a smile. All teeth. Her eyes remained hard. "Classified," she said. The major's head tilted in a sick mockery of clinical observation as she waited for his next reaction.

"Bullshit," Langston said.

He could barely contain himself. He scanned the insignia among the gathered CC soldiers. Redacted, every single one of their insignia was redacted. While Zhou's name was visible the entirety of her commandos were operating completely incognito.

No unit number or company assignment, no nothing. It was more rule-breaking nonsense, but it was yet another thing that defied logic. This wasn't a Wilds outpost where CC could smash and maim while being unidentified and lawless. This was a Central Core luxury station.

Lawless bloodhounds. CC's complete disregard for the rules they enforced gave him indigestion. Their cult-like allegiance to the Pact supremacy gave him heart palpitation. Langston had heard enough of Aurora's soap-box speech to agree that CC was little better than profiteering hired gun, rabid dogs off their chain.

To make matters worse, they had a deeply problematic, snake-eating-itself style relationship between the Pact and CC leadership. They seemed to be able to get away with anything.

Langston pressed further. He said, "The closest CC ship was just under two sols out. Who approved a jump? Cause we both know that the only way you got here. How the hell did you get here so fast?"

"Classified."

"Bull. Shit."

"Yes, you are correct. My bowel movements are also classified." this pixie whistle of a woman delivered this retort with an unshakable deadpan. Respectable if it wasn't so frustrating at this moment. Scratch that. He did respect it. That made it worse.

Aurora interrupted to redirect the conversation back to the station captain and safer ground. "Ahmed, on whose authority were they allowed to even land? Esaa is under strict lockdown and we should've been contacted for approval for any Command Corp ship looking to anchor. Why weren't we made aware of this situation earlier?"

Ahmed's pinched eyebrows communicated his tenuous grip on professionalism. This pissing contest had catapulted him well past his wit's end. "It was a damned system override," Ahmed said, "We were just on the bridge and next thing we know---"

"Classified," the major interrupted. The slip of a commanding officer then strolled past him, his crew, and his shattered dignity into the auditorium. She slithered in and out of the assembled members of his team without a care for personal space or decorum. A crocodile loves muddied waters. As she scanned the auditorium with a bored sort of curiosity, she looked like she didn't have a care in the world.

Langston was done. "Listen, you can classify every person, place, and thing you want, but until I get direct orders to stand down I'm--"

Behind him, a jarring bellow of a laugh came from the company of CC soldiers. It was a first lieutenant of the CC who was now holding up a thick war compad on display-mode. "Sorry, Detectives, but truly, this one is out of your hands." The lieutenant presented an official Oya-Vearro Pact-sealed Orders Script. He flicked through the script with no care to allow them to read the document. Even without reading the specific legalese of the memo, the message was clear. "Command Corp, Black Division will be taking over the remainder of this investigation under Treatise, Section 25. You are ordered to return to your ship and await further instructions."

Langston had heard water-cooler gossip back at HQ about some nightmarish scenarios where SI units were pulled off a case in order for CC to be given room to "work their magic". Section 25 was a carte blanche, boogie-man-in-the-closet clause. Translation - no one involved was ever heard from or seen again. While he was short on details, the original concept was that Section 25 gave the highest-ranking Command Corp officers near-total discretion to investigate, detain, and generally meddle in whatever they wanted at the drop of a hat. It was supposed to be a failsafe, in case insurrection or mayhem arose. The power of Section 25 was a cudgel against Langston's throat.

The Lieutenant smirked, putting away the order. "You see, the 'who's who' list of the dead made its way up the food chain and this is officially too much jelly for one crew."

Aurora's restraining hand raced out to pull back on Langston's bicep. It had the additive effect of silencing him as well. "Ok," she said, nodding slowly. "It looks like we got off on the wrong foot. Our team has been embedded for just under ten hours. I'm sure we all agree a swift closure to this investigation is what we are all after. Try to understand-"

A familiar voice stopped Aurora's soothing tap-dance of cajoling words.

"No, Detective Harlowe, it's you who needs to understand."

As a unit, their collective attention ping-ponged from the Lieutenant in front of them to the Major behind them in the auditorium. In her palm was a holocomm of Colonel Dean. Dean looked as if zhey'd gobbled down a barrel of olives and peanut butter. "Treatise Section 25 is clear. Your compads have been disconnected from the SI network and any Esaa secure access granted to your GIM has been revoked. Go back to your ship. Major Parker Zhou is in command." The scratchy, no-nonsense quality of Dean's voice brokered no discussion. No one in SI ever liked orders like this, but Dean was responsible for holding the line at times like this.

Aurora's mouth snapped shut. Her eyes widened a tick. Her fingers loosened and sagged on his arm. Langston physically felt his partner give up at that moment.

He knew that the odds of recovering this assignment back were next to nil but, hey, today he woke up and chose fight. He wouldn't roll over with a try. "I don't--"

"Yes, you would be right, LD Aster. I *don't* care about your opinions on the subject. I expect reports that say that you were nothing but cooperative and unobtrusive in Zhou's write-up. Is that understood, Aster?" Dean's tone brokered no room for negotiation.

"Yessir."

"Harlowe?" It was insulting. That additional display of uniform acquiescence communicated distrust from their superior officer burnt the frayed edges of Langston's control.

"Yes sir," Aurora said.

"Then you are... relieved. Return to your docked vessel until this investigation is concluded or your next orders come through." Dean's holocomm connection staticked out and Zhou closed her fist around the device.

Langston's professionalism appeared for the first time in this conversation. "We've already done extensive forensics and crime scene analysis, do you--"

"No." Major Zhou's deadpan continued to sting, crispy and taunting.

"We've got--"

"No authority. Yes, I know." Zhou's eyebrow arrowed down in sharp malicious glee. She had her back to them at this point. Didn't even give him the dignity of looking at him. Her attention was a silent signal to her goons swarmed past the amassed group of Socrates officers. Their group was small compared to a full CC squadron.

Before he attempted to make one last play, Aurora's hand that had never quite left his bicep tightened its grip. She moved in front of him to salute Ahmed. "We are dismissed."

Ahmed shook his head but nodded to them both, before following behind the CC squad into the auditorium.

That was the end of that.

Except it wasn't. Not by a long shot.

Performance Program of *An Inch of Flesh,* 2065
Soon to premiere at the Santos Opera Hall of the world
reknowned Esaa Seltenta Space Station and Resort

2 - DUET

(def) 1. (*esp for instrumental compositions*):
duo a musical composition for two performers
or voices
2. *an action or activity performed by a pair of*
closely connected individuals

00:00:00 VST

LOCATION

SANTOS HALL AMPITHEATRE, ESAA SELTENTA SPACE
STATION & RESORT, GEOSYNC - QUO

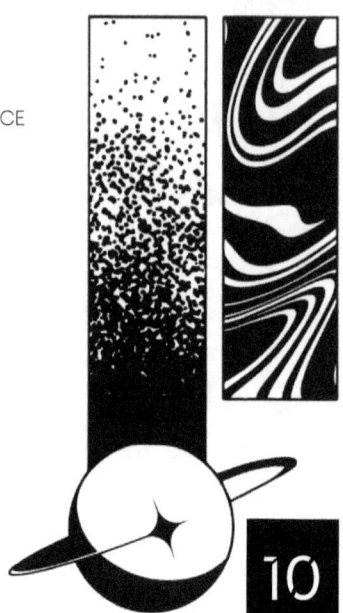

FEAR AND ADMIRATION

KIERAN

The Command Corp team settled into the bloodstained auditorium with sloppy and inappropriate sort of gusto. Feet propped up on seats, they eagerly pulled out the game consoles that he had gifted them to secure their silence. The irony of bribing government officials with goods he'd stolen from government impounds was the cherry on top of it all. He was less than impressed by how jubilantly they played their games amongst the burnt embers of death that surrounded them. The stench of dead bodies and the sulphuric remains of the bombing did nothing to dampen their enthusiasm.

The CC grunts were happy to look the other way. The gory scene before them didn't meet the bar of their concern or disgust. They had seen worse. Hell, they had almost definitely done worse.

Kieran was unfamiliar with the moral high-ground he could occupy over these white-suited neanderthals. The fact that it was him of all people who could claim ethical superiority over anyone was a testament to CC's overall integrity, or lack thereof. It was downright damning.

Major Parker Zhou, beside him, stood sentry at the theatre doors, glaring at the last of the SI squad scurrying away. Her performance wasn't for his benefit. She came by her dislike of System Intelligence officers organically.

Once they were out of sight, the serrated smile that cut across her face flaked off, leaving no discernible trace of emotion. There were just those blank brown eyes in an absurdly angular face. She jutted her chin up to look *way* up at him. A brief flare of annoyance flashed across her face as her eyes skimmed over the designations on his uniform. She was such a zealot. The fact that he wore the uniform of her second in command, a CC lieutenant, stung at her dogmatic zest for the Pact's honor. When he had decked himself in the regalia to signify the status of a Lieutenant, he saw her wince with each additional pin.

Unfortunately, donning the uniform hurt him as much as it hurt her. It was a necessary evil for today's performance as ***The Lieutenant***.

THE LIEUTENANT

It had been several years since he had worked together with Zhou. And "together" was a bit of a generous interpretation. She had just been getting her sea-legs back then. A new cadet fresh in the Corp with only the flickers of the obsessive Pact-gospel that had metastasized in her now. Today, in many ways, was just like before. Despite how she had clawed and stabbed her way up to this rank, today she would be the one taking orders — just like last time.

"What next?" Zhou asked.

The Lieutenant looked down at his compad and pulled up the seating diagram of Cherie's mission brief. "It'll be over there. Center seat of the center row."

He led the way through the aisles of sticky-hot seat cushions, Zhou trailing behind him. Based on his specs, the smoking-gun evidence that could connect all the dots from plan to perpetrator hid within the lining of the back cushion of Asa Greene's seat.

The Lieutenant pulled out a regulation CC blade and cut through the cushion. His digging fingers searched for a tiny-little-billionaire-killing surprise that should've been exactly where he was looking.

But there was nothing there. They'd already found it. Industrious little pricks.

He sighed.

"What are you looking for?" Zhou asked.

"Something that isn't there." The Lieutenant rolled his eyes and tugged down at the chest plate of his hard-plastic disguise. If the SI unit had already found their little surprise and that meant that they knew about Asa. "That's a complication. But half a dozen this way, the plan doesn't change. We'll just need to move faster. Perhaps with a little less finesse. All *you* need to worry about is that you just do what I tell you and in ten hours or less, I'm out of your hair. First up, we go grab Dummie #1."

He was up and moving towards the exit, ready for the next step in the plan.

"Maybe fuck your plan..." Zhou said. Her voice was hesitant, but firm. He was sure that she meant what she said with every fiber of her being.

Now, even The Lieutenant could admit that she had grown up since he last saw her. Zhou had become a bogeyman in her own right, perhaps. Perhaps in certain circles, her name alone incited fear. In some circle... but not in his.

"You are too far up shit's creek to have misgivings like that, Major. You've made your grand entrance and there's no going back after that. You, whether or not or you like it, are going to get exactly what's coming to you. Including the money we commissioned you with, your debt with us cleared, and all the prestige that arresting terrorists comes with."

He crossed the distance that separated them. He got close, really close, hunching his shoulder and craning his neck at a semi-uncomfortable angle to meet her eyes. The Lieutenant wanted to say this next bit while looking directly into her eyes. He saw Zhou's pupils dilate, heard her breathing arrest and hold. "But let's get to the heart of the matter. If this goes side-ways... If you go off script. Just know, I refuse to kill you. In fact, I promise, you will be alive, breathing and cognizant of everything I do to you. Death is an escape. And if you fuck this up, there is no escaping me. You got that?"

She tilted her chin up in something that was a sickening mix of fear and admiration. She nodded with fires in her eyes. Nothing like the threat of torture to inspire a sociopath.

She nodded, a new hunger burning in her eyes. "Yes, Kieran."

He turned again to leave, "It's *'Lieutenant'* now, Zhou. Please, we mustn't forget decorum. We've got work to do."

11

DEAD FISH

AURORA

Aurora couldn't feel her cheeks.

In all fairness, she wasn't sure if she could ever feel her cheeks, but in this moment, that realization was jarring. Her cheeks were numb in the same way that the rest of her was numb. It was a disassociated... accepting kind of numbness.

She knew who she worked for. She knew that at the end of the day, the VP program was still a part of the greater Systems Intelligence machine. Still linked, ball and chain, to the unstoppable force of the Oya Vearro Pact. Decisions like this were part of the job and the bargain she had made. So her cheeks were cool and clammy, not red hot with rage. She would categorize this dissociative episode as self-care and put all her rage in the back corner of her mind that she didn't dare to think about.

A body bumped against her side; it was Matias, one of the Socrates' analyst. Aurora could see that her unit had been following along behind her aimless wandering, thinking she was

118

guiding them. The Socrates looked to her for new orders. They huddled around her as directionless as she was.

Where was Langston?

She was under the vague impression that she was, at some point, following Langston's lead back to the ship. But he clearly wasn't in front of her anymore. A quick glance around her located Langston, who was a few paces behind them with Liya. He was whispering in her ear as she furiously typed on the compad. Almost as if he felt her gaze, Langston looked up, caught her eye, and nodded once.

He returned to the group, and the team swarmed Langston with questions layered on top of anxieties. What was next? What did this mean? How could this be legal? He gave a short order to hold; this silenced them like a bated breath, ready to burst open with more questions at the next available opportunity.

No details or instructions followed. Instead, he grabbed Aurora's arm and dragged her to a secluded hallway by a bay of windows and a waterfall feature.

He pulled out a dual set of locowear pins from his utility belt and a closed-circuit commlink from his pocket. It was the gear they typically used in solo missions or surveillance ops where SI-issue compads would be too conspicuous. He stuck out his palm to offer over half of the set to Aurora. "Plan the Plan. Fly the Plan," Langston said. His hand waited outstretched between them, a patient and implicit offer for her to grab the gear and get with the program.

"I say we just do this old school, hard interrogations with the goal of a swift confession. We have the undercover gear and we'll need it if Dean haslocked our system access. No fancy tech today, just good old-fashioned police work."

"What?" Aurora's face scrunched up. Her eyes, her ears, and her brain were not on the same page and she was in no mood to take either the bait or the mission tech.

"Oh, do catchup. We're on borrowed time here, partner. That's actually a good point." Langston flicked his left arm up to check the time on his GIM. "We have a head start since Zhou decided she didn't want the evidence we've uncovered. Cause, clearly, that's the *'smart move'* if you're an idiot."

Langston pressed the external commlink into his ear. Aurora followed his sure, rapid movements with her eyes, the glassy excitement whirring within him quickening his movement. He was chomping at the bit to get back in the arena. Whereas she was just exhausted. But by the looks of it, Langston would not be giving up anytime soon.

"Hmm, we'll have to split up."

"What?" Aurora asked, but she wasn't really asking. He had a plan, most likely a very bad plan, for their careers.

It was at this moment that a lightning bolt of empathy for Langston skidded across her psyche. The complete reversal of their position was comical, not in a "ha-ha" kind of way, but a cosmic irony kind of way. She was emotionally transported back in time to Hwei, where it was Langston who asked bemused questions as she gave an impassioned soliloquy.

And she saw it there, glimmering in his eyes. A speech about justice and doing what's right, just waiting to be passionately delivered.

She hadn't even heard the speech, and she was exhausted by just the glimmer of it in his eyes. She never realized how dreadfully exhausting that kind of righteous indignation could be. And Vearro help her. Even she could admit that she played that card all the time.

But today, for both no particular reason and an endless, unforgiving, constant deluge of reasons, Aurora was tired. She was too tired for the games she "always" played.

Langston, as a testament to his kindness, didn't point this out. He raised a brow but otherwise wasn't phased at all.

"So, *yeah*, we split up," he said slowly. Perhaps he thought a slower delivery would get her on board. "There's the usher and the son. There is definitely enough evidence to make both of them prime suspects, even without another footage review. I say we interrogate them both. Half an informational interview, but we press them hard and get answers. There's that time element peaking over the horizon, so half-answers won't cut it. The only open question is: who'll take which suspect… You know I'm open to your input but I think while I might be better at blending in with the penguin suits out there, I'm probably a bit too keyed up for gentle conversation so--"

"Stop. What are you doing?"

"Preparing for the next step in our investigation," Langston said.

"The one we were summarily removed from a little under two minutes ago?"

Langston closed his eyes with the first sign of fatigue from him and shook his head. She saw him stare past his reflection in the glass, out at the wide-open darkness of space. He was so still at that moment. From all the energy raring to go,ready to tackle all-comers, to a rare showing of tar-like calm.

"We are doing this," he said, each word careful. "We are going to do this. Off-books, if we have to. But it's happening. Cause.. **come on**, this is fishy. How in Oya's blue balls did they get here so fast? There is something here." He said it all under his breath, like they shared a brain. Like there was a chain connecting every wavelength and thought pattern in his brain to hers. He said it in a way that he couldn't be sure Aurora would understand, but in his gut, he knew she would.

He was right in a lot of ways.

She could understand it if she wanted to. She could pull that chain and follow the logic pattern and get onboard with the idea that they were doing this.

But she didn't want to.

Yes, they could do this.

The two detectives from Hwei who saved lives and fucked up and made a mess but did what was right. **Those** two detectives *would* do this.

Aurora just wasn't sure that was her today.

Not at this moment.

Not when she finally saw what <u>doing this</u> would cost. She rejected the chain that tied them. She rejected the wavelength and the understanding. Cause the world is cruel and unfair and full of injustice and today that just wasn't her problem.

To be fair, this was not her choice, it was **theirs.** She didn't give up; they took away it from her. Twice within a single sol she was close to loosing everything. And she didn't have much to loose. And today, she was done fighting and Langston would have to just live with that.

Aurora couldn't feel her cheeks.

She just blinked at him.

Langston whipped around to stare out towards the lobby. The view was slightly obscured from by the perpetual waterfall babbling along. Aurora watch him from distant eyes as he wagged his finger towards the auditorium door where Zhou and the CC squad had finally emerged.

"You know... It had to be a jump. Logically, there is no way, no matter what, no matter who died and what's on fire, Command Corp would *never* authorize a fuel burn like that on a jump when a VP team was already on sight. Not for anything." He curled his finger into a fist and dropped to his hand to his side, "So, you see. We can't just let it go. Especially not to that rottweiler of a menace at the helm... It's this feeling in my gut, Roar. It's just this feeling."

She wasn't gonna touch that. She couldn't. She wouldn't lie to him and say she didn't feel it too (because she did). But it was untouchable.

This was not their problem anymore. It was no longer their fight.

This was over.

"So, you want to break rules again, Langston?" Aurora asked with an arched brow. Rules: Langston loved rules.

She knew that implication would bother him. He was all about covering their ass with semantics and fancy footwork between the lines. But continuing this investigation was not bending the rules; it was breaking them.

A disbelieving laugh burst out of him. "Oh, **really**, Roar." He said, every syllable dripping on mocking disbelief. "**Now**, you wanna follow the rules. I forgot you are Detective Harlowe: Keeper of the Rule, Law-Abiding Officer of System Intelligence. Hah. Great. I'm glad *that* Detective decided to show up for the party." Langston huffed out a final exasperated breath of air before piercing through her with a solid glare. " We don't have time for this. Spit it out. What exactly are you saying to me?"

"I'm saying I'm following orders. I'm done. They say I'm done. So I'm done. That's what I'm saying." She twisted away from him to give her words a sense of finality. Now it was her turn to glare enigmatically out the window. She couldn't bear his gaze. She could barely stand his words.

"Oh, you're not done. Not by a long shot. You're going to let some chihuahua take you your place. No, I don't believe it." He refused to be ignored. He crowded into her space so he was between her and the glass. A 6-feet and some change solid wall of stone-faced confrontation. "Let's finish what we started. We owe them that much."

The accusation stung. "Who? Who do I owe? What do *I* owe *them*?" Her head tilted up steadily to match his gaze. Her jaw tightened, her nostrils flaring out with hot, angry breaths.

"The same people as yesterday and the day before that and the day before that. All of those people who died tonight. They deserve justice. The future victims, they deserve safety. If the guilty person isn't arrested, violence like this will continue unchecked. And, honestly, our team — *us*. Roar, we will always owe our people our level best. This is what we do. That's the job."

Aurora couldn't look down, couldn't look away, and was unwilling to take a step back. But her voice was quiet. "It appears that today it isn't."

"You don't want to go there. Let me tell you from experience, walking away like this does not mean that you're absolved of anything. Walking away just means you give up control. It just means that the poor schmoe that that meat-grinder will pin this crime on, yeah, that poor schmoe's day just got a lot worse. But for us, decisions like this ripple. After Hwei, after **this**, it's over. If you think following orders will stop them from disbanding The Socrates, you are dead wrong. If we walk away and let me be clear, that is not an 'us' decision, that'll be on you. No one from our investigative unit will ever find another serious job in law enforcement. It's the end for them. Are you really that selfish?"

"You are going to want to reassess that tactic," Aurora growled out.

"Really? Cause I like the nerve I'm working. I'll just come out and say it. This isn't about you." Langston let emotion shine through his eyes. It wasn't malice or even irritation. It was pity.

Pity burned Aurora's ire worse.

Langston let that grenade sit between them before he finally stepped to the side out of her immediate bubble. Shoulder to shoulder with her now, he stood at her side to look out at the lobby as she looked out at the space beyond.

"It never is. It's not about the past, or who wronged you, or how you can see the evil in their eyes. It's just not about you or how great you are and how ungrateful the world is for not recognizing your talents. It's about *them*."

She caught her own gaze in the reflection in the glass. "Well, it's not about you then, either."

Langston closed his eyes, dropped his head back in exhaustion. "Drop the act. It's just us. I'm not the posturing macho team lead, and you aren't the all-knowing ethereal sooth-sayer. This is --"

The saliva in her mouth soured with her own hurt. She didn't know why she was continuing to run from this. She twinge seeing the phantom ache of Langston's isolation. All because she was too scared to join him on the path. In the attempt to do the right thing, whatever that meant. Even so, she couldn't say anything.

"We can't just do nothing. Something is sideways here. And

'just following order' has never been us. Only dead fish go with the flow. So I need you to be my partner. Cause I've read you, Aurora. You are neither stupid enough nor cruel enough to confuse laziness with free will. And that's what going back to the ship is. Laziness."

"Why?" Her voice was fragile and so easily pushed over the edge.

"Why what?"

"Why is this so important to you?" Aurora asked with genuine curiosity.

The question is fair enough. This conversation had gone off the rails long ago. Even though she knew there was no way he could know, she knew he knew she wasn't saying half the things she wanted to. But she was almost surprised with the haymaking hit Langston had pulled out of the woodwork. Yes, she knew he was right. But he was invested. And so she was curious. She questioned if he was seeing something she missed.

Langston paused for a heavy beat before a truth tumbled past his lips. "I refuse to be the kind of man who walks away — who leaves the door open to the darkness."

That level of honesty from Langston shocked her. She turned to him full-on. Met his gaze. She slowly blinked open the infamous Ohahlian *True* eyes, the opalescent silver owl-like second-lens. The ***Truth*** in her eyes made them noticeably different and potentially hypnotizing to anyone who wasn't prepared for their display. The secondary lens enlarged the size of her pupil and iris to a little under double its original size and added a dark black halo around the shimmering yellow-purple-pink-silver pools of the iris.

Scientifically, the ***Truth*** in her eyes was a vestigial function, a hereditary predator-response developed in about 35% of the Ohahlian population during the Time of Healing. Like an bird, it gave her a larger field of vision from a binocular view of 74% up to 90%. In all the ways that mattered, it was just a flashy by-product. It was the only physical trait that demonstrated what made the people of her planet so different from their Anhkaena and Gherrean neighbors. It was the physical and symbolic manifestation of the Ohahlian Truth Seers. But unlike the temporary blink-flash of her *Truth* behind her lids, her abilities as a Truth Seer were something she couldn't turn off.

On a day-to-day basis, she didn't have complete control over the *Truth* in her eyes. It was instinctual, like a blush or a sneeze, something that was both learned and intrinsic. But with some small amount of effort, she could intentionally flash the quick-silver lens at will.

With her gaze steady, Aurora said with as much conviction as was possible, "You could never be that man, darling." Another blink and her eyes are back to their usual warm medium brown with normal-sized pupils. She smiled, small and apologetic. "Plan the plan?"

"Fly the plan," he finished. Accepting the half-apology for what it was. Partners till the very end.

She nodded and turned with him to gaze out at the wider lobby and their team. He once again offered her the mission tech, and this time she took it. Finally onboard, she reiterated the plan with a few revisions. "Ok, you take the usher, Jamie Pope. Social profile than a hard interview. I'll take Azul. We can't include the team in on any of this. But if we move fast and one of these two suspects actually did it... we might be able to get away with all this. Do you think the crew will cover for us? How much should we tell them?"

"Honestly, nothing. While I'm sure they would cover for us. Keeping them in the dark means plausible deniability. Though I'm reasonably sure that they'll do us the solid of refraining from reporting us missing."

"Oh, well then, I'm not worried about that angle at all. Liya will cover for us, keep them all in line."

With the big details settled, Langston moved to walk back into the lobby to give last orders to the squad. Aurora stopped him with a quick hand at his elbow. "Thank you and I'm sorry."

His smile in response was warm. He understood more than she knew. Langston had always been more than a partner. He was more like family. "Don't you forget it." The group of techs and forensics stood at attention as they approached. Langston barked out, "Return to the ship! I want all of our evidence bagged and tagged and organized in case Major Zhou over there decides to wise up and not waste hours of information."

They were clearly a little surprised to be heading back to the shuttle. Where were the avenging angels from Hwei? This was not the message they were expecting, which rang both as a mild insult and as a complimentary note of their own loyalty. She decided she was more proud than insulted.

Shuffling from side to side, they looked among themselves before Liya was the first to break. Liya helmed the crew back through the crush of opera attendees and the overall opulence back to our humble little lifeboat.

With the squadron out of sight, they both calibrated their exo-commlinks to a secure channel and to set up their locowears' GPS to their current location. The locowears were a fail-safe protocol in case an operative went missing in the field for some reason.

"Ping your location every half hour. Report back at oh-one-hundred hour?" Langston asked.

"Roger."

Langston gave a mock salute before he headed to the far right service entrance hidden behind the bar. Her suspect would be in the lobby.

The fun had just begun.

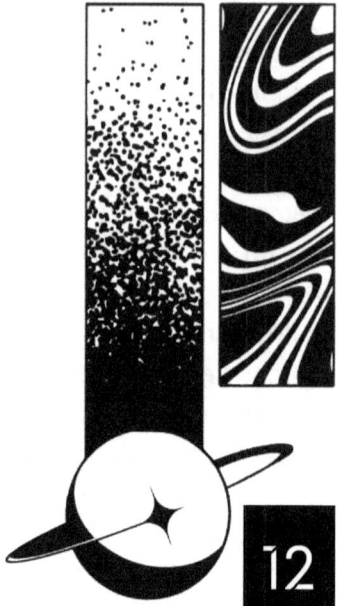

PRAYING TO THE PORCELAIN GODS

AURORA

Aurora tucked herself quietly along the edge of the lobby. She observed the scene with fresh eyes. The lobby, the grand stairway, and the balcony walk-around. The anxiety of the crowd had settled from it's previous heights.

That was all thanks to the Esaa Core management team who had single-handedly made the smartest decision of the night. They reopened the bar.

For better or for worse, boozy billionaires were more manageable. Loose lips and public naps were far preferable to a storming of the gates.

The fatigued lull of the crowd made her job just the slightest bit harder. Calm waters troubled easy. She'd have to avoid detection or causing ruckus that might risk drawing the attention of the CC squad. Luckily for her, Major Zhou seemed to enjoy showboating in a rather grotesque display of power. The amount of pageantry from the woman seemed to imply a certain amount of Napoleonic overcompensation.

She hadn't gotten a good read on Zhou except for the vaguest whiff of frothy loyalty. It was a common CC trait among the mid-tier officer class. Aurora wouldn't want to risk getting on her radar.

So, a covert operation would be best.

Aurora slunk through the shadows along the edge of the room. Looking among the bejeweled elites, Aurora came to grips with a thought both tragic... and stupid. Painfully stupid. Fireably stupid. If only she hadn't been summarily dismissed not minutes ago, this latest revelation would've called for immediate termination.

She did not know what Azul Greene looked like.

They were betting the whole enchilada on this one. Aurora and Langston had made the dangerous decision to openly and directly disobey orders in a last-ditch effort to solve the case and prove their worth. Their careers teetered on the edge of obsolescence. And she had one job.

Interrogate Azul Greene.

And, not to put too fine a point on it, she didn't know what the hell he looked like.

By default, she reached for her compad. The AUTHORIZED ACCESS DENIED lock screen taunted her. Dean knew zheir detectives well enough to know that locking them out of the system would be a smart move. Either way, she doubted Dean expected the totality of how off the deep-end Aurora and Langston had jumped. However disrespectfully distrustful Dean's actions were... all things considered, here she was, breaking all the rules, so the distrust was well earned.

She growled and shook the compad in frustration before refastening it to her belt.

Her eyes darted from face to face. From tuxedo to four-piece suit, hoping against all hope for some miracle, maybe Azul was wearing a neon blue suit with his full name embroidered in red on the back. But no luck. Her brain was empty of any useful remembrances. Hissing air through her teeth, Aurora tried to comb through the hay-stacks of her memory for a clue.

She had seen many pictures and articles of Asa Greene, the mother, so the best she could hope for was that Azul looked a lot like the male version of his mom. Or, if she was lucky, perhaps Azul appeared in one of the press photos. If her subconscious had stored the information away, maybe she could figure some sort of something out.

However, all of those possibilities were contingent on Aurora having a better memory, which she did not.

She fought the urge to laugh hysterically. The urge to give up and head back to the ship with her proverbial tail between her legs. She reached into the recesses of her mind and latched onto the thing that kept from running scared in the past: the gargantuan chip on her shoulder. While it may have thawed some, that good ole chip followed her ever since she had got her first chance in the Pressure Cooker. Both a saving grace and a fatal flaw, she knew the chip would get her out of this situation. Though the annoyingly self-aware devil on her other shoulder couldn't help but acknowledge that it was that same chip that Langston had so artfully manipulated not a few seconds ago. So, while it might be able to get her out of trouble, it was definitely the reason she was in trouble in the first place.

So, here she was; this was the path she had chosen. First things first: figure out who Azul was.

There were only so many options on that front, but clearly the most obvious was to ask someone. If they were still on the case officially on the case it would be a matter of milliseconds to ask Liya to pull up his SI citizen profile.

That was not currently an option open to her.

Currently, Aurora's only option was to ask one of the billionaires milling about. One of the billionaires wearing the bow ties cut of silk that cost over one million credits easy.

Thoughts like that could make a person fidget with the rolled cuff of their third-hand bartered shirtsleeve. Perhaps the first thing to do wasn't just to find Azul.

First things first: she needed to blend in.

If she had any hope of wandering through the gathered masses, nosing around, and finding Azul, she couldn't be wearing what she was wearing.

Ah, that was the perfect opening to a thrilling premise. Her assignment in the VP unit had, much to her disappointment, never called for the intrigue of undercover work. But the silver lining of not doing official work is that perhaps those official rules and regulations could also be thrown out the window. Thus presenting a perfectly reasonable opportunity to embrace the idea of a disguise.

If Langston were with her, he would laugh and make her dispose of such wild machinations and plots. But he wasn't with her so, hello independence. If they were going off-book for this mission, a certain amount of coloring outside of the lines was to be anticipated, if not preordained.

The only question was where to find her new "mask". Creativity would be necessary to pull this off. The patrons were wearing black-tie attire, so her bolo-tie would not cut it.

This opportunity needed some skills she had gathered before she was "welcomed" into the ranks of SI ranks. She scanned the room for items to "borrow".

Aurora went about pickpocketing several minor items with ease. Her efforts to refurbish her attire were culminating into a fashion success. Or better yet, something that doesn't noticeably place her socioeconomic light-years away from the "poorest" attendee at this opera house.

She'd scored a black satin sash that had been discarded by a sleeping debutante and a pair of midnight stilettos cast-aside by a woman flirting by the east banister before she found her YETI.

Yes, Every Thing Included. YETI.

The big one to pull the whole look together.

Drunkenly stumbling alone towards the balcony bathroom was a woman wearing a stunning sequined gown and a calf-length black-on-black embroidered cape. It was chef's-kiss perfection. That cape was going to pull this whole look together.

Skulking through the crowd, she gathered the goods, the sash and the stilettos, as she made her way up the stairs to the bathroom. It was easy to weave through the patrons as they were too used to ignoring the help, hyper-focused on their own vanity.

Aurora slipped into the bathroom — four stalls and a deluxe powder room. The sound of vomiting greeted her.

The stall with the vomiting damsel was occupato but with unlocked door as the lovely mark was half in and out, kneeling on the floor. The other three stalls were thankfully empty. She locked the main entrance to the bathroom and made her initial approach.

On her way through the powder room, she grabbed a crystal champagne flute that sat on the complimentary bar cart. She dumped the champagne and filled the flute with water before giving a quick knock to the ajar stall door.

It swung open under the gentle pressure of the knock. The heaving ingenue curled over the toilet bowl, paid the door and the knock no mind. Gone was the class, the elegance, the refinement.

Praying to the Porcelain Gods was life's great equalizer.

Without a response, Aurora tiptoed in without an invitation. "Easy does it. Get it all out. You'll be fine," Aurora said, her voice soft. She smoothed a hand across the back of the woman's back before she gathered the woman's hair out of the way into a loose knot at the back of her head. Using an old trick she dipped her fingers into the glass and flicked lightly, sprinkled the water on the woman's face. A couple more heaves before the woman rested her head against the toilet. The woman hummed in pleasure when the cool water hit her overheated neck.

"You ok, hun?"

The beleaguered woman grunted before another hiccupping heave propelled her forward. However, her hand shot straight up into the air from its death grip on the toilet with a thumbs up.

Aurora snorted out a quick laugh. Our ingenue was down

but not out. She loved a woman with a sense of humor. This girlie would be just fine.

Aurora rubbed light circles on the woman's shoulder. "Now you'll never forgive yourself if you get last night's dinner on tonight's dress. Let's get you a little more comfortable, huh?"

Arms flailing, the woman abruptly pushed back off the toilet to flop against the stall wall like a fainting madonna. Her glazed eyes assessed Aurora beneath eyebrows scrunched in confusion. The woman was an ageless beauty in the way only good skincare can produce.

She spoke with the honey-sweet twang of the southern Anhkaena citizen. Probably unnoticeable in regular conversation, but as she slurred and hiccuped through her tirade, it became more and more apparent. Probably more of a social climber than old-money.

"Yeeooo! Mishish Kind Lady Person! Argh mah besht friend. And aye will luuoaf you ugh— hiccup — until mah dying daaaay. Whish is NAUGHT, whish is absolutely not tood-yay." She lurched forward to crawl a bit closer to Aurora.

While it tempted Aurora to move back based on the powerful odor coming out of the woman's mouth, the proximity place her goal firmly in her crosshairs.

Get the coat-dress.

"Aye — hiccup — ullmost DIED today. I wash VISH close. PHAM. BOOM. And noww.... Hiccup... all I can STOOPID fhink about ish STOOPID DOMINEEK! Dooo — hiccup — do-do— doooo you fhink... he loafths mee too?"

The woman continued on in a frankly hilarious description of a young person by the name of Dominic, who was playing a cat-and-mouse game with our poor ingenue's heart. The woman got closer and closer to Aurora, eventually leaning on her as she waxed poetic through a loud summary of her love life.

This made easy work for Aurora's objective. A clasp here. A shoulder wiggle there and she wrestled free her prize.

"Darling, if he has any sense at all, he will love you forever and never let you go. You are, without a doubt, a hoot and a half," Aurora said as she guided the woman up and to the sofa in the powder room. "Now rest."

Aurora smiled and returned to the bathroom. There was an official disguise to don.

13

A FAVOR

AURORA

There is magic to be found in armor. In the right shade of lipstick and the new perspective from high heels and higher ambition. Protected by new wolf furs, Aurora was ready to sneak amongst the pack and find her target. Proud of her new off-the-shoulder coat dress, cinched at the waist with a sash over her embroidered pants that reminded her of mama. She would deny that there was an extra sway in her hip as she approached the banister to gaze down at the patrons below. She double-clicked the small thumb-sized locowear. The first half-hour of her time was gone.

Now to find Azul Greene.

There were only 500 or so people in this room. So, as far as haystacks go, it wasn't necessarily an overly large haystack, and she had probably almost definitely seen this particular needle before. Scan, scour, observe and should come to worst, interact with one of them.

"Now that is a gorgeous frock."

135

Startled by the unfamiliar voice so close to her, Aurora didn't move — she assessed.

The woman to her left had slipped past every one of her defenses and normal situational awareness. Draped in floor-length lavender silk, she leaned against the banister with her full attention trained on Aurora. As Aurora studied the newcomer, the newcomer studied right back. Her grin taunted Aurora as the laughter danced behind her eyes. She gave away nothing but her smirk.

"Thanks..."the detective responded.

This woman was either genuinely complimenting her on her outfit, hitting on her, or doing something else entirely. Aurora couldn't fathom which of those options were correct, but she didn't have time to find out. She needed to end this now. In fact, Aurora wasn't even going to let whatever this was get started. With a tight grimace smile, the detective nodded and took a step back, intending to disengage.

That smirk still firmly in place, the stranger sipped a taste from her champagne glass and swept the cascade of waist-length micro-braids over her shoulder. Aurora couldn't shake the feeling that this woman was taunting her.

"And, honestly, I much prefer the way you styled it," the woman said.

With that sentence, she now had Aurora's full attention.

Vearro-damnit, she was a Harlowe, not some simpleton Pink-Panthering around and stumbling into brilliance. While this moment might not be her pride-and-joy, most shining-est moment, she was still a goddamn professional. To be so easily discovered by a civilian was a tremendous blow to the ego. And lately, to be honest, Aurora considered swapping out her ego for a punching bag for all the use she was getting from it.

So, Aurora could hypothetically wave off the idea that this woman could catch her unawares as she attempted to observe a massive gathering. But her words and approach showed that this woman had been watching her. She had been watching her for quite some time. That was a concept was deeply unsettling.

But there was something between her smirk and the fact that Aurora didn't actually want to move away from this woman that bothered her. Despite her bother, this enigma intrigued her. As with all great enigma, it cloaked the woman in questions and mysteries.

Aurora didn't like not knowing things. Despite what her career would imply, she hated a mystery. She liked that answers came easy to her. This woman was already making her think too hard, even in silence.

While the gears in Aurora's eyes whirred away, this enigma laughed. She turned to lean against the banister and survey the lobby's main floor below. "Fashion is not for the weak. That silly little waif was letting the cape wear her," the woman said. She was acting so casually, as if this was just a casual conversation about style, not unmasking an off-duty cop caught red-handed going undercover.

With amusement bordering on mirth, she saluted Aurora with her glass. "But where are my manners? I'm Cherie." She sipped and maintained perfect, unflinching eye contact. "The polite thing to do once a person has introduced themselves would be to return the favor," she prompted.

"I'm --"

"And please don't lie. I hate that. It's a horrible way to start a friendship. And I would so like to be friends," she said before Aurora could spit out a passable alias.

The stillness crackled between them. Aurora had to decide on her next move and, tragically, Aurora was of two minds on the subject.

Call the bluff and lie or take the bait.

"Thank you for the fashion advice, but I don't see friendship in our future."

The woman — Cherie — pouted as an expression of humor rather than displeasure. "What a shame. I enjoy interesting friends with interesting stories. And I can only imagine the legendary tale of how an Ohahlian became a Pact Officer."

Aurora heard ringing in her ears. This explicit admission that this unknown entity knew who she was, what she did and then *chose* to behave the ways she was behaving raised every fire-alarm, red-flag and bad feeling Aurora had ever known. Her statement, a gauntlet of a throw-down was a massive power move. Cherie was proverbially flashing her teeth.

Aurora couldn't decide if this was a smart move on Cherie's part.

No, smart isn't the right word. This was creative, which was decidedly more dangerous than simple intelligence.

Aurora was willing to take the bait. She wanted to see what matter of monster was on the other end of this fishing line. Cherie seemed to have her advantage of the moment, as she had just shown her ability to manipulate Aurora to a certain degree. But Aurora had a monster within her, too. And Aurora's monster had questions too, and by Vearro she'd get some answers. "You've been watching my team."

"Not your team. You."

Yet again, Cherie's words flattened Aurora to the ground. Perhaps it was the detective's fault. She should have never taken the bait, so now she was playing Cherie's game, whether or not she liked it. Aurora was unwilling to make another waltz into whatever trap this enigma had waiting for her. No, two could play that game. Aurora waited for Cherie to say more. She glared, and she waited.

Like a bomb.

Every uncanny conclusion made it clearer and clearer that Cherie had... an end goal. She wanted something. This was not simple curiosity. So Aurora could wait because she would not walk head first into the verbal land mines that Cherie had sprinkled throughout their conversation.

So she waited.

Tick.

Tick.

Tick.

Tilting her head with a sardonic eyebrow raise, Cherie's smile grew over the course of the widening silence.

Cherie braced her elbow on the railing in front of them. "So, I don't suppose you'd indulge me?" She flicked her gaze back to Aurora conspiratorially, as if they were sharing secrets now. Which, in all fairness, was an accurate description of what they were doing at this point. "While we can probably warm up to your life story, is there any way you would consider telling me the deeply fascinating story about how you got from over there" — Cherie pointed to where the gaggle of CC troops pointlessly pace like caged dogs they were by the Theatre entrance — "to over here?"

"No," Aurora said without a trace of that jolly energy Cherie wanted to share.

Cherie was unmoved by the steely silence Aurora used as a defense. She laughed, a soft hypnotic melody. "You caught my eye the moment you entered the grand lobby. In fact, I was standing right about here when I first saw you. A surviving Ohahlian out in nature, in the flesh. It was just fascinating. And your team was so cued into your rhythm, your signs. The man you were with, your partner, I assume. He was keeping the lesser mortals distracted while you, you held the world on a string," Cherie said, with her gaze locked on Aurora. No coy or subtle breaking of tier gaze as she continued her explanation. "It's like you have a gravitational pull. All your little teammates draw closer to your warmth. I mean, look at me. Even I got pulled in. And you're aware of it too, aren't you? You use it on occasion, but you don't abuse it. Fascinating!" Cherie said as she again saluted her with her glass before she finally finished the champagne.

"But then, the plot thickens later in the night. You have a fight with Mr. Partner guy, he goes storming off, your team is sent away with their tails between their legs and then you steal poor Barbie Sanders cape—"

"I didn't steal it," Aurora said. The defense sounded weak even to her own ears.

"Oh, yes, of course. My mistake." A lush giggle snort escaped from Cherie. "I feel like if we're being honest with each other, we can both admit that... whatever it was you were doing... it was all a bit weird," she said. Her eyes sharpened before she added, "Almost as weird as finding an Ohahlian in SI uniform."

"Listen, Miss —"

"Call me Cherie. All my friends do."

"What the hell do you want?"

"Hah! World peace... and your life story. How about this? You tell me how you climbed the Pact ranks and I'll... I'll help you blend in just a little bit better. While you did an admirable job... if we don't do something about the finer details of this get-up, I will not be the first person to suspect something underfoot." Cherie's light, almost mocking joviality, was consistent and damn near contagious. Aurora was at once annoyed, intrigued, and soothed.

It miffed Aurora to have her cover made so quickly into her little jaunt. It didn't bode well. Perhaps some help wouldn't be unwelcome.

"I'm not sure it's a fair trade."

Another laugh. "Life isn't fair. But it will keep you entertained. So?"

"Deal." Aurora caved to her inhumane demands. The detective didn't like to share.

Cherie gently adjusted Aurora, so that she was facing her straight on. Starting at the top, the hurricane of a woman grabbed onto Aurora's ensemble to rearrange and fiddle with the pleating and bunching of where Aurora had sloppily tied things into knots. It was quite invasive and presumptuous. But... Aurora couldn't deny that it looking like Cherie was making positive progress.

"Well, let's start easy. A name?"

"Detective Aurora Harlowe, junior investigator on VP005, System Intelligence."

"Well, it's a pleasure to meet you, Detective. What's your story?" Cherie asked.

Aurora sighed and watched the carefully precise weaving

technique of Cherie's fingers coiling through the silk. "Well, it's clear that you won't believe the honest truth that I applied, got in, and succeeded."

"Oh, I believe that's exactly what happened. I'm sure you are the best. Better than your rank and assignment indicate. I'm still looking for the 'why.'"

Aurora felt the answer like a raw wound on her side. But should couldn't say it out loud, not to a stranger. Not to anyone. But a deal was a deal. "It's just… It was how I was raised. It's what I'm good at. Law, order, all that bullshit."

All the while, Cherie finished on her makeshift dress and moved towards her face. She pulled out a multi-makeup applicator from her purse and went to town on her face. "Say more."

"The war's over. I know that. We lost. Quite spectacularly. So I needed to find my place in this world. I'm making a new life and I want — I can honor my family's memory by living the lessons they taught me."

"Hmmm." Cherie clearly didn't agree with Aurora. She clearly had more questions, but at long last, the woman seemed to be done with the makeover and the tortuous personal questions. She stood back to hold up a medium flip open a small mirror from her bag — "There. Now, you'll fit right in. For better or for worse."

Chagrin, as Aurora was to admit it, she was now indistinguishable from another guest. Cherie imprinted that look of effortless, unblemished perfection she carried herself onto Aurora.

She handed the mirror to Aurora before she took a step back to admire her work. Cherie nodded with satisfaction before she finally clocked Aurora's slightly horrified expression. "Well, I guess I have my story and you have your polish, so this is where I'll bid you adieu," Cherie said while waving around her empty glass. "Despite indications to the contrary, I didn't mean to be a nuisance. I was just… obeying the laws of gravity. I'll let you get back to your work. Good hunting, detective."

Cherie turned and walked away.

Cherie was a bag of snakes. There is definitely a time and place where it's helpful to have, but only a stupid person puts their hand into a bag of snakes. Aurora would hypothetically like to say she wasn't stupid, but her back was against the wall. She needed to find Azul and... anyone capable of painting Aurora into a corner had a keen set of observational skills that might be to her benefit.

It was a risk. Arguable, a gargantuan, neon-sign-do-not-enter kind of risk but perhaps one that might also pay off.

She hesitated, let Cherie put several meters between them, because the unknown was Cherie's motive. Completely unknown and undeniably dangerous, there was little to no chance she was harmless. Everything about this interaction was deeply suspicious. But, and it was a big 'but', Cherie wasn't on her radar prior to this interaction. The likelihood that she was in any way involved was low probability.

But still within the realm of the possible.

What Aurora was considering was massively unwise. But she needed a magnet in order to find this needle, and this mission had an expiration date that was quickly approaching.

"Wait."

Decision made.

"How about another deal?" Aurora called out to Cherie, "I am looking for someone."

Cherie turned with an eyebrow raised and a smile a mile wide. Graciously, Cherie walked back over to Aurora, not one to make her close the distance. She appeared to do her level best at containing any outward signs of gloating. "Well, you're in luck. I am great with faces, names and intentions. But what do I get this time?" Cherie said.

"Name your price."

"Let's just call it a favor. It's always beneficial to have interesting friends in interesting place owe you a favor." Cherie held out her hand to close the deal.

Aurora rolled her eyes but shook her hand. "Deal. Now, Azul

Greene. I'm looking for Azul Greene."

"Ugh," Cherie muttered, "Miscreant." Cherie narrowed her eyes and turned to the banister. Her hand hovered beside her mouth and she scanned through the patrons below. "You should've seen the fuss the Greene's kicked up during intermission. At the time, I would've bet money that their little scene was going to have top billing in tomorrow's gossip rags. Hmm, it's terrible how tragedy contextualizes all this drivel we partake in."

She pointed down to where she had spotted him. "He's... there. Sleeping by that massive glass fountain." Close to the men's room and the main bar was an ornate glass fountain surrounded by a bench style lip. Several groupings of people littered the edge of the bench separated by a polite amount of distance. A curled up figure was wrapped in a swath of shimmering velvet taking a nap. Apparently, that was Azul Greene.

"Do you know him? Personally?" Aurora couldn't help but ask. Desperate for even an inch more leverage going into this interview.

Cherie bobbed her head in indecision. "Know? No. Had my hand halfway down his crack measuring inseams. Of course." She pulled at her earrings before she continued, "And yet, despite that level of intimacy, I bet he wouldn't remember me. The Azul's of this world never do. Now, he might remember my boss, Cotillard. I'm here as her guest tonight. She's a major designer. Did the costumes for the show."

Nodding, but not trusting, Aurora refused to take the bait of Cherie's alias. While intriguing, she had bigger fish to fry. Aurora steered the conversation back to the topic at hand. "You said there was a fuss? With the Greene's?"

She didn't answer, but looked back and forth between Aurora and Azul for a second. Laughing, Cherie clapped, "Oooh, he's a suspect!" Her focus then pinned Azul's sleeping form like a laser. She tilted her head and let out a quiet considering 'Hmm'.

"He's just a person I want to have a conversation with,"

Aurora said, thoroughly regretting putting her hand in a bag of snakes. "I'll have you know I'm a charming conversationalist."

The answer earned her a smile brighter than before as Cherie said, "I wouldn't doubt that for a second... How intriguing. Now Azul, I always thought he was... a few beavers short of a damn. But I guess stupid doesn't mean benign, huh, Detective?"

"Miss--"

"Cherie, please."

"Cherie. You mentioned the Greene's during intermission. Can you tell me more about that?" Aurora gently guided the conversation back to solid footing.

"Yes, there's always a bit of flash with that family. Asa's so dramatic. Living her life like some grand theatrical production. Honestly, Detective, she could've lowered her voice if she gave a flying fuck about decorum. Now, I didn't hear specifics. But I saw Asa practically drag Azul into the auditorium by his ear."

Aurora immediately latched onto the detail. Azul had entered the auditorium during intermission. Why did he leave? How long was he there? How did he survive? Aurora damned the fact that she wouldn't be able to review footage and have hard facts on his whereabouts prior to his interview. His disappearance, while notable before now, became even more suspicious.

"This was during intermission, yes? Was it close to the end or the beginning?" Aurora asked, digging for more information.

"Hmm, I... can't be sure," Cherie's eyebrows drew together in remembrance.

"What were you doing during the intermission when you saw the fight? And then after. When did you return to your seat?"

"So...I was... having a conversation with the show's producer. He was in the middle of a hilarious ramble about wanting to leave before the end. Honestly, he was freaking out something awful. But he took the spare minute to stop and point out the Greene-eyed gossip unfolding behind me. Asa was practically screeching at Azul and dragging him down the hallway... Me and Marius gabbed for another... two or so minutes, mostly about the show and early predictions for reviews, and then I headed in to get to my seat."

"Intermission was 15 mins... so it was close to the end." It was damning for Azul to have been in the auditorium, the epicenter of this attack, and then to walk out unharmed seconds before detonation. "That's great information. Really great." Aurora said.

Internally, Aurora debated whether or not any or most of it was true. Cherie had proved herself to be incredibly helpful. Perhaps suspiciously helpful. But there was nothing for Aurora to do about that except to pin a red flag on any future movement, reference, or actions from Cherie. Given her utter lack of resources, this was a blind bet she'd have to make with nothing but faith and optimism.

"For you, toots," said Cherie as she shoulder bumped Aurora like good friends. "Anything."

Thankful for the help, Aurora remained wary. This was not a normal interaction... But this was also far from a normal investigation.

Aurora looked straight into Cherie's eyes, holding them, and said, "No, really, thank you. This has been exceptionally helpful. I owe you one."

For a second there, there was a flash of two emotions that sparked in Cherie's eyes: greed and humor. Neither made much sense, and Aurora had to let it go. She had bigger fish to fry.

One fish, blue fish. Then we get a clue fish.

She nodded before she headed to the main staircase to have a charming conversation with Azul.

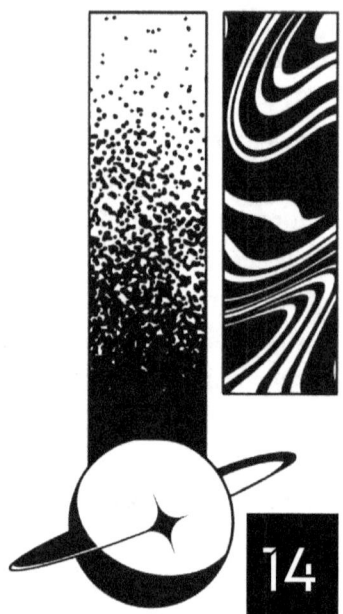

SON OF A BITCH

14

AURORA

Despite her recent fashion transformation, Aurora still felt like a boil on a bum. As she walked through the lobby toward the glass water fountain, the crowd split around her like oil separating from water.

There was a subtlety to wealth that seemed like a forever gatekeeper keeping her out. She had felt it throughout her life, from the guards at the refugee ships, from her instructors throughout her secondary education. She could never find the words to describe it, yet it was constantly present.

Aurora hypothesized that every trust fund came with an encyclopedia of codewords and phrases so that they can easily distinguish the privileged from the pissants.

Perhaps they didn't invent judgment, but they had perfected it.

Curled into a liquor-soaked heap on the edge of a fairly ornate fountain, was Azul — dead to the world. Without the occasional snuffle and shift from below his suit jacket blanket, one might think he rested in peace. Drunk and tired, she rarely had such an easy target.

The image he made was a familar one. Before she approached him, she considered where she had seen this pose before. She smiled and made a quick course-correction to divert her towards the nearest bar. She flagged down the bartender and ordered 2 glasses: a water and a vodka. Her memory had supplied plenty of circumstances to where she had seen Azul's pose before. She, and most people, had seen someone curled up like that on a park bench a thousand times before in a thousand benches and transit stops on a thousand worlds. There was no confusing Azul for some vagrant.

The hunch of his back lacked even an ounce of shame. Just the same, by the smell of him, she had whiffed from quite some distance; he had had enough alcohol to fuel a yacht.

Limbs arranged with the unabashed thoughtlessness of a man who had never questioned his place in life. She almost envied him. A cruel dark place in herself probably did envy him. But then there was that other part of her, the part that knew what came next in his tableau, that laughed and felt something more akin to pity.

Game time.

She crouched before him and took a moment to observe his face.

A Botox perfect, wrinkle-less face without blemish in sight. An homage to what money can buy.

"Pick your poison," she said. The beckon accompanied a shimmy of ice in the crystal highball glasses. Her voice was loud enough to shake him from his slumber, but in a tone that was more akin to whispers.

Azul's eyes squinted out at the crust to look over to her and then the glasses. "Whazzasht?" came Azul garbled inquiry.

Aurora gave a quick and practiced giggle. Holding up the glassed evenly, she said. "Your salvation. The Most Sweet Elixir and an opportunity." She shook each glass tantalizingly. "Could be water... but... it could be something more exciting? So. Pick your poison."

As she spoke, Azul slowly rose from his heap with his eyes entranced by the glasses. With unerring precision for someone seeing double, he reached for a glass and took a gulp.

Hair of the Dog. Water of the Gods. He chose vodka. Moaning out his pleasure, Azul decreed, "You're a goddess."

Aurora's answering smile was easy and bright. A touch alluring. He was used to girls with easy smiles, so she might as well communicate in the language he was accustomed to.

"Remember you said that," she said at the end of another calculated titter.

Azul stretched out as he returned to the land of the conscious. More careful sips as he took in the world around him. He moved to put his coat over his shoulders before he realized that there was a person in front of him. He gave her a head-to-toe once over look like a hungry goat. "Well, look at the legs on you," he said. "Where have you been all my life, darling?" His voice was clear and if she couldn't smell the drink, she wouldn't know he was 5 sheets to the wind.

Despite Aurora's overall ability and comfort in giggling like an idiot, her opinion of him was circling the drain with every work. If this was his modus operandi, he treated women like pieces of meat. It was despicable and predictable. It made him an easy target. It was laughable how easily she had slipped past his pathetic defences.

Aurora raised her hand to smooth down the messy strands of the hair framing his face. "You seemed under the weather there."

He gave a half-laughing huff, half-frustrated sigh, "Well, it's been a helluva night."

"Especially for you, I've heard."

Azul rolled his eyes as he looked around at the room of the milling socialites, vaguely spitting in his disgust. Azul said, "Pact of rabid fishmongers, that lot of 'em."

She popped down into the seat next to him. Their shoulders pressed together like co-conspirators. "But rumors are only rumors, if they're not true."

However, the persistence of the comment drew his attention. "I don't think I caught your name."

Ever easy, wicked quick, she answered. "Aurora. And you?" She offered him her hand to shake.

He examined it, but took the hand and kissed the back of her knuckles.

"Azul." He said, smiling. "Look at us. Azul and Aurora. The A-team. We could be one hell of a crime fighting duo, you and me."

This sparked the first genuine laugh out of her. "As long as I'm not the only one in spandex, you are on."

"Deal."

No matter the levity of the moment, her faux casual demeanor clung to her skin as wet as it was inauthentic. She turned her gaze away from Azul, towards the puttering glob of ground beef CC officers by the theatre doors. "Maybe we could solve the clusterfuck of what happened here if we really put our minds to it. No chance of those dolts doing it" "

Azul's devil-may-care facade collapsed. He flagged down a waiter and gestured towards his glass, his spare hand churning to motion a refill. He chugged what remained.

A waitress approached to fill his glass, but he grabbed her wrist in order to take the bottle from her. She charged his wrists for credits as Aurora frowned and issued a profuse apology that the waitress waved off as she well used to this level of affluent assholery. She headed back to the bar, but Aurora's frown remained.

"Do you have anything to confess?" Aurora said into his ear, the 'ss's hissing air across his ear lobe sparking a jolt of goosebumps across his skin.

Noticing her proximity, Azul leaned back from her, his eyes widened. "Excuse me?" he asked. Azul, for perhaps the first time, locked eyes with her.

"Did you get enough rest?" she said for the first time. Her face was bland, not giving an inch away. His inebriation worked against him and even though he realistically knew what he heard, he wouldn't press. They were at a bit of a stalemate. His prey response seemed to kick in and tingling. That sense urged him to see beyond her delicate wrists and pretty eyes. However, Azul had long ago abandoned instincts. It went the way of his liver, overburdened and never heeded.

After a beat too long, he shook his head before he answered. "Clearly not." He tore his gaze away from hers and leaned against his knees in a hunch. "I can't believe they have the gall to hold us here against our will and in complete discomfort," he said.

"Well, no rest for the wicked, they say." She mirrored his pose. Arms rest on thighs, head scanning the crowd. "Did you lose anyone tonight?"

The air in his lungs caught. Quick exhale, then resuming the steady and heavily intoxicated breath pattern from before. Azul drowned whatever emotion rose at the top of his lungs with more alcohol.

That silence, heavy and uncomfortable, sat between them. Aurora knew that this silence was an answer of sorts. An answer that should satisfy a casual acquaintance who would leave it at that. A random stranger would not poke. But this wasn't random. Regardless of the unsanctioned nature of this interrogation, it was damning. So, the silence hung and pushed and crushed all efforts of subterfuge.

Azul traced his thumb over the skin on his middle finger. Worrying the place where a ring previously sat in a nervous habit.

"I'm 44. I'm 44 and I'm just..." Azul said, nearly a stutter with his mouth processing thing ahead of his heart and his mind. He grasped at words but was unable to say them. Based on the size of his pupil, the drugs in his system weren't making him more erudite and eloquent. He dropped his head into clasped hands for a second before he stormed up to his feet, indignant. "I thought I would be ecstatic when the old gerbil bit the dust. But... this doesn't feel right?"

Another ugly silence as the world spun around them.

"Why?"

Aurora's face was empty of judgment. A blank slate between listening ears gave Azul the space to unload.

Sneering as he looked to the theatre over his shoulder, he started up mid-thought, "At least it was dramatic enough. She always loved a huge scene." He fumbled in his pocket for a cigarette and light. His woozy hands shook from alcohol and a pinch of anxiety. Deep inhale of toxins, he blew the smoke out. "At the last trustee meeting, she put on this one-of-a-kind display. Read that silly little producer for filth. Just gutted him. Right there in the conference room." Azul shook his head in a move that seems like a habit, a regular reaction to familial antics. He said, "They were lovers, you know? And she always does that. Airs all our fucking business in public. Just for fun."

Azul looked at Aurora like he was looking into a mirror. "It was never fun."

With a slight tilt of her head, she pierced his gaze. "Asa, right? Asa Greene was your mother."

Laughing, he corrected her. "You mean the Great Magnanimous, Incomparable Asa Greene. There was a woman who believes her own fucking legend."

"And you didn't?"

"I didn't then. But, now..." Azul pursed his lips with a hint, then shook his head, "Still no, I guess."

"I heard you had a fight earlier tonight," she said. Her tone was gentle and open as she tried to coax out more information.

He nodded and said, "Yeah, when me and Am'ma got together, it was always explosive. If you excuse the pun." He did not want to be excused. He wanted to be berated to be censured and called a cad. Aurora didn't rise to the bait.

"What about?"

"Excuse me." It wasn't a question as much as it was a statement intended to shut this conversation down. Azul adopted an aghast tone of uncomprehending high society horror to shield himself from scrutiny.

"What did you fight about?" Aurora said again.

"No." Azul's last vestiges of self-preservation were kicking into high gear. "I just realized I have no fucking idea who you are. And also, excuse the fuck outta me. Why are you questioning me about my last conversation about my recently deceased mother?"

"I'm Detective Aurora Harlowe. I'm investigating the terrorist attack tonight, as well as the possible assassination of your mother."

The statement poisoned the air between them. While the best and brightest minds in the galaxy regularly surrounded him, Azul wasn't one of the prime thinkers of this generation. He didn't even watch enough crime TV shows to know enough about the implications of a detective approaching you. He was clueless, which he was used to, but also nervous, which was new.

Aurora watched as the sputtering wheels in his brain revved up and came crashing to their natural conclusion (which wasn't a good one).

Azul fidgeted in front of her, leg bouncing, eyes darting, terror racing through his body. He tried for casual when he said, "And why are you wasting your time talking to me?"

"Do you consider yourself to be a particularly lucky man, Azul?"

He rolled his eyes and nodded and raised his glass to salute his own lucky star.

"I agree," Aurora said. "You, Azul Greene, are one lucky, lucky son of a bitch. But the question is, how lucky are you? Because we've identified that the Metabolic Partiphaser bomb that killed over 500 people tonight was placed underneath your mother's seat. The seat you were supposed to be sitting next to the whole night. The seat you would've occupied if you hadn't been,"-- paused for dramatic effect— "*luckily* somewhere else during the bombing. The bombing that was actually an assassination of your mother, Asa Greene. I guess I'm wasting my time talking to you cause I want to know how lucky you really are."

Azul's eyes dilated, his hands clenched together in front of him as her words sober him up. His muscles clenched, froze and released as he stood petrified. Out of his element, with no idea what to do next.

She drove the point home with this last question: "So, were you born lucky or do you make your own luck?"

In a rush, he closed the gap between them as he said, "But — that doesn't make... Asa and I... you can't possibly —."

"Where were you during intermission, Azul?"

He took a step back, his breath labored and unsteady. "I — I want my ---"

With hands like lightning, Aurora reached out to grab his forearm in a light, warm pressure. "I'm going to stop you there." She didn't move closer, but she lowered her voice, drawing him closer to catch her whispers, "This is a casual conversation. Between two people. One of which is a detective investigating a bombing and the other who was strategically, suspiciously absent when said bombing occurred. Now, lawyers are nice. I'm sure you have real nice lawyers. I'm sure Asa had phenomenal lawyers. However, this doesn't look great. Not to the public. Not to the lawyers."

Azul grunted out like he was punched in the diaphragm, "You can't intimidate me."

Even he didn't believe that lie.

"I doubt I could intimidate you on my darkest day," Aurora said. "I'm simply giving you a summary of what's happening. Currently, I'm just asking where you were and why you weren't sitting next to the bomb. You call a lawyer. This conversation happens at Command Corp HQ with 7 meatloafs, putting you through a sausage grinder. Cause a lot of important people died here tonight. Someone might've been targeting Asa, but they got a helluva lot more bang for their buck."

"You can't prove anything."

"You are damn right, on that count. That's why I'm asking

questions. I'm looking for facts. Facts like why you and your mother were arguing about money tonight, Azul, heir to the HausVert empire. Facts like how you got the drugs you're currently floating on smuggled into this facility. I'm fact-finding and you'll find I'm particularly good at my job. Are you good at yours?"

His words were watery and desperate, he pled. "I would never... could never kill Am'ma."

"Did you help someone who did? Did you know about the bombing in advance?"

"I — No," His voice picked up in the end, reedy and anxious. "I didn't I could never be involved in something like this."

Aurora considered him. She measured the anxiety swirling together with the cocktail of drugs in Azul's system. She realized this would be both easier and harder than she expected. His defenses were low, but his reactions were a live wire of intense mood swings. But there was this sliver of squishy underbelly. He wasn't sure what she knew... which wasn't a lot, but was definitely enough. Currently, all she had was a mountain of rumors, conjecture and a bit of body language psychology mumbo jumbo.

But he was a liar. She knew liars, knew them well.

"I'm going to tell you a little something. I'm a Truth Seer." As she slowly blinked her eyes closed, she reveals with a seductive grace and opens her eyes to reveal the metallic, shimmer pearlescent of Ohahlian *True* eyes.

This was Aurora's party trick. The reason that despite the brutal massacre of her people, the Pact coveted her gift enough to let her rise through their ranks. 'The enemy you know' was a constant mantra on both sides of her relationship with the government.

As long as she crammed all the anger and hurt that the pride of the Ohahlia had been reduced to side-show attraction, it was enormously effective during situations like this. Because her party trick, a flash of the *Truth* in her eyes, called to the memories of the Truth Seers and the tireless Yavrron.

The Truth Seers had the extrasensory ability to detect lies

154

with complete accuracy. Outside Ohahlia, folks knew more of the legend than the reality. It had gotten worse as their numbers dwindled down to the dozen, but frequently, the Truth Seers were bundled up together with the more famous and legendary subcategory — the Yavrron warriors, who specially trained to use that ability in combat.

The Yavrron was the stuff of legend; legend as in 'of the past', as in extinct. The Yavrron, at least. On a technicality, there were still some Ohahlians and Truth Seers kicking about, Aurora included. Though few remembered the distinction between the warriors and civilians.

Ohahlians were a race endangered, to say the very least. No longer able to return home, they lived as nomads across the system. Nothing unique in their story. The Oya-Vearro star system swelled with migrants and vagabonds.

However, whispers and rumors of meeting one of the last Ohahlian Truth Seers were prime cocktail hour small talk. There was a level of exotic and dynamic mystery because of their tragic past. Because while it had been nearly 15 years since the Centennial Carnage massacre, 13 since the end of the war, fact had faded to fiction and some version of truth and lies became a monstrous amalgamation of legend.

However, at times like this, it was to her benefit.

"Do you want to know why the Yavrron didn't win the war?" Aurora asked rhetorically. "They didn't win the war because the truth doesn't fucking matter. People are always lying. Some big lies, but mostly small. Most Truth Seers don't understand that just an ounce of untruth can spoil an entire sentiment. Back home, it was either a truth or a lie. I... miss that. The clarity. It was refreshing. But they didn't understand how you people communicate. They didn't understand that you could lie to protect, lie to soften a blow, lie to yourself. So, if I were as stupid as you think I am, a simple lamb easily fooled by petty lies, I would immediately run to my superiors over there in white and ID you as the most likely suspect in this room. Do you want to know why I'm not doing that?"

"Because I'm not lying."

Genuine laughter bubbled up from her stomach. Aurora threw her head back before she reached out to grab Azul's hand in a tight, vice-like grip. His eyes are pinned with an unwavering gaze. Her laughter crashed upon his unhearing ears like a wave against unyielding cliffs.

Aurora brought their clasped hand to her mouth to deliver a quick kiss to the back of his hand, dragging his gaze to lock with hers. "Oh, darling," she said on a sigh.

A quick huff of anxiety flared his nostrils wide. Their gaze chained together in a standoff. His hand gripping hers just as tight, he went in for another attempt at an answer. "Because you know I didn't do it?"

A quick, blink-and-you-miss-it smile flicked across the corner of her lips, across the edges of her eyes. She graced another kiss on the smooth skin on the back of his hand before bringing their joined hands down to her lap. He slumped into a heap of nerves beside her. Breaking eye contact finally, Aurora patted his hand quickly and efficiently as her eyes moved out to observe the churning crowd in front of them.

"Azul, why weren't you in the theatre when intermission ended?" Her question stood stark. The heart of the problem would not be missed.

"Me and Am'ma got into a fight."

She pulsed her hand in a quick squeeze of understanding. He continued. "It wasn't the worst fight we'd ever had, but... she threatened to disinherit me. Said I wasn't worthy of the HausVert legacy. She said that I didn't bleed green."

Calmly, all the warmth and gentility drained from her voice, Aurora stated plainly, "Well let's start from the beginning, from when you landed on Esaa station. Start from there and tell me exactly what happened."

15

BONES AND GLORY

LANGSTON

Langston was on minute thirty of meandering through the squeaky-clean service hallways and felt confident that he could write a two-thousand-word epic poem about sanitation practices on space stations. Traversing through the endless maze of pristine corridors, Langston would be more than happy to eat a five-course meal off these floors. They were that clean. Everything smelled distantly of forests in far-off lands and disinfectants.

But no matter where he turned, each turn in the endless hallway looked identical. Not just uniform, but horror-movie level identical.

In all honesty, most hallways in space stations looked pretty similar, but there was something nightmarishly indistinguishable from every square inch of this section of the ship. Seamless, curved white walls pocked by portholes without a doorway insight. While the familiar peaks of the blue-black expanse of space outside should've given him a sense of ease and relaxation,

157

it proved to unnerve him and enhance the overwhelming sense of... limbo. He'd been walking in a variety of directions in an attempt to find some staff people for what seemed like an hour. This hour had been fifteen going on twenty minutes, and he would know cause he was checking his watch religiously. Based on the basic map posted along the hallways, he should've been able to walk right into the staff barracks from where he exited the Santos Hall's lobby. But nada.

He wouldn't call himself lost (though that was a realistic assessment of his situation).

Langston could've sworn that he had heard a door closing several times as he walked through these halls. However, the click and swish of the door were always right beyond the next turn and out of reach. Each time he arrived near where he thought he heard the sound, there was neither a door nor a person anywhere in sight. Limbo.

Another five or so minutes of directionless walking and the clock said that he had to ping his locowear with his location. This moment wasn't necessarily a breaking point for Langston, but it was clearly not a high point. He was half certain that he might be hallucinating the sound of doors closing and, despite his seventeen years on the force; he wasn't able to locate the damn staff quarters. So, he wouldn't say that he had quite reached the point of just comm calling Liya to get a GPS-guided map uploaded to his compad, but he was close. Of course, using the compad was impossible because of the authorized access lockout courtesy of Dean. But he kept on walking. He was an intelligent human and he could figure this out himself.

Because it wasn't like his entire career was on the line here. Seven or eight minutes more minutes of searching wouldn't kill him. Langston laughed out loud at his own internal dialogue cause damn if his sarcasm didn't annoy himself sometimes. Again, he couldn't emphasize to himself enough that this wasn't a breaking point, and he wasn't laughing at lame jokes while contemplating the nature of purgatory.

The laugh echoed down the stupid, endless labyrinth of hallways.

So he walked faster. Then slower. Tried jogging. Tried sneaking around corners. It was ridiculous, but without the resources of his team and technology, he was it his wit's end.

So he spent five more minutes of aimless wandering, matched step-by-step with mindless introspection. Why hadn't he had Liya send him the map when they arrived at the station? Just because he never needed a map before didn't mean that he wouldn't need one now. Clearly, maps were a mandatory essential that should never be overlooked. Further contemplation circled back to the more esoteric theory that perhaps it was a curse of the human condition that one never had a map when one needed one. Also, was he a stereotypical male for not asking for direction before heading out on a search? Was being a stereotype really so bad? In this moment, he cursed that, but in general—

"A little lost there, Boss?"

Liya's sultry voice echoed through the sterile halls like a lightning stike.

There she was.

Liya had changed out of her uniform into plain clothes, leaning a hip against the wall with her tablet dangling precariously from her fingers — the very embodiment of smugness and something else that punched him straight in the gut.

At once, he felt both an enormous rush of relief that was quickly chased away by annoyance, worry, and anger. Liya was not supposed to be here. In hindsight, of course, this is exactly where she'd be.

His hand pulled down over his tired eyes. "Shiiiiiiiit."

She sauntered over to him, eyes peeking out from under hooded lids. Just enough sway in her hip to be intentional for him to notice. He rolled his eyes and raked his nails across his scalp. He regretted the damnable passing thought that posited that her presence here would make things easier. There was a matchstick's chance in hell that she would make things harder... in a literal sense of the word. "Liya. Come on. Does my authority mean nothing to you?"

"It means something. Probably not what you hope it might, but definitely something, boss man," she said, arms folded, smirk honeyed and alluring.

"I'm working." Langston took a step back from her with purpose. "You are supposed to be on the ship."

Defiance flared into her eyes as Liya leaned into his space. "Well... you're not officially working... So, technically peaking, so should you." She was close enough to see her heartbeat in the hollow of her neck.

The centimeters of space between was a minefield on a volcano in the middle of a thunderstorm. But Langston wasn't one to be dramatic. He... just—He couldn't think with her this close. With her being everything, she was. Smarter than him. Insightful. Soft skin, thin beautiful fingers. It was her fingers that broke him of any notion that it was simple lust. Or perhaps more specifically, the straw that broke his back was when he saw he had found him accidentally been writing a small haiku in celebration of the beauty of her hands.

That was his sign to take a step back. Because that kind of nonsense was inappropriate. No pining, no innocent caresses, absolutely no haikus. Yes, more space. Yes, more professionalism.

"Stop." The words were whispered out as he took a giant step back.

Over time, he had created a precarious set of rules to prevent any... unfortunate sniffing. Most of the rules were just a clear articulation of what could be defined as professional space. This could also be easily defined as never talking to her alone in deserted hallways where she looked edible in all the best kinds of ways. She owned all the real estate between his ears and he was starting to think that she knew it.

Though she would deny it, Liya pouted. With a quick roll of her eyes, she seemed to meditate for a second before shimmying the tension out of her shoulders before once again her gaze returned to his, sure and direct. She stood straight up.

No more seduction lingered in her eyes or hips. *So, at least she understands the seriousness of the situation.* "You and Aurora. You're off-book using locowears and frolicking about the station. Does that seem like the wisest decision you've ever made?" she asked. Well, to call that a question was a bit of an exaggeration because while it was phrased like a question but it wasn't.

But Langston was not to be outdone, in a competition of smugness. "Well, it's just the day for bad decisions while frolicking, isn't it, Liya?"

Her gaze dropped in defeat, and her head flinched slightly in an aborted shake. *Somehow, they had gone from inappropriate flirtation to barbed personal insults in a matter of seconds. He could never master professionalism with her the way he should.* His victory felt hollow.

Langston's hand swiped across his chin. Attempting to soften the barb and to bring back a modicum of banter and their usual flow back to the conversation, he offered a light, "And for the record, I'm doing the furthest thing from frolicking."

"Please. I'm two seconds away from slapping a tutu on you and calling you Ethel," she said, graciously accepting the apology for what it was without passing up an easy opportunity to mock him.

Crossing the veritable small ocean of space between them, she stood to this side and crowded into his space. She pulled out her compad to show him something while he was still trying to calculate if this was another trap of temptation or a simple practicality. As Liya's fingers danced across the tablet, she pulled up the multiple schematics and blueprints for the hallway and ship sector they were currently occupying. The 3D blueprint of their hallway was placed next to a holo of the blueprint of the ship section. Her finger draws a bracket on the blueprint. "See that there? That's your problem."

Langston huffed a laugh and dryly delivered "But of course, it's times like these that I curse the gods that I never got that community college architecture degree."

"Ha ha," — rolling her eyes, she nudged him with her shoulder, and pointed to the important parts — "So this hallway is what, the standard 3 feet wide, yes? But these blueprints have this hallway located flush against the shell of the ship. The blueprints also have this listed as 15 feet wide, 5 times its actual size. So where are those extra 12 feet?"

"Now that is something."

"And that something is about to get a whole lot more interesting." She then dragged a new tab into view on the compad. It showed his locowear dot in a mockup of the ship's schematics. "So, of course, we got ourselves a port window looking into the expanse right there, so you'd assume that this false hallways was flush against the outer hull. But your loco-dot locates you 14 ft from the hull. So..."

"This is not a port window," Langston approached what, even upon very close inspection, still looks like a port window. It looked great, but it was the feel of the thing that gave it away. It was warm to the touch, not hot, but approaching it. No matter how luxurious, how well-kept a space station he had been on, he had never in his life experienced a warm hull. By design, it was impossible for the overall stability of the gravity stability tech and oxygen maintenance systems to insulate the outer hull to anything past a cold metal slab.

"Exactly," she said, her voice aglow with excitement. He heard her blow out another centering exhale behind him. "You are still investigating. You're looking for Jamie Pope," Liya said, like it was the most obvious thing on the planet. Like they weren't in direct contradiction to their commander's orders.

He didn't turn to address her. He doesn't want to see her expression. Even if she doesn't know it, her face... her emotions do something to his resolve. And he couldn't at this moment afford some things to interfere with his objective. "Thank you for your help. Go back to the ship," he said. His voice was icy.

"I can help."

Clearly, Langston thought as he huffed out a laugh devoid of humor. He had spent close to an hour lost with his finger up his bum and not a hope in hell that he was going to find Jamie, and in under a minute, she had given him new insight and a pathway to investigate. Her helping hands weren't the problem. "I know you can. Go back to the ship."

"So you are just going to stay here, frolicking in this stupid maze of fake hallways and not let me help?" she asked.

He whipped around quickly. He didn't have time for this. "Yup, I will frolic all up and down these goddamn hallways. Just call me a frolicking freak as long as you remember that I am your commanding officer and I am ordering you to return to base."

"Well, that would certainly make it more interesting for your observers," she said.

His next fiery command froze in his throat as he considered her words. Her words were so unexpected that he chooses to just ignore them. Liya's face is a stone testament of stubbornness.

"Liya --"

"Someone is watching you. Did you know that?"

Her words shocked him out of his own determination. "Say that again now?"

"That's why I came to find you, only to discover you weren't on the bridge. Someone's hacking the CCTV feeds all across the station. Anywhere that you and Aurora pop up, they're watching."

His head was spinning. There was no good answer to this question, "Do you know who?" It could be SI, Command, the Esaa Corp execs. But no matter who it was. The answer wasn't good.

"No, that's the weird thing about it. The feed was embedded into the system as it currently stands. It's not a big guess to assume that whoever's hacking this knew about the bomb, at the very least."

He pressed and asked, "If you really tried, could you find out who it is?"

Liya's head tilted back and forth in an unhappy waiver as she grimaced out, "Yes and no. The only way to truly identify the signal will be to find the device the footage is being viewed on. The signal is not being broadcast outside of this station."

"So, it's someone still on this base?"

"Yes?"

Liya's tone told him she wasn't sure. However, he knew from experience that she would say nothing with surety unless she knew it to be completely factual. Langston would always appreciate her directness and surety. "I'll take it. It might be a piece of evidence... eventually. Assuming we find this dickswab"

Mockingly, she offers the commentary. "See, I'm very useful," she said.

He laughed. "Go back to the ship." There is no heat in his words, just a request from a friend. "Me and Roar, we can take the heat, no matter what ends up happening here. You don't have the clearance." His voice stumbled over this next part. "I can't protect you if anything happens. Please." Langston motioned back in the vague direction of the ship, hoping this vulnerability will finally push her to listen to him.

Her eyes narrowed for a second in a curious confusion. She was always so quick. "Wait," Liya asked, "Where do you... think you're going exactly?"

"To find my suspect and interrogate them."

"Yah, I got that, but like, where are you going?"

"The staff quarters," he said. "Rhys had mentioned that because of the lockdown, all non-essential staff is gathered there until further notice."

Full-bellied laughs barked out of her as she walked away down the hallways, "Oh Oya, I forgot you were a civvy. You know, that explains a lot. You're right, you don't need me at all. You go to your '*staff quarters*' and see how that works out for you."

"What do you know?" Langston asked. This was unimaginably worse than asking for directions.

Falsely slapping a hand over her heart while continuing to back out of the hallway, he followed her. "Oh, I wouldn't want to overstep," Liya said.

"Liya, give me a break." Langston stopped in his tracks. If she asked, he would beg for the break because the end of his rope gave out about 15 mins again and he was somewhere between groveling and simply keeling over and dying. Whatever got the best results at this point.

Laughter still clinging to her words, she gestures for him to follow. "It's just so funny. I forget that in the end, you are such a *civvy* sometimes. A squishy little Gherrean soft skin who grew up in the Central Core. Soft and looking for "barracks". It's a wonder how anything gets done without Harlowe." Liya stopped walking and approached the fake port window. She folded and stored her compad in her belt before beckoning him closer. She ran her hands around the port window, looking for something that he couldn't tell.

"Willing to share with the class?"

Liya continued her meticulous hand search on the metal rim of the false window. "So, there are barracks, run by the 'big man' — station chiefs, security personnel, etc. They're official and sterile and empty. Those housing units are more like a sanatorium than an actual living area. No one actually lives there. So the staff barracks are 'official' but anyone who grew up soil-less grew up in the Hallows. Every working ship has Hallows, it's the place where people actually live. If they're a service crew on board, there are definitely Hallows. But, hell, every station in the Wilds past Anhkae has Hallows. They come unique — different sizes or shapes, but nine out of ten times they're hidden behind double-walled insulation. Just like this. Hallows are special, but one way or another they all end up... smelling like home. It's obvious to anyone who grew up in the Wilds when they see blueprints, when they see blueprints like this. 12 feet of empty, hidden hallway like that is a dead giveaway."

Liya's right hand stops along the lower left side of the metal rim of the false porthole. She caressed her hand up and down, smiling at what she felt under her fingertips. She grabbed Langston's hand in hers and guided it to the window rim, tracing the lower section. He can feel the indentation in the shape of characters, an inscription. Once faster, a second time slower, Liya guided his hand so he could understand what he was feeling. It was Kaetyene, the old Ankaena language.

"You feel that? The inscription?"

Langston ran his fingers over the character a few more times. "**Qoh'amkeses**," he said, sounding out the phrase. "It's Kaetyene, right? Do you speak it... know what it means? Cause it sounds damned ominous."

Her head tilted with what looks to be nostalgic. "Yeah, it's not proper. They likely don't teach this in language classes in the Central Core. It's a loose, creole-jumbo version Kaetyene. Basically, it's kinda of like the unofficial language of the Hallows, of the people who work. But **qoh'amkeses** isn't ominous at all. It's from an old stellar prayer that I probably was forced to memorize at some point but I can't recall the whole thing. **Qoh'amkeses** means between bones. The full poem goes on about something about 'between bones and glory, you will find your home.' Something like that. When all of this is over, I'll have to read it to you sometime. It's truly very beautiful. All the Hallows entrances are marked with this phrase. From the dark edge to Vearro, there are doors between the bones of the station's scaffolding."

She brushed away his hand before placing one hand against the rim and the other on the wall beside it. She took a beat to look at him for a second. "Don't — just know that... we don't let the outside... in... ever. No corporate suit, no ship captain, CC grunt or SI investigator has ever entered any Hallows in a professional capacity. You just don't enter other people's Hallows without an invitation. So just..," her words faded out. He couldn't say he understood, but he would always respect her perspective. He was asking her to do something unprecedented.

He didn't quite know what to say to her, but without a response from him, she nodded and went back to her task. Liya applied pressure to the lip of the metal till it gave way in a slight indent. Her grip on this new indent, she turned the ring of metal counter-clockwise until the panel of the wall with the window popped forward. She smiled and took a small inhale, closing her eyes. "Smells like home."

She pushed the doorway open.

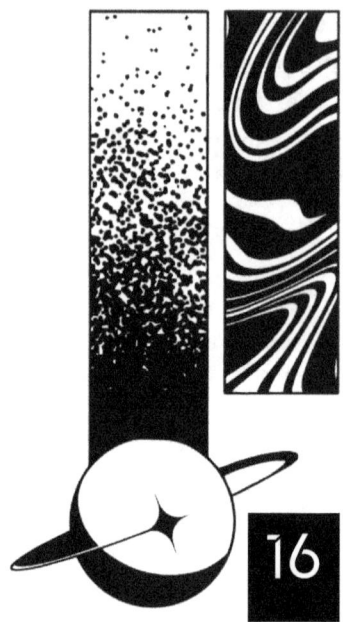

16

HERITAGE

LANGSTON

With a few steps, they walked past the door, through a portal into a new world, between the crevices, tucked in the gap hiding secrets. It was a dark corridor underneath a canopy of glowing plants, forming a tunnel that opened up to something bursting just beyond.

Langston ducked his head as the bio-luminous leaves rustled against his hair as he walked. The vines dangled from a cage of plastic and copper pipes woven together above their heads. He squeezed through the tight corridor with Liya in front of him.

The sterile hallway behind them had been mausoleum quiet, so the whirr of life was startling to hear hidden bursting out from behind the secret door. A thousand voices, accents and conversations layered on top of each other, combining into the humming buzz of life.

Liya paused at the edge of this entrance corridor. Langston

could see over her head that there was a procession of bodies moving past their entrance in a steady flow of traffic. She peered her head out, turning left and right cautiously before she looked back at him.

"The look on your face," Liya said. Her voice was unspeakably soft and thrumming with brightness. Her voice was whisper soft compared to the muted roar behind her. He could just barely hear her with her face in profile with twinkle gleaming in her eye. She reached out for his hand in a warm, soft grasp and pushed into the flow of bodies, heading in one direction.

The flow forced them to walk with the crowd until Liya could find them a space to hold up and get their bearings.

The gentle lullaby-like quality of Kaetyene carried through the air. Mixed with the common tongue, it was the preferred language in these parts. Academically, he knew that the language was mostly used by the poorer Ankaenan who ended up migrating off-world for work. It was today that he connected the dots that this wasn't some dying language. It was a living, breathing thing. Liya even kindly muttered, "**_Adon'ib_**" as she squeezed past an elderly man and "**_Ogo shebu_**" as she nodded to a passerby.

They slipped into some squeeze of space between two separate huddles of people. Liya took the time to look around to get her bearing on where they were exactly. Langston just looked around, tried to get his bearings in general, and figure out what this was exactly.

Langston had seen worlds across the galaxy. He had seen the crackling chartreuse lava falls of Hwei, 100-ft waves crashing over a dome on Yemaya, the Diamond belt in the Tether. He'd met people from every corner of this system. But he had never seen something quite like this.

He marveled at a uniquely obvious balance between creativity and productivity. Within this hidden world, these Hallows were a sanctuary. The structures themselves, intermixtures of salvaged material and rusting debris, burst across his eyes with a jolt of dazzling vitality. What had once been,

Langston could only imagine, a dingy 12 foot tunnel passage had become a vibrant piece of living art. Where the decor of Esaa Station proper was awe-inspiring in the precision detailing of handcrafted nano-ceramic tiling, these crafted shanty buildings belted out their uniqueness. Spray-painted murals on corrugated metal siding beside chunky hand-woven tapestries came together to make a hovel into a home. Not an inch of space was wasted. Second floors formed bridges overhead, connecting homes to one another. What should be chaotic, a thousand different cultures mashed against a million different perspectives, wasn't.

It wasn't a cacophony (loud, disharmonious, grating)— it was gospel. An emotional outcry of a collective singing together as one. Singular and haunting, something like this was made of feelings, not words impossibly limited by their two-dimensionality.

Langston's eyes darting every which way. A gaggle of young women sat together in plastic chairs — some pregnant and sweating, with their shirts rolled up over sizable bumps, others bouncing chubby-fingered toddlers on their knees while laughing exuberantly. Two men in spirited conversation over mugs filled with a steaming liquid. While everyone in these Hallows was logically Esaa Corp employees, they had turned their generic uniforms into something extraordinary. The uniforms draped and tied across their bodies and layered with vibrant fabrics draped around them in the style of provincial Gherrean sarongs, topped with the unique metal jewelry style he had seen out in the Wilds. The elaborate skin art of the Ohahlians seemed to be adopted broadly by the younger folk who rushed back into the crowd.

Liya leaned her head against his shoulder so he could hear her voice. "Do you smell that?" Across from them was a kitchen front with folks milling about the various counters and stoves communally cooking.

He nodded his head, looking closely at the three giant boiling pots on the back burners, woks, and pans shuffling food in the air on the front burner.

"Close your eyes, and take a big ole whiff," she said. He obeyed without thinking. Her voice was the only thing he could hear. Everything else took a back seat. "You can smell it in the air. History. All of their homelands baked into their food. Today they're cooking... in the Far-Oceanic Gherrean style. Have you ever had it?" — he shook his head — "Almost all their food is flavored with blue squid-honey. It's a sticky sweet ink they smother everything with. You can smell it a mile away. Just this side of cloying to your nostril hairs with an intoxicating, heavy sweetness. I love it. Everywhere you walk, you can smell their heritage. Saffron from Gherrean Inlanders. Huacatay from the Deep Z migrants. Midnight pepper from the Anhkaena city ravagers. And all those scents are carried away by... I call it the *dew*."

He turned his head down to look at her. Her face was so relaxed and open as she looked right back. There were no barriers between them at this moment. She was sharing something important.

There was a delicate vulnerability edging in the corner of her eyes. He knew he didn't have to ask the question. That she was offering this vulnerability with the distinct knowledge that it was too real. Too unforgettable. It was the kind of thing you shared with only one person and the hidden places in your soul.

"What does the dew smell like?"

"People. It smells like so many people in too little space. Like all their body heat combines together and evaporates into the air."

Confused, but swept away by her enthusiasm, he asked, "And this is a pleasant scent?"

"The very best," she said easily. "It's not body odor. It's people odor. Just you wait. You won't notice it while you are here, but the next time you are in a Hallow, you'll smell it."

He couldn't help but run his thumb over the edge of her jaw. "I bet I will." His hand left her check when Liya was jostled by an ash-covered man rushing past, pushing in the opposite direction of the flow of people. Langston dropped his hand and schooled his features.

"So, you think we'll find Pope here?" he asked. Desperate for innumerable reasons to get back on track. The reason he was focused on was that he had bet all of his marbles on this escapade. On solving this case before Zhou and earning his place back in the sunlight of SI's good graces.

Liya did that head shake thing she was always doing when he let himself get too close. Like she was shaking loose illusions of... of a something out of her head and remembering reality. He could relate.

This whole situation was unfair to her. Which is why he was scum. In all the ways, which is why he had to stay in control. Cause he was scum, and playing hot-and-cold with her was unfair. And he was her boss, and he was better than this and he must remember the case. To focus on the case.

She looked to the right, down at a few bricks. "Yah," she said, "I think if we make our way down to the Center Tri, we should be able to find an elder or two. After an event like the bombing, they will have already taken attendance and probably identified some likely suspects among their own ranks."

The implication of her words vaguely shocked Langston. Liya, having never set foot on this station, had insight into the service workers' internal cultural governance system.

For not the first time in this mind-shattering fifteen minutes, Langston was confronted with the fact that he knew nothing about these people and their world. Their world which was half an inch from his face, his entire career if not his entire life.

While he had been learning to challenge the Gherrean savior complex, in his heart of hearts, Langston had gone into this line of business to help exactly these people.

It was his purpose in life. Something that centered him on hard times. Honestly, in times like these, where all the cards were stacked against him. He just thought about how he could give up cause this was his Vearro-be-damn purpose in life. To help people.

But he did not know these people at all. They were supposed

to be his. His chosen… family. These were the people he wanted to help the most. It was stomach-churning to know with such clarity that he knew nothing.

Liya grabbed his hand and pulled him across the two lanes of people down to where an elderly woman was sitting in a pouf on the ground. Above her head was a neon sign that had Kaetyene glyphs written on it.

Liya kneeled next to the woman on the open square pillow beside her. She bowed her head in greeting. "*Āshyamni.*" Liya tugged on his pant leg and Langston sat down beside her and muttered a broken hello in Kaetyene as well.

The old woman had clear and lively eyes shining out of a crinkled shadow of a face. Her midnight skin matching his own, she looked like what he imagined his grandmother would look like if she was about 35 years older. Non-planetary gravity was kind to the skin, so to see someone so weather-worn and carved by lines indicated extreme age. She nodded as her eyes pierced Langston with an unwavering attention.

Liya started talking swiftly in a way that Langston couldn't quite catch, explaining something to the woman in front of them. While normally Langston would try to keep up, he was hesitant to break the intense focus directed on him by the hunched-over lady in front of them.

She shook her head no, "***Mojinm khet oeph. Tyn ku'phelhta ka?***"

Her voice was a scoured-soft rasp. Her eyes remained pinned on Langston. Unwavering. Piercing.

He opened her move to clarify that he didn't speak Kaetyene, that they needed help that — Liya silenced him with a tight squeeze against his forearm.

"***Hæm'alo sah Command oeph. Ftemuelo-azh, āmnam th'qol ogo. Yavroo-al āhk khet pha'kæia-ib, Māathta yavroo-ib. Hæ-ib Liya Grimae. Hæ-al āhk-ka. Oi'ilo cheej a'urrbān.***"

As Liya spoke, the woman's eyes shifted to lock on hers. Her intensity did not dim or wane, but burned.

The silence did not stretch or bend but crackled swiftly through the air.

The woman frowned deeply and nodded. "We shall see, won't we, Liya Grimae? We are preparing for the inevitable in the Center Tri. 48 bricks port that way. Be swift. We have many uninvited visitors today. The dogs are barking at the door."

They reached out to each other and gripped their hands together in a tight grip. Liya bowed forward to kiss the woman's knuckles. "***Imnohta ka.***"

Swiftly, Liya stood, and Langston followed. They headed in the port direction. Liya had a bounce in her step as she led the way. Proud to have solved yet another puzzle on the journey toward the center of the mystery.

She was a genius, a lovable quick-witted genius who deserved more than this world could give her and certainly more than he could ever offer. The precariousness of their situation had crept back into his hindbrain. The distraction of an entire world beyond his sight had let him forget that this wasn't some tourist excursion. She shouldn't be here. He had had a bad feeling since that hallway and it just refused to go away.

It was almost like he was being watched.

Which fair? Liya had just recently told them they were being watched. Langston couldn't help but wonder whether these Hallows were monitored as closely as the rest of the station. But that was an academic issue where there were bigger fish to fry at this moment.

He needed her help (clearly) then he needed her to return to the ship (safety) so that he could finish the mission (keep her safe). Semantics.

He closed the distance between them and placed his hand on her mid-back. Leaning down to speak into her ear, so she could hear above the din of a thousand different conversations happening around them. "Tell me about Jamie Pope."

Her face burst open with conspiratorial glee as she matched her pace to his. "If I was a more devious woman, I would suggest that you are asking me to steal into a back door of the SI network, access black data from government servers and break a couple of Pact regulations in order to give you the upper hand in this investigation."

"That's exactly what I'm asking," Langston aid.

Shock splashes across her forehead. "Oh," she said as she nodded. She whipped out her compad from her back pocket. "I actually didn't expect you to be that direct." Trusting in Langston to guide her through the crowd, she hacked through secure national databases in a matter of minutes. "All things considered, neither of us is on the case. So, really, this is just some recreational hacking by two concerned citizens moseying along dark secret passageways in search of a dangerous terrorist. Nothing too nefarious or any reason to raise any alarm bells."

"Well, put."

Clicking away, she compiled the information into a report format, "Ok." She held up the screen for him to view as they walked. She scrolled through the information she had snatched from secure databases. "Born 2043 to a family commune on Yemaya. Commune assigned to the HausVerte Lavender Domes. Pretty normal social media profile. Nothing overtly political, just the typical generically horrid thing all teenage boys like. Pretty tame sexual profile for a Dome doi too. He was active in science fairs in the public school system. Won or placed high in several competitions. Pope enlisted with a scholarship to the BaseX Private Academy in 2053. There he stayed until he later dropped out, just two years shy of his degree. Returned to the Lavender Domes. Where he then disappeared another two years after that. Complete dropped off the map with a couple of minor pings in the system. Popping through checkpoints at various outposts and trading stops, but no permanent jobs. No red flags."

"What did he study at BaseX?"

She handed Langston the device over to him with a grimace, "Molecular Engineering."

"Ok... This profile basically has a neon sign, 'I'm the bomb maker' written all over it. He actually used his real name in the employee file?"

"Yup."

Pope had a long, soft face. Soft, barely there eyebrows pitched up in a look of constant confusion or like he was nervous. He had kind eyes, though, but wasn't much of a smiler. It all combined to make him seem a bit sad. Forlorn in a hopeless way that went bone deep from a lifetime of degradation. Or something like that.

"Here, I think I found an article that was released about the HausVert Lavender Domes about the same time Pope dropped out of BaseX... oh shit," Liya looked up at him with wide, round eyes in shock.

"What is it?" Langston didn't actually want to know.

Liya read through the article, "It... it looks like there was a crack in the dome during a hurricane, everything was flooded out... However, a section of workers were tethered.. locked together... no one unlocked them and they drowned."

"Yup, that would do it. Can I assume Pope lost someone in the tragedy?" he blew out a breath. Sad eyes. Not that he was empathizing with a terrorist and mass murderer. That would be unprofessional. Langston had to limit his unbecoming unprofessionalism to breaking the law, rather than coddling criminals.

"Nothing conclusive or obvious. It's a fair assumption based on the close familial bonds and communal parenting in Domes," Liya said.

Langston handed the pad back over to her. She folded it and tucked it back in her pocket. The only thing that truly made sense was Pope had assumed, however erroneously, the investigative team would see none of this information. Or that he would be long gone before the information was uncovered. So, Pope was either ill-prepared or under-informed. Or perhaps he didn't care, and he wanted to get caught so he could promote his manifesto. Anyway, you cut it, there seemed to be some pretty major tactical flaws on

Pope's part.

"Overconfident little bugger," said Langston in conclusion.

They approached what could only be the Center Tri that Liya and the old woman had referenced. Where the rest of the space was a simple tunnel crowded, plastered with shanty structures, the Center Tri had no major structures or buildings.

While there was no structure, this large open space was in the shape of a pyramid. It was in the open bazaars style he remembered from home. Folks talking and bartering and relaxing in a way that was so familiar it made him ache. The familiar nature of the scene was punctuated by a strain of tension.

They found their way to the edges of what was a cloister of folks blocking the exit from the tunnel into the Center Tri.

Langston could see the shadows of a warm red swathe of light shine across Liya's cheek. There was a great red lantern connected to a maze of fairy lights hanging at the entrance of the palazzo. What was all the more unusual was what appeared to be a bright natural light source emanating from the pinnacle of the pyramid. Having grown up soil-side on Gherre, daily exposure to fresh sky filled with blues and gentle whites was something that he missed dearly.

Never, not from the barebone naval ships to the highest of high-end luxury cruisers, equally had he ever seen anything that could replicate natural light — not till today.

Illuminating every nook and cranny of the Center Tri, it was interesting to see how the light could brighten certain parts of the face while casting shadows and angles on the rest. Every person in the Tri was easy to see at any distance. So it would stand to reason that Langston was equally visible to them. Langston took a step meaningfully back towards the tunnel, coaxing Liya back with him.

Compared to the easy churn of what seemed like the typical daily life of the Hallows tunnel they had left, there was a distinct sense of unease in the air. Soot-covered survivors milled together, shivering against the onslaught of recent terrifying events. Several folks wearing patterned shawls rendered first aid to the crying, grieving groups slump unorderly through the space. Some wandered aimlessly, seeking comfort where any sliver may lie. With so much movement within, it was easy to observe and identify folks in the crowd. Langston mostly observed while he left, finding these Elders for further questioning to Liya.

She tugged his shoulder to direct his gaze right to the very heart of things. The elders. They weren't arguing, but there were hand gestures and fast-talking a plenty in the huddle of 5 people, all of them at least 80 years old.

When Langston really thought about it, he had almost never seen someone over the age of about 50 working on any ship ever. It was easy to guess their age as noticeably more ancient than the norm.

Langston observed a meeting of minds with craned necks and tensed shoulders; they must know where the inevitable *conclusion* would lead investigators. Smart money was always to bet against the help.

Classist but nonetheless smart money.

Langston could imagine with this "secret" network of existence buried an inch deep behind the scenes, having investigators poke around would be the last thing they needed. The obvious next steps would be to either identify the perpetrator and turn them over or close ranks and stand strong. Both had merit. Given this crime, in particular, the morality of the options on the table was fairly simple.

It was then that Langston caught sight of the youngest man among the Elders.

There, sweating, shaking and pale, was Jamie Pope.

He didn't speak. His eyes were glassy and vacant, but he was there all the same. He was completely covered head to foot in gray soot. His once neon yellow hair was unrecognizable. Pope's stomach and arms being smeared with knobbled layers greasy black char.

Squaring his shoulders, Langston nodded to himself. He

didn't know what he would say when he got there, but the time for fun and games was over. He would get answers from Pope one way or another. Elders be damned. He headed toward the center of the Tri pavilion.

"Wait. Fuck." Liya whipped him around by his arm and dragged him away from the try over to a kitchen stall by the edge of the tunnel. She pushed him firmly against a pillar holding up the second floor of the hut.

She peered around his body and the pillar before pointing discreetly. "Hamburger helper, 7 o'clock."

Langston's blood drained from his face. His neck tightened ramrod straight. He snagged Liya's compad off her belt and held it up to use the camera as a mirror. Right there at 7 o'clock on the other tunnel entrance into the Tri was the telltale white uniform cutting like a hot razor through the crowd. Command Corp soldiers let by the terror, Major Zhou.

They were making quite the entrance.

Aggressively using battering sticks to beat back the milling tides of people, the squadron surrounded Zhou and her towering six-foot gyro-spit of a guard on a pathway to the center. As the surrounding people caught on to CC's entrance, the panic spread as folks started rushing towards safety or the exit.

While violence seemed like a periphery source of enjoyment, the squadron was intent on their beeline towards a single aim.

To Jamie.

The Elders formed a wall of bodies to shield him from view.

Langston was academically interested in whether it had always been their decision to defend him or if the unprecedented entrance of CC troop in their sanctum had codified that decision.

"Damn," Langston said as he handed the compad back to Liya.

He closed his eyes to think.

There was no obvious move.

No clear next step. He slapped his hands lightly like a drum on his cheeks.

With Liya tucked against him, he could feel her rising up to her tiptoes, leaning around him to take in more of the situation. He rested (banged) his head against the back of the pillar. "Give it to me straight," he said.

"I've got eyes on nine rottweilers on crowd control. Then there is that super tall, objectively incredibly hot, lieutenant with the psychopath eyes. And then there is Zhou. It looks like the lieutenant is doing the talking to the Elders. Zeroing in on Jamie. Gotta be honest, I am low key shocked that they identified Pope as a possible suspect so fast. Honest to god, I thought they were... stupider than that."

"You and me both," Langston said, checking his belt for ammunition and his badge. It was clear these CC meatballs were smarter than the average pork sausage. "But I'll be damned, even if I didn't underestimate them... also... so just everyone knew about Hallows except me?"

Liya took her eyes off the scene to look back up at him before returning to the track the developments with CC. "Honestly, I thought you knew. It's... everyone knows. You just don't talk about it outside of the Hallows. Ever. It makes sense that folks who grew up on Core Planets don't know about the Hallows but. Yeah, as you grow up you know that Hallows is something you absolutely never talk about."

Langston shrugged it off. There was so much wrong with this situation he didn't quite know where to start. He was completely out in the deep end without the security of rank and backup on the highest stakes mission of his life in unknown territory where, to make matters worse, everyone spoke a language that he didn't. They could actively choose to switch into Kaetyene and exclude him, playing upon his knowledge-gaps. It was a new weakness that grated at him. And things were moving fast.

It had been weird at the time that Zhou hadn't taken the evidence they had collected or their investigative notes. CC wasn't an investigative organization by nature. If this was a normal case,

CC would've been up shit's creek without a paddle.

But instead, defying everything he assumed to be true, Zhou had made the investigative leap of the century and found Jamie Pope in just under an hour. Then fresh from the investigative leap of all time, Zhou then makes the seemingly radical move to storm Hallows in full gear.

These were the actions of a woman drunk on confidence.

Langston didn't have time to make logical matrices of how they could've possibly gotten here before him. His gut was all that he had at this moment. So... if Liya was to be believe Zhou had crossed some significant if unspoken rule to get to Jamie Pope in Hallows.

He couldn't imagine she would do that on a whim or without hard proof.

His conclusion: somehow... Zhou knew beyond a shadow of a doubt that was Jamie Pope was guilty.

He let that thought sink in. Considered it. Weighed it in his gut.

It was a conclusion his gut would support. So what next? Langston would have to move with equal amounts of fearless tenacity as Zhou.

Langston considered his next moves. All things being equal, if they knew Pope was the perp, one might consider that they took a luxuriously long time getting here. So, Langston considered himself lucky to have gotten this far.

CC hadn't spotted them. For all intents and purposes, this was it: a point of no return.

He had risked so much to get to this point, but ultimately, it would make sense to pack it up and slip through the cracks between walls back to the safety of The Socrates.

Or he could not.

It was difficult to even game out what the alternative would be. A confrontation with Zhou was definitely an alternative. Snowballing his career into a unrecoverable pile of garbage was inclusive in that alternative. So no pressure.

The answer to what he should do was obvious. Langston wasn't sure that he wanted to do the thing that was obvious.

Unaware of his internal dilemma, Liya asked, "Maybe they are the ones who are watching you?"

What a terrifying possibility. But… on brand for the CC, more on brand than the idea that the deductive genius' over at Command Corp were able to solve something more complex than 'what's for lunch'. It was a more obvious answer to the mounting list of uncomfortable questions. Nodding, Langston said, "Maybe."

Langston shifted so he could see how things had developed in the Tri. The crowd was getting antsy. Those who hadn't fled stood static by the barricade around the elders that some enforcers had set up. Not static, as in still, but static as in a buzzing anxiety of stasis. One elder genuinely looked second away from a very public bathroom break. "This still smells to high heaven. Hell, if I was running this investigation, I would just have him summoned to the bridge, rather than coming down here. It's just not their typical operating procedure. Command Corp is just not investigative by nature, and even if they were, this is not how they'd do it."

Movement near Zhou drew their attention away from their conversation and back to the scene. The Elders stood aside and let a mournful soot-covered young man take center stage. There was not an drop of the will-to-run-fight-live-continue left in him.

It didn't look like Pope was doing much talking, but the group exchanged more words. It was hard to tell who was instigating it, but the growing apprehension of the room swelled with each second. Two of the bulldogs on crowd control moved to Jamie. They slapped some cuffs on him and they stood sentry with their hands anchored on his arm. More talking, more anxiety. Then the lieutenant rushed forward to sucker punch Pope in the stomach. He crumbled to his knees like a bag of potatoes. The crowd blood pressure elevated as a group. It was getting out of hand.

Hypothetically, Zhou had the entire area on lock down. Her

goons had cleared enough space out around Pope and the Elders under the specific the threat of their high-powered gun and an itchy trigger-fingers. Thanks to Langston's interagency training, he knew each guard could respond with lethal force given half a second response time. And they had every corner of the pavilion covered. CC was infamous for turning this specific type of situation into a massacre.

"I just... can't catch a break," Langston said.

Langston weighed his options. Option A: continue to try against the mounting odds to interview their primary suspect and in-so-doing reveal to the pixie-goblin of a CC commander that he had disobeyed orders and step into whatever shit storm of bureaucratic disciplinary action that that might incur. Option B: don't do any of that. Slip into the shadow and leave Aurora out to dry, like the coward he is. Claim that the odds were against him (which they were) and there was nothing he could do (if didn't want to get into trouble).

Admittedly, these weren't great options. He was way out there, in the way out, juggling moral platitudes and heavy promises between coworkers. Because without her stupidly large, owl-sized hazel eyes staring at him, it was hard to remember what commitment he had to Aurora. They were technically just coworkers. Yes, she'd saved his ass from near certain death on several occasions. Yes, he... thought of her as a sister. But... he was a coward and the easy way out had convenient labels that added a smooth veneer of professional distance.

So, while he hadn't yet technically committed to any course of action over another, the vague sense of earnest commitment he had to his own wobbly sense of being a decent human being weighed on his decision-making process. Try as he might to take half measure and equivocate, this was a point of no return. One step forward and there was no going back. There would be no easy return to the stable comfort of Gherrean geniality. He'd be what he always wanted to be.

Or rather, what he always said he wanted to be.

So, unfortunately, he knew there was only one option. As the old saying goes: when there's nothing left to lose, you must set yourself on fire. Even then, with all that being said, he'd be damned if he got Liya dragged into the muck with him.

"So, now we'll have the true test. Can I, Detective Inspector Langston Aster, charm my way out of a paper-bag... or federal criminal charges?" He could tell by the way Liya's eyes seemed to double in size she didn't love these options either. Langston gently grabbed her hand and placed his gun between their hands. "Hang back. I can't take you with me on this. I'm not sure how this is going to shake out. If I'm in the clear and Zhou is on my side, I'll give you a quick signal and you can join me. If not, wait 15 minutes, then head back to the ship and give Aurora as much heads up as you can. Keep hidden for now."

Now was not the time to say the things they specifically had never said before. Someone should've told Liya that because as their eyes locked together, he could see the words they weren't allowed to whisper screaming at him. He hoped she could see the same within him.

OBSTRUCTING
JUSTICE

LANGSTON

Time to meet the Meat.

Langston zigzagged through the milling crowd, making his way towards the front of the laser barrier. He could feel Liya's eyes track his movements from behind. With significant effort, he refused to turn back to look at her, to reassure her. He had a vague fear that if he looked back now, he might not move forward at all.

As he reached the laser-tape barrier, he saw Zhou was absorbed in a heated conversation with one of the Elders. He waited to take more of the scene in before he entered the fray. As he scanned the group of officers he made direct eye contact with the Lieutenant without any specific name. The towering dark-haired Lieutenant followed Zhou around like a bad taste and was her right hand.

Ignoring the penetrating gaze of the Lieutenant, Langston continued to observe the actions of this hellish squadron. This Lieutenant, in particular, was a puzzle. Now there was the obvious question: could Langston take him in a fight? And the answer was, he sure hoped he could.

Physically, Langston had maybe an inch or two of height and a fair amount of bulk over the officer. But there was something wily about the Lieutenant that gave him pause. A kind of "bringing-a-bazooka-to-a-knife-fight" wily energy that Langston's fight-or-flight instinct was wary of. But the way the man shadowed Zhou implied she had him on a tight leash.

But a mad dog leashed by a wild owner was a hollow relief.

After measuring him up, Langston acknowledged the Lieutenant with a quick raise of his brow. The man didn't respond. So, Langston cleared his throat just to be annoying.

Zhou's head snapped up and landed her gaze on him. He met her gaze head on across the distance. A slurry of annoyance and surprise settled across Zhou's face. The Lieutenant whispered into Zhou's ear. She flashed a smile at whatever he said. The Major barked out a couple of orders that started a flurry of activity. The soldiers on crowd control started the forceful push to clear the Tri inch by baton-battering inch. Two grunts grabbed him in a tight hold and frog-marched him up to Zhou. Langston didn't even give a token protest.

"Why hello there, Road Block," Zhou said in greeting. "It took you less than an hour to break no less than three Pact statues. I'm disappointed, I was hoping it would be a nice round number."

"Oh, you know me. I live to disappoint." Langston squirmed against the bruising grip of the meatball bracketing him. Perhaps all hope for a working relationship between the two of them was dead if they had cute nicknames for each other. However, in his head he knew "Psycho Bloodthirsty Barbie-Q" wasn't a nickname Langston wanted to say to her face.

A snarl twitched the corner of Zhou's nose, but otherwise she didn't react. Among the chaos of panicked people protesting the clearing of the Center Tri. Against the growing objections of the elders voicing their complaints against the treatment of Jamie Pope, she stood, glared, and remained unmoved. Call him petty.

He didn't want to break the silence first.

So they glared at each other.

Zhou's eyes flicked away to catch some action behind him. She gave one of her grunts a sharp nod. Langston turned his head as much as could to catch what had pulled her attention behind him. Jamie Pope. The man of the hour. Still crouched with his hands cuffed in front of him, his head bowed against the ground.

He returned his attention back to Zhou. "I can help with that."

"I'm not the one who needs help here, Road Block." What must've been Zhou's attempt smile reminded him of shattered glass. It wasn't comforting in the least. She flicked her hands and the behemoths holding him searched him for weapons, finding his gun at his hip and ankle. They passed the weapons into the waiting hands of the judgemental Lieutenant.

Manically, Zhou twirled and flipped his ankle gun through her hands. With more glee than was frankly kosher, she pointed the gun square at his chest. "You strayed too far from the beaten path. What happens next is on you. You have my pity."

Langston's neck flexes as the blood rushes to his face. But he didn't take his eyes off her. He couldn't. He kept his eyes off the barrel of the gun pointed at his heart. His eyes met hers, unflinchingly. He knew in the end he (probably) wasn't in any genuine danger. While she was off her rocker and a psycho. He hoped this was just Zhou's versions of a high-stakes game of chicken. "Look at where you are. We are both pretty far from the beaten path. You need my help. I *can* help. Let me."

A wave of red-hot emotion spread across her eyes as every muscle in her body tightened. Noticeably, the hand holding a steady grip on his gun ticked up towards his face. "How chivalrous." Zhou was not amused.

"No, I--." Langston was getting nowhere with her. Stuttering, he softened his approach, making himself a tad more pleading. "With the investigation. With him." Again jerking his head toward the suspect to his side. Appealing to her CC structured roots, "I trained under General Montgomery James in the art of interrogation. I can get an air-tight confession out of this prick that will hold up in any court in the system. This is too important to let your ego get in the way. I can help. Let me help."

"This is my investigation," she said. While not a question, he knew his agreement, fervent and unquestioned and would be important to how this "relationship" between them would go.

Nodding, Langston moved slightly closer to her to the protest of the CC grunts hold him. "Yes." The word hung between them. He let the words settle over her before he made his play, "You give me five minutes and I'll gift wrap this case up in a bow for you. Easy." All he needed was five minutes.

Zhou's head tilted in consideration and she dropped her hand, holding the gun to hang in front of her. Rolling her shoulders a bit, she whipped around to face away from on him. The lieutenant kept his eyes burrowed on Langston while he tucked his head down towards Zhou to catch her words. He gave a swift, silent nod and made his way behind Langston.

While he couldn't see the Lieutenant, he could feel him. The way you feel a chill clinging to your bones.

Her head turned to speak in profile. "I guess we'll see then, won't we?" Zhou span around while tossing the gun in the air for a bit of a scare. Waving the gun around like a pint of beer before she leveled it with Langston's left eye. "Five minutes."

She clicked the safety back onto the gun and waved the CC guards off of him. "Gentlemen, let's give this master some room to work his magic."

The guard moved back to form a circle with the other guard around Zhou, Langston, and Pope. Holding the Elders and the remnants of the crowd back. Shaking the circulation back into his limbs, Langston took in a quick survey of the room. He was impressed overall by the level of control they could strangle out of the crowd. This was the Command Corp. This is what they did. A history of violence was putting it mildly.

He turned to Pope. The man had his hands cuffed, clasped

in pray above his head. Pope slowly and repeatedly knocked his head against the steel floor. A pang of familiarity shot through him. He knew that pose, the futility. It had been a couple of hours ago when he was banging his head against a table. He shook that feeling off. He wasn't a mass murderer; he had nothing in common with Jamie Pope.

It wasn't clear if Pope was aware of what was happening around him. Not because he was dumb, or crazy more... he seemed overwhelmed. A portrait of a man in over his head, out of his depths. The skin on his hands and back of his neck were singed and black. The uniform, soaked with all different liquids, sliding off his shivering bones.

Langston knew his job was to make this poor fragile lump of a man crack like an egg. Thin shell hiding the ooey-gooey bit of information that he needed to extract while keeping the yolk intact. Reaching into his wrist guard, he pulled out a single cigarette. While he didn't smoke himself, this was one of the fastest ways to a criminal's heart.

Coming down to Pope's level, he crouched casually in front of his prone form while lighting the cigarette. He waved the scent in front of his nose. Like a dying man to water, Jamie's head followed the tantalizing trailing wisps of smoke with his nose almost unconsciously.

With what were the last vestiges of his strength, he rocked back into a seated, kneeling position. Hollowed, hunched body in despair. His eyes trained in unquenchable hunger on the cigarette that Langston held in front of him. Jamie's fingers twitched in phantom reaches towards Langston's offer, but years of conditioning had trained out the mongrel survival instincts in the face of authority figures.

Langston deposited the cig into Jamie's hand and, like the first gasp of a dying man, Jamie sucked the smoke into his lungs as his eyes rolled back in nicotine-driven relief.

It was a temporary and despairing reprieve from what was to come.

"So you're Jamie Pope," Langston drawled. Jamie doesn't react a whit to his name being said. When individuals generated enough renown, enough infamy, people said their first and last names like it means something. This was one of those times. Before today, Jamie had probably never been First-Last named like he was someone before. But now, like it or not, Jamie had become Jamie Pope, a trivia answer more than a flesh and blood person. "The man of the hour."

Pope's eyes were miles away and his pupils blown wide. He took another life-giving drag of the cigarette.

"I'm Detective Langston Aster. Behind me is Major Zhou. We'd like to have a word with you," Langston said. He needed something, anything from Pope. A baseline. A twitch. Something to read. As he looked at Jamie, all he could see was a wash of fatigue and defeat. A blankness that left the man a blank canvas. There was that hollow gape hidden behind his eyes, but nothing else. Pope gave him nothing.

"Nothing to say. No hello," Langston said with an inappropriately light tone. Leaning back on his heels and fidgeting, Langston knew his time was running out. He literally did not have the time to coax a conversion from this guy. He was going in with pliers and intention. "Well, you're famous now. Probably don't want to mingle with me, a sorry nobody. From dome doi to detonator of doom. Those headlines really write themselves, don't they, Jamie-boy?"

"No," the whimpered objection escaped his mouth without his intention.

"No? As in, you weren't responsible for the bombing tonight?" Langston prodded. Again, no direct response. Pope shivered a bit as he rocks a bit on and off of his feet. His jaw clenched and unclenched repeatedly. "Well, then you sure seem pretty nervous there for someone who did nothing wrong tonight."

For the first time, Pope's dancing jittery eyes darted and caught Langston's gaze before hurrying on. "Not nervous. You– I'm–" Pope said.

"Well, if you did nothing wrong, you have nothing to be frightened about," Langston lied. More than aware of the fully loaded, heat-seeking ballistic rounds in every weapon surrounding them. Being scared was just a sign of intelligence at a certain point. But lie he must. "This is just a conversation, Jamie. Nice and easy. Just tell me what happened tonight. What happened?"

Pope's nostrils flared as he attempted to center himself, needing more than paltry nicotine to soothe his nerves. He looked behind him at what Langston could only assume was Zhou. They stayed in Zhou for a long moment. Langston couldn't be sure what he saw in her if it intensified the fear or made encouraged him to work more closely with Langston, who might be the sanest person in uniform in the room.

"Ok," Jamie's assent is more of a surrender than an agreement.

But Langston will take what he can get.

"Why Asa Greene?" Langston started.

No answer. Pope's anxious rocking intensified to hurricane levels of motion.

"Oh, and we were so close there, Jamie boy. Why Asa Greene?"

Shaking his head, he dropped like a rock. Pope flopped forward, forehead first, to the sandpaper rough ground with a sickening *shmoosh*. Pope's bowed form revealed the looming figure of Zhou. She had moved to stand directly behind Jamie. What she lacked in height she more than accommodated for in menace. Zhou's face didn't move beyond a slim, calculating tilt of her head. Calculating. Measuring.

He was running out of time.

Langston reached out to place a firm hand on Pope's shoulder. Steadying with pressure, his large hand covered a huge portion of the kid's back. It was almost like a hug, but it was yet another source of pressure. Pope's tumultuous quivering paused beneath his hands. "It's ok. We know all about the Lavender

Domes. About what he did to you. To all of you. We know about the family you lost there. We get it. Asa Greene. We know all about Asa Greene. But we need to hear it from you. We need you to tell us why."

Sightlessly, Pope's hands reached up and out to land on Langston's forearm. He gripped onto Langston like a lifeline. Langston was clearly remarkably close. He hadn't even done anything particularly advanced or probing. But here was a man who wanted to confess. A feather could've pushed him over the edge.

Pope remained silent still. Needs must, Langston pressed on. "We know you had your reasons. Tell us why."

Choking over his words, Pope's voice was crackling with hoarse, smoked raspiness. "I don't know — I ruined everything. I'm sorry." His words were heavy. Tangled in both a sense of absolute disgust and this empty sense of remorse showed guilt, but not an outright admission. Pope looked past Langston to the CC squadron behind him before he looked back. "I can't help you." But his hand remained hooked into Langston's forearm, his short fingernails and burnt marbled fingertip skin biting half-moon marks on the detective's skin.

Years of training, unconsciously and sharply, drew Langston's attention up. Up to the slate grey barrel of a standard issue CC sidearm that moved into his periphery. Unlike the minutes before, when Zhou pointed his own gun in his face, he saw the finger on the trigger. That was enough to get his immediate attention. Even if it wasn't inches away from his face, as a uniformed Pack officer, they didn't put their finger on the trigger unless they were one hundred percent ready to shoot.

His reaction felt tar-slow. He looked up. He --- was not quick enough to provide an appropriate response.

Point blank. Zhou pressed her gun to Pope's forearm. Click.

The blowback of blood sprayed across him. Langston could feel the **thump-thump-thump** of his heart bang through his sternum. His vision blurred. Was there blood in his eyes? The sound of the scream sounded just like Jamie. It was Jamie.

Jamie was silent no more.

A rough a belch of pain tore out of Jamie. Before both of them stared dumbly at the new hole in his arm. A whistler's round from a CC sonic pistol tore through skin, blood, tissue, and bone in a matter of milliseconds.

The screaming that followed - Langston would never forget those screams. A wet cry clawed past lips clenching in a bleeding bite against pain. The noise crescendoed and swelled. It was like something in Jamie just broke and out burst incredible wails. He rocked back through the pain of a bullet in his arm raced through his nervous system. Pope flailed pathetically, desperate for a position that would ease his pain. He found none. He curled belly-up, squirming in submission, his knees and body wincing to provide cover to his damaged limb.

Langston had realized that he had never seen someone actually shot before. In all his years of training in the field, traveling far and wide across the system, he had never seen anyone shot. All of SI used plasma stunners, and he had never had the misfortune of crossing fire with the rabid ranks of CC.

Shock.

Jamie's screams stuttered into whimpers, which faded to glassy eyed muteness.

The thumping in Langston's eyes slowly faded from a cosmic roar to a similar muteness. He then recognized the growing sound of chaos building in the atrium. Looking away from Pope flipped on his back like a dying cockroach to his surroundings. Where the crowd had once been cowed by the presence of the CC guard, they swirled and paced on the edges of the laser-rail perimeter, fully enraged by the unprovoked violence of Zhou.

Two guards approached them. The Lieutenant quickly injected Jamie with something into his injured arm before his limp body was hoisted up and dragged out of the auditorium by the pair of them with the bulk of the deployed guards.

Langston sat on bent knees and stared at his hand. He

rubbed his fingers together, feeling the sticky remnants of drying blood.

She was crouched in front of him. Reaching down, she dragged her hand through the thick pools of blood Pope had left in his wake. "That's some technique you got there, Road Block. I should've taken notes." Piranha-fast. Her hand clawed to his shoulder with a steady, debilitating press of her nails into his pressure points.

His eyes were laser focused on hers. Her continual cool facade cracked across the edge of a black sneer. Her contempt for him was palpable.

"Here's where you made your first mistake. You underestimated me. I am Command. I bow to nothing and I will eat your beating heart out of your fucking chest. I will win. Unequivocally, savagely, and thoroughly. *This.* This is just a warning. **Take it.** Be as smart as you *think* you are and do not get in my way again. My mission was to detain the scum who killed 592 people today. And guess what? I just did it."

She stood and stepped back from him. His eyes followed her. He had learned the hard way that this was not a woman you took your eyes off of. He slowly blinked pushing through the murky fuzz of his brain. His eyes blinked into focus.

Zhou laughed above him. Langston wished it was a sour, joyless laugh, but it wasn't. It was buoyant and full of genuine humor. He was disgusted by the sound.

A set of guards bracketed him between the rippling rolls of their arms. Zip ties whizzed by his wrist.

He glared up at Zhou. "You won't get away with this. You are overstepping," he said.

The words were cliche and ineffective. But they were the last straw he grasped for in an uncontrollable situation.

A new bellow of laughter rasped from her as she shrugged off her outer jacket. "Oh, no? What? Was I overly aggressive during arrest?" Her eyes flared open in a mockery of shock, her hand covering her mouth. Her point was punctuated by the joint-

194

ripping wrenching of the guards at his arm.

"You have no right to---"

"Road Block, you'll find I have more rights than you've even imagined. I'll be just fine. You, however, are under arrest." Zhou walked ahead of him and the guards dragged him behind.

"For what?!" Langston choked out.

"Obstructing justice. Best of luck, Road Block."

THE BRIG, ESAA SELTENTA SPACE STATION &
RESORT, GEOSYNC - QUO

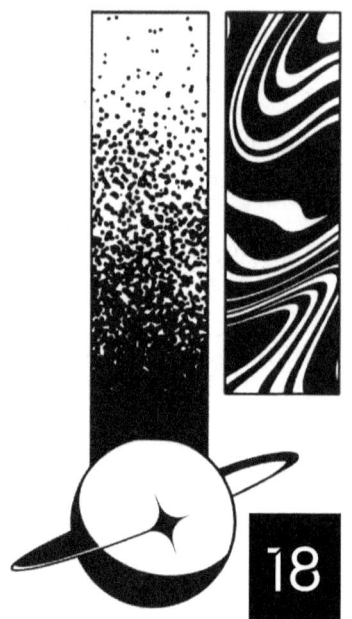

BURNT FINGERTIPS

18

LANGSTON

Now, Langston didn't think his current circumstance was funny…

But… tragedy + time = comedy. So maybe one day, he'd look back and laugh.

And one day he would look back at the day he sat for a solid fifteen minutes, each minute a solid sixty seconds long, with each second filled with a symphony of pain wrenched out of one Jamie Pope. A clarinet-whine before the oboe-groan over the drumming panic. Fifteen minutes and counting before the volume dwindled and the facts settled in.

While Esaa Station was an admittedly gargantuan base, Langston knew there was no way in hell that it would take a medical team longer than five minutes to arrive in the brig. It just wasn't possible. They hadn't come; they weren't coming; they had probably never been sent. It shouldn't have taken him this long to reach that conclusion, but blame, the fall from grace or the screaming, Langston wasn't thinking straight.

So, it was fifteen minutes of whimper-scream-crying that Langston came to his realization that no one was coming to help him, to bail him out. It was just him and the broken and bloodied Jamie Pope in this cold cell. Just enough room for two men and the remains of a tattered ego ready for another beating.

To quote Roar, Vearro willing and the creek don't rise, do what you can't not do.

Langston let himself sit with that thought in silence.

Silence.

No more screaming.

Jamie's huddled figure rocked as he mumbled to himself, "This is no place to die. This is no place to die. This is no place to die. This is no place to die."

Jamie, sure as shit, wasn't wrong. Langston clocked for the first time that somewhere along the lines Pope had become Jamie. Oh, the intimacy of shared trauma.

While it wasn't rare for Langston to be wrong about something, the turn of events since he left Aurora in the lobby unmoored him. Since Hallows. Since discovered a civilization teeming with culture an inch away from his face. Since Zhou proved once and for all that, he was utterly useless. Since getting arrested. He couldn't think. Or rather, he didn't want to think. Because there were two things he should be thinking about.

Option One: make a plan.

Option Two: sulk... Option two had some obvious benefits.

Langston's sulk led him inevitably to Angel, or as he was better known now as Lieutenant Colonel Michelangelo Kos, his first partner. He'd grown up with Angel. They'd managed to be in the same calculus class every year in grade school and then entered the Pressure Cooker together. Langston was riding shotgun when Angel had totaled his dad's FTL rig when they were 16.

At one point in his life, he would've said that Angel was a brother to him. So now, in the bitter crevices of his sulk, he had to admit to himself, if Angel were he there wasn't a shot in hell that he would've been arrested, let only sitting in a cell with an alleged terrorist.

Then again, before Zhou, Angel was the dirtiest officer he had ever met.

So, the irony of him leaving that partnership and still landing in handcuffs was soul-crushing. It was piss in the peanut butter. It was tripping at the starting line. It was borderline too much.

It still burned against his soul that people like Angel and Zhou just rose higher and higher and higher through the ranks.

Angel lived by one simple rule, people are fundamentally no good. While frequently and frankly Langston agreed with that maxim most of the time, Angel took it as a carte blanche to be worse than the rest. By rest, he meant the rest of the system in its entirety. Angel slipped into a logical sinkhole where nothing was so evil or wrong or morally depraved that couldn't be justified by a person's own innate evil. He would frame someone for a crime to call it even cause the lady was an 'asshole'. He had several blackmail schemes running out in the Wilds because they 'would've spent the money on drugs, anyway'.

And each time Angel smashed through justice for his own benefit while Langston did nothing, a bit of humanity flaked off of their decrepit hearts. Yet, because of that inhumanity, because Angel knew how to play the game, his former partner rose higher and higher until finally he got an offer to be a Sergeant at HQ for System Intelligence. Langston was relieved more than anything else. Angel wasn't going to be his partner any more and he wasn't going to have to make the hard decision. The decision to say something about what was the secret to Angel's success. His brother's success.

Several partners and a handful of months went by before Langston got the opportunity to be the commander-in-chief of a VP vessel. He could pick his own partner.

So, he chose Roar, the best person he knew. She had been the one he had confessed all his Angel-shaped baggage to when he was in the red-hot center of the corrupt shit-show his life was.

She had listened - hadn't voiced any judgment even if there was some - and she tried to help.

Aurora was like Angel in a couple of minor ways. But one of the most significant ways was their innate understanding of how the justice system worked. Angel played it to his advantage. Aurora found loopholes to extract true justice.

Where did that put him? Pondering the virtue of corruption in a jail cell with someone who was almost definitely a mass murderering terrorist.

Well, fuck that. He would not do nothing. Not anymore. Not again.

First things first: don't let Jamie die (without a confession).

Langston slid off the bench to kneel in front of Jamie. He gripped his shoulder and pushed the limp and sweating torso up so that he could examine his wound. The scraps of fabric Langston had wrapped the arm in when they had first arrived in the cell were doing their level best. The packing was holding, though. Langston laid his hand over the wound, adding a bit of pressure.

Jamie's breath hitched, but he continued his lost muttering: "This is no place to die. This is no place to die. This is no place to die."

"Jamie, stop. No one is dying," Langston said. "So, don't go getting esoteric on me there, Jamie. It's not a flesh wound but... you aren't dying.. So, just..." Langston's words trailed off because honestly, he was surprised that Jamie was still conscious. A wound like this, bleeding this way, Jamie should've passed out minutes ago due to blood loss alone.

Jamie stared at him, wide watery eyes filled with pain. They were filled with pity. Pity for Langston, which was strange and discomforting. "I underestimated Zhou. And I'm sorry. I won't make that mistake again," Langston wanted to scrub the pity out of Jamie's eyes.

Jamie's hand whipped out to grasp Langston's hand in an iron grip. Their combined hands like a vice over the bullet wound, startling in its strength. Langston's eyes refocused on the blown wide pupils of Jamie. "You already have," Jamie said, his voice simple and steady, as it wasn't in his panicked mumbling. It was clear as much as it was a warning. Like Jamie was trying to protect Langston. The detective bristled at his assessment, but wasn't entirely sure Jamie wasn't correct. Perhaps the warning was well received.

Jamie's grip and body then went lax. Flopping forward, energy drained, and he curled back into himself. He transformed into a study of hopelessness.

Langston couldn't let little things like poignant warnings, hopelessness, and pity get in his way. He needed the Oya damned confession "We are going to get out of here," Langston said. "Jamie, you are not going to die. But there are questions to be answered."

Though Jamie was unmoved by his word, he instead dropped sideways on the bench. Langston had to remove his hand else it get wedged between the metal slab and Jamie's body. His eyes flinched behind closed lids.

"Jamie? Jamie--"

"The air doesn't move," He rambled on, his voice echoey and far off. He wasn't speaking to Langston, he spoke through him. "It's... it's pushed around, but it doesn't move. There is no life in the air. Back at Dome, you could feel a swirling hurricane of life constantly brushing against you. The atmo-hole keeps you connected to the swirling chaos right outside the glass. It was so alive. I don't know how Wilders do it. How can they stand it? The weight of dead air. I can't stand it. Living without air. This is no place to die."

Langston understood on a visceral level. He said nothing in response.

The tide of can-do-attitude receded and Langston rested his back against the metal bed.

They were approaching a full hour. Jamie had napped on and off for just under 20 minutes. Langston had rested his eyes as well. It was a waiting game at this point. The next moves were going to be made by others. Esaa Corp execs might have a thing or two to say. The Pact would act through Zhou. And hopefully, Aurora was working on a way to save him as he sat there uselessly in a jail cell.

Jamie was sitting up again. He looked slightly more clear-eyed and wasn't mumbling any longer. Hands sluggish, he peeled away at his sticky wound rags. By the time, he had gotten through the outer layer before Langston saw and chided.

"Stop picking at the bandages. It'll get infected."

"Sorry." Langston's words had the effect of cutting the cords surrounding Jamie. Immediately, the baby-faced terrorist's head fell back against the wall, his hands fell unmoving on his lap. He wet his lips as he stared blankly up at the ceiling, "Well, I'm certainly good at following orders."

"No, no-no-no-no," heated, Langston stood and turned to face Jamie, looking at him directly in his face, "**No**. Fuck you."

Langston paced the borders of the cell, not sure what he needed to say but regaining the fire in his belly, the fuel into his bones. As he caught glances of Jamie, a wry half smiling expression plastered itself across Jamie's sweaty brow. Apparently, his rage was comical.

"Are you kidding me? What is this? Some kind of stunt? Jamie, look at where we fucking are," Langston said, exasperated. Any effort or attempt at eloquence had left the building. The once put together and suave operator had been knocked down more than a few pegs. Langston was on the wrong side of the jail bars, and he had never been so low. So, yeah, his back was up. He hadn't hopped aboard this rapidly sinking ship for nothing. In the last hour, he had some time to think. To dig into the clusterfuck of a situation he found himself in. He knew where his mistakes were, where his responsibilities and failings had resulted in the current situation.

He was far from perfect. But Xajan fuck, he wanted answers. He was going to solve this case if it physically killed him.

Which at this point, there was a higher than zero percent chance of that happening. Just given his current lucky streak.

"Jamie, we are so far up shit's creek," Langston said. He stopped to stand across from Jamie, making unforgiving eye contact. "And so I'm so far beyond pretending like I don't know you did this. Do I have proof? No. But your eyes, man. It's eating you up inside. How could you do this?"

Jamie squinted for a half second. The sound of both of their labored huffs echoed in the space between them. Jamie spoke.

"I'm sorry. The shitty thing about it is that I've been asking myself the same thing." His hand white knuckle clenched and unclenched, rubbed and fidgeted, shook. "I let them down. I let them all down. I would love to say that I realized my mistakes too late. But, I should've, I should've known better all along. I just," his labored breath faltered. Eyes closed, Langston saw a man before him who was utterly defeated. Jamie wasn't going to get back up in the metaphorical sense. If the med team ever came, they might clean him up, they might stop the bleeding. But they would never get him back to human. This... crime, this sin had scraped away the inside bits of his personality.

"I did — I can't tell whose skin this is. Mine or theirs. It was so hot. I tried to grab as many people as possible and drag them back. Drag them out. Our skin... it's ours. Melted together. Forever. Together. Little pieces of them that I'll carry with me until the end. It's the least I can do," Jamie plucked and caressed at the skin on his hands. His fingertips were warped and black underneath a layer of his own blood. Jamie's hands were a memento of the many tragedies from today. They were marbled from the flames of the fire bomb, soot covered from the ashes that follow, and stained brown-red from his own drying blood.

Jamie hiccuped out a dry sob, disjointed and haunted. He clenched his hands together with one last measure of finality and raised his eye back to Langston's horrified gaze. "I don't have any answers for you."

Pushing back the disgust and pity that warred within him, Langston spat out, "God, I wish I could be sympathetic right now. I wish I could put on the veneer of professionalism and coax this confession out of you that you are clearly dying to tell me but... I just can't muster up the effort. You killed people. Maybe you had a change of heart. Maybe... you know, fuck it. It doesn't matter. You killed a lot of people. Hundreds. It's unforgivable. So, if you are any kind of human at all, you'll find some answers, because that's what your victims deserve. Their families *deserve* answers."

"The answer won't make it any better," Jamie pleaded.

Langston scrambled, wild. Not externally. Externally, he was a rock. All well-intentioned eyebrows, and a firm disappointed frown. Jamie wouldn't be able to so easily convince him that he didn't have a story to sing.

"Jamie," Langston said, "Yes, you saved as many as you could. And I am so thankful. But it's not enough. Cause the blatantly obvious fact is that you didn't do this alone."

That truth froze the tension between them. Jamie's body tightened like a bow. Ramrod straight he got a bit shiftier. His eyes dodged Langston. Looking wildly around the room for escape that wouldn't come.

"And while, I may never be able to respect you for what you've done, your remorse, your accountability is important. I don't think the others are like you. Tell me who you were working with," Langston said, a steely authority in his voice that was hard to counter. "Cause they don't feel sorry and they won't stop. They'll hurt more people and you won't be there to stop more people from dying."

Jamie's eyes were pinned away from him. Transfixed on the upper right corner of their cell. Langston would give him time. Time enough to marinate on his confession. Time enough to consider the wisdom of his words. Jamie would need to make the next move. Langston could hold this space, tow the line. He just had to wait the little bugger out.

It could've been hours, but it was more like the longest six minutes of Langston's life.

His terribly dirty, forlorn shoulders release some tension on a sigh. Deep breath. Eyes to the sky in defiance, Jamie nodded. Langston won.

With a quick cough, Jamie whispered out, "It's complicated. What you have to understand is that there was a plan. It was a good plan that I believed in and started with Asa Greene. But what actually happened tonight... well nothing went according to plan. That was something else entirely —."

The brig door slammed open, interrupting Jamie. A med team rushed into the cell. They had a gurney and several guards with them.

Upon entering their cell, two guards quickly detained Langston, bringing him to the opposite end of the cell. The four-person team of medical professionals swarmed around Jamie. They immediately gave each other orders and worked to stabilize him after more than an hour of slowly bleeding out.

One doctor called out to bring a sedative.

Langston pushed against the guards, tried to strong-arm his way out of custody closer to Jamie. "Wait, no!" Langston said. "Give me a second. He's—"

Jamie was sedated. His eyes never once leave Langston's till his eyes are fully closed.

The words died in Langston's mouth: He was going to confess.

A SPECIAL BRAND
OF PSYCHOSIS

AURORA

O ver two stiff drinks with Azul, Aurora got the agi-heir's story of what had happened.

Azul's story wasn't particularly unique. Nor was it particularly... interesting. It was, however, convenient.

And Aurora hated convenient stories. They were so full of holes. Similar to Swiss cheese. She hated both Swiss cheese and convenient stories.

Azul started from the beginning, from his visit to Esaa Station, which had been a terror from the word go. At the last minute, Asa had insisted that Azul attend the board meeting for Santos Performing Arts Collective, the non-profit behind the theatre company, and the opening night gala to follow. Never one to turn down the splendor of Quo's brightest gem, Azul came prepared to have rollicking good time. He even flew in a day early. Asa, however, was midway through a messy break-up with the Artistic Director and Executive Producer of the Collective, Marius

Bell.

From all reports, Asa had a type or perhaps an M.O. is more accurate. She liked them smart, pretty, and loud. The infamously inappropriate Marius fit the bill. Asa and Marius' relationship had lasted longer than most. Azul added the editorial note that the longevity of the relationship was because of Marius' familiarity with old Gherrean literature. Asa not only shared that passion, but practically spoke in poetic verse. As her son, Azul had grown up listening to Asa read from Shakespeare and Adichie as bedtime stories. Azul hypothesized no one left a relationship with Asa without a few killer ancient quotes under their belt.

Asa had initially purchased the tickets with herself and Marius in mind to celebrate the young man's new success. Asa had bragged that they were the best seats in the house. Then, when the lover's inevitably short honeymoon phase came to a cataclysmic end, Asa gave Marius' ticket to Azul. With a sold-out gala with high-rollers by the dozen, Marius was then relegated to the cheap seats for the opening of his own show at the last minute. It was a spiteful move that was a classic of The Greene-eyed Monster.

From Azul's perspective, he had assumed he was just a prop in some bizarre lover's quarrel. It was then a great surprise to him when Asa started yelling at him. Azul couldn't pin down the origin of their argument due to the boatload of drugs in his system. But the public dressing down in the middle of the lobby during intermission was one of the worst he's ever had with his Am'ma.

"So, of course, I told her she could fuck right off." Azul was always sure to cast himself with as much leeway. "Which didn't improve matters any cause that just set her off more. Am'ma had a fucking fit that I had the nerve to sleep through some of the boring parts of the play, so she decided to publicly launch into this laundry list of all the shit I've done wrong in my entire life. And all of this was typical, cause when aren't we having loud public fights?"

"What was on the laundry list of misdeeds?"

"Well... she wasn't a huge fan of the..." Azul raised a finger to his nose and huffed a bit to reference the drug use.

"Ah."

"But—but, that's not even fair because she won't even let me touch anything in the company. I never invited to any of the *real* board meetings or planning subcommittees–"

"But you were this weekend, yes? Asa had asked you to attend the Board meeting for Santos Collective?"

Azul opened his mouth in response, cut his eyes swiftly to her before he looked away and picked up where he last left off. "She was being horrendous. Embarrassing in front of everyone. Which she *always* does. Page Six just loves us. Cause she'll just scream at the top of her lungs about that one time — one time — that I accidentally pissed myself during a meeting with the CFO. And that's when things got interesting, because the producer-ex-lover-pansy-fucker boy then chimed in with the little gem that perhaps 'golden showers kink' was a family trait."

"How did Asa react to that?"

Azul chuckled. "Not well, I'll tell yah. She basically just turned the color of a tomato and ignored him. And just kept hammering at me. It was brutal... I can't believe that that was our last conversation... We said terrible things to each other."

"Like what?"

"I... might've called her a bit of a slag... she slapped me... I apologized but... I said what I said and now she's dead..."

Aurora could tell that most of what he said was truthful. There was some editing to downplay his own behavior, but nothing too severe. She had him convinced that working with her would serve his best interests at this point.

"And then when you got to the auditorium, away from prying ears, what did you two talk about then?"

The man clearly had a self-preservation instinct hidden in there somewhere, because Azul was thinking so hard it looked like it hurt. Sweat beaded along his face in between the growing layer of 5-o'clock peach fuzz.

"Come on now, Azul. Don't trip over the finish line now. If you don't tell me the truth now and I find out the truth later from someone else, that will be worse for you. The truth now, all of it."

"She... Basically, we talked more. I really still didn't see what the issue was. She said I wasn't worthy of the HausVert legacy. That I was unforgivably incompetent with no hope of redemption. She said... she said she was going to disinherit me. Take it all away."

"Define all."

"The houses, the inheritance, the company when she dies... all of it. All the money I currently have and probably... honestly, all of it could be whatever the fuck she wanted it to mean."

That was an incredibly compelling motive, all things considered. Money motivates.

He had reached the end of his story and his glass of scotch was filled with a fair amount of tears and snot. Which didn't prevent Azul from drinking it. "She actually whispered that she loved me. Said she was sorry... I called her a bitch, and I ran to the bathroom... where I promptly took enough drugs to sedate 300-ton sefaphatula."

He promptly sobbed uncontrollably, which drew eyes to their current situation, which Aurora didn't love. Realistically, this was clearly a time to cry as his mother recently died in a fiery blaze, but try explaining emotions to the rich.

While rubbing a soothing hand across Azul's back, she saw the side door Langston had disappeared through hours ago slammed open. It wasn't Langston as she expected but rather Liya. She was disheveled and breathing heavy. She was frantically looking around when guards approached her.

"But I didn't kill my mom, Detective. I swear," Azul pulled Aurora's attention back to himself as he pleaded his case with an earnestness that was foreign to him.

She measured him in her mind for a second. He simply wasn't creative or smart enough to do something like this. That much was clear.

He was, however, dumb enough to be an unwitting pawn. Or a believable patsy. That's where she would put her money. An interesting avenue she'd have to investigate further. But, from the looks of it, Liya needed her. Aurora needed to wrap this up.

"I want to believe you, Azul, I do. Tell me why. Why should I believe you?" Aurora asked.

He looked at her earnestly. Azul searched his soul, his innermost consciousness, his heart, his gut, and every particle of his being. He dug deep. He had the look of a man who found what he feared he would find. Nothing. Nothing but the truth.

He shook his head and held her gaze resigned. "I've got nothing. But it's true. It's... true. It will always be true."

Aurora's eyes smiled.

Right answer.

"I have to go now. Thank you for telling me this. It's been invaluable. We are going to find the people responsible, Azul," Aurora said. "I promise you."

"Will I see you again?"

"Most likely, someone will be by to get you oficial statement and," — Aurora waved over a server carrying glasses of water, plucking one of the tray and handing it to Azul — "hopefully in a more official, less inebriated setting. Sober up."

Aurora cut through the lobby to make her way over to Liya. The guards were already upon Liya, but Liya, being Liya, was skillfully talking her way out of the guard's suspicion. By the time Aurora was by her side, Liya sat on the ledge of a bench, catching her breath. Aurora laid a hand on her shoulder, a soft rub to ease the tension that was there. "Liya. What's wrong?"

"It's Langston — Detective Aster," Liya huffed out, urgency in her breath, "He's... he's been arrested."

Despite the round-about, less than legal shenanigans they knowingly were undertaking, Aurora was genuinely surprised by this information. Langston had always been teflon. Nothing stuck to him. "Not ideal. What happened?" She said as she took a seat beside Liya, who had just about caught her breath.

"Zhou happened," spat Liya. "She's fucking crazy."

"Well, that's not very female affirming of you," Aurora tsked with several gallons of humor poured over her words.

"Well, I'm just being accurate." Liya sat up straighter to communicate the seriousness of the situation as she met Aurora's eyes. "She point-blank shot an unarmed suspect for literally no reason in front of a heavily populated gathering of civilians. There is only one word for that and it's crazy, Harlowe. It's absolute shit-eating madness."

Quickly, Aurora followed up. "Wait, is Aster ok? How was he involved?"

"He wasn't shot, no. He was going for Jamie Pope when I found him. He couldn't find the Hallows, so I showed him how to get through the bone entrance--"

"Wait, why weren't you back at VP005?" Aurora interrupted.

"Is that really important?" a frustrated Liya sassed back.

Aurora was not to be sassed often, even if she also had a soft spot for Liya. Eyebrow raised, "I don't know, you tell me."

Liya rubbed a face and nodded. "Yeah, actually. Someone is watching you two. There is a backdoor in the surveillance system and someone is only tracking and watching the two of you since we landed. Given your extracurricular activities, I thought a bit of a forewarning was necessary. I was letting Langston know when I got roped into the whole shenanigan."

"Do we know —"

Liya gripped Aurora's hand. "Langston is sitting in a jail cell at the mercy of a sociopath. Both things are important, but can we please get back to that?"

Aurora pressed pause on the lever of the hypothesis whirring in her head. She motioned for Liya to continue.

"We found Pope at the same time Zhou did. Aster told me to hang back, and he engaged with Zhou. I was out of the way observing, so I couldn't hear the conversation, but it was insane. Zhou pulled a gun on him. Like pointed right in his face. I really don't know what conversation they could've been having, but eventually Zhou dropped the gun and I think Aster moved over to interrogate the suspect. Aster was talking to him for barely a minute when she shot Pope in the arm. Then just — chaos. I was pushed back by the stampeding people. I couldn't see much, but I saw Langston in cuffs and getting walked out right behind Pope."

"How long ago was that?" Aurora asked, checking her GIM for the time.

"Twenty mins give or take, once I was clear of the crowd, I ran through the service hallways to get to here."

"Do you still have access to the security grid on your compad?"

Liya hesitated, "Not legally, but..."

"Ok... Tap into the feed and I want to know where Zhou is and how Langston is holding up," Aurora said, before her eyes went soft, a shade, and she truly looked at Liya. "Can I assume you are *in* this now?"

Liya gives her a stupid, silly, exhausted grin. A signature Liya grin. One that meant trouble and home and adventure. "10-4, Roar. You got me."

"Wouldn't want you in any other corner than my own," Aurora finished with a much needed side hug. She stood and shook herself a bit, getting ready for what's coming. "Now that we are both in this. Step one is all you." To which Liya nodded and hopped to her business, tapping across the scene.

First up was Langston.

The security footage had a high angle from the upper right corner of their cell. Pope seemed to pick at a clump of rags covering his wound. Langston was sitting on the floor, resting. So not much was going on on that front.

She did not want to be him. Being arrested was basically any person's nightmare, but it was a bitter one for Langston. Aurora didn't envy Langston the orgy of time to contemplate his misdeeds, real and imagined. Nothing like cooling your heels behind bars to gain some perspective.

Next was Zhou.

Which was an equally straightforward task to accomplish because she had returned to the scene of the crime. Right outside the gate of the amphitheatre. Give or take 150 meters away from their location.

Aurora knew what was going to come next, and she was exhausted. So before heading over to Zhou, she took a second in the company of a friend to let the walls fade a bit. She held her hand to her face.

Counted to 5.

That's all she had time for, but she'd take the seconds she could get.

"Ok... Ok. O-fucking-Kay. O. k," Aurora said to herself. Turning to Liya, she had her game face on. "From now on, you are a ghost. There are a lot of moving pieces today and I can't afford to lose you. So at all costs, you stay on the board and off the radar." — she laughed a tick, unable not to lighten the mood — "Don't get caught." Liya laughed too. It had been a whole day.

Aurora wordlessly asked for the compad and quickly wrote out six names. She handed it back to Liya. "Here's a list." Liya's eyebrows shoot up in shock, but she takes notes as Aurora continues with her list of priorities. "No one sees this list. Least of all the people on this list. I need detailed backgrounds and profiles on all of them. You know who you can trust. Get the information where you can. Also..." Aurora paused a bit. "In the opposite diection, see if you can get any inside help... maybe Rhys back at the Esaa Station sec-deck. Maybe he can help. I want to know who's spying on us, and the easiest answer to this riddle is finding where our sneaky peekers are tapping in. And... and... We didn't have time before, back when we found the soil aerator. I still need the footage of the orchestra pit and stage lip to get a better look at the audio detonator. So, yeah, definitely get a hold of Rhys."

Aurora gave Liya the look. They both huffed out a breath together. Aurora smiled and nodded. It had been a damn day.

"What about Langston?" Liya asked.

"Leave *Lieutenant Detective* Aster to me," Aurora said with a hint of teasing, "Don't worry, getting that man out of trouble is my fondest hobby in life."

"I thought your passion was getting him into trouble."

"One passion fuels the next, my friend. Priority number 1, finding the source of the security feed. I need that," Aurora said.

"Then you'll get it."

"Never had any doubt." Aurora steeled herself and headed over to the theatre doors.

Zhou's laughter was just this side of manic. "If I detain a complete set of SI assholes, do I get a prize?" Zhou asked.

"No, it's more of those sandwich punch-card type deals. You get cuffed yourself once you hit 10 arrests," Aurora quipped back. The brigade of CC hamburglers circled around her. "Nice to see you again, Zhou. I'm impressed by your lack of progress."

"Well then, you are direly misinformed," Zhou said. "The perp is cooling his heels in the brig, and I feel pretty fucking comfortable."

Aurora slow-clapped while shaking her head in feigned amazement. "Outstanding police work, Zhou. Two thumbs way up."

"Walk away before I arrest you on basic principle," Zhou barked.

Throwing her hands up in surrender, Aurora backed up a couple of paces. "Of course, I can tell you are someone who doesn't like to be questioned. Questions aren't really your forte, are they?"

"Stop," Zhou said, her voice booming as a couple of her officers going into lock step to block Aurora's exit. "Spit it out. Now."

"Spit what out? While of course, I, like all citizens of Oya Vearro, am at the complete disposal for Command Corp, what could *I* possibly do for *you*?" Aurora's eyes blinking widely in mock innocence.

"Just say it." Fully exasperated, Zhou shifted from side-to-side, annoyance vibrating through her core.

Aurora's record preceded her. She wasn't ever one to brag, but it occasionally came in handy in situations like these. Today happened to be chalk-full of situations like this. "I'm not a mind reader, Major. That would be against department policy."

Zhou reached for her sidearm and quickly drew it to aim it directly at Aurora's head. Her gaze doesn't waiver. However, Zhou had forgotten where she was. This wasn't Hallows, safe and secreted away. This was the main lobby, surrounded by civvys. Zhou couldn't do what she wanted with little fear of recrimination. A roar of surprised gasps behind unblemished soft hands. The coiffed flowers of the upper crust were simply aghast by the CC officer's behavior. The once gentle milling patrons of the ill-fated opera stood stock still, as all eyes were on Zhou and Aurora.

But Aurora wasn't surprised. Somewhere along the lines, Zhou had slipped her chain of command. She was off regulation and currently making her own psychotic rule book. Aurora knew you didn't keep a dog on the iron chain if it didn't have rabid fangs.

"Don't make me repaint this fancy wall with the inside of your skull."

"Make you? I'm quite sure that I couldn't make you do a damn thing." Fast, Aurora's hand darted out against Zhou's, pushing the gun in her outstretched arm out. The gun flipped out of Zhou's grip and into her own.

Aurora had the gun.

The surrounding CC grunt moves toward retaliation when Aurora then aimed Zhou's confiscated gun below her own chin. Aurora taunted, "I am at your disposal, darlin."

Zhou glare darkened. Her head tilted up a fraction in rage.

"You say jump," said Aurora as she cocked the gun nestled at the crux of her neck.

It was a theatrical move that Aurora had designed for a woman who dealt purely in tactics of shock and awe. The towering lieutenant beside Zhou placed a quick hand on Zhou's shoulder before laughing. "What a pair you make. A special flavor of crazy from each of you."

Aurora doesn't spare the man a minute of her time. Solely focused on Zhou, Aurora asked, "So what could I possibly do for you today?"

"Stop gloating." Zhou reached over to reclaim her gun, only to have Aurora side-step and keep the gun perilously pointed at her own head. Zhou continued to glare up a storm. "I've heard of you, you know. The rumors of the rogue Ohahlian whisperer. The last Truth Seer. 'You better watch out, she'll divine all your secrets.' So, Detective Aurora Harlowe, tell me my secrets."

"I can't tell you where your skeletons are hiding, but I can tell you right now. You messed with the wrong team," Aurora closed the distance between them, breathed the same air as the enraged major.

"Arresting Langston it's not something I will forget or forgive. From here on out. Let us both remember exactly what decisions we made that led us to this point. Zhou, I'm sure that this is *new* information, but you can't just arrest someone without evidence. And I'm not even talking about LD Aster here. Maybe you could get away with these back alley bullshit, thug antics for some small op out on the Wilds. But some of the most powerful people in the system died today. If you think Jamie Pope, that doe-eyed little idiot, orchestrated a multi-ton fusion bomb in one of the most heavily guarded stations that exists, then you better have something to **prove** it. I don't know what you're into here, but pinning this with a bow on Jamie Pope is a mistake. And I will crow from the heavens the second I can to anyone who'll listen. Now, I can't threaten you--"

"Yes, threatening me would be a mistake," interrupted Zhou.

"And clearly, we aren't making mistakes today, are we?" Aurora paused, glaring daggers and ready to continue. It was a second that felt like an eternity.

Zhou's eyelid twitched.

"I am not standing here like an idiot with a gun pointed at my own head for my health. Cause I imagine that like all CC officers I've ever met, you're one of those zealots who thinks that this festering boil of a civilization deserves saving. So, let me make this clear for you: this" — Aurora pointed in towards the crime scene in the theatre — "is a bad beginning. It's a problem. You don't like problems, do you?"

"I've been listening the whole time, asshole, no need to soapbox at me."

"You've heard me so far, but only time will tell if you listened."

"Well, Harlowe?" Zhou growled out.

"Pope didn't work alone. That much is glaringly obvious. I have conclusive evidence to prove that the other assailant is still on station. Now, it took you... by my watch, a full thirty minutes to find Jamie. I'm sure perp number two should be no trouble at all. So. That's all the help I can offer you. Find perp two... on you own... if you can... I'll leave you to it," Aurora finished her prophecy by offering Zhou her weapon back. Gun laid flat on an open, giving palm.

Aurora would give no more than an inch. She wasn't technically on the case. Her partner (her family) was in custody. That fairly obvious conclusion was all Zhou would get without some concessions.

She wouldn't hand them to keys to the universe for nothing. Zhou would get nothing from her. Not without giving something in return.

"I hate you," Zhou said, rolling her eyes and snatching back the gun. With a final huff of aggravation, Zhou knew what Aurora wanted. "I'll trade you. Aster's release for assistance with the second assailant. It's a fair trade."

Aurora swallowed quickly, thankful that Zhou knew how to play this game, too. "The word *fair* is doing... quite a lot of work there, isn't now?" Aurora questioned, "What's going in your report as far as Aster's *temporary* detainment goes?"

Zhou's eyes considered her the red heat of her anger cooling to the regular even keel of homicidal psychosis. Zhou stated measuredly, "The report will document that this was a prearranged interrogation scheme devised by Aster and myself in order to get Pope's confession. Which, if he's as good as he says he is, he will be working on it presently. I have some techs on sec-deck monitoring his progress."

"Good," Aurora agreed. "And he is. He's better than he says he is."

Zhou rolled her eyes. "What next?"

"I go get my partner out of chains and then we help you close this case," Aurora said, heading toward the main staircase and the exit.

"Specifics, you colossal egghead." Zhou called out to her retreating figure. "Who's the next suspect?"

Aurora knew she needed time, so she did what anyone would do. Aurora sent them on a very helpful goose chase. Aurora gave Zhou a deliciously tempting morsel of truth. Zhou's "next suspect" would be Azul Greene. Bless his heart, he'd have to endure another decidedly less pleasant second interview. He was a very promising suspect Zhou would love to investigate as the 2nd assailant.

Perhaps is Zhou glared hard enough she might be able to squeeze a false confession out of the poor billionaire.

THE BRIG, ESAA SELTENTA SPACE STATION & RESORT, GEOSYNC - QUO

STUPID DOESN'T LIE

20

LANGSTON

A slow clap roused Langston from the semi-sleeping state he'd entered while sitting on the cold cell floor.

Langston looked up to see Aurora. She had somehow snuck into the brig while he was unawares.

Annoyingly, she was lounging against the wall that faced his cell and grinning. It was a rare occurrence to see such a wide smile on Aurora's face.

His shoulder dropped about two inches and he took his first deep breath since they slapped the cuffs around his wrists. A sickening amount of relief shivered through his spine. If Aurora was smiling like that, things were looking up.

"The Pride of Gherre," Aurora proclaimed.

He really couldn't blame her for a bit of fun. He couldn't keep the twist of a begrudging smirk off his face if he tried. "Oh, fuck off." Langston dusted himself off and stood up from the floor. Quick to dust off his previously pristine slacks, he approached the bars between them.

He clocked Aurora was wearing quite the outfit. It looked expensive as hell. Not that this was the first thing he noticed, but it was definitely the second or third.

"You look... like you smell very nice," he said.

Another bubble of a laugh popped out of her. "Thank you. You will be pleased to hear that I smell exactly the same as how you left me," Aurora said with a quick, gracious tip of her head. "But now to the more pressing issues. I'd just love to hear how this little escapade is my fault. Cause Vearro knows, I'm the problem child in this partnership, so bless stars and garters, who would've thought that it was you behind the bars."

"Yeah, yeah, laugh it up, Roar," Langston said

Aurora held up her hands in twin 'L' shapes to frame him in a faux camera. "Let me get a good look 'atchu," she said, tossing her head back with a true Aurora roar. Her smile stayed, but dimmed a tick in the silence that followed. She inspected him. Her eyes glided over his bedraggled clothes, blood-stained hands. She took a serious look. "All your fingers and toes accounted for, my dear?" Aurora asked.

"I'm fine." Langston's voice filled with a warm reassurance. He held out a hand between the bars as evidence.

Rushing to close the gap between them, Aurora grasped his one hand in both of her own, gripping his hand to her chest. Aurora wasn't one to stand on ceremony or be overly gushy. She was easy to talk to but hard to read. She was an easy veneer of soft smiles. So, this small crack in her armor was like a vote of confidence.

Looking into her eyes, Aurora saw into the very center of Langston. Saw that all joking aside, this had cost him. She pulled him into a close hug, even with the bars between them.

Her mouth whisper-close to his ear, she promised, "She'll pay, Langston. Mark it. This... there more to this and I swear to you I will make them pay." Her voice still quiet, she pulled out of the hug, her hand still wrapped tightly around his. "You are my family."

Langston's skin tightened and prickled as her words washed over him. He would never admit it, but the moisture level in his eye rose by an estimated 15%. He could feel a heavy beat of his heart pass, especially slow to mark the occasion. Letting that feeling linger: acceptance.

Aurora's devotion produced a violent, heady, drug-like haze within him. Easily addictive. Loving someone like this was dangerous. It blinded you.

He might as well have handed Aurora his eyes and let her guide him through life.

Loyalty was met with loyalty. Honor with honor. She was his people, and he was hers. He was glad that today he had proven his worth to her. He was thankful that she was who he thought she was.

The moment hung between them. Lingered in the claustrophobic gray prison. Their fight wasn't over, so they cherish the morsels of brilliance created from the ossified chains of fidelity they bound themselves together with.

Aurora shook her shoulders and pulled away from him. She stared behind him at the bloodstain that should've been a bloodstain and a suspect. She had undoubtedly noticed that they were down a terrorist. "I thought you were sharing a cell with Pope."

"I was," Langston shrugged in defeat, "I had him dead to rights on his own involvement. This damn close. I almost had him, everything but the confession and his assailants' names out of his lips."

Aurora slapped excitedly on the bars, "Ah, my thoughts exactly. This was never just a one-person job. I have Liya working on hard proof. Too bad about the name, though. Anything useful otherwise?"

Langston shook his head, turning away from her to lean against the bars. He stared without sight at the bloodstain. It mocked him. "I had him on the ropes. He was opening up, then the med-crew arrived. They put him under and charted him out."

"Hmm, seconds away from a confession, and Pope's sedated and carted away. Call me paranoid, but… that's… suspicious timing, no?"

"I can't tell. Yes and no," Langston said. "He was bleeding like a stuck pig for over an hour. I had dressed the wound, but a bullet wound is a bullet wound is a bullet wound. Honestly, the fact that I had so much time with him to begin with was a bit of a miracle. By the time the EMTs showed up, I had half suspected that Zhou was going to let the poor asshole bleed out pre-trial."

Aurora's sassy left eyebrow agreed. "I wouldn't put it past her. But the timing… it's almost like you were being watched."

There it was, the 300 ton sefaphant in the room wearing a hat and glasses in a disguise hoping we wouldn't notice him. Their observers. He waited for her to say more or to elaborate, but there was nothing more to say. They both knew what they knew, but clearly Aurora hadn't had time to dig into that bit of intrigue, either. He didn't press; he moved on.

"Any luck with the son?"

He heard her huff behind him. "It's complicated. Honestly, if Pope weren't such an obvious assailant and fall guy all wrapped up into one, Azul, the son, would be the perfect Patsy. Artfully placed, damning motivation, stupid as a bag of rocks. He checks all the boxes."

"I'm sensing a but?"

"Yes, a big booty 'but' indeed," Aurora said, tapping her fingers against her upper lip. She frowned. "He's the perfect patsy… but I feel like we found him by accident. Like the evidence was all set up to point at him, but it doesn't actually point at him. It just doesn't quite line up…" As her words trailed off, a devil of a smile cut across her face. She suppressed a cruel laugh. "I — I set Zhou on him. Just to keep our faithful major preoccupied while we do some real police work. If she throws out the rulebook like I suspect she will, Azul will give her answers the same answers he gave me and that will lead her right where I want her. But hey, stupid don't lie."

Langston considered that idea: *stupid doesn't lie.*

Every element, every piece of evidence has been singing from the same sheet music. The puzzle pieces were simple and organized and barely hidden. It was difficult to rectify the melodrama of the "clues" with the obscurity of the motivations and overall conspiracy.

"I can't help coming back to this... this a stupid crime?" Langston dragged his blunt nails in circles across his closely shaven head. "Yes, it was clearly effective and a bit... melodramatic, so these weren't no dumb-dumbs. Let's face it, Pope, regardless of his obvious guilt, at the very least, had high-level mechanical and chemical expertise. This was quite literally a hard crime to commit. But --"

"Yeah, right," Aurora picked up on the thread he began, "These clues, veer a touch towards the bizarre. If nothing else, it seems like the Asa assassination element was right on the money. It fits well within her basic bio."

"Hmm, effectively the clues end up being more like schoolyard taunts than actual hard evidence."

Pointing at him, she paced in the slip of space available in front of his cell. "Yeah, yeah. Gotta go back to stupid, right? Definitely has the flavor of technical genius paired with a profound social dysfunction."

That added up. It definitely completed the picture of who Jamie Pope was. Thinking back to his anecdotal experience with Langston, he agreed. "Mass murdering aside, he was a sweet kid. Thoughtful. A bit broken. And in the midst of a fairly unsettling disassociative episode, that's for sure. Oddly enough, I'd probably describe him as an empathetic people pleaser. Which in no way, squares with the terrorist bits but, if the homicidal shoe fits."

Langston sagged back against the wall and propped his feet against the edge of the bench. He watched Aurora pace and glare. Her fingers twitched as moved in front of her in a silent dialogue with herself.

Interrupting her mental gymnastics, "Ok," Langston said, his hands over his knees as he counted it out on his fingers. "We've got the audio detonator, the soil aerator, the video clip of Pope's actions, a partial, inadmissible jailhouse confession from Pope, motive and access for both Pope and technically Azul Greene, and enough to circumstantial evidence to tie them both in a knot and deliver them to SI with a bow."

"I love it when terrorists gift-wrap themselves for the authorities. It's just so damn helpful," Aurora singsonged, but her face dropped into a dry, lackluster expression. "You buying it?"

"Not with my last credit."

Aurora bobbed her head, both nodding and processing.

However, there was only so much overthinking in circles they could do at this point. Langston settled on his own opinion. "I think our best bet is a full confession and the naming of the other assailants from Pope."

Aurora finally moved to the brig datapad screen by the entrance. She tapped away to process his release. The lock popped and the cell door opened. Roar swung the bars wide and presented his freedom with a sweeping presentation of arms. "Well let's get at her."

Finally, on the right side of the legal system, Langston did some perfunctory stretches. "Where's Liya?" Langston said... casually, very casually.

"Look at all of that self-control. You lasted 5 full minutes before asking about her. I am impressed," Aurora tossed her head back with a guffaw, slapping him on the back in a quick shoulder shaking hug. "She literally *ran* to get me when you were detained. Ran. High knees, good form and everything. I sent her back to sec-deck to see if she could enlist Rhys to get to work on our peeping Tom and the cyber angle. She's doing her thing. She is fine."

His lung capacity once again expanded less tightness in his heart allowing for my air in his lungs. He bowed in a gesture of guidance towards the exit, "Well let's get at her," Langston echoed.

"If the med crew took Pope, then he should be in Med Bay under armed guard. I'll message ahead and we can meet the team there. Cause you and me buddy, we are back in action."

21

HOPE

LANGSTON

As requested, Liya, Dev and Rhys were waiting for the two detective in front of Med Bay doors.

Immediately upon entered the hallway, Liya glanced at him — ran her eyes over him before making eye contact. Her gaze, direct and reproving, harpooned his very soul. Quicker than he would've like she turned from him. Look at Aurora and pretended he wasn't even there.

He had some groveling to do if it weren't for Aurora's no-nonsense debrief.

Before she'd come to a stop in front of the trio, Aurora dove straight into details and updates with Dev and Rhys. Talking fast, the two had quick responses for all of Roar's rapid-fire questions. The trio fell into a productive flow. Langston wasn't quite following but it seemed like the tech squad had been able to impede their cyber-stalkers from enjoying the view for the time being. They hadn't located the Peeping Tom, but they had stopped the signal, which was a relief.

"How is Zhou doing with the Azul interview? Was he able to sober up beforehand?"

Langston knew someone responded.

But their response, their words was of lesser importance. He instead directed every sliver of his attention towards Liya.

She stood stiff as a board beside him. He'd bet his right lung that the roaring in his ears blared at a similar frequency in her head as well. They both half-heartedly followed the happenings in front of them, like the back and forth of a lack luster game of youth tennis.

If he reached out he could grab her hand in his. Of course, he kept his hands to himself. But he wondered if her hands were cold or warm.

He stole a glance over to her. Her head tilted up in his direction in response.

Liya's voice was quiet but sure. She said, "Don't do that ever again."

Langston choked out a hollow laugh. "I didn't — yeah. I promise. Never again."

Liya's chocolate-sweet eyes met his own. Her exhaustion and anxiety still shown through. "Ok."

Aurora pulled their focus back to the case. "Liya, I need you to head back to the ship and manage the case files. I want everything in order in case we are able to squeeze out a confession."

Dev asked, "Ooooh, a confession out of who? I've missed so much!"

Aurora ignored Dev with an eye roll and turned to Rhys and Liya. "I had hope Liya could delegate some basic research over to you and your team. Did you two coordinate on putting together a social profile for Asa Greene?"

Excitedly reaching in his pack for a holoscroll, Rhys handed the profile over to her. "Yes! I got a lot of public and private information from the web. Thankfully, Greene put it *all* out there. Almost everything she did was splashed across the news."

Langston looked over Aurora's shoulder as she scrolled through the compiled information. She had given him a summary of her conversation with the son on the walk up to this level. Her basic summary was that she believed 80% of what Azul had said (which was high for her), but wanted some confirmation.

"Ahh, and there's that public humiliation kink that Azul mentioned." Aurora had paused on a clip from a gossip rag publication featuring Asa and her intentionally leaked sex tape with a former lover. She apparently had included the sex tape during a PowerPoint presentation as she accepted a fairly prestigious award ceremony.

Rhys reached over to scroll down to the next article with similarly atrocious behavior. "Can't help but think the dried up old slut had it coming."

Wow.

Utter silence descended. A pin dropping would cause an avalanche in the barren horrific silence of his faux pas.

Rhys had integrated with their team so smoothly that he hadn't even clocked that he was, for all intents and purposes, an outsider. But that atrocious language was not in any way part of the culture of their team. They joked around and made jokes at the wealthy's detriment, but slut shaming is a big no-no.

Langston growled out, "Unacceptable. We don't speak that way about other humans or verbally judge their sexual expression, acts or preferences. Got it?"

Rhys blanched and took a step back. Probably clocking the seven-to-eight inches of height and 80lbs that Langston had on him. "I — I'm so sorry. I didn't... I just. I'm sorry. I'm not a bad person. It was just..."

"Don't do it again. Not in front of my team. Not ever."

Swallowing loudly on a dry throat, the surveillance tech stuttered out. "I understand. I'm sorry."

Aurora hummed, but her eyes were fierce as she assessed him. "Thank you for your understanding. It's just a sensitive subject for our whole squad given the violence we deal with against women."

Langston held out a palm up to Rhys in acceptance. "No shame in not knowing, I grew up in Central Core and truly didn't get it growing up. But once you see the power the words have, there is no turning back. No hard feelings. Live and learn, yeah?"

The waifish Rhys clasped his hand in the formal Gherrean handshake with clammy, shaking fingers. Langston nodded and smiled, though.

"Bygones, Detectives. Bygones," Rhys said, eager to keep his place as a part of their group. He was an odd guy.

With all that mumbo-jumbo wrapped up, Aurora confirmed up with Liya on their next set of assignments. He was already behind on the finer details so he didn't both listening to closely. He geared up for this next conversation with Pope. Langston was confident that he'd make progress this time. And quite frankly, post-incarceration, he needed a win. Langston had primed the pump in the jail cell; this confession was his for the taking.

Aurora finished up and shooed the trio away from the entrance doors of the Med Bay. "Now, back to the ship. We don't have any time for dawdling."

Liya smirked, "Well, then. You better get to work then."

"Don't miss us too much, Detectives," Dev called out.

Rhys feigned a semi-feint into Dev while clasping his hands against his heart in false hurt, "Parting is such sweet sorrow."

Langston rolled his eyes and laughed at their antics. He pushed open the bay doors before heading in.

Aurora didn't follow him, though. Langston went back to hold the door open for her. The trio as gone but she as glaring at the end of the hallway still. There was something wary or nervous in her gaze.

"Roar, let's go. They're going to be fine. Zhou's on our side now. We've got solid leads and at least one bad guy's already arrested. No one else is likely to be shot or whatever. Everything bad that could happen has already happened. Don't worry so much. I'm mean, at the risk of saying it. What could possibly go wrong?"

She shook her head out of a wayward thought. "I--- just... Well, I guess you said it." She shook her head and gave him a grim smile. "Let's go find Pope."

Med Bay was in a state of utter chaos. The small medical facility was way past their capacity and straining under the burden of numerous fatalities and life-threatening burn victims. Nurses, patients, grieving guests and orderlies whirled up and down in every direction, a disfunctional swirl around the circular reception desk and nurses station at the entrance. It had been hours since the bombing, but the med team was still in triage mode.

Weaving through the throng of directionless traffic, Langston tried to flag a nurse down.

Eventually by literally waving his badge in the air, one of the nurses got the picture and directed him, "Oh, you here for the detainee? All the way to the back, the last hallway. The one with the guard." She quickly grabbed some charts and brushed by him in the opposite direction.

The pair follow her directions towards to back. It got quieter the further they made it back from the reception area.

They turned the corner onto the intended hallway but stopped in their tracks.

Where was the guard? There should've been an armed guard at the door. Should have been — as in, there wasn't one.

Aurora quickly took several steps back into the main hallway and bodily blocked a nurse to get her attention. Her SI badge in hand, "Ma'am, I need an answer. Jamie Pope was transferred from the brig up to MedBay with a bullet wound. He's a suspect in our investigation. What room is he in?"

The frazzled nurse clicked across her compad, "Room 2, just make that left and the room is at the back of the hall." The nurse then walked around Aurora to grab a gurney.

Langston leaned out to make a quick glance down the hallways. His unease escalated.

"That can't be right. Where's the guard?"

"That's all I've got. You can find the Charge Nurse or just check yourself but that's all I know." The nurse pushed the gurney as she made her way back to the packed trauma bay. "Anyone from the brig goes in that hallway. The room down there all have roboguards on the doors. Just go check."

He glanced at Aurora and saw the same thing reflected in her eyes. The no-good lurch in your stomach when you know something just doesn't add up. Both detectives booked it down the hallway to the assigned room.

The door was open.

No guard.

No lock.

No Pope.

They stared at the room blankly, stunned. Their dumbfounded silence was broken by the shush-click of the door behind them closing and locking. It was the door to the service stairwell.

Langston raise his GIM over the scanner for the entrance. The heavy door cranked open at a painfully slow pace. They could hear the echoes of staggered, clumsy steps on the stairs below. They raced down after the noise.

Langston called out. "Jamie? Jamie!" His voice echoes through the stairs.

Heart pounding in his ears, Langston took the steps three at a time. Aurora, fast on his heels, they were a half a minute behind Pope. The perp had maybe 150 meters on them, 200 tops.

They could catch him.

Pope slipped out of the stairwell.

Shush-click. The door closed and auto-locked behind him.

Frustrated beyond belief, Langston crashed into the door and slammed his wrist on the scanner to unlock the door. Aurora stopped short of colliding with him. Another couple of seconds of the door opening was an eternity before they were off down the hallway.

The hallway was long, long, long, long.

Right at the end of the corridor was Pope. His sweaty hospital-gown clad body stumbling, barely able to put one bare foot in front of the other in his attempted escape. Langston spotted a scalpel glinting in his hands. Pope swung his arms in wide, loose circles for balance. His escape attempt was hindered by his inability one foot in front of another. Langston assumed that he had been loaded up with a gargantuan amount of sedatives to treat the laser-bullet.

Both detectives drew their guns. They fell into the easy choreography of SOP, they settled into a safe distance to engage an armed combatant as per their training.

They had him. Jamie wasn't going anywhere anytime soon.

The blond detainee turned to his right at the end of the hallway. Langston wasn't worried. Drugged to the gills, he was slow and they'd arrived in the nick of time. Not that he could've gotten far on a station in lockdown.

"Turn around with your hands in the air."

Jamie's hand made a slow slash out to his right. His mouth was moving, muttering something incoherently and too quiet for Langston to hear. He faced out toward the path of escape and didn't even appear to acknowledge Langston's words or Langston. He stunk of desperation.

"Jamie, we don't want to hurt you." Langston took slow, careful steps while lowering his gun. Aurora kept a steady aim. "Drop the weapon and face us. You've got nowhere left to run. We can talk about this. It's gonna be ok."

It was all over now. Even Jamie could feel it.

He'd come in.

They'd get the confession.

End of story.

"Jamie, ---"

Three shots rang out.

Shocked, Langston whipped his head back at Aurora. But it wasn't her. Neither of them fired their weapon, but Jamie was hit by three bullets to the chest.

Every atom in Langston's muscles tensed at once and exploded into action.

There was a shooter in the dead end hallway.

Aurora rushed to Jamie, pressed down on the bullet wounds, administering first aid. She waved Langston on, so he chased down the hallway behind te shooter.

He chased hard.

It was a matter of seconds but the crucial scrap of split-second shock had cost him distance on the shooter.

Langston was going to run the assailant down.

It had been a long day. It would be a longer night still, but exhaustion wasn't an option.

He ran.

He ran harder and faster and without a passing consideration for any but that one driving forward thought. Langston would not let this asshole get away with this.

The perp: a bony, lean frame wore nondescript black clothes, simple slacks and a turtleneck. A full head mask covered their hair and face.

Faster.

He had to run faster.

The shooter knew every turn and met no resistance on their chosen route. Every door was open, not a lock or security measure in their way. Langston path was not so easy. His body slammed hard, catching every corner. With clawing fingertips and crushed toes, he barely managed to slip past every slowly closing door.

The runner was well prepared. Their escape was perfectly planned. Right as the shooter passed through the door, it closed behind him. The coordination was seamless, without an ounce of give to get. So, Langston couldn't stop.

He couldn't think. He ran

He couldn't make a mistake.

He couldn't aim.

He just ran.

There was just the chase.

Run.

One foot in front of the other.

Hope.

Hoping that his intuition and motor-memory were enough to catch this asshole.

Each door, each hairpin turn, was another opportunity to be a second too late for those spitefully well-timed security doors to separate him from the shooter. He needed to be faster.

Push harder.

Move.

But he made it. He kept slipping through a closing door. Gained momentum in the straight hallways.

Until he didn't.

A single inevitable second-long-delay stole the finish line away from him. He was too late. The locked door clicked as he slammed into it. A second too slipped through that last door. Fumbling, Langston smashed his wrist GIM across the scanner to get through the door. An empty hallway.

Not to give up, he continued to run through a couple of

hallways. Stalled and delayed even further by every locked door. Finally, he reached a stairwell with too many door and not a sign of the perp.

They got away.

"Fuck."

Langston's sweating head smooshed into a metal door in defeat while he panted heavily. He let himself take a few seconds to catch his breath and let the crushing feeling of failure rush over him. Once last huff and he turned to go back the way he came, only to find himself in the same endless white halls he had gotten lost in what seemed like lifetimes ago. He had gotten lost in these identical hallways that felt barren and hopeless like this before he had ever met Jamie.

Now he had (probably) lost Jamie permanently. His last hope of solving this case slipped through his fingers.

"Fuck."

The way back was immeasurably longer, harder, and more desolate than the chase out. He jogged lightly out of a sense of desperation, fighting against a sharp, bleak sense of desperation attempting to weigh down his steps. This investigation was so close to the close.

Langston arrived back at the hallways where it all started. He saw Aurora crouched at the mouth of the hallway, Jamie's body supine beside her.

She was on her knees hunched over Jamie's torso, her now-bloody hands brushed gentle and soft through dirty blond strand. "***Eel-ib. Ghoibal āhk al'nixe***," she whispered. Their faces were inches apart with her her ear by his mouth. He could just barely hear Jamie's words.

"***El'esses, ptiāt'hat maāt ka-ib. Pharrjhat ka khet. Hopalo sah oolo im'sah ftem. Hæm khet ānya***." He stopped moving soon after. His body got cold on the unforgiving floors. He stopped breathing that cruel unmoving air.

Aurora placed her hands over Jamie's chest. Her face was sad and cold as she stared down the bullet holes left behind.

Langston took a step away from scene, turning his back to the body. His lungs felt like they were filled with stones. He slammed the side of his fist against the wall. His forearm throbbed from the impact. He wanted to yell, to rage, to destroy. It wasn't fair. He slammed his arm against the wall till it stopped hurting. Then nothing.

Aurora exhaled harshly.

"I called for help. I tried to get... anyone. No one came. I even tried to drag him back towards MedBay." Aurora rubbed the sweat off her face with the back of her arm, the only part of her not covered in dying blood. "I lost him."

"Lost mine too. This is bad. We're fucked," Langston said. He collected his composure and returned back to her side. He held out his hand to her, helping her up. As she stood, Aurora shook out her limbs and rubbed the drying blood on her black pants. Langston cracked his neck. "These coincidences are getting a bit out of hand."

"Yeah." Aurora agreed with utter defeat, her eyes never leaving Pope's corpse. "They really are."

"Our passive observers aren't so passive anymore. These eyes in the sky got real involved with the shooter." Langston waved a quick circle with his finger to the nearby security cameras. "It was like the shooter had the keys to the kingdom. Every door they tried was open for them and closed behind them like it was on a timer. They're embedded within the security system, that's for sure. Everything about this case has stunk to high heaven since we landed on this yacht. Killing hundreds to assassinate one. The staff files. Fucking Dean and the compads. It's all bad news."

Aurora nodded in silence, chewing her lip. "We're missing a puzzle piece and a big one right at the center. I think it's Zhou. Something about Zhou. She has an angle, some motivation that we can't see. And I don't think we can trust her. I think... I think she's involved somehow."

"Hey... You just heard me, I agree this stinks to high skies. But we are all Pact. Not trusting CC is just common-sense but it's a high stakes investigation. Hell, she fucking arrested me and shot someone, so, I'm not defending her... but... let's be frank here, you are systemically predisposed to a prejudice against power-mad psychopaths," Langston cautioned.

"Well," Aurora muttered, "It should concern everyone how large the overlapping Venn-diagram between psychopath and Command Corp officers intersects."

"Roar." Langston shook his head. They didn't have time for this bullshit. He'd been down this road with her before. Everything was systemic. Everything was institutional. He understood, but they worked for SI. The Pact. Langston loved everything, every single thing, about his job. Of course you press for progress, but the job was the job. "Don't make it personal. Not today. We aren't talking about history lessons. We are talking about this investigation today. If I can get over being arrested, well, you can get over your bias. I'm just asking you to give me something concrete. Something real. No gut feelings or intuition."

Aurora's eyebrows leaped up in disbelieving arches, and her face froze in that moment. She couldn't hide the genuine sting his comments left. But it needed to be said, so he said it.

"CC is what they are and I'm not arguing that. But they arrived on station after the bombing. They're assholes who are definitely up to something but they are being led around by this perp the same as us... As insane as she is, Zhou arrested Jamie. She wants this case solved as badly as we do. So. Move on."

A leaden silence hung for a second before Langston pushed through it.

"What about Jamie? It looks like you might've gotten something outta Pope in those last few minutes with him."

Aurora frowned deeply and swallowed several times. She pulled out her compad and clicked rapidly while pulling up the footage for the crime scene that they had been looking at all night. "Yeah," Aurora whispered. She was annoyed, and she was hedging. "I did."

Langston peered over her shoulder as she fast-forwarded and rewind through the footage, pausing seconds before the equalizer explosion and rewinding it. Looking for something she knew was there.

"And?" Langston pressed.

The pounding boom of steel-toed boots on steel hallways sounded at the opposite end of the hallway from where this had all started in the Med Bay. Zhou had apparently finally caught on to the current situation. Her stampeding pack of dogs charged behind them to their location.

Aurora glanced up from her compad to clock the incoming CC puppies. She shook her head and said, "Those coincidences are killer." Aurora turned to meet his eyes. "There's no time... and I think I have it figured out. But it's almost like I'm at the end without any idea how I got there. Lots of gut feeling and intuition, unfortunately. I need you to trust me."

His attention pulled away from her before he could give an answer.

Half-way down the corridor, with more piss and vinegar than Langston thought was possible to hold in her five-two frame, Zhou voiced her displeasure. "What the hell happened here, detectives? I wanted a confession, not an execution." She waited an impatient half a second before demanding, "Report."

Langston, out of equal measures of embarrassment and habit, gave a summary. "When we arrived at his Med Bay room, Pope had already escaped. We followed him down the stairs into this hallway, but he was pretty out of it because of drugs in his system. He was about to turn down this next hallway when an unidentified suspect shot him 3 times in the chest. I gave chase while Detective Harlowe administered field medical assistance. I went after the shoot but lost the perp in the service hallways behind a locked door on floor two."

"Description of the assailant?" Zhou barked out.

"Five-seven with a fast runner's physique. They wore standard deckhand black trousers and boots. Most likely male based on build. Black tactical masks and a black turtleneck. It was a coordinated escape. The locks on the doors were all timed out to assist with the getaway. I lost them, but I know that there were security cameras every 10 meters that should be able to pull eye scans and get a solid ID if not a partial," Langston concluded.

Zhou's jaw ticked several times as she ground her teeth and swallowed before she dropped her gaze and hesitantly gave them the bad news. "We were hacked. All the surveillance for the past fifteen minutes was looped, and we saw nothing on the four floors surrounding and including this one. By the time we realized what had happened--" Zhou shook her head in self-disgust — "Well, we got here as fast as we could. He dead?" She kicked the body that separated the space between them with the heavy toe of her boots. Excessive, but what about Zhou wasn't at this point.

"Yes."

"We get anything new?" Zhou perked up with a bit of anticipation.

Langston couldn't keep the petty in his mouth if he tried. "So, we're a 'we' now?"

"We are exactly what I fucking say we are, Lieutenant. Where are we in this investigation?"

He rolled his eyes, not willing to have this fight with her now. This pint-size megalomaniac had fucking arrested him, yes, and he wanted see her fail and be miserable yes. But on the other hand, he wanted to catch this terrorist so badly it hurt. He nodded his head in Aurora's direction. She was the one to get the confession, Jamie's dying words. Let her be the one to tell Zhou.

Aurora shifted a bit before she clicked her heel twice firmly on the ground. She clicked her heel. ***Heel click.***

Their signal.

Over the course of their partnership, it had taken them a while for them to figure it all out. But, eventually the pair had developed a series of auditory and visual signals to make the most of out Aurora's little party trick. In general, Aurora was... a blunt instrument and wasn't the best option for formal interrogations with suspects they wanted an admissible confession from. She oscillated between revealing too much and just putting the fear of god into whoever she was grilling.

But as a Truth Seer, Aurora's ability to verify the truth and unfailingly distinguish a lie wasn't a talent you took off the board. So they developed signals.

If she cracked her knuckles, that meant it was a half truth. A lie wrapped up in the truth or a truth wrapped up in a lie, but either way a sign to keep digging.

If she clicked her heel, that meant there was a significant lie uttered by the suspect.

So, heel click equals a lie.

Well... she asked him to trust her. And he did. And now she had given him a clear signal for a lie... If he was a gambling man, he'd bet that she was about to lie to a superior Pact officer during an investigation.

Aurora's eyes were near unblinking. A bout of silence hung around them. Zhou glared right back at Roar. Langston closed his eye to prevent anyone from seeing him roll them in annoyance.

"Please continue to speak at a snail's pace. You know how that thrills me." Zhou spat out. A chorus of hollow barks from her squadron echoed behind her.

"I was with Pope as he died. Went through the medical response procedures, but the hack and delayed support response clearly prevented a more advantageous outcome," Aurora said slowly.

Aurora was stalling, waiting for something. What, Langston could only guess.

Zhou's nostrils flared in annoyance. "And?"

Aurora sucked her lips in a tick. "He was drugged within an inch of his life and suffered from what I can only assume was a rapidly collapsing lung so I couldn't hear him very well... he tried to make out a couple of phrases, but I couldn't make heads or tails of it cause his speech was so garbled, utter nonsense... so... nothing. No leads."

Well, heel click indeed. There was that lie she promised him. Because that was total and complete zazaa-shit. Jamie's voice was rusty and harsh, but he was talking till the very end in what seemed like complete sentences. Langston damned himself a fifteenth time for not knowing anything but tourist Kaetyene. She was lying. It was a lie. A pretty good lie, in fact.

He'd asked for her to put the investigation first. She had asked for him to trust her. And he did. But he couldn't help wishing that they had more time to talk, cause Langston didn't like where she was taking them.

More silence hung in the air, filled with the copper, sludgey smell of drying blood on the floor.

"Disappointing." Zhou pursed her lips and gave a haughty final assessment of the scene. "Well, I guess it good thing that we already know who the second assailant is." She nodded her head in acknowledgment and turned to exit back toward MedBay.

Langston couldn't believe what he was hearing. He scrambled past two CC goons buoying in the halls as he followed the major. "Mind sharing that conclusion with the class."

"We are not of the same class, Lieutenant."

She was so fucking smug.

Aurora laughed a bit as she said, "Oh. You think it's Marius Bell, don't you?"

Marius Bell? Langston almost couldn't see straight. He was so frustrated by his lack of insight. He recalled the producer from earlier in the night but failed to see how both Aurora and Zhou could consider him a likely suspect. Was the man pompous, crass, and slimy? Sure. Mass murderer? Well, it appeared that Zhou and Aurora had enough information to make that logical jump without dragging him behind them.

They were both so smug, equally smug. He was doomed to be surrounded by smug women.

Aurora's quick-witted-ness in this moment annoyed Zhou as much as it annoyed him. Zhou stopped in her tracks. Aurora had her attention.

"Yeah, I had that same chat with Azul too," Aurora's voice was quiet, but carried the distance to Zhou.

Based on the tension scurrying across Zhou's shoulders, Langston almost expected her to turn around and confront Aurora. The silence was instead broken by the eight-ton gorilla of a Lieutenant who inappropriately chuckled at Aurora's retort.

Zhou half turned away the two detectives, but she didn't speak. She had her eyes on the Lieutenant for a tense second before she shrugged and nodded. "I think you've both done enough here. One dead body is more than a fair contribution to this investigation. You're dismissed. Again. Your team can help clean up Pope's body. It's genuinely the least you can do."

With that, the CC unit's exit behind an efficient Zhou was as quick and their arrival was disastrously slow.

Langston pressed the balls of his hands firmly against his eye sockets for several long, long, torturous minutes. The door shutting behind CC meant that there was no lingering sound in the corridor except for himself and Aurora's breathing.

This was as bad a worse case scenario as he had warranted to hypothesize on.

Aurora let the silence hang between them. Her eyes were closed, blinking rapidly behind her lids as her finger twitched like she was counting.

No answers, explanations or apologies seemed to be forthcoming without a bit of prodding. The silence stretched and station personnel in scrubs trickled through the main stairwell. They moved with an efficiency around them as they stood like statues waiting for someone to break the ice between them. They took photos for the file while others prepared Jamie's body for the morgue.

"I've got it."

"Wait, what?" Langston's patience was at his wit's end. "Got what? What the fuck was any of that?"

Aurora heaved out a breath and her shoulders fell from her faux confident posture. Her eyes were closed as she started talking. "To make this right — if we... Ok, we're losing time. I think I've got it..."

She opened her eyes and pinned him with the full-force of her cartoon-princess big eyes. "Now, I can convince you that I've got it. I can lay all the cards on the table but that would take time. And we're losing time and... and... I think it's a fair assumption to assume that I would convince you — if I tried — I would eventually end up convincing you that I've totally got this. A plan. A good one. I've got it. So assuming that I do convince you, I will have lost at least 5 minutes of time catching up to Zhou and I've gotta go catch Zhou. So, so... simply put —" She was talking so fast that she literally gasped out trying to get the words out.

"Too late. You are not making any sense, Roar."

She huffed and slowed down. "Hah... You have two options, Langston..." She pulled on he sleeve of his jacket, nagging like little sister. "The hard way or the easy way. The hard way is... well, it's hard, but... it's got a better chance of success by my guess and I'm sure you would prefer it the hard way if I told you exactly what the easy way entailed but... yeah.... Hard way or easy way. Your choice."

Langston measured her expression. Aurora used to ramble when they first met. It was like her words couldn't quite keep up with her mind. With time, after the Pressure Cooker and around her second or third year on the force, she slowed down. She moved intentionally. But this kinetic energy of hers in this moment was both familiar and new. She was alight with the adrenaline of the moment.

She asked for his trust, and he gave it to her. That's how it worked with them. She was damn good at her job. And if Aurora was this on edge, she was on to something.

So hard way it was.

"Ok. You owe me, but sure. Team Hard Way, here I come."

She smirked. "Do I owe you? It's shocking how easily one forgets who recently rescued whom, quite heroically, from the brig?"

"Point well made," he said, laughing before his eyes caught the body bag on the stretcher floating past them. Langston's face hardened into a scowl. "Well, Detective, what's our next move?"

"Go to Liya. We need you prepped and ready to interrogate Marius Bell and get a confession out of him in 30 minutes," Aurora said this while checking her GIM for the time and heading to the door.

Langston followed her. "You think he did it?"

She made a face and tilted her head in what could only be described as the halfway point between a nod-yes and a shake-no. "I need you to get a confession out of him."

He rolled his eyes but continued to follow her. Once they hit the stairwell, which was relatively clear of lingering personnel, she started jogging up the stairs. He paused at the landing, watching her ascent. This was a woman who loved intrigue.

"And where are you off to?" he called up to her.

"To make a deal with the devil."

Esaa Seltenta Station Postcard, 2021

3 - FINALE

(def) 1.the last part of a piece of music, a performance, or a public event, especially when particularly dramatic or exciting.

SANTOS HALL GRANDE FOYER, ESAA SELTENTA
SPACE STATION & RESORT, GEOSYNC - QUO

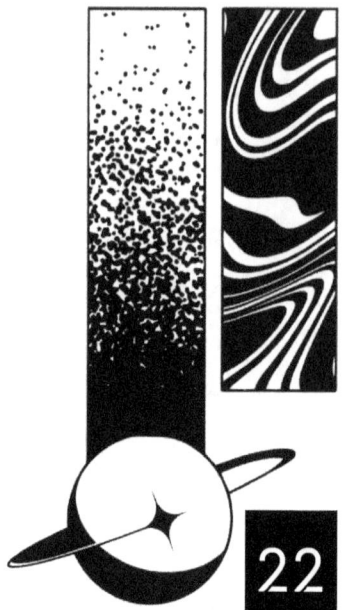

RUNNING OUT OF LEASH

KIERAN | THE LIEUTENANT

22

T he Command Corp squad arrested Marius Bell with their usual level of delicacy and discretion. Which is to say there was none.

The lack of decorum was exemplified by a particularly nasty bit of theatrics produced when one of the pitbulls clocked the producer in the face so hard his feathered hat flew off into a nearby fountain. The volume of the resulting tirade ended in a locked mouth-guard being attached to Bell's face. Bell, cuffed and muzzled, was dragged straight through the lobby, suspended up by his armpits. Zhou strutted behind them, soakin in her victory.

Left alone with the remainder of the squad, the Lieutenant barked out some pointless orders to the remaining grunts so he could get back to his real job. His next "official" duty as a lieutenant were to follow Zhou back to the security deck. Bell's interrogation was next-up on the agenda. It was an interrogation that promised entertainment but no value.

But for the pre-show, the Lieutenant had bigger fish to fry, a higher calling than CC duty.

The unfortunate death of Pope was yet another fly in a rapidly souring ointment.

He split away from the squad without a word. With the relative confidence that the grunts would follow their orders without his glowering supervision, he had bought himself maybe 10 minutes tops before anyone noticed he was gone.

He skirted along the edges of the crowd and crept into an empty corridor on the outer rim of the lobby. Behind a set of frosted glass dividers and waterfall walls was a secluded enclave framed by floor-to-ceiling port windows. It was the most privacy he could find in this venue. The enclave was bathed in a tranquil pink luminescence from Quo below.

In less than a minute, the Lieutenant felt her slip from the shadows to his side.

Cherie.

She looked expensive which was disconcerting. From laser-proof flax vests to a purple shiny gown, her wardrobe change was *weird*. Perhaps weird wasn't the right word. The fact the finery did nothing to lessen her overall air of intimidation was impressive rather than odd.

"Fancy meeting you here," he said.

Cherie let out a husky giggle-bark before knocking his hip with hers. "Oh, you are having entirely too much fun. Hanging out with murderous thugs agrees with you."

The Lieutenant tugged at his CC uniform as he rolled his eyes. "Birds of a feather and all that garbage." A comfortable silence settled between them, allowing both of them to have a brief reprieve. He knew he didn't have time to unwind. No time for meditative silences when things were going from bad to worse.

The Lieutenant broke the bad news. "Dumber killed Dumb."

Her breath hissed out heavy and hateful. "By Dumb, you mean...?"

"Pope. Yeah."

Spine straight, head high, the news shattered the finessed disguise she had slipped on for the mission. The slouching high society snob vanished and before him stood the leader, he would beg, steal, borrow, or die for. Cherie was the architect of this plan, and it was not going according to schedule. Th set back was clearly a blow. Her lips pursed as she takes in a deep inhale through her nose. She glared down through the window at the maelstrom of a planet below.

He understood her frustration. The loss of Pope was not part of their design. Beyond his obvious engineering acumen, Jamie was a sweet one. Cherie had a soft spot for Jamie. Even he could see that.

Yes, the poor dummy had fucked everything up, something awful, but it was easy to remember him at his best. He was an idealist in the gentle way that most people all wanted to be. He was someone who had survived too much pain and was deserving of a better death.

Another silence buzzed between them.

Jamie's death was regrettable, especially considering they still had lingering questions. Why had he deviated from the plan?

Because of his betrayal, she says nothing in epitaph.

Cherie nodded once. Her mind settled on something as she pulled a compad out from somewhere beneath a fold in her dress. She tapped away, scrolling through their back-door access into the live security cams of the station. She found on the camera recording the hallway where Pope's cooling body lay dead. SI was back on the case and they were swarming all over the hallways. The Lieutenant saw her zoom into focus on the male detective talking to some analysts.

The Lieutenant roughed a hand through the stubble that had accumulated across his cheek. "Those SI good-boys have actually been pretty johnny-on-the-spot... I can't... figure out the female detective, Harlowe. She's got something up her sleeve and I have very little doubt that, given a sliver of an opportunity, she'd probably find answers. I can put an end to it, but it's a new loose end. My guess is she already knows too much." He hesitated before he pressed on. Cherie had assigned him this job, needing him to play the role of fixer. And things... were at the brink of slipping beyond his control. "My primary concern is the effect Harlowe has on Zhou. The damnable woman knows exactly how to manipulate Zhou. Which I'd respect if it wasn't so damn inconvenient. If this doesn't end quickly, well... I'm running out of leash."

As a new voice echoed out from the entrance. Hair-trigger response activated, the Lieutenant drew his gun and had the intruder in his crosshairs between heartbeats.

"I'd be insulted by that sentiment if I didn't agree."

It was Zhou.

The Lieutenant moved his finger off the trigger but didn't lower his gun an inch.

Very little leash left indeed.

The new steel in Zhou's gaze didn't bode well for an easy resolution to his plans.

"So good of you to join us, Zhou. It's been too long," Cherie said. She didn't turn to greet Zhou and her voice, despite the words of welcome, was icy and sharp.

"This isn't what I agreed to," Zhou said.

The Lieutenant laughed. "Oh, did you think this was a partnership? Interesting."

His laughter caused Zhou to shiver a bit. Good. She had a stony poker face and didn't seem phased by his violent outbursts as they gallivanted around the station. He had been worried that prolonged exposure had led to a dulling of the intimidating vibe he was going for.

Zhou started again, "There are rules —."

"Not for us. You remember, don't you? That's how you got into this mess. We don't play by the rules. You know this." Cherie's response sounded light. It sounded non-threatening, almost factual. It was none of those things.

"I was — I — I am a Pact officer. I have... a duty. If my actions here endanger the Pact. Our future. I won't have it. You said that we were here to clean up a mess. Not make one. I did not agree with this and I won't have it," Zhou said.

Kieran was impressed. Once she got going, she didn't even stutter once. Bravery and stupidity sure shared a lot of similarities. Zhou was showing a fair amount of both qualities.

Cherie finally turned around. She skewered Zhou with her gaze. "Major Parker Zhou. You are one of our most important Pact allies. Allies work together. I'm sure we can... compromise. Give a little to get a lot. For both of us." Her voice was soothing while her eyes remained raging pits of disdain.

Zhou let out a hiss. Her shoulders shifted back, a tick from tense to standard military attention. "No more deaths and no more games. I want this last one in prison, to be read their rights and face Pact justice. No more back-alley bullshit."

Cherie's eye tightened at the edges, and Kieran shifted. He shifted with the intention of drawing Zhou's eyes to his actions. A move designed to make her quickly do a risk assessment. "Back alley bullshit?" It was a threat more than a question.

"Excuse me. I just — I want order. I want clean, uncomplicated justice. My apologies for my... passion, those were not the right words." Zhou quietly and quickly vomited the words out with an impressive amount of professionalism and terror.

Cherie tilted her head. There wasn't an expression on her face to give away what she was thinking. After an aching pause, she said, "Sure. No more deaths, games or back-alley bullshit. You have my word... Now get out of my fucking sight."

Zhou nodded before doing her best impression of someone who wasn't scurrying in fear. It wasn't a particularly interesting impression.

With Zhou was out of earshot, Kieran said, "But I love fun and games." He holstered his weapon.

Cherie rolled her eyes and turn back to the planet swirling underneath the window.

"So, what do you want me to do about Dumber? Dear Pretty-boy, Mr Cheekbones McGee?"

Her eyes stormed over, nostrils flared. "Kill him."

SANTOS HALL GRANDE FOYER, ESAA SELTENTA
SPACE STATION & RESORT, GEOSYNC - QUO

23

MOTIVATION

AURORA

Faster than a jog, slower than a sprint, Aurora was hustling. She arrived out of breath and just in time to witness the arrest of Marius Bell. Bell was being escorted out of the main entrance of Santos Hall, doing his best to shriek past the muzzle the Command Corp had fitted him with.

Neither Zhou nor her second-in command were with Bell as he was perp-walked into the main stretch of hallway. She'd have to look for the Major inside the lobby and hope for the best.

Aurora shook her head at the over-the-top antics of the arrest as the CC goons dragged Bell to the brig. Seconds after their exit, the last of the laser-rails dimmed out, signaling the official end of the Opera house sequester. Patrons rushed out of the foyer, cheering their freedom from luxury bondage.

They swarmed together as they all tried to exit at once. Aurora didn't have time to wait. All five-foot-four of her forced her way through the stampeding elites. She waded against the converging masses down the grand stair while her eyes darted around looking for Zhou.

Put this down to her overall annoyance at the inconvenience of her current predicament, but Aurora thought ending the lobby sequester was an unseemly bit of overconfidence on Command Corps part.

Yes, Jamie was dead.

Yes, Marius was in custody.

Command Core and Zhou were operating as if they collecting gold at the end of the rainbow. But an arrest is not a confession. Any Pact officer worth their jet fuel should've known better.

There is no victory without certainty.

A smart woman would only claim victory *if* perhaps, let's say, Jamie confessed and ID'd the 2nd perp with his dying breath. *That* would've been a victory for a smart woman.

It was a shame there were not more smart women in the Pact.

Or perhaps it was lucky for Aurora.

Arresting Bell and releasing the patrons on a mere hunch was cocky and typical.

She shook her head to focus. With so many moving puzzle-pieces and double blinds, she didn't have time to get philosophical. She tugged at her hair before checking her GIM again. She was likely five to ten minutes behind Zhou. Aurora was running out of time.

Adrenaline from the run was finally fading from her veins. Aurora anchored herself to the banister to survey the lobby and find her target. On her second or fourth searching-pass over the hall, Aurora spotted Zhou at the far end of the lobby near one of the scenic view enclaves.

The sooner Aurora could get on the other side of this surge, the more time she had to make her case.

Aurora made her way to the bottom of the staircase to intercept Zhou.

"I finally made sense of it," just a hair out of breath, Aurora launched into her pitch.

At the sound of Aurora's voice, Zhou slid into a defensive stance and her hand twitched towards her sidearm. It was an insane over-reaction.

After a beat of tension, Zhou's stance immediately settled into something more appropriate. Which considering her past shoot-first-ask-questions-later approach to Jamie's interrogation, Aurora was relieved to see her hand fall back at ease away from a deadly weapon.

"What... do orders just mean nothing to you? 'You are dismissed' is a full sentence that I shouldn't need to explain that to you, Detective. Return to your vessel. Immediately," Zhou said as she stepped around Aurora and trudged up the stairs.

"Pope's last words. I made sense of them."

Zhou froze.

Stalk still, she stood frozen, either with fear or curiosity had stopped Zhou in her tracks. Aurora was making a calculated bet that it was curiosity. If it was curiosity, she was right. Her plan had a very high likelihood of working. If it was curiosity, then this wasn't a stupid thing to do.

The major didn't turn around in those first sets of painful seconds. The lobby had finally emptied, basically void of people. Which wasn't great for Aurora, considering that Zhou had almost pulled a gun on her not a few seconds before.

Aurora felt a presence approach her from behind. She spared a quick glance to clock the Lieutenant approach from that same alcove Zhou had vacated. Without a name plate, she had to rely on the rank on the Black Badge's uniform for identification. This particular Lieutenant seemed to be Zhou's right hand. He did fairly more talking that the rest of the unit, and seemed to think himself a bit of a comedian. That and a professional lurker, he was a big fan of the lurking. She was irritated not to attach a name to all that lurking.

As Zhou turned to look down at her, her gazed took in the scene of Aurora with the Lieutenant at her back. Her face was the usual mix of disdain and harshness that gave away nothing. But Aurora could swear that she could spot the most helpful hints of curiosity in that gaze.

"Is it enough to confirm the ID of the second assailant?" Zhou said.

Her question revealed her tentative curiosity. The plan was a go.

"It was garbled but… I'm pretty sure I heard the phrase — 'Asa's lover'. He said it a couple times in the end. With the collapse lung and all, I could barely make it out but I'm moderately sure," Aurora said, overplaying he hesitancy and uncertainty to a comic degree.

A relieved smile cut across Zhou's face. "Exactly. The 2nd bomber is Asa's lover. Way to confirm what we already know. Marius Bell will face justice." The major nodded before she headed up the stairs, more assured than before.

Aurora was quick to follow. Forceful and talking fast, Aurora said. "Seeing as Pope's dead, of course, I would be prepared to go under oath and attest to that. However… it's just hearsay without Jamie. In fact, without Jamie, this whole thing pretty much falls apart, don't you think?"

The Lieutenant who followed at a much more relaxed pace behind the two women spoke up. "Give yourself some credit, Detective. I'd say your word is believable enough."

"But consider the mess of it all. Pope was lured out of his room and executed in front of two SI detectives." Aurora shook her head. "It's messy, and it's not a very compelling case. I wouldn't count on a conviction."

Aurora could almost see her words plucking away tiny pieces of Zhou's confidence in her case, in her action.

"And don't forget the lack of evidence, of course. Together well, it makes the arrest seem… well, I won't say it cause I understand… but I'm just not sure that those recently traumatized citizens who survived this attack will be satisfied with these half answers. There were some pretty important people here today. It's always been my experience that important people don't like half answers." Aurora heaved a melodramatic sigh.

Zhou's pace slowed to a stop. Aurora had followed her up the stairs to landing by the main entrance. Aurora was running out of time. If Zhou got past the main doors, Aurora wasn't sure if she'd get any more of Zhou's time. Aurora estimated she had maybe... three minutes to convince Zhou.

Aurora rushed out, "VP will help you out as much as we can. For our part, we can identify that it took at least two people to place the devices. Could be more, but at least two. Now it's a hairy chance that there are *more* than two people involved in the attack. And... with the stakes this high, those chances are a bit too hairy for my taste. I'd prefer a confession. But that's just me. If it was my career was on the line, surety would be something of a personal goal." Aurora could practically see the seeds of doubt being planted in Zhou's head by a chorus of dancing cherubs.

"But..." Zhou whipped around to face Aurora head on. "It's enough. It's obvious. It's Asa's lover. You said so yourself. All the evidence makes sense with Bell. And honestly, how many people on this goddamn canoe fit that description and having fucked Asa Greene?"

"Oh, it's definitely a short list." Aurora's face was placid, but her eyes were alight with mirth.

"No, it's one person," Zhou threatened.

"That you know of," she helpfully added.

Frustrated, Zhou had reached an end of her rope. "Oh, give me a prize winning bull. Only one person fits that description and we all know it. It's Marius Bell. End of story. He had access. He had motive—"

"—well, it is technically a motive provided by a recently-deceased known-terrorist and a thoroughly inebriated, disinherited heir... both who had their own potentially more compelling motives to kill Asa. I wouldn't say either witness is terribly reliable. Without any evidence... or a confession. Well, damn...," Aurora said, full of false dismay.

Zhou was enraged. She was passed enraged. What was slightly comical was that it was that the Aurora seemed to have that recurring effect on Zhou. However, after a night of shenanigans and so many fits of rage that at this point it actually seemed like she was plum out of froth. She was in a dry, frothless rage.

Aurora struggled not to gloat or bask in the general splendor of annoying Zhou.

"I said it twice now, real nice. Maybe the third time's the charm. You. Are. Dismissed. Get out of my fucking sight," Zhou said, turning on her heel and made it out past the grand archway doors.

"You better hope you're right," Aurora called out.

Again, Zhou paused. The Lieutenant walked past and around Aurora to flank Zhou. He whispered in her ear. Zhou nodded, but didn't walk on.

Zhou had the option. She could continue walking down that hallway, out to the brig, beat a confession out of Marius Bell, and get a chest full of medals and awards for the fine police work she did today.

She could keep walking and hope she was right.

But Aurora could sniff it on her from the second she met Zhou. There was a reason she hated Command Core with the passion she did. It was because she understood them. Their motivation. Why they did the ugly things they did?

As she suspected, Zhou didn't walk away. Her shoulders tightened. She didn't turn back to Aurora, but she turned her head a tick and waited.

She'd give her this. As much as Aurora understood Zhou, it seemed Zhou had a similar understanding of Aurora. The major was waiting for the next carefully worded bait.

Aurora approached Zhou slowly, like you would with a predator in a laser trap. "You better hope that you are right, Major. Cause Marius Bell, *if it is* Marius Bell, and remember there is literally not a shred of evidence past a garbled, deathbed confessional of a medically impaired terrorist that would in any way support the idea that it was Marius Bell behind this attack. But, sure, let's say it is. Marius Bell will take a quick, cold walk into some deep dark space. And if he did it, that shouldn't be a problem for you at all... Unless, of course, it wasn't Marius Bell and the other terrorists are still out there."

Aurora took another step up and continued to drive home her message, "Because Marius Bell is an easy fool. Lover's revenge is nice and tidy. It'd be nice if you and your squad, your superiors, hell, the whole damn system would have the confidence of knowing that Major Zhou got it right. Justice was served fresh and without complication. Beyond the shadow of a doubt. And thank Vearro for that, because we all know that terrorists start small, don't they? If this was a terror attack, if this is just the beginning... If that psycho who did this is still out there, the next time it's not an opera house and six hundred people. It's more."

Aurora stood to the other side of Zhou, across from the Lieutenant. They both stood perhaps too close to comfort on either side of Zhou. Aurora's voice slid into Zhou's ear like a tickling wind. "So I just hope that you are right. Cause I am not nearly creative enough to think what 'more' could be. But you, Zhou, you seem like a creative soul. How bad could 'more' be? Do you think the Pact could take 'more' of this? They say that balance is delicate. But I don't know, I've always been the betting type."

Zhou purses her lips and turns to face Aurora, looking at her coldly in the eye. "What do you propose?"

"Give us ten minutes with Bell. Langston'll get a confession. Ironclad. It will be more than enough proof."

Zhou raised an eyebrow. "I've heard that before and been disappointed." The woman just couldn't let the opportunity for a passing pot shot go by.

"Oh, don't worry. Don't think your conduct will ever be forgotten." Aurora stated this simply. She wasn't rising to any bait today. She was a woman on fire. "You don't have any direct evidence of a second co-conspirator. You don't have any evidence.

Full stop. Period. You need a confession."

Zhou flicked her eyes towards her Lieutenant who shook his head. "I could beat it out of him. I have done more to people who've deserved it less," she whispered.

Aurora had gotten Zhou to question her surety. This was a woman who wore surety like an armor. But she wasn't a soft-hand. Based on her size, on her rabidity, she was station bound and bred.

Aurora needed to close the deal. She quoted an old hymnal, "Oya sings peace."

A hum escaped from Zhou, and she nodded. Her eyes were glued to the ground. "Vearro bleeds justice." Zhou finished the phrase, nodded again. When she turned back to Aurora, her glare was vociferous. "Ok. Ten minutes with the suspect and that's it."

Aurora smirked. "Let's do the full ten this time. None of that two minutes and then let's shoot the suspect when we get bored bullshit."

Zhou was off, charging back out towards the Med Bay. "Well, perhaps your partner should do a better job of keeping me entertained. It's not my ass if we get nothing, Harlowe."

"No," Aurora called out, "It'd be the thousand innocent civilians who die next attack who'd pay that piper."

Zhou didn't respond.

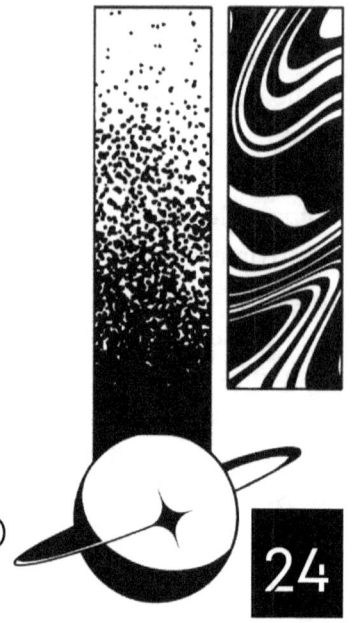

THE WHOLE GOOD COP SCHTICK

24

LANGSTON

"I don't like being blind-sided."

Aurora didn't look at him when he spoke, and he didn't look at her. Tension festered between them. The two detectives stood awkward and tense, waiting halfway up the staircase that led up to the viewing room of the security deck. A dim glowing blue from the screens in the room above cast more shadows than light. The shadows danced around them, threatening consumed them. Langston heard the faint sounds of their team prepping for interrogation in the room above.

Aurora stood a couple of steps above him and stared penetratingly at the wall. She tugged at her fingers in an absent-minded way, not nervous but just barely.

She dared a glance at him before she returned her gaze to the wall. "Yeah. Sorry about that. But... you did pick the hard way... and this is it."

"Do you know what you're doing?"

She didn't immediately respond. He could tell she was thinking over her answer. Her brow furrowed deeper with each passing second. He knew she wouldn't lie. Not again. Not now. That didn't make the prolonged wait for her answer any less nerve-wracking.

"Yes." Aurora answered definitively and turned to look him in the eye. "Remember that... I will never leave you hanging out to dry."

These words both reassured and left a bitter tang in the back of his mouth. Aurora had insisted that Langston lead this final interview. And Langston was pissed.

His anger was to be confused with regret or doubt. Langston burned to find the remaining terrorist. His rage crackled through his blood.

The image of charred bodies would never leave his mind's eye. The visceral inhumanity of it was seared like a brand across his psyche. But Langston was becoming increasingly unmoored by the lasting image of Jamie, cold and dead in an empty hallway.

Mass murdering and the engineering genius aside, Jamie was bright in all the ways that made a person great, but none of the ways that made a person smart. There was a kind of airy, poetic something about him... It was a waste. It made him a useless, used-up boy with more knowledge than know-how. Langston was convinced — Jamie was going to fold, turn, confess, rat out. Jamie Pope was not a good man, but he would have done the right thing, eventually, had he not been murdered. But Jamie couldn't have known his partner in crime would kill him versus leaving him alive to confess. So, now, Dead Jamie Pope must bear the weight of infamy alone. Because despite what Zhou insisted, Marius Bell was no terrorist.

At least to Langston, the identity or even a hint of suspicion towards the second assailant was an utter black-box mystery.

All that to say, Langston couldn't let it go unsaid. "I don't think it's Bell."

"That's cause you're smart." She shook her head a bit and

shrugged. "What I *can* tell you is that for this to work, I need you to make the people in the room see you interrogate Bell like you won't leave this station without a confession."

She didn't say more, but he guessed that meant she had a plan. A plan he couldn't know for some reason. He raked his fingers against his scalp, hesitant but ready to do his level best. "How hard should I be pressing, then?"

"As hard as you can. If you can get him to crack. Crack him."

He whipped his head up to her, tried to catch her eyes. He could see nothing past the contrasting darkness cast from the dim light. This was unlike her. This whole day was very unlike the both of them. There was so much left to say between them. He tried not to be stung that she wasn't telling him the full story. He tried not to see it as a lack of faith.

He couldn't stew with these feelings any longer. Whatever she had cooked up, she was undeterred by his displeasure. While he did not know what was going through her mind and why she was keeping him in the dark, he was just going to trust her. Like he anxiously hoped she was trusting him.

He trudged up the stairs past her. She said nothing more. Aurora just followed him like a shadow.

The room was more of a stage at this point. A careful mirage produced to instill fear and paranoia into the suspect. Light creeped through the crevice and highlighted the battle-smudged, bags-under-eyes exhaustion on the faces of the gathered cavalry.

Zhou had wanted everyone present to witness the full impact of their "collective" evidence against this last suspect in their investigation. So she gathered the collected force of the complete investigative unit of VP005 and the Command Corp squad came together at last. Clearly, Zhou was also of the mind that the show of force was of additional benefit as supplementary evidence, as well as a helpful little intimidation tactic. She'd arranged the gathered agents into a seamless wall of uncompromising justice. Beefcakes and investigators shoulder to meaty, uncompromising shoulder. Its melodrama and presentation were perhaps a bit much, but Langston couldn't protest, as he knew that such showmanship would be effective in today's unfortunate audience.

Marius Bell.

Langston took his position. A nod from him signaled the start of the action. The muzzled executive producer was dragged in from the back holding cell. His stuttering breaths and fumbling feet were the only sound in the room.

This was the main course. And the gallery was hungry. Gone were the doldrums of typing and whirring of machines. All screens were off, all eyes were on Bell for the big interrogation.

Langston remembered the pompous producer from when they had first met at the crime scene. The posturing, the peacock feathers, the sleaze, were hard to forget. All of that was gone now. Ironically, since they'd last met, Langston and Marius actually had something in common. CC had arrested them. It had humbled them both. But perhaps, like Langston, it was an unjust arrest for Bell as well.

He pressed the muscles in his should back and down, re-centering himself in the here and now.

Bell's eyes darted across the room like nervous pickering seerkats; his pupils dilated to the size of needlepoints. The wall of glowing holoscreens reflected off the beading sweat on his upper lip and forehead in a pale yellow-blue sheen.

Aurora had worked with Rhys to compile a series of images and clips from the bombing to use during the interrogation. Rhys has specifically stitched together all the camera angles to give them an immersive 360 degree image of two stills from footage. He had used a software that allowed you to toggle through the actual image in a pseudo 3-dimensional walkthrough. With the complete picture in view, the puzzle pieces slid fatefully into place.

Bell sat in a steel chair in the center of the room, his cuffs chained to a loop on the ground, across from another chair that sat empty. Langston stood stalwart behind the chair, with Aurora barely a meter behind them. About 3 rows of Pact officers caged them in a 3-sided semi-square shape around the holo screen.

The stage set. The interrogation began.

Langston pulled the chair back a bit to sit down across from Bell. Aurora walked behind Bell to remove the gag before returning the sentry behind her partner.

Langston let him stew in the silence for an eternity of seconds. Leaning back in his chair, the interrogator's face remained impassive while Bell's breathing eventually evened out without the muzzle. The suspects anxious remained at peak freak out mode.

"How are you doing over there, buddy?" Langston kept his tone friendly, but his features were hard and impassive.

Bell's eyes zapped to Langston. "I'm not supposed to be here. You've made a mistake."

"What mistake?" Langston tilted his head. He made his expression and movements carefully blank to lure Bell into a bear-trap of false curiosity and open intentions.

"Well, whatever happened that made you think I need to be here is clearly a fucking mistake. I'm not angry. We all make mistakes." Bell shifted to the edge of his seat as far as the chain would allow him. He teetered on the edge of his naturally caustic personality and an ingrained self-preservation instinct that everyone in the Oya Vearro system had learned because of Command Corps method. Every muscle in this arm flexed and shook with tension. His eyes focused on Langston like a lifeline, while remaining perpetually aware of the bulldogs that surrounded them. "Really, it's ok. It happens but — But — You've gotta — I need to. Please. I can't be here."

"You were pretty insistent earlier that we should've ended the lockdown. Let everyone go about their days. That begs the question: if you're not supposed to be here, then where are you supposed to be?"

"Not fucking here."

Langston shifted forward. From a relaxed lean to a seated position where Bell was the center of his complete focus. "I'm in a rough spot here. It's not just the Esaa Corp looking for answers, it's System Intelligence, it's CC. It's the Pact in its entirety. The whole Pact needs to know what happened here. I'm sure you do too, right? I know what this show must've meant to you, Marius. What it must've cost you. All the effort you put into both the art and the audience. From all reports, you are a brilliant producer. You've gotta help us out here. Cause we have questions and we knew you would be the best person to ask. It's a very serious investigation, so please excuse my friends for their… enthusiasm."

Bell breathed deeply and nodded along as Langston spoke. His panic visibly draining from him with each of Langston's words to be replaced by a heady sense of importance and righteousness. The whole "Good Cop" schtick wasn't necessarily his favorite technique, but when dealing with suspects who had the misfortune of slipping into CC's good graces, there was rarely an alternative option. So, Good Cop would take the day today.

"What's your official role as far as this production goes?" Langston asked.

Sniffing away at some of the snot that had accumulated on the edge of his nose because of all the sobbing, Marius fixed himself up. His eyebrows adopted a superior slope. "Officially, I am the executive producer of tonight's entertainment as well as the Creative Director for the Santos Arts Collective, which is the nonprofit that operates the Santos Opera House."

"When did you arrive at Esaa Seltenta Station?" Langston asked.

"Over three and a half months ago."

"Why?"

Bell visibly gulped before he answered. "I was helping out with the final financing options and dealing with some actor's contract issues."

"Are you ***proud*** of the work you did here?"

Bell remained slightly on edge based on that question, but answered. "I guess you can say that. Overall, I'm immensely proud of all the work that the Santos Art Collective has undertaken."

"Of course." Langston looked down at the papers on his laps in an effort to nonchalantly utter this next little breadcrumb. "You should be proud. *Happy* even, by all your work."

"Yeah... I guess you can definitely say that."

Behind him, Aurora cracked her knuckles. A Signals.

Cracking her knuckles meant that the truth was a bit wobble-dy in order to help Langston seamlessly navigate the interview.

The timing of their Signal was never precise because Langston had to do interpretation on the fly.

Based on the context here, it could mean 1 of two things. Option One: Bell's early arrival was outside of the norm or standard procedure. Interesting. Something he could work with and on. Option two: the calling back to the phrasing of the terrorists calling card using the phrase "proud versus happy" flared some recognition in Bell. While perhaps it did immediately raise the red-flag-I'm-guilty-o-meter but it warranted further questioning. Perhaps there was also a third option. That both were true. His early arrival was in some way suspect and... repeating that section of the murder's calling card did resonate with Bell.

Langston pressed deeper. "Did you notice anything significant concerning the auditorium, its security or the venue in general prior to tonight?"

"Yes, in fact, everything was just awful," Bell's nose tipped up as he side-eyed some of the assembled ranks. "About 3 weeks after I arrive, those Wilder pissants go on strike and all hell-breaks loose. Now, I'm not one to speak out of turn, but clearly every competent roughneck worth a damn has a high sense of moral integrity. Because, my god, the incompetence of the scabs they brought in was just horrendous. In fact, knowing what I know now it seems inevitable once you let untrained trash in that the whole production goes up in flames."

"What is your relationship with Asa Greene?"

Bell's face blanked out in surprise, completely caught off by the shift in direction. He coughed out. "Uh-what?"

Langston gave a cursory look down at the file folder sitting uselessly on his lap, giving the impression that this was a perfunctory question. "Asa Greene. What was your relationship with Asa Greene?"

"She was… she was a newer member of the board of directors." Bell's words were measured as he looked at Langston's hands and nodded to himself. "And, I think — I think she was at the show tonight. Yes, I saw her…. during intermission. Nice enough lady. We've met before."

There were several poorly concealed coughs from the peanut gallery. Some of the undersexed, overworked surveillance staff had discovered that there were a couple of sex tapes available in the Asa Greene's social profile. Sex tapes featuring the one and only Marius Bell in flagrante delicto with Greene. They had been gleefully watching the tapes and critiquing them with gusto until The Socrates squad had arrived to prep for interrogation. Their lack of professionalism was not appreciated.

Having heard these unsubtle chuckles at his expense, Bell jutted his chin forward obstinately. He calmed in a way, thickened his skin, ready for 1,000 cuts. Or, from Langston's perspective, all the work he had just put in to lower the man's defenses was now

"What is this about? Why are you asking about Asa?"

Langston gave him nothing. "I think it would be best for both of us if you left the question asking to the professionals. Tell me about the last conversation you had with Asa."

Bell's hands jerked up to his face to wipe away the gallons of sweat that accumulated there, only to be stopped by the cuffs. Because Bell was chained to the floor. He didn't have the option of not answering. Even his silence was just a token protest.

Langston repeated: "Tell me about the last conversation you had with Asa."

His eyes were closed, lids fluttering rapidly. "We didn't talk necessarily. Asa was gloating. She had to make sure I knew that she'd won."

Langston leaned forward. This was progress. "Gloating

how?"

Marius' sigh was tinged with shame. "She shopping for a new toy."

Now was not a time for half truths of unstated ambivalence. Langston needed direct answers. "To use your language, who was her last 'toy'?"

"I--" Marius stuttered and looked Langston directly in the eye. There was a soft sort of gentle hatred and apathy in his gaze. Like a trapped animal who knew that wriggling only meant pain, not freedom. "Me. It was me. Toy is perhaps... a polite but realistic term for our relationship."

But Langston had his orders, his role to play in this clear charade. Break him, she said. "So, you didn't directly speak to Asa at all tonight?"

"No."

"Were you on good terms with Greene?"

Trapped like an animal, Marius weighed his options but ultimately admitted. "It's complicated."

"I see," finished Langston. He shuffled through the file on his lap, giving Marius the time to fill the silence, which he did.

"No, you don't — you don't get it." Marius' hands fluttered as he meaninglessly implored Langston, "Yes, Asa was an asshole. And, yes, it's complicated because I swear we were on good terms. Asa took pleasure in using and abusing people. It's just what she did. I've been around enough times to know she has a gambit. I wasn't surprised or upset when she did it to me. I read the gossip rags. I've seen her do it before. She plucks out nimble young men from nowhere and gives them the world. It's what she does, it was she's always done. Did I think I was special, going to break the mold? Yes, of course. I'm a hopeless romantic. And love isn't logical. But I knew her MO. I knew what was coming. Asa basically gets off on public humiliation. It was better than sex for her. But that was fine for me. I genuinely didn't give a shit. I swear."

"This humiliation routine. She did this to you? When? At the board meeting before the premiere?" Langston asked.

Marius blew out a dejected breath. "Hmm, yes and no. We had a big blowout on vacation about three and a half months ago. It ended with her kicking me out. I had nowhere else to go, so I came here. I thought she was going to pull funding from the collective. A final 'fuck you'. So, at the board meeting. Honestly, I was just thankful that it was just more gloating… It wasn't, well, it was, but. It… It was just what she did. The revenge porn was nothing. But if she had pulled funding for the show, it would've destroyed me. But Asa kept her words so we were just fine."

Langston could feel the desperation pour out of Marius, but he kept on pressing. "Are you implying that Asa was bribing you? Is that why you resented her?"

A quick, hoarse laugh burst like a dam in Marius's chattering teeth. He cannot believe he is in this situation. "Not enough to kill seven hundred fucking people, that for damn sure."

"Maybe enough to help someone else plant the bomb to kill seven hundred people."

"No!" The word shot out of Marius like a fish gasping for water. He searched for any inch of leniency in Langston's eyes and found nothing. Droplets of sweat collected on his upper lip. He explained, "This was my night! It wasn't about Asa, or my feelings for her, or anything. It was about the triumph of 'An Inch of Flesh'. I wouldn't have ruined this night for anything," Marius finished on a half-choked sob. Fists clenched knuckles-white in their cuffs, he looks down at his hands as fury sparked then died within him. "This was my night."

Marius was clearly performative and dramatic. While being a bit of a ham would lend towards a talented liar. But this was not a lie. He glanced back at Aurora. He had seen enough footage of a false confession to know that he was on the precipice here. A couple of psychological nudges here, twisted words there. All that in combination with the actual horror Marius probably experienced in the "care" of the CC squadron. He was at the bend before the break.

Aurora's eyes are sharp and predatory, but they were not

trained on Marius or himself. Her attention was pulled. Curious. Whatever her plan was, she wasn't ready to reveal it to him or anyone else. And so here he sat... with the innocent Marius Bell and instructions to crush his resolve.

"So, you arrived at Esaa Station three and a half months ago after Greene publishes your sex tapes and kicks you out. The labor strikes result in a degradation of security procedures. The day before the show, Greene again humiliates you on your own turf. Is that accurate?"

Marius muttered out a slim agreement, bereft of much of his former hoighty physical vitality.

Langston turned to the holo projection behind him. He clicked a few buttons, pulling up a close-up image of Marius' face in his former glory, bedecked in peacock's feathers but not self-assured, not victorious. He looked only slightly less petrified that he did now (facing an interrogations for terrorist charges). "So. What are you doing here?"

The image zoomed out a tick to reveal Marius hovering in the shadow of the pews and biting fingernails in anxiety.

"I don't know. Being nervous and looking fabulous."

"I agree. You do look nervous. One would think, it's your big night, perhaps you would look proud on your big night. Perhaps even happy. Proud and happy."

Click. The footage then zoomed out to give a wider view of the scene. It was the moments before the bombing at the top of the Second Act when the lights were dimmed. The framing was such that you could see exactly what Bell was staring at nervously. Directly in Bell's crosshairs was one Asa Greene.

The clip played through for Bell. The footage played in the empty silence of the room. Just the sound of heavy breathing to score the dramatic replay of the crime. The angle of the footage was from across the seating section, so Asa and Bell were in frame, but not much else. Bell's face was shadowed, but visible. His furrowed brow and gnawing mouth working at a pace. Then an enormous smile slid across Marius' face. And the bomb exploded.

Then there is silence.

Marius pulled his eyes from the screen in genuine confusion. "Is there more? Is this all the evidence you got?"

Marius scoffed, completely flabbergasted by what he's just seen. Langston can't really blame him. It was indeed flabbergastingly circumstantial evidence.

He saw Zhou shift uncomfortably to his right.

"All of this, because of that?! I'm not staring at Asa, you neanderthal. I'm staring at the general fucking audience, gauging their reaction. Getting a feel for the room. This is the big scene. I wanted to observe how the aria landed so I could report back during Post-Show Notes for the cast."

Langston rewound the tape to where Marius's grin overlapped with the first explosion. "We need an explanation why you are gleefully smiling while you stared at the soon-to-be-assassinated victim while the first bomb detonates during your big scene. The soon-to-be-assassinated victim who had spent the last several months humiliating you."

Marius clucked a bit in complete speechlessness.

"Explain why you are 'strategically' out of range for both blast zones with enough of a running start to 'luckily' escape untouched by the imminent carnage."

Marius frantically cried out, "I wouldn't call it luck. It... it was a coincidence. I— I wouldn't hurt Asa. I wouldn't hurt anybody. This just looks bad!"

"Really?!" Langston approached the man. His sharp features marked by bruises, sweat and panic. "That's your best defense. It just looks bad?"

Marius curled his body down to hide his face behind his cuffed hand, shaking back and forth. With a harsh measured exhale, "She was a fucking investor," Marius said. "This theatre, this work is my very soul. I would never do anything to harm that. I would never kill an investor. I couldn't kill anyone. I wouldn't kill hundreds. Please."

"Of course, you wouldn't orchestrate an elaborate plot to

get this performance at the top of every newspaper in the system. You would never do that. And remember, love isn't logical, is it, Marius?" Langston pushed hard on the suspect. He squatted down in front of Marius to get his full attention. "I'm not proud, but I am happy". What does that phrase mean to you?"

A tear mixed with the sweat and slipped down his jawline. Marius shook his head. Langston wavered in his belief in Marius' innocence. Because that tear was damning.

Marius knew that phrase. He had a connection to it.

Langston reached into the file and pulled out a clear picture of those words painted in front of Asa's seat. He held the image in front of Bell and it was like an invisible force punched him right in the gut. Marius Bell had been showing the gamut of facial expression depicting pure terror throughout the interrogation, but there was a certain desolate twinge to his current expression. He knew this phrase. This phrase connected him to Asa.

"This was the last thing Asa Greene ever saw. This is evidence. This was left by the terrorist at the scene of the crime. If you know its significance, tell me now. Your time is running out. Because the list of people who wanted Asa Greene dead is long. The list of people capable of such an act of violence is short. The list of people who know the significance of this phrase wanted Asa dead and are capable of such brutality... for your future, I hope that list doesn't include you. Help me. What does it mean?"

He hung his head in utter desolation and shook his head, unwilling to say another word.

"Or did you really just want to get rid of Asa the second she had lived out her usefulness? Is that right?" Langston asked, his voice now soft and cajoling.

"I — Please, I just," Marius Bell had no more explanations, no more words.

Langston needed a confession. Not details of the crime (because he is sure Marius didn't know details) but an acceptance of guilt. That's what all the best false confessions were made of. Langston choked back the bile of his own actions and pushed forward. "You just wanted what? Revenge? Closure? Vindication? What did you just want? Did you want to be happy?" Langston took a hold of the cuffed hands and brought them away from Marius' face. "You did this."

"No," the producer whispered.

"Look at you," the detective moved beside Bell and pointed up to the screen, to the damning smile. He held Marius' jaw captive, so he was forced to look at the screen. "You watched your carefully orchestrated plot fall into place, all the puzzle pieces aligning, stage direction, bringing each element into place. Jamie, on the other end, ushering the house crew to safety. Careful that no one that you actually care about is injured."

"No. No," confused and desolate, the tears poured out of Marius' eyes.

Langston closed his eyes. He kept his face turned to the on the screen. Not on Aurora, not on Marius, just on the screen so he could keep pushing like it was an exercise back at the Pressure Cooker.

He could keep pushing. He could get Marius to confess right now. A good investigator knows when they've got someone past the point of reason into the territory of pure unadulterated fear. Where there is no exit, no way out, just the authority of his position and the suspect. However, a confession wouldn't be what he would be getting out of Marius.

He knew bone deep that this wasn't right.

Zhou would be satisfied with this confession. Colonel Dean might be too. SI and CC would join hands and sign a happy little diddy that this investigation was wrapped up within a thirty-hour day cycle on Quo.

Without a doubt, Langston knew he could push this shivering mess of a human to say the words and accept responsibility for these crimes. It wouldn't be a confession. It wouldn't be the truth.

It sure as hell wouldn't be justice.

He looked at Aurora one last time.

She had pushed for this. Pushed hard. He had seen her, backed her up as she used most of the tricks in her tricky little pocket to mold Zhou into agreeing to VP005's final interrogation. She had the new evidence, the fresh cuts of the footage that reveal new angles and hidden views of the crime.

She had pushed for this conversation to happen this way and with these people and he hadn't the foggiest idea what was going through her mind.

Langston wasn't a dummy, but he had nowhere near the raw analytical brain power that Aurora did.

If he had serious doubt, close to straight up disbelieving Bell's guilt, he was absolutely convinced that Aurora had exculpatory evidence.

She met his gaze finally. Her lips were a grim line of determination. She nodded at him. Aurora played games upon games, but perhaps now was the time for her to reveal her cards.

She stepped forward into the yellow-blue light, away from where the assembled force stood.

25

VANITY

LANGSTON

"No, Marius, you're right." Aurora leaned forward to lay a gentle hand on his face.

Her dark finger swiped away a tear from his cheek. She frowned at the suspect in a way that was sweet, almost. It was considering comfortingly. She hitched her head to the right to motion Langston out of her way. The lead detective rose out of his seat, handed her the remote to the surveillance footage and gleefully retreated to her vacated space among the rest of the squad.

"Whoever did this, their wounds were raw and unstable. You are too much of a realist. The person who did this didn't know what Asa was like. Not like you. They didn't fly in the same circles as you. They didn't expect her melodrama. No, in a lot of ways, they were not like you at all. The person who did this wanted to hurt Asa, wanted to hurt something she loved. And from what Azul told us, she did legitimately love your production and this Opera House. No. But I suspect the true culprit wanted to be there to see her take her last breaths."

Sharply, Aurora stood and walked away from Marius towards the wall of monitors. "Rhys?" she called out.

He eagerly stepped forward, his face an open and helpful plateau. Still the perfect little helper. His shiny black hair, still coiffed without a hair out of place. "Yes, Detective?"

"Did you notice anything out of the ordinary between the start of intermission and the detonation?"

"No, sir," Rhys answered with a hint of confusion, "I would've immediately noted it in my log."

"Oh," Aurora said. Her face transformed into a textbook expression of confusion. It was a false expression, as much as her surprise was obviously false.

Aurora was up to something. Langston's gaze shifted as he played back her words in his head. She was onto something, and he'd definitely missed it.

The Truth Seer frowned, but she kept her back to Rhys. Her words were clearly meant for him still. "But you weren't taking a log during the bombing."

"Sir?"

Standing close to the holos, Aurora pressed a series of button on the remote. The screen flashed backwards and forwards, zoomed in and out before it settled on a giant still of the entire Opera Hall in the seconds before the bomb. They still captured every detail of the auditorium from behind the stage to the entrance doors. And right then, Langston saw the full picture, the last puzzle piece finally slotting into place.

It was the footage they had been staring at all day. But it was a jumbled mishmash of angles. It was a bird's eye view from a slightly wider lens than Langston had previously seen.

In the early stages of the investigation, they'd rushed. They'd cobbled together as many angles and options as available. They'd made do and made excuses.

This new fully compiled image revealed the gooey center between the mystery of this case. Aurora zoomed in on the silver of space between the orchestra pit and the front row of the audience. It was perhaps a five foot section of carpet. Likely, it was a blind spot for at least of couple of security cameras in the auditorium.

Because, clear as day, front and center, was Rhys stood in the center of the Opera Hall just out of range of every bomb that would detonante in mere seconds.

"That's you, isn't it?" Aurora asked, her inquisitive voice deceptively light. "You were right there. Right in the center of it all. What were you doing?"

"A security check," Rhys rushed out.

"Oh, how helpful," Aurora said. A dark laugh rumbled past her smirk. "You are always so helpful and thorough, aren't you, Rhys? When it benefits you. Always so helpful and thorough. Except it's funny, we've never been able to access this view of the footage before now. That's your job but it was always a 'processing error' and logistics and fancy tech words. Before we had a suspect in handcuffs, before we all together, in alignment, started hunting down evidence to prove Marius Bell's guilt. We never got to see the full view of the auditorium. But now, we see it all. It's right there. The full picture. Now that Marius Bell is arrested... we see you." Her voice was so even and calm and eerily plain it drove even Langston towards the edge. Rhys reacted with suspicion.

Aurora flicked her head to the far right corner where Captain Ahmed stood sentry. "Captain Ahmed. Is there any job duty that would require a security technician to ever leave their post behind a monitor?"

Ahmed answered with his typically brusque, "Never, Detective."

"So," Aurora said, looking towards the screen, not Rhys, "What were you doing, Rhys?"

Rhys shuffled to stand beside her. Langston lurched closer, he didn't like the little slimeballs proximity to his partner at all. She shook her head and allowed the invasion of her space. His hands trembled and his mouth formed a thousand excuses that didn't make it past his mouth.

"I noticed that one of the cameras— one of the cameras in the west wing, yeah. It was askew. I was just heading down to correct it. I was just being thorough. Please excuse my inaccuracy of language. I just thought, I said... I was just saying security check— because it was easier. I— I thought— it would make more sense."

"Try again."

"Excuse me?" Rhys now turned to Aurora directly. His head tilting down to meet her gaze. Aurora ignored him. His facade of helpfulness flaking away at the edges.

She didn't turn to him. Yet she matched his intensity. Aurora enunciated each word, "Try. Again."

From where he stood, Langston could only see half of her face when she did eventually grant Rhys the dubious grace of her full-attention.

"That lie is even less convincing than the first, Rhys. Why were you there during the bombing?" — Aurora's finger jabbed towards the holoscreen to highlight his unique placement. She clicked to zoom out to show that he was standing directly within Asa's line of sight — "There is no good reason for you to be there. So maybe a good lie would work. So, try again."

Rhys licked his lips and glared started to scratch its way across his perfectly manicured brows.

Maybe it was the angle or how the arrest and sobbing had cleaned off the make up from Marius' face. But Langston could see it now. Langston finally clocked the physical similarities between Rhys and Marius. Waif-thin yet lean muscled bodies, with shiny black hair and simple patrician features, large red lips that stood out in stark contrast with pale, Caucasian features.

Asa had a type.

Aurora turned back to Marius. Gave him a half smile and uncuffed his hands and feet while she asked, "Marius. If you'd be so kind, I think we are going to need an answer to that question. What does 'I'm not proud, but I am happy' mean to Asa Greene?"

Marius' gaze locked on Rhys. Marius saw what Langston saw. Strip away the frills and the garnish and Marius and Rhys were intensely similar looking. Marius whispered, shock and horror clouded his speech. "It was the last thing she said to me before she kicked me out on my ass. I was begging her to let me take some clothes. To give me money for the flight home. She laughed, shook her head and said, 'I'm not proud, but I am happy'. I ended up looking it up later it's a quote from some Gherrean epic 'The Count of Monte Cristo'. The way she said it, it just stuck with me."

Aurora nodded and helped the producer out of the seat and guided him over to Liya's who stood waiting with the keys to his cuffs.

Her attention drifted back to Rhys. The security tech was stiff as a board. Langston could practically see the fight-or-flight adrenaline ricocheting through his synapses. His gaze darted between the exit, Bell and Aurora. But surrounded by practically a full battalion of trained militarized personnel, no option would be easy. So Rhys stood frozen, hot steam of hatred whistling out of his ears.

Aurora considered the close up of Rhys, the bright blue light shining back on her face. She nudged Rhys with her shoulder. "You know, everyone says that Asa had a type. And of course, there is the hair. And the whole perfectly symmetrical face thing. The obvious. We all see it. But do you know what I think it really was?" Her every word carved another furrowed wrinkle of fury into Rhys's face. "Vanity. I think Asa was attracted to vanity. Cause you didn't have to write the note. You didn't have to frame Marius Bell. But I'm guessing you *really* wanted to. Your vanity demanded it."

Rhys took a step away from her to face her head on. His face contorted. He still wasn't saying a thing. Was looking every which way, but his gaze kept landing on her. She didn't look back at him.

"I mean, look at you there. You just had to come and enjoy the show. Even though you knew Asa was going to die, you couldn't resist the urge. To gloat. To see her take her last breaths. To treat her with the same disrespect that she showed you."

"No."

"No?" Aurora hisses the question softly, like a threat.

"I would never hurt anyone," Rhys was uncomfortably trying the reign in the pulsating rage beneath the surface. He tried to pull his persona back on but has difficulty donning it like a wet coat.

"No. You wouldn't want to get your hands dirty. Those soft hands couldn't do a hard day's work if they tried. And killing is hard work. But... Asa showed you the high life for a time. She taught you that anything you want done, you can pay to have someone do it. So you found Jamie."

"No!" Rhys hotly denied.

"Look. Look at you. Right out of reach of the explosion. You went out of your way to make sure that you were present during your own devastating outcomes. You wanted to witness 687 lights extinguish at once. You disgust me."

"I'm innocent," he growled out.

"You know every inch of this theatre. Every nook and cranny. Every camera angle, every security patrol. You probably could've done it without getting caught, too. But you just had to brag. And then... you needed to get rid of the dead weight. You didn't give a shit about a poor sap like Jamie Pope. No, this was you. Your pièce de résistance. This was your vanity," Aurora accused.

Rhys retreated a step and looked around at the gathered law enforcement officers. The faces surrounding him are a mix of confusion, calculation and growing hostility. He would find no friends here.

"You had everything figured out, but you wanted to see it in person." Aurora said the next part quietly, carefully. She walked around Rhys to sit in the chair Langston had originally vacated, giving Rhys the illusion of space.

"It wasn't political for you. It wasn't about the humanitarian worker's claims like it was for Jamie or as a favor to Azul to protect his inheritance. It was for love. You did it exactly as Asa trained you to do. Death wasn't enough. This was scorched-earth, salt the fields and piss on the grave kind of affair. Total annihilation. Of the highest and most thorough degree. It wasn't a terrorist attack for you."

Langston caught five microexpression morph across Rhys' face as Aurora laid into to him. Her words ate at the hollow resolve that the man tried to maintain.

"You just wanted to destroy Asa's whole world and the things she loved the most. Honestly, bravo," Aurora's sarcasm was delicious.

Continuing Aurora ramped up talking faster and quieter, drawing Rhys into the bear-trap of her analysis, "You've done a phenomenal job. If only you had been less petty. Less stupid. Maybe more focused. Instead, you tried to frame both Azul and Marius and damn near every asshole from here to Old Ohahlia. It was that vanity that led me back to you. I would've never even considered you until I talked to them. Azul told me all about Asa. Her passion was literature. A passion she clearly shared with you. You've been quoting poems, plays and classics all day and it wouldn't have crossed my mind if I hadn't heard it from Azul. Then with Marius, we all became convinced that of course it was a spurned lover. And in the end, that's exactly what are you."

Rhys gave up trying to stare down Aurora. His eye wildly darted around the room looking for support. His hands quivered anxious looking for something to do. But Aurora didn't stop. Settled into the chair, loose body pose, she eviscerated him. She went for the jugular and Langston knew she'd get this confession one way or another.

"You were so convinced that you were safe. So convinced that you had won that you just handed me the footage you had worked so hard to conceal. So convinced that we had followed your breadcrumbs to Bell's door that we wouldn't even think to actually look at the evidence that you handed us. You gloat. Just like Asa, you gloat. But, of course, I had hunches. I had guesses. I could smell something wasn't right with you, but honestly, I had nothing. Yes, there was the literature. The looks. But the nail in the coffin was always going to be Jamie Pope. You had to get rid of him, so you killed him."

Tugging at his hair frantically, "You— there's no evidence. You've got nothing. You can't prove shit!" he tried.

"You are so sure of yourself," Aurora's voice edged with sympathy and derision, "You covered your tracks for this massacre fairly well..." Aurora shook her head and frowned a tick. "But then there's Jamie."

"Jamie's dead," Rhys spat out, his jaw jutting forward in frustration.

"Yes, he is. But that wasn't the original plan, was it, Rhys?" Aurora sat forward with her head in her hands contemplatively.

There was silence. Rhys' jaw clenching and unclenching. Eyes darted around before he locked his gaze with Aurora. Spare grey eyes behind dark brown skin. In her eyes, Langston saw Rhys crack like many had before him.

She made them want to tell her all their secrets. To be understood by her was the ultimate validation.

It was to know a universal truth.

He was there on the edge. He just needed the right push.

Langston stepped back into the fray. Boxed him in. "Jamie was cracking," he offered gently. "He was an unlit match in a tinderbox and you didn't have time to get him off of the station and quietly dispose of him. We were hot on his heels and he would've broken sooner or later. In the Hallows. In the jail cell. At Medbay. He was going to tell us everything. That was an inevitability from the word go. You couldn't have that. So you killed him."

"I — I would never kill, that's --" Rhys swallowed thickly, a hand ruffled his one perfect hair. "Jamie was my friend."

"That's no way to treat your friends, Rhys." Langston pushed. Rhys had his eyes pinned on Aurora. He just wetly looked at her. So, Langston pushed. "Jamie wasn't a friend. He was a tool. And he broke. What do you do with broken tools, Rhys?"

A round tear sludged out of Rhys's foggy blue eyes. And another.

"What do you do with broken tools..." Langston asked again. "Liya, were you able to unencrypt the footage from the service hallway in the 5 mins during Jamie Pope's death?"

"Yessir."

Langston hooked a heavy hand on Rhys' shoulder. "While we might have to work on that mass murder terrorist charge, for the murder of Jamie Pope, you are done."

Rhys jerked his head back, butting Langston directly in the nose. The security supervisor then kicked out into Langston's gut, pushing him back several feet to the ground.

Rhys turned, pulling a gun from his inner jacket.

He drew the gun up towards at Aurora, aiming dead between her eyes.

Bang.

In the wake of the thunderclap shot through the room. All eyes were on Aurora, looking for a gaping red splotch and crying and pain and a gunshot wound.

She sat trembling, but utterly unharmed in her seat.

It was Rhys' body that lay dead from a gunshot to the head on the floor across from her.

It had been Zhou's shadow. The Lieutenant. The towering mammoth of a man that had stepped forward and shot Rhys in the skull before he could make another move.

Before the echoes of the Lieutenant's shot could fade and, in alignment with the typical CC brutality, the lieutenant shot him twice more in the chest, just to be sure.

It's over.

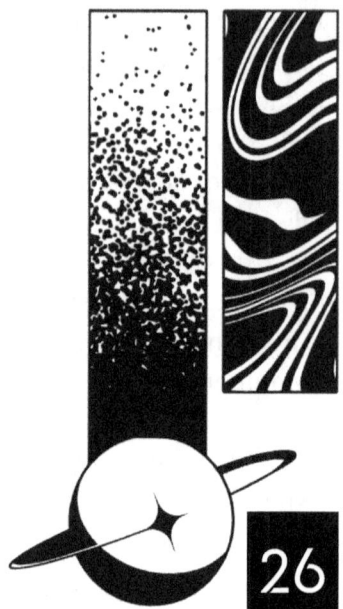

A LOYAL DOG

26

LANGSTON

With both terrorists dead, things moved fast.

Zhou jumped on the opportunity to claim credit for the "resolution" of the case. Her every action picked at the oozing scab of resentment left behind from his recent arrest. Zhou did nothing. Without Aurora, there was a high probability they would've arrested the wrong man. CC had been direly close to ice-ing Bell without blinking twice.

Zhou's investigation... or rather, interference had solved nothing. It was her, not Langston, who had been obstructing damn justice.

But a silly little thing like the truth would not impede Zhou's peacocking. Zhou touted the fact that "she" had saved the day when, again in actuality, it was her spooky Lieutenant, not Zhou, who brought the investigation to a conclusive end.

His complicated feelings about what had occurred aside, Langston would celebrate a win as a win.

In the final phases of the investigation, the win became even more obvious. The Socrates crew brought up Rhys and Jamie's personal effects to the sec-deck to be searched. They found a veritable orgy of evidence in Rhys' bunk. The mask from the MedBay shooting. The chemical kit and paintbrush used in the message in front of Asa's chair. Falsified access cards and more. An honest to Vearro orgy of evidence. And with an orgy afoot, it was all hands on deck. There was more than enough grunt work to go around, so ultimately, the CC and the Socrates units were working harmoniously for once in order to get everything settled faster.

Zhou, Aurora and Langston all took a noticeable step away from the rest of the investigation, which seemed to help. It lowered the temperature to everyone's undying relief.

With his free time, Langston did his own strutting. They had solved the case in just under a sol, half-day early. He could work that little fact into every conversation and practically every other sentence.

Sure, there would be no trial. But hey, The Pact and CC were never a huge fan of airing dirty laundry. So there would be no complaints from the higher ups.

Faster than two shakes of a lamb's tail, they wrapped it up. Each unit quietly packed up, readying themselves to clear out and return to their shuttles.

Langston was sorting through the last of the evidence analysis holos when Zhou crept up beside him like a bad dream.

"I'm not going to apologize."

Zhou's voice maintained its usual coarse neutrality; but her evil, little fists clenched and unclenched so tightly to where Langston heard the cartilage pop in her knuckles. Her appearance and her general level of high-strung-ness were enough to make him worry. Even with the case closed, Zhou had a bad habit of genuinely surprising him with her actions.

"Well, can't say that surprises me," Langston shrugged, but didn't let his attention or gaze linger on her for too long. While Langston might not have asked for an apology, he was positive he deserved one.

He wasn't much interested in anything she had to say, even an apology Vearro forbid. No, he could happily never speak to this woman another day in his life and die a happy man.

"Because I'm not sorry," she said.

"Again, consider me monumentally unsurprised." Langston focused on the mind numbing sorting work in front of him and cherished the idea that every second he was closer to putting distance between him and this psychopath.

"You are so smug. You really think you accomplished something here. That you figured it all out," Zhou spat the words out so fast it was hard to catch some of the many (pretty unwarranted) critiques.

Langston couldn't help but raise both eyebrows while he continued on with his task, not missing a beat to her tirade. Half-ignoring her seemed to have the added benefit of fully annoying Zhou. "Well, if your man hadn't shot the perp, we would've." He kept his eyes on the task in front of him.

Honestly, he was hoping she would just walk away. She did not.

She shifted a bit in front of him but didn't walk away. The rhythm clench-unclench of her fists intensified. Her mouth would occasionally open and close with the attempts at more 'conversation'. After about 4 open-shut attempt, Langston couldn't help but interrupt her efforts.

"Can I help you with something?" he asked with genuine earnestness built from frustration. "Because if not, I'd love to wrap this gem of a conversation up and shove it out of an airlock."

"Rhys and Jamie planted the bomb. They killed Asa Greene," Zhou said.

"Tell me something I don't know."

"Well, I'm trying so..." Zhou said, her eyes closing in defeat. A couple more open-shut attempts at saying something. "I'm not sorry."

Apparently, an apology was not something that she wanted

to say, but, "We've gone over this before." Langston said. His hands and attention were off the deck on the table in front of him. Annoyed and pissed as he was, her attempts at conversation had sparked some shell of interest in his brain.

"I'm not sorry... But... between two Pact officers, one who might've wrongfully imprisoned the other," — while she said she wasn't sorry, her face was carved with guilt in the tense wrinkles at her eyebrows — "but both... who... want to do good — I wouldn't pat myself on the back for a mission accomplished on this one."

Yet another insult vaguely surprised Langston. Her words didn't match her tone or that gut feeling within Langston that told him that this "something" she was trying to tell him was something he needed to hear.

"What?" he asked.

"I just... sometimes even when the math adds up --" she turned to face him. Her eyes were sad and resigned and guilty as sin. "This isn't over." She had yet to apologize for the whole arrest thing. Her words sounded like an apology. It sounded ominous as hell.

"Is that a threat?"

She nodded with a fierce earnestness. Her eyes burned into his. "...I'm afraid it is." Her gaze dropped, and she flexed her fingers in and out of fists. "I don't know what to say to you."

Langston laughed "Clearly."

"You... It's only going to get more complicated from here. I don't think you'll ever be free of this. I think your partner... she might be an albatross."

He was used to people saying many things about Aurora. Mostly racist, sexist, terribly limiting and awful things about her. Langston was well trained in the art of defending her honor, or backing her up as she kicked racist, sexist asses all up and down a flight deck. The way she accused Aurora of being an 'albatross', it didn't sound like an insult. Like half of the things in this conversation, it sounded like more of a warning.

"I don't know what any of this means."

"Fuck." Zhou scrubbed her hands across her neck in frustration. She shook her hand like she was trying to shake the words out of her mind. She pulled the ends of her uniform down and tight, regaining some of the wobbly weird footing this conversation had taken them to. "Well... *Try*. Try to figure it the fuck out, I guess. And... Don't stop... and I guess. I'm sorry." Zhou said it like she meant every word. With a last nod, she turned and walked away.

So he believed her. "Ok."

She stopped and turned back, her expression a bit hopeful. It transformed the serrated sociopathic edges of her normal expression into something more... normal. "Ok?"

"Yes," Langston smiled. "I'll try and I won't stop... and if I ever make sense of this conversation... I'll forgive you."

Her head tilted up. She didn't smile, but it seemed more content than any faux smile could've on her face. "Square deal."

Rolling his eyes, Langston shook his head. Aurora would adore psychoanalyzing this conversation. He looked around to find her chatting with the Lieutenant.

AURORA

"You could've aimed for his legs or torso," Aurora called across an empty stretch of corridor toward the Man of the Hour. The Lieutenant. This was her first moment alone since the interrogation, and as soon as she could she had immediately sought him out. She didn't quite know what she wanted to say, but firmly believed that just talking might shake something loose in her brain.

The Lieutenant kneeling down to pack up a large, black go-kit that probably wasn't up to standard CC-issue regulation. Even for CC, this man seems to shirk authority and order like he had an allergic reaction. He smirked, but didn't stop his motions. His quick glance communicated how wholly un-bothered he was by her overall abruptness.

"Hmm, what an unusual way to say 'thank you, I owe you my life. You're my hero."

His response gave her absolutely nothing.

"He might be alive. Alive he would've been able to stand trial, to face justice," Aurora said. She couldn't help stop stating obvious facts to this man. Obvious facts that he appears to be aware of but ultimately unconcerned by.

The Lieutenant's laugh churned like a motor turning over, grumbling out from his belly with genuine mirth. He stopped what he was doing to finally look up at her. His coal black eyes gave her a once over. He gave a faux-pouting frown. "Oh, but you seemed much smarter than that."

"Excuse me?"

She was a bit thrown off by the noticeable shift in his demeanor. Throughout the investigation, she had dismissed him as a simple sidekick who added the occasional savory seasoning to Zhou's aggression. But here he had abandoned any attempt to display some military orderliness. His persona was monstrous.

With all his intimidating muscles and menacing scowls, he had checked all the obvious boxes for "scary". Aurora could understand why most people, even herself, failed to identify the truly unsettling part about him. If you missed the spark of brilliance in his eyes, it would be easy to mis-categorize the type of monster you were dealing with. He was masquerading as a blunt object, but that intelligence sharpened the way he hammered things out.

His decision heightened Aurora's unease, his "truer", scarier self with her... alone in this corridor. Before he saved her life, before he shot Rhys point-blank in the head, she hadn't paid him much attention. She had seen what he wanted her to see: a loyal dog.

But the man was in front of her now was no domesticated

animal. This was a wolf, a predator, and a survivor.

She saw him. It reflected poorly on her that she was at once a bit more comfortable with him without the mask.

Without her response, the silence yawned.

He considered her as she was considering him. He seemed to see her, too. It was curious if the Lieutenant could always be seen her or if something had changed in this moment. His head tilted with concentration. "Ah, there it is. I can see it now. You still believe in the 'System'. You might think you are tough and jaded and pessimistic... but you still think that '*good*' is possible." Derision dripped from the last word. Shrugging, he returned to packing his pack. "Nothing to be done, but wait that shit out. It'll wear off before long."

"What's your name?" Aurora asked. She couldn't hide her genuine, rabid fascination. The overall nameless of this CC (hell of the whole unit) was frustrating and ridiculous.

Another rasped laugh before the Lieutenant said fondly, "You're an odd cookie, aren't you?"

Aurora was beyond exasperation. It had been a long day as anyone can attest to. She just wanted a goddamn name, and she was determined to figure out a piece of his puzzle. "You're a hero. You technically saved my life. I don't get a name?"

"Yes, I **gave** you your life. You'd think that'd be enough. But, sure, here's a name: Aurora Harlowe. You have my respect," the Lieutenant hauled his pack onto his back and slowly backed away from her. His expression was soft. Gone was the derision and vinegar he had snarled out throughout the day. A gentle smile spread out across his face. "I... You know what? I hope we never meet again."

"You say that like it's a compliment."

"It is." His mouth hardened, but his eyes were clear. There was a seriousness in them that expressed an earnest, yearning warning.

Her light smile faded off her face as she tried to dig deeper into those fire-blue eyes. She... felt like she was looking into the abyss. Black and full of stories and danger and fear and nothing to be trifled with.

Behind them, from the busy hub of the control deck, Langston called out to her. "Harlowe, we need you over here." Aurora turned her head to take in the turmoil on deck, knowing that this conversation would draw to a close. But her reason for stalking him down remained. She was unwilling to be put off by relaying the gratitude she initially came over to convey.

He jutted his chin out in Langston's general direction. "Go on. Give em' hell," the monster's grin was bright and deadly spread across his face. A mask. A wolf in a hot-dog suit.

Tilting her head and locking her gaze with him, she answered, "Always."

She settled disappointingly to take his threat or warning or whatever it was as an act of kindness that he intended it to be. At the very least, Aurora appreciated an armistice of subtleties when presented with one. There was a widening ocean of things unsaid spread between them. That would have to just be ok.

She smiled because in a different life. In a different world, she could see them as friends. The darkness that cloaked him was mirrored in her. Hers was simply well-leashed and tightly chained by her overwhelming dedication toward the pursuit of justice. Still, she was dark and stormy and appreciated this small ounce of comradery.

The tension around his eyes softened. They nodded to each other, and she made moves to head back to the control deck where she was beckoned.

As she retreated, she did some calculations in her head. She realized a couple of truths. One, this was not a man who would kill someone to save a life. Two, he didn't shoot Rhys to save her. Three, his reasons were most likely part of the plan or a strategy she was unaware of and probably would never understand. Four, none of this matters to her. She was still grateful.

Turning back to him a final time, Aurora found his gaze was still laser-focused on her.

"Thank you," Aurora said it quick, she didn't linger. A quick nod and she was back on her way to the security deck. She almost didn't catch his response.

"Kieran."

His — Kieran's — voice reached her like sandpaper on soft wood. She had finally had a name for the face.

A mega watt smile lit across her face with a chuckle. She turned to him again without breaking her stride. His face held a fond respect tempered with an intense seriousness. Aurora had quietly and easily achieved a feat that few could boast of Kieran's respect. For this was not a name to be forgotten, or one that was given lightly.

"Kieran," she said. "It's been a pleasure."

His grizzled laughter reached his eyes but didn't escape his mouth. With finality he turned to the landing bay in the opposite direction muttering, "A pleasure? You know what, I agree. A pleasure, indeed."

YOU'RE FIRED

AURORA

The last bit of paperwork finally signed on the Sec-Deck rendered their case was officially closed. The 'i's were dotted, the 't's were crossed, and the crew was waiting on VP005. Together, two detectives made their last trek through the renowned Esaa Seltenta Luxury Space Station. It was officially morning and the main stretch of grande hallways was empty for perhaps the first time since they arrived. Even billionaires needed their rest from this excitement.

The walk was tired and the silence companionable.

About a hundred and fifty meters out from the loading dock, a sound teased against Aurora's eardrum. It was the sound of water babbling against soft-smooth rocks. It was something slow and gentle, lazy waterfall. Her eyes followed the temptation of her ears and she turned to see the entrance of the tropic oasis resort center. It was a few tantalizingly short meters away from the Loading Dock.

Aurora cased the hallway. No one was behind them and

just their dedicated and understanding team waited for them on VP005. No attendants, no staff, no nothing… to stop them.

She bumped her should against Langston's before she made a quick U-turn into the oasis entrance. She threw him a quick smile before she split into a jog towards the entrance. Aurora avoided eye-contact as she was entirely unwilling to accept the possibility that Langston might show some unwelcome sense of decorum. By her estimation, a few minutes in a wonderland for the detectives who saved the day wasn't going to hurt anyone.

Stepping past the circular doorway, the warm, sun-soaked heat hugged her skin. The entrance housed a lobby that had a shockingly accurate habitat model of a rainforest. The mimics of birds cawing through surround-sound stereo speakers and a squishy soil flooring were fully immersive and utterly perfect.

Deep inhale, Aurora slipped off her shoes, rolled up her pants, and waded into the small lagoon centerpiece. The large mossy rocks and the sway of artificial currents seemed real the way a dream feels. The large check-in desk behind the waterfall punctured her illusion, but she refused to let it detract from her overall enjoyment. She traced the balls of her feet against the pebbles of the basin.

She heard Langston join her, and her smile ticked up another notch. He plopped onto one of the rocks behind her in a similar position — shoes off, pants cuffed.

"What a day," she said.

Langston chuckled before responding, "Not even a day, if you can believe it. Less than thirty hours."

She waded back over to the rocks and dropped down beside him. "Time flies when you are having fun, I guess."

They didn't say much after that. Aurora titled her head back and savored the kisses of artificial stellar rays through leaves warm her face. It could've been on those rocks for a minute, it could've been twenty.

"There you are."

Liya's exasperated voice broke the silence of the oasis.

Aurora lolled her head back to see Liya stomp towards them.

"Hello Liya," Aurora greeted lazily. Liya was just the person she wanted to see. This was the perfect time for Aurora to spring her surprise.

Langston jumped up from his rock to turn and look at her. His arms opened wide, Langston proclaimed, "How good of you to join us!"

The analyst rolled her eyes, huffed a bit before she ignored both greeting. "Everything ready for takeoff, we are just waiting on a destination and you two diligent professional to mozy on over so we can take off."

"Well, we're not going anywhere special. Just back to headquarter," Aurora said. She got up, made moves to dry off her feet and put on her shoes. She smirked over at Liya. "We're gotta pick up a new senior analyst."

"Haha," Liya said in a deadpanned a laugh before holding her hand out to Langston to help him over the rocks. "Hilarious."

"I'm not being funny. I am joyously, *utterly* serious. This was your last mission with The Socrates."

Liya's face glitched. She was so shocked by this very serious statement, misjudged his weight and Langston went splashing back into the fountain.

A soaked and outraged Langston demanded, "What the hell?" He scurried and flailed his way out of the water to stand beside Liya. Both glared confused daggers at Aurora.

"Yeah, what the hell?" Liya chimed in when Aurora didn't provide an immediate answer.

She loved these two doofuses. "You're fired," she said. She pretended that a large shiver scurried down her back. "That was fun to say. I should fire people more often. 'You're fired.' Hah! What, you two aren't coming?" Without delay, she made her way towards the exit and the Loading Dock where VP005 was parked.

Langston picked up his shoes and charged after her. Liya was a pace or two behind him. She was trying to both keep pace and stomp, which appeared to be hard to do.

"Aurora! What the fuck?" Liya shouted. She was normally so prim and proper on a case, so Aurora silently congratulated herself on making her composure crumble.

"Liya, be reasonable," Aurora's voice was gratingly calm and perky. She stopped just shy of the exit to turn back and look at the pair. "Think about your behavior today. Disobeying direct commands for your XO, illegally hacking Pact databases, unlawful entry into the station's Hallows without authorization and with a grounder. These are not the actions of a System Intelligence Senior Analyst, Liya. You didn't think we wouldn't notice."

Liya's eyebrows seemed to be permanently pinned to the top of her forehead in shock. "Aurora — Detective Harlowe, I — most of that I did with —."

"Oh, did you think your not-so-secretive canoodling with the LD over here would help your case or hurt it?"

"Aurora, I would never--" Langston's strangled gasp barely squeezed out of his throat. He seemed to have moved past his shock to find his own voice. Good for him. The fact that his tone was both chiding and embarrassed in equal measures made it all the sweeter.

"Well, like I said — this is your last mission with The Socrates. You've clearly demonstrated that this is no longer a good fit." Aurora turned away from the two to pick up the last bit of gear. Langston seemed to have forgotten in his panic. Langston and Liya trailed behind her, their eyes blinking owlishly in a panic. The same smile she had on since Liya arrived remained plastered on her face when she turned to them and looked Liya dead in the eye. "*You deserve better.* We're heading to HQ with a strong letter of recommendation for promotion and immediate transfer to the cyber security division."

At this conclusion of Aurora's terrible prank, Liya's emotions were precariously balanced at their tipping point. Aurora could practically see the gears churning in her brain as she processed the words and the news. A tear accumulated in the corner of her eye. She tutted and huffed out a breath in a wobbly smile. "Oh."

"You earned it, lady. Enjoy."

"Oh." It seemed like this was the only word Liya could produce after such emotional upheaval. She laughed before tackle-hugging Aurora. Quick in the attack, she retreated from the hug in under a nanosecond and righted her uniform.

Aurora couldn't help but pat herself on the back for a prank well executed. She once again headed back towards the exit of the oasis center without Liya and Langston. "It also conveniently removes any... conflicts of interest or power imbalance or ethical dilemmas that might prevent certain horizontal pursuits I imagine you were interested in... pursuing."

Another straggled gasp of "Aurora" escaped from Langston. The second gasp was no less embarrassed than the original.

Smiling, she left Liya and Langston standing in front of the fountain of the oasis center.

A waterfall behind them. Birds cheering and cawing in the distance. They looked like idiots just standing there. Smiling, being in love. They were, inarguably, idiots.

Fools in love.

THE END.

AUTHOR BIO

Audrey Sechrest (she/her/hers) is an American author and playwright currently living in Chicago, Illinois though she is always and will forever be a California Girl. She graduated from the University of California, San Diego with a degree in Communications. Her first play, As Luck Would Have It, premiered at the 2016 San Diego Underground New Play Festival. In her spare time, she loves DIY art projects, traveling, and spreadsheets. This is her debut novel.

www.audreysechrest.com | @audacitylights

NOTE FROM THE AUTHOR

Thank you from every corner of my heart for picking up this book. This is one of the truest passion projects I've ever undertaken. From a dream I had when I was 17, to writing in earnest ten years later, I've poured love, sweat, and a fair amount of tears into this – my first-ever novel. I am unbelievably proud of this book and if you are reading this you are now a part of my journey and I couldn't be more grateful. However, unfortunately, due to the general… negativity of being a millennial living in America in the current apocalyptic era, I personally couldn't afford to professionally edit this book. I've done my darndest to make this the best quality for you all… but grammar was never my strong suit. Apologies for any errors/flubs.

So, here is both a promise and a challenge. If I ever sell 100 copies of this book (both very possible, highly unlikely and also a cute lil challenge), ***I do hereby swear that I will formally edit this book and re-release it.*** All the original squad (people who previously purchased) will get a free copy with a special gift (tbd). Sending you all the love!

A TRAVELER'S GUIDE TO KAETYENE

(NOW INCLUDING A KAETYENE PHRASE BOOK*)

*This phrase book includes all Kaetyene dialogue from Borealis Burning + the complete poem referenced in Chapter 16.

HISTORY OF THE LANGUAGE

Kaetyene, the native language of Anhkae, became a universal language during the Divine Era. The Divine Era, which spanned most of the 17th and 18th centuries, was marked by the extreme religious zealotry of warring nation-states of Anhkae. It started in the early 1700s when several national leaders anointed themselves as gods. The period was known for the doctrine of state-sanction conversions and cultural genocide. By the end of the Divine Era, all Anhkaena nation-states adopted the divine language, Kaetyene, as its official language.

Kaetyene remains the official language today.

After the Fall, as Anhkaena survivors migrated back into the cities, Kaetyene underwent a linguistic revolution. Due to the historical context of the *Sanuelo Elku* (the Bright War), trust was low between neighbors and outsiders. Extreme xenophobia was rampant across the planet. Travelers developed a transitory short-hand code made of different line-drawings. This was colloquially called "glyph".

Today a modernized alphabet form of glyph is the official written form of Kaetyene.

PHRASE BOOK

KAETYENE	ENGLISH	#
El'esses. El'esses. Oeph khemhio.	Please. Please. No more.	CH 1
Āshyamni	Hello	CH 16
Adon'ib	Excuse me	CH 16
Ogo shebu	Good night (greeting)	CH 16

KAETYENE	ENGLISH	#
Mojinm khet oeph. Tyn ku'phelhta ka?	You don't belong here. Why would I help you?	CH 16
Hæm'alo sah Command oeph. Ftemuelo-azh, āmnam th'qol ogo. Ya'vroo-al āhk khet pha'kæia-ib, Māathta ya'vroo-ib. Hæ-ib Liya Grimae. Hæ-al āhk-ka. Oi'ilo cheej a'urrbān	We are not Command. Despite (subtract) his authority, this man is good. I trust him with my life. Believe my truth. I am Liya Grimae. I am you. In the old ways and the new.	CH 16
Imnohta ka	Thank you	CH 16
El'esses, ptiāt'hat maāt ka-ib. Pharrjhat ka khet. Hopalo sah oolo im'sah ftem. Hæm khet ānya.	Please, you must believe me. Find them. We have blood on our hands. He is a monster.	CH 21
Eel-ib. Ghoibal āhk al'nixe	I promise. I'll make it right.	CH 21

ABSOLUTION FOR THE DAMNED, A POEM

KAETYENE	ENGLISH
Hæm th'kæ'aina unio cheej Hæhtan al'oeph Sah, hophtan al'oeph yavrro Maāt'hæmalo sah rrobi a'āchron Oeghænalo no'irralem, ibyialo i'bu'ād cheej	This world is forever lost It is not ours, it holds no trust We are but ruins and frost Starving for redemption, dreaming of stardust
Pharrjalo-befiji no'sah, āzhughælo no'shyl'ām? Sah, værreealo ty'jo māmta, xexerrān cheej Hæhtan al'guith no'ttobbi, zhohul iodin? Oeph. Oeph irralem. Oeph ftell kan-leyft i'kæia	An escape for us, a hunt for peace? Us, who have seen horrors, endless strife. Is it mercy for the deserving, an earned release? No. No absolution. No refuge from the storms of life.
Ghom. Ghom. Kāajhta yavrro im'htoi. Urr'ānhta yavrro oi'ftāneesh, nakht-hta yavrro im'rranā Th'yush, th'pheett, th'eel pha'uhlee Maāt'ñianalo sah. Maāt'ephoo-alo sah. Maāt'liomalo sah.	Remember. Remember. Etch the truth upon your skin. Sow it in the mind, scar it on the land This ode, this indictment, This promise to kin We must endure. We must rise. We must stand.
Aiāmem, qoh'oolo a'phirreesh Befiji, **qoh'amkeses** a'albef Hæmalo sah oeph sheefoj, Hæmalo sah xe Maāt'hæmeealo sah oeph Āhk, maāt'hæmeealo sah cheejog	Wrath, between blood and friends Home, **between bones** and glory Our is not the lullaby, ours is the end We are not the self, we are the story

PLANETARY MAP OF THE OYA VEARRO STAR SYSTEM

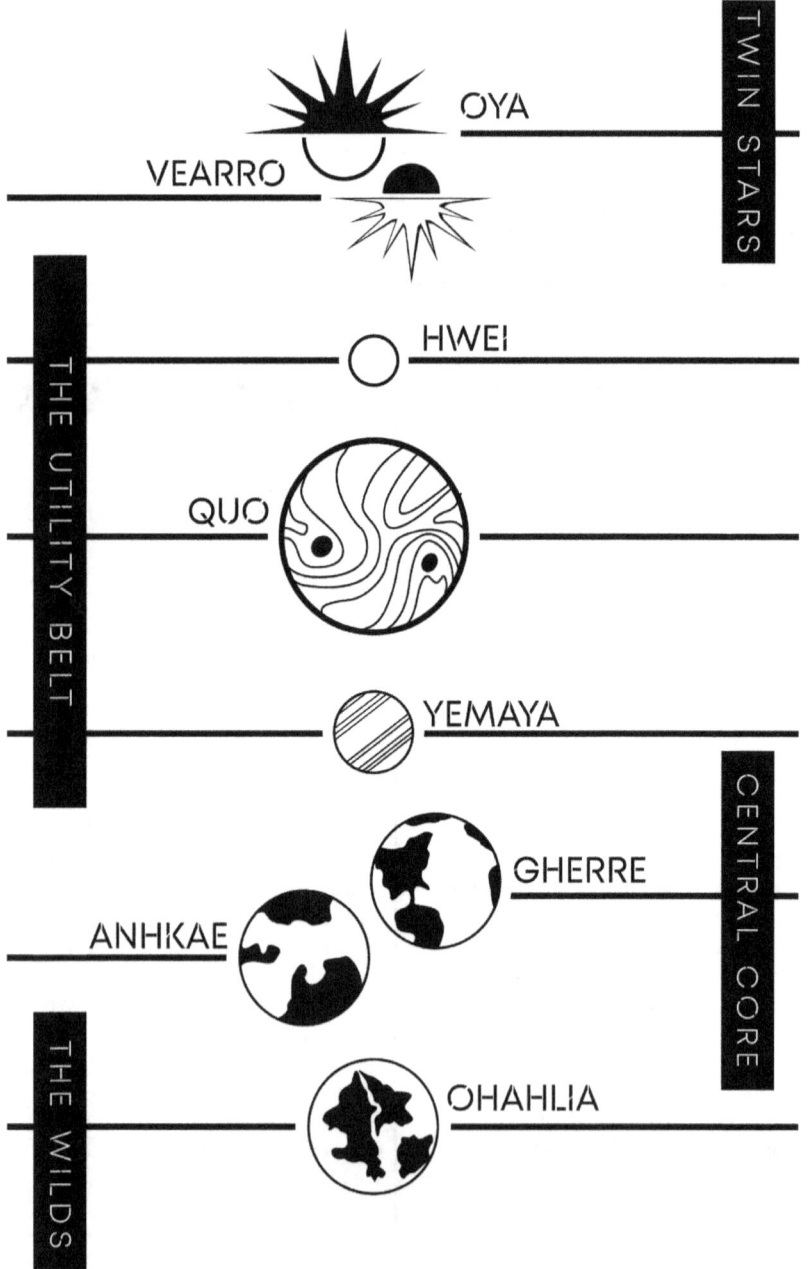

POSTCARDS

Wow! Look at you! All the way at the back of the book! Hot-cha-cha! I'll take any and every opportunity to thank you for participating in my impossible dream (to create work that people enjoy). So thanks again!

If you liked the art that appeared on the title pages for Overture, Duet, and Finale, you are in luck!

Use this QR code to get access to your free digital downloads!

www.audreysechrest.com/free-art

High quality prints of all art is also available for sale on my website